THE
HASHTAG
SERIES

The Hashtag Series Finale

by Cambria Hebert

#HEART Copyright © 2015 CAMBRIA HEBERT

Published by: Cambria Hebert Books, LLC

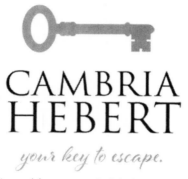

CAMBRIA
HEBERT

your key to escape.

http://www.cambriahebert.com

Interior design and typesetting by Sharon Kay of Amber
Leaf Publishing
Cover design by MAE I DESIGN
Edited by Cassie McCown of Gathering Leaves Editing
Copyright 2015 by Cambria Hebert

ISBN: 978-1-938857-78-2

DEDICATION

This book is dedicated to my readers. The real live #nerds who have shown this series so much love in the past year that we have all become #family.

This book is written for you, as not only a finale, but a thank you. I hope it's everything you want it to be and more.

What an incredible ride it's been.

This might be the last book in the series, but we aren't over. Family doesn't quit each other.

We are #OneNerdPackUnited!

THE
HASHTAG
SERIES

SHE SAID YES! TIMES TWO

(AKA PROLOGUE)

#AndTheAwardGoesTo
Romeo for the most romantic proposal of
all time. Shakespeare has nothing on him.
Some #Nerds have all the luck.
#WaitingForTheWedding

#BuzzBoss

ROMEO

Best game of my entire career.

Yeah, okay, it was only my first season. And yeah, okay, I still had a lot of games in my future (God willing), but I knew without a shadow of a doubt that nothing—no game, not even a Superbowl title—would ever beat out today.

Congratulations went around the locker room. I got slapped on the back, the ass, and in the head so many times you'd think it would get old.

I was too happy for that.

I was even too happy to be bothered by the ribbing and snide remarks I heard from a few corners around the room.

Fuck them.

Rimmel was going to be my wife.

I felt my mouth pull into a wide, toothy grin. Hells yeah.

I thought back to the moment I first realized she was it for me. The night at the animal shelter when she sat on the floor, soaking wet from the rain, and Murphy crawled into her lap. She'd pulled her hair out of her face and looked up at me.

It was game over from there on out. I was hers.

Even so, I'd been a little nervous tonight before the game. Asking a girl to marry you on live television, in the middle of a giant football game, was sort of a gamble. Especially for a girl like Rim.

She liked her privacy. She liked to blend in.

Rimmel didn't know it, but she was destined to stand out. Without even trying, she'd become the darling of the football world. The cameras loved her and got at least one shot of her sitting in the stands at every game she came to.

They watched her clothes, her hair... Hell, they even talked about her glasses.

She was an unlikely fixture in the center of a football game. She wasn't a model, a celebrity, or even someone who wanted to draw the public eye.

And for that, people loved her. She was the girl next door, the one that everyone knew. People related to her in ways they couldn't to all the other football elite.

I'd been planning to ask her to marry me for a while now. I'd just been waiting for the right time.

Then shit hit the fan at home.

Zach was released, he went after Ivy, tried to kill her, and almost did. Braeden made it just in time to save her life.

When I walked into her hospital room and saw her lying there battered and bruised, it served as a heavy dose of reality. We weren't guaranteed any amount of time on this earth. We weren't promised another day, another chance.

It sealed the deal for me. I couldn't wait any longer to claim Rimmel in every possible way.

I called up Ron Gamble and told him I was ready. He'd been thrilled. Back when he set up a false press conference for me and basically helped me nail the bastards trying to extort money out of me in exchange for Rimmel's life, I'd made him a promise.

I promised when I proposed, I'd do it during a game. He wanted huge media buzz, and he knew this way he'd get it.

So tonight during the game, I did it. Right there in front of thousands of cheering fans.

Goddamn, she looked so adorable in her purple Knights hoodie and glasses. The surprise in her eyes was real and so was her emotion.

The second I slid that ring onto her finger, my entire world felt complete.

As soon as I finished changing I tossed all my shit into my bag and headed for the door. I wanted to see my future wife.

"Someone's getting laid tonight!" one of the guys hollered as I walked toward the door.

"Hells yeah!" I yelled and left them all to their dirty jokes and exaggerated moans. Those guys were a bunch of pervs.

I loved 'em.

Well, almost all of them.

I stepped out into the quiet tunnel that led to the parking lot. I imagined Rimmel waiting out there for me and quickened my pace.

Some movement in the shadows against the wall had my steps faltering, and a small figure stepped out into the light.

I grinned. "How'd you get in here?"

She mock gasped and pressed a hand to her chest. The rock I'd just put there glistened under the light and shone brightly. "Don't you know who I am?" she intoned.

I pretended to think it over. "Can't say that I do."

She started forward, her eyes never once leaving my face. "I'm the future wife of the best player on this team."

"Ahh," I drawled. "I thought you looked familiar."

I dumped my bag at my feet and held open my arms. "Get the hell over here."

She laughed and ran at me. I caught her midair, and her legs fastened around my waist like she didn't even have to think about it anymore. She just knew where she belonged.

"Mrs. Anderson," I growled.

"Not yet," she sang.

"Soon." The word was almost lost between us when I covered her lips with mine.

Her lips parted instantly, and my tongue sought hers eagerly. My fingers tightened on her hips as we went at each other right there in the tunnel. Rim's hand fisted in my hair, and my mouth assaulted hers.

A few steps and I pinned her back against the wall, using my chest to hold her in place, and ripped my mouth free to trail hot, wet kisses down her neck and then up to nibble on her earlobe.

Her core rocked against my waist, and she groaned with need.

Impatient, her hand slid between us and started traveling low, but she couldn't reach the part of me she wanted most. The distressed sound that tore from her throat made me laugh.

I stepped back just enough so she could slide down my body. The way she felt rubbing along my front was damned intoxicating. When her hand found and squeezed the rock-hard erection beneath my sweats, my body jerked.

"Come on," I said, hoarse. "I got us a suite at a nearby hotel. It's got lots of nice amenities, but we're not gonna use them."

Her teeth sank into her lower lip with anticipation.

"Show me," I demanded, possessiveness flaring inside me like some incurable disease.

Rim knew what I wanted and she lifted her hand and held it out between us.

The engagement ring took over her small fingers. I'd gotten as big a diamond as I dared, knowing if I went too big, she'd refuse to wear it. Hell, I knew the three-carat stone I'd gotten was probably more than she would have wanted, but I didn't care. That ring represented so much to me.

It represented my love for her.

It represented me.

It represented what we were to each other.

And yes…

I admit.

It was also a large warning to any guy who ever dared to look at her. Hell, they'd be able to see the glittering center stone and smaller stones around it from across the room.

It was a giant SHE'S TAKEN sign right there for every man to see.

I liked it. It brought out my primal side. It brought out my continued need to claim her.

"You like it?" I whispered, taking her hand and lifting it to my lips.

"I've never seen anything so beautiful," she whispered as I pressed a kiss to the ring and her hand.

I grunted. "I have."

She bestowed upon me a brilliant smile.

I picked her up and moved over to dangle her upper body over my bag on the ground. "I need my bag, Mrs. Anderson." She laughed and picked it up. Her laugh turned to a screech when I pulled her up and flipped her body so I was able to carry her against me.

"You can't call me that. We aren't married yet," she said, settling my bag in her lap.

"Wanna fly to Vegas tonight?"

She laughed, but when I didn't join her, she glanced up and sucked in a breath. "You're serious?"

"As a heart attack."

"We can't just fly to Vegas."

"The hell we can't. Tomorrow is my off day. We could be married by morning."

"You'd marry me tonight?"

I laughed. "I'd marry you right the fuck now if I could."

"I love you," she said, her eyes filling with tears.

"Whoa," I pulled back when she tried to come at me for a kiss. "What's with the waterworks?"

She giggled and blinked. "I just can't believe I'm so lucky."

"Is that a yes to Vegas?" I asked, hopeful.

She chewed on her bottom lip and then nodded once. I actually jolted in surprise. My feet stopped working and I stared at her in shock. "Did you just say yes?"

"No, silly." She laughed. "I already said yes, out there on the football field."

My heart actually turned over. "You'd marry me tonight?"

"I'd marry you right the fuck now." She echoed my own words.

I love it when she says fuck.

I grinned like the goofiest motherfucker on the planet. She made me so stupid happy. I never in a million years thought she'd actually agree to go to Vegas and marry me tonight.

Goddamn, it was a powerful feeling to know she loved me as much as I loved her.

I started running to the car.

She squealed and hung on to the bag in her lap as it knocked around.

Outside, there were a gaggle of reporters all hanging around, just waiting for us to emerge. My steps slowed to a quick walk when I saw them.

I should have thought about this. I should have expected the press to be right here. Hell, they were always around.

They rushed us, shoving cameras and lights in our face. Rimmel shrank against me, and I tightened my grip. I didn't want to deal with this right now. I wanted to continue being stupid happy.

But these people were stupid annoying.

But I smiled anyway and turned to face them all, holding Rim. "Just practicing for after the wedding," I joked.

They all laughed and snapped some pics.

One of the female reporters pushed close. "Let me see the ring!"

Rimmel glanced at me and then held out her hand. More camera bulbs went off.

"If you'll excuse us," I said, "we have plans." I spun and deftly moved through the crowd.

At the Hellcat, I tossed the bag into the backseat and then more carefully placed my life in the passenger seat, taking care to buckle her and let my knuckles skim across her breasts.

Once that was done, I rushed around to the driver's side and threw the Cat into motion.

Rimmel laughed like she was totally amused, and I tossed her a smile.

We made it to the hotel in record time. It was the nicest one in this town. I booked the honeymoon suite and asked them to fill it with white roses. When I told them my name, the lady almost pissed her pants with excitement.

So I chatted her up, charmed her, and got Rim a couple more dozen roses for free.

What can I say? It's a gift.

I pulled up to the front entrance and tossed the keys to the valet as I jogged around to get my girl. It was the first time I'd ever let a valet driver handle my car. Right now, I could barely think straight. I wanted to be alone with her so bad.

I grabbed her hand and all but dragged her inside to the sweeping three-story reception area. A huge glass chandelier hung down in the center of the room, and two grand staircases with wrought iron railings filled the back wall, each staircase leading in a different direction.

Rimmel's breath caught and her footsteps slowed the second she saw the opulence. I left her there to stare as I checked in at the desk and claimed the room keys.

The woman at the counter was all smiles and went on about how she watched mine and Rim's moment on TV and made sure the room was set up perfectly. I made sure to slip her an extra twenty before retreating to Rimmel's side.

"This place is amazing," she breathed out as I ushered her into the elevator, craning her neck so she could see every last sight before the doors shut us in.

Our suite was on the top floor, so it took a couple minutes to make it up there.

"Wait." Rimmel frowned when the doors pinged open, and I took her hand and led her into the hallway where there was a single set of white double doors. "I thought you wanted to go to Vegas?"

The elevator closed behind us, and I picked her up, holding her out in front of me like she was a doll, her feet dangling above the floor. "You'd really go?"

Her eyes softened. "I'd go anywhere with you."

I gathered her close and folded my body around hers. *Damn.* Sometimes she just got me exactly where I was the softest. The raging lust I'd been feeling dimmed to a dull roar and emotion swelled up within me.

There were just no words to describe what she was to me. Oxygen to a suffocating man. An umbrella in a rainstorm. Light in the darkness. None of those even came close to the way I loved her. To the way she made me feel.

I hugged her tighter for long seconds more and then pulled back. She tipped her chin and looked up.

"As bad as I want to fly to Vegas and claim you right now, I can't." I groaned.

Her forehead creased, and I leaned forward to kiss it.

"I can't be that selfish. You deserve better than a quickie *I do* with some Elvis standing in front of us. You deserve more than a bouquet bought at some cheap chapel that imports flowers by the dozen. I want you to have the wedding of your dreams with all our family around us."

"I don't need fancy flowers and a huge fairy tale." She smiled. "All I need is you."

"And that's exactly why you're getting everything." I kissed her nose.

"You're just scared of what your mother will do if she finds out we eloped."

I grimaced. God, she'd have my balls.

Rimmel laughed.

I growled and backed her against the room door. "Woman, are you saying you think I'm scared of my mother?"

"I am." She teased.

A little of the laughter left me. "Aww, baby."

"Shh." She pressed a finger to my lips, and I sucked it into my mouth.

It didn't escape my notice the way her hips tilted toward my body as I massaged her flesh with my tongue.

When I released her finger, her eyes were heavy with desire once more.

I swung her up into my arms and slid the keycard in the door. When it clicked, I held it open a crack with my foot. "How about we set a date tonight, then go home and tell everyone tomorrow?"

"I'd like that," she whispered.

"How fast can you put together a wedding?" I asked.

She laughed. "Fast."

I kicked open the door and carried her in the room.

She gasped the second her eyes left mine.

I was good.

Like really good.

The suite was the entire top floor, with a huge wall of windows that looked out over the lit-up city. The view was incredible, and all the lights on the buildings looked like stars against the night sky.

If the view wasn't amazing enough, the room was glowing with the soft radiance of candles the staff had lit before we arrived.

White roses filled the space. Vase after vase sat everywhere, and the entire place smelled of fresh-cut flowers. I took a chance with the roses. I knew they weren't her favorite because Zach has sent her some to lure her out one night. But those were red. Not the color of love for us, but the color of blood. These were white. Pure. Just like her and the way I'd always feel about her.

"Oh my goodness, Romeo." Rimmel breathed and all but jumped out of my arms to go over and finger one of the large bouquets nearby. "Did you do all of this?"

"Like I said, I want you to have everything."

"*You* are everything. All of this is just..." She looked around once more. "It's extra."

She looked gorgeous standing there amongst a sea of white roses and candlelight. With her in the room, I didn't notice the million-dollar view.

God, I wanted her.

As if she could read my mind, Rimmel reached for the hem of her hoodie and T-shirt. Slowly, she stripped them away, letting the clothes fall to the floor.

Next, she reached for the button on her jeans, popping it open and sliding down the zipper. I watched silently, need hammering in my veins as she stripped.

Once the jeans were gone, she stood before me in nothing but white lace panties and a bra. Her dark hair fell behind her shoulders like a dark backdrop for the creaminess of her skin.

Holding my gaze, she reached around behind her and unclasped the bra to let it slide down her arms and fall away.

My mouth went dry.

My eyes fastened on the perfect roundness of her breasts. I ached to touch them, to fill my mouth with her flesh and feel her body arch against mine, offering up even more of herself.

I stepped forward, and she made a sound of protest.

With a wicked little smile, she reached for her panties, stripping them away with painful precision and blatant lust, standing completely naked before me.

I watched with rapt attention as her little hand slipped over the flat front of her abdomen, across her hipbone, and down past her belly button. I licked my lips when her fingers delved into the dark patch of short curls right above her entrance.

"Rim," I growled. I was going to explode in my damn pants like a fifteen-year-old. Not only was she going to be my wife, but she was giving me a strip show, and now she was feeling herself up?

Damn.

She smiled a little as her hand moved farther down, disappearing between her thighs. She let out a soft sigh, and her nipples tightened.

I practically tripped over my own feet rushing across the room. I saw her about to tell me to stay back, but fuck that. I was done listening.

My hands spanned her narrow waist and I lifted her and tossed her over my shoulder. She giggled as I carried her back to the bedroom, but the second my hand slid between her legs from behind, her breath caught and she lifted her little ass to give me better access.

That was better.

Much better.

If this was any indication of how married life with Rim was gonna be, then I was one lucky bastard.

RIMMEL

Best night ever.

And...

As if the memory of Romeo proposing in the middle of a televised football game, literally sweeping me off my feet, and then making love to me on a literal bed of white rose petals over and over again wasn't unforgettable on its own, there was this huge sparkling diamond on my finger that would remind me every single day for the rest of my life.

I'd been staring at the diamond for hours, never growing tired of the way it sparkled. The center diamond was round and, frankly, too big and was surrounded by smaller diamonds. The band was thin and simple, with more sparkling diamonds. Sometimes when I stared at it, I wondered how such a delicate band could support such a large stone.

With a happy sigh, I sat back and turned my head toward him. My hair smelled like roses because of all the time we'd spent rolling around in the petals.

Romeo's large, warm hand covered mine, and I smiled.

We'd taken an early morning flight back to Maryland. Most of the Knights were flying back to the state today as well, but we weren't going where the team was based. We were going *home*.

Romeo only had one "off" day a week, and today was that day. Coming home for one day wasn't something he did very often, but he'd been doing more of it since everything happened with Zach. I knew the travel and the sleep he wasn't getting was going to catch up to him, and I worried about it, but telling him not to come home would be like telling him to hold his breath for twenty minutes.

It wasn't going to happen.

Going to his away games was something I didn't do very often either, but lately, it just seemed more important to be with him as much as possible. Lately, it had been even harder to be apart.

We'd all changed a lot in the past year and a half. More than I ever really thought possible. We'd grown up, become a family... We had learned what was most important in life.

This would actually be Romeo's last short trip home, because his first NFL season was almost over. Soon, it would be the offseason, and he'd be able to come home and stay there longer than a couple days. I looked forward to that day fiercely, but I was still so incredibly proud of the way he played this season and the success he'd achieved. I couldn't wait to see what the next season, and the ones after, would hold for him.

A few minutes later, the cab pulled onto our street, and I smiled. I knew Braeden and Ivy were going to be surprised to see us. They wouldn't expect us to show up so soon after he proposed. That was partly why we dragged ourselves out of the opulent hotel room after getting no sleep at all and boarded a plane.

The other part was because even though neither of us said it out loud, we were still really worried about how they both were doing. It hadn't been very long at all since Ivy's car accident and Zach's death. Being home was just the place we needed to be most right now.

The second the car dropped us off in the driveway, I hurried to the front door, fumbling in my bag for the keys. Of course, I dropped my bag, and half the contents spilled out all over the porch.

"Whatcha doing over there?" Romeo asked, clear amusement in his voice as he stepped up onto the porch behind me.

"You know me," I replied as I tried to scoop up my stuff that was scattered about. "Graceful as ever."

His large feet and jean-clad legs appeared before me. I paused in reaching for my ChapStick and smiled a little because of the déjà vu I was experiencing.

I craned my neck and looked up his long, muscular body standing over me. He was smiling, and I could tell by the look in his eyes that he was remembering the moment we met as well.

He bent down to help me pick up my things, and our hands brushed together as we both reached for the lip balm. I paused and looked up.

It was still there.

That jolt of electricity, that surge of chemistry right to my heart.

Even now that I was wearing his ring, he still affected me like that first day.

I hoped it never changed.

But unlike that day, he didn't hurry to scoop everything up and stand. Instead, Romeo fell back on his butt and pulled me into his lap. My things still littered the concrete, and the air was cold and brisk.

I didn't notice any of it. All I felt was his large, warm body beneath mine.

"I should have pulled you into my lap that day," he murmured, stroking my hair out of my face. "I should have looked into your beautiful face and known just how badly I needed you."

I pulled my knees closer to my chest, and Romeo wrapped both arms around me, holding me close. "We were from two different worlds," I whispered. "I was out of your league."

"No. I was out of *yours*. But we created our own world, didn't we? A world I wouldn't trade for anything."

"I love you," I answered softly.

He groaned and pressed his forehead against mine. "You're killing me, Smalls."

I smiled.

He kissed me like we weren't sitting out in the open, like it wasn't below freezing outside and neither of us had any sleep. He kissed me like we hadn't kissed a thousand times before, but this was the first time. The only time.

His lips were full and soft. The way he moved was lazy. Everything around me went hazy. Everything inside me went missing. It was only him and me. The past, the present, and the future swirled around us to create a cocktail of promise. A promise I knew we would both keep.

When he finally pulled back, I sighed deeply and snuggled into his chest. His lips brushed over the top of my head. "Your hands are cold, sweetheart."

"I didn't notice," I murmured.

In one fluid movement, he stood and set me on my feet. Within seconds, he'd scooped up my belongings and opened the door with the keys. I went ahead. Hearing the low sound of the TV, I dropped my bag on the floor and hurried into the family room.

Ivy's blond head peeked up from the couch, and her eyes filled with surprise. "Rimmel!"

Braeden's dark head jerked up, and he spun around. I smiled at him, and a huge grin took over his unshaved face. He gave a shout and jumped up and leapt over the back of the couch, sank low, and scooped me up to spin me around.

I laughed.

"There's my baby sis who's gone and got herself hitched!"

"Engaged, not married," I told him, smiling. He stopped spinning me, and I pulled back to look at him. His lopsided grin was so cute I laughed.

"You look good," he said, gruff. "Happy."

"I am."

He made a big show of kissing me loud and rather sloppily on the cheek before squeezing me again and then finally putting me down. He turned to Romeo, who was standing in the doorway, amusement clear in his eyes, and scowled.

"You," Braeden growled. "Don't you know you're supposed to ask for a blessing before you go giving out rings?"

Romeo made a rude sound. "I'm pretty sure I don't need your blessing to get married."

"That's my sister."

Romeo glanced at me, and I giggled. He rolled his eyes and sighed. "Braeden, would you please give me your blessing—the guy you've known almost all your life and ten times longer than your *sister*—to get married to the only woman I've ever loved?"

Braeden didn't miss a beat. "I'm not sure you're good enough for her."

I gasped, and Romeo gave him the finger.

Braeden cackled. "Blessing given."

"My life is complete," Romeo muttered.

"Rimmel!" Ivy called from her place on the couch. "Ignore those boneheads! I need to see that ring. I need details!"

Ivy looked small sitting in the center of the couch with a thick blanket piled over her lap. Her blond hair was pulled up into a messy topknot and her face was free of makeup. There was a white bandage on her forehead, covering the stitches still in her head, and her broken wrist was cast and lying in her lap amongst the blanket.

She looked pale and tired. Even though most of the bruises from the accident and her struggle with Zach were almost faded, she still looked a little battered and worn around the edges. It was to be expected really. She'd had a really hard past several months. Frankly, I was shocked she looked as good as she did.

I smiled at her and stepped up beside the couch. She handed me the coffee mug in her free hand, and I sat it on the white table we'd painted together. When her hand was free, she made an impatient sound and wiggled her fingers.

I laughed and held my hand out between us.

She gasped loudly. "Oh my God! This is gorgeous!"

"I know," I giggled.

Braeden leaned over the back of the couch to look at the ring. "My man has good taste."

Ivy was captivated by it, and she turned my hand this way and that, watching it catch the light. "It's perfect for you." She smiled and looked up. "I watched the whole proposal on TV!"

"They're gonna start talking about romance and flowers and shit," Braeden told Romeo. "It's bad enough I was sitting here watching the fashion channel with her."

"Hey," Ivy said, a little hurt in her tone. "You said you liked it."

Braeden's face softened and he leaned over the couch to kiss the top of her head. "'Course I do, baby."

"We'll give you two a minute to be all girly and shit," Romeo said and winked at me on his way past. "Want some coffee, Smalls?"

"Sure," I answered and sat gingerly on the couch near Ivy. I was afraid of jostling her body too much. I knew her broken ribs were still really tender.

Braeden snagged his mug and Ivy's off the table and followed Romeo toward the kitchen.

"So…" I began right away. "How are you feeling?"

Ivy grimaced. "I'm fine. I'm tired of being a prisoner to this couch, though."

"Didn't the doctor say you could go back to classes?"

She nodded. "Yeah, this week. I wanted to go today, but Braeden wasn't having it."

"He still hasn't left your side," I mused, thinking about what a good boyfriend Braeden made. I'd always known he would.

"No, and he's bossy as hell," Ivy grumped. "But…" Her voice softened. "I really do love him."

"I'm so glad you two are together."

"Me, too." She paused, and some of the light went out of her eyes. "When I think about everything I almost lost…"

I put my hand over hers. "But you didn't. You're still here. So is B. It's over now."

"Is it?" she whispered and swiped at her eyes.

Worry crept up the back of my neck. Why wouldn't it be over? Why would she think it wasn't?

Before I could ask, she smiled brightly and sat up a little straighter, holding her side as she moved. "Tell me all the details. Every last one of them."

I opened my mouth, but she cut me off. "And I'm sorry I wasn't able to style you for that game. If I had known it was going to be *the game,* I would have dragged myself out of bed and told Braeden to shove it when he said I couldn't go to the boutique."

I laughed. That would have been fun to watch. "It's fine. Besides, I think it's rather fitting I was wearing a hoodie and jeans when he proposed. That's the real me, you know?"

She nodded. "Yeah, it is, and you're right. It's perfect."

After that, she grilled me about every detail, stared at my ring, and started going on about all the different ways we could have our wedding.

We were still giggling about flowers and dresses when the guys came back into the room. I glanced up and met Romeo's eyes. He smiled, and my heart swelled.

"Rimmel!" Ivy said and grabbed my hand. "Pay attention. Color is very important."

Romeo winked at me before I turned back to her lecture on color selection for weddings. She looked more refreshed than when we first walked in, color in her cheeks and a smile on her lips. Braeden seemed to notice, too, and he gave me a grateful look from her other side.

This is why Romeo and I came home.

This is why we wanted to be with our family.

Because together we were better.

Together we could handle anything.

Cambria Hebert

GUILT, BRUISES... & ORANGE JUICE?

(AKA PART ONE)

CHAPTER ONE

Sometimes the echoes from
the past turn to screams.

#BuzzBoss

Two months later...

BRAEDEN

The odor was pungent.

It burned my nostrils, and I could feel the bitter tendrils in the air all the way down into my lungs, where it filled me up and created a burning sensation in my chest.

Even through the distinct sounds of groaning metal, the loud, rapid dripping of the god-awful-smelling gasoline, and the smooth purring of the Hellcat's engine several yards away, it was the silence that was the loudest.

The absence of her.

Her voice.

Her struggles.

Her life.

I blinked away the blurriness in my vision, willing away the intense urge to panic and the sudden moisture filling my eyes.

"Ivy!" I roared, rushing around the wreckage, ignoring the fact my foot stepped right in the center of a puddle and my shoe sucked up the liquid like a sponge.

Every cell in my entire body was focused on one thing.

The woman I loved.

The reason my heart even beat.

She didn't answer even when I asked her to, when I begged.

I screamed up at the sky, as if letting out a warning to the heavens that if she were dead, there would be hell to pay.

Only the stars winked back at me, making me think of her. Making me choke back even more tears and fear.

The slight squeeze of her fingers wasn't even enough to assure me she was still alive. It could be a trick, another sick mind game of Zach's.

Fucking Zach.

I shoved myself onto the ground and into the shattered window. Sharp pricks of glass cut into my arms, stabbing me in the stomach as if warning me to turn back.

I wouldn't walk away from here. Not without her.

She was responsive when I first saw her battered body inside the car, but by the time I pulled her out, she wasn't.

I rushed away from the heap of metal, my lungs and chest tight and seizing from the sharp smell of gasoline. I laid her on the ground.

She was so bloody.

So pale.

So still.

Her eyelids looked purple against the rest of her ghostly face, and her lips…

They were blue.

"Ivy!" I panicked. "Baby!"

Nothing.

Sheer terror grabbed me like icy, sharp talons. My hand shot out and grabbed her chin and pulled her face toward mine.

"Open your eyes right now!" I demanded.

She didn't.

I squeezed her chin until my fingers hurt, but not even that made her wake.

She was too pale, too still... too blue.

"Noooo!" I screamed, my voice hoarse with emotion and strained in defeat.

She was dead.

Ivy was dead, and I was here... alone.

CHAPTER TWO

#Fetish

Odaxelagnia:
Arousal from biting

#BiteMe

#BuzzBoss

IVY

It was happening again.

I knew it before he even started moving. The tension coiled in his body, the way his fingers gripped the blankets with so much force it was a wonder they weren't torn in two.

I'd become attuned to sleeping with someone who was haunted by nightmares. I'd become attuned to reading all the things Braeden never said.

There was a lot.

A lot of torture.

A lot of pain.

A lot of fear.

When he started thrashing about, I moved on instinct. Not away from him, though, toward him. Even during a night terror, when he was clearly out of his mind, I wasn't afraid of him. I would never be afraid of him. I loved him far too much for that.

I didn't think twice when I reached for his hands. The granite-like strength of them beneath my palms didn't faze me even a little.

"Braeden," I whispered loudly. "Everything's okay."

"No," he half groaned, half sobbed. The sound tore at my heart. It did every time.

I tightened my hold, but he started fighting against it, against me.

I was knocked away, my body caught by the mattress, and a pillow skidded over the side and landed on the floor. Prada untangled herself from the sheets and looked up at me with wide eyes.

"It's okay, pretty girl," I crooned.

She glanced over at Braeden at the same moment he flung out his arm. She leapt off the bed and went to her dog bed in the corner.

"Don't leave me," he sobbed. The guttural sound, the sheer pain in those words was a knife to my heart. I froze, momentarily stunned by the grief and torment in his voice.

It was the first time he'd said that during a nightmare. But this was the longest one yet. Usually, I could quell the worst of his upset with a touch or my voice. Usually, his eyes would spring open, unfocused and blurry, and find me.

Tonight, he was too lost for that.

He thrashed again, and I ducked out of the way, narrowly avoiding being shoved off the bed. I thought about yelling for Romeo, worried maybe I didn't have the strength to subdue him.

I didn't, not really. Not physical strength anyway.

But I had another kind of strength that far outweighed muscles.

And I wouldn't call for Romeo when it was me Braeden needed most.

I moved fast, straddling his hips and pressing my body over him. The weight of me sitting on him made him pause in struggling.

"Braeden," I said, firm.

Both his hands caught my wrists and squeezed. He squeezed so hard it hurt, but I said nothing and I didn't flinch away.

I wanted to press my hands on his shoulders and pin him down completely, but I couldn't disengage from his grip.

"Braeden James, look at me," I demanded.

His eyes snapped open.

My heart broke.

Tears swam in their surface. Real, raw emotion. He looked up, reality crashing back into his world as a single fat tear fell from the corner of his eye and trailed down the side of his face.

Inside my chest, the beating of my heart slowed to a heavy thud.

I think most people want to find a love that's so strong nothing can break it. I think most people fantasize about becoming someone's entire universe. The feeling is almost like a drug.

But just like any drug, there are side effects to a love so unflinching.

Pain.

Weakness.

Fear.

I'd never seen Braeden cry. Until now.

Until the reoccurring nightmare of me dying in his arms won its first round.

I wanted so badly to wipe that tear away. His grip was still so tight, almost unbearable, yet I acted as if I didn't even notice. I leaned down close to his face.

"I'm here, my love," I whispered, gentle. "I'm right here. Warm and breathing."

I didn't know exactly what he dreamed almost nightly. He never would admit the details. But I knew it was always about the car accident the night Zach died. I knew in it, I was always the one who died.

His grip relented, and I took his face in my palms after brushing at the wetness on his cheeks. I couldn't even tell you what it did to me to see such a strong man cry.

"I'm right here with you, B. Exactly where I belong."

"Ivy." His voice was gravelly, like he was in danger of losing it.

I nodded, and a few long strands of silky hair fell over my shoulders and dangled between us. One of the strands dragged across his chest, and he sighed.

I wore it straight and long a lot these days. It was a lot of extra work, but I found the way it brushed against him as a quiet caress at night calmed him in ways my words could not.

True to my thoughts, his fingers found the strands and he carefully wrapped his hand around them.

A sigh of relief filled the space between us, but I knew it wasn't going to be enough.

Not tonight.

I still saw it in his eyes. The emptiness. The horror. The darkness he tried so hard to keep hidden.

"You're here," he murmured, tightening his hold on my hair.

I nodded and caressed his face. "I love you, Braeden."

He made a sound deep in his chest. The wariness in his gaze hurt. Not because he was unsure if this moment were real or just another dream, but just the fact that he had to wonder.

He was tortured.

I reached up and untangled one of his hands and laid it against my chest. "Feel that?" I whispered.

He nodded.

"See, I'm alive. You saved me. Everything's fine."

His hand spasmed against my chest, and his molten eyes flared. Suddenly, the fear in the room turned to desperation.

I gave in, instantly. After what just happened, I was feeling a little desperate, too.

His ability to move fast always surprised me. Before I knew what was happening, he was on top of me, his heavy, sweat-dampened body pressing me into the mattress. He braced his hands on either side of my head. The look in his eyes was fierce.

I spread my legs.

His nostrils flared, and then in one hard, fast stroke, he plunged into my body.

I cried out, not because it hurt, but because it was so sudden and he was so incredibly hard. He usually didn't penetrate me this way. Despite me telling him over and over that I could handle it, Braeden was still very careful with me.

My cry must have broken a little of whatever emotion he was lost in, because his body went taut and he stared down at me.

I didn't give him the chance to think. I tilted my hips up, forcing him deeper inside. And just like that, he was lost again. The little bit of clarity left his gaze and his eyes slid closed. His face was both a mask of pain and awe as he started moving.

My inner walls felt tight compared to his throbbing, solid length. It was almost like he'd grown bigger or I'd grown smaller since we'd last made love.

But tonight was different.

Tonight, Braeden needed something from me, something he never asked for. And though my heart felt bruised for him, I was also oddly endeared.

This was just another way he was opening up to me. Another side of him he was finally letting me see. Almost our entire relationship, Braeden was nothing but strong. Nothing but unbendingly protective, almost impenetrable.

And even though right now it was his steely cock literally pounding into my entrance, it wasn't me who was being penetrated. It was him.

I was finally getting into that very secret, very unknown side of him. The side where his deepest feelings lay.

The place B himself likely never acknowledged.

Above me, his body forcibly shook. I felt the tremble in his arms as his cock speared me over and over. He was anything but gentle; tonight he was greedy and rough.

When his hand fisted my hair, I allowed myself to be jerked upward, my head leaving the pillows so he could assault my mouth with his.

Our teeth gnashed together, but neither of us pulled away. This side of Braeden was addictive. I kissed him back, meeting his demands—keeping up with them even—without making any of my own.

I wanted him to have everything.

I wanted him to take it all.

He ripped his mouth away and growled—the sound more animalistic than human—and he buried his face in the side of my neck. He tucked one arm beneath me, flattening the palm of his hand beneath my ass and thrusting my hips up so I was tilted even closer against him.

I whimpered when he hit a spot that sent chills racing up my spine.

His teeth scraped over my collarbone as his other arm flung out. I felt him grip the top of the headboard, bracing himself against the bedframe.

With the angle of my body and his newfound leverage, he pushed so deep I felt the tip of his swollen and pulsing head at the entrance of my womb.

I opened my mouth, but no sound came out.

I failed to breathe. I failed to think.

He'd never been so deep.

And that spot he'd hit just moments ago?

His cock was now pressed against it, rubbing as he thrust as deep as a man could go inside a woman.

A guttural sound left his lips, and he started to pull back slightly. I snaked my arms around his back and kept him where he was. An orgasm was building inside me, teasing me with the sweet promise of bliss.

It was almost painful how strong my need was to release. Something in the back of my mind whispered I should let him pull out just a little. But then the rest of me, the harlot who wanted insane pleasure, told that part of me to shut it.

I knew when I fell, it would be the most powerful climax I'd ever known. The walls of my core were flexing so firmly around him I wondered if he could feel it.

As if to answer my unspoken question, the hand holding my ass in place tightened. His palm filled with my flesh, and he shoved deep with a hoarse cry.

I made a sound and clung to him, holding him tight as an orgasm ripped me in half.

I didn't know I was biting him until, right next to my ear, he said, "That's it, baby. Use your teeth."

Still completely in the throes of an earthshattering orgasm, my teeth sank farther into his shoulder.

He growled, and I literally felt his cock pumping his release. I whimpered as my body milked him, demanding every last drop he had to give. Even after his muscles relaxed, he was still hard.

I collapsed against the bed, embarrassed that tears dashed to my eyes. Emotion so swift and strong rushed into my chest; it was all I could do not to cry.

What the hell kind of woman cried after sex?

The kind of woman who has powerful, barrier-busting sex.

I squeezed my eyes closed as he moved inside me, a few more long strokes that felt like a sinful massage after a hard day of work.

When he pulled out and collapsed beside me, I couldn't move. I knew I needed to clean up, but I just didn't care. In that moment, feeling the evidence of his release against my thighs was so satisfying.

It was assurance that Braeden got whatever it was he needed from me.

"Ivy," he breathed and reached for me.

I cuddled up to his side, and his arm fastened around me. His lips brushed over my hairline in a gentle caress, and then within seconds, his breathing deepened and sleep claimed him once more.

CHAPTER THREE

> #WheresRomeo
> It's NFL off-season ladies.
> That means #24 is back in town.
> Keep your eyes open. U just
> might see him on campus.
> #BuzzBoss

ROMEO

Getting out of bed sucked.

Especially when it was early, cold out, and my sexy ass woman was pressed up against me, naked.

I thought about slowly waking her up, teasing her folds open with my lips, and penetrating her with my tongue until she was drenched, breathing heavy, and ready for my cock.

Yeah, the idea had merit.

Okay, it was the best idea I'd ever had.

But I held myself back.

Ever since I'd put that ring on her finger and I came home for the off-season, I'd been on her like yellow on a taxi. She never complained. Hell, half the time, she started it. I actually didn't plan on giving her much rest either, but this morning I would. She was sleeping so soundly when I slipped out from beneath her, I knew letting her rest was the best thing.

But there were no breaks for me.

I pulled on some workout shorts and went into the gym, pushing the door around, but not latching it.

Closing it all the way only resulted in Murphy sitting outside and meowing like he was being tortured. Last time I did it, he woke Rimmel, and she'd come bursting into the room without her glasses, no pants, and wild hair, thinking there was some emergency.

It'd been funny as hell.

However, she didn't think so.

So now I left the door open slightly so Murphy could satisfy his curiosity by looking in here and then disappearing.

I started out with some light calisthenics and then pushed some earbuds into my ears and pulled up a running mix on my phone. The off-season was time for players to let their bodies heal from the constant abuse they were put through during football season. We were told not to train too hard or too long, that our bodies needed time to recover just like our minds.

I still worked out almost every day. I wasn't about to lose any of the conditioning I'd worked on for the past several years. My arm was back full strength, and I'd finished up the season really strong. So strong that I had another three-year contract already signed.

And damn, the money was fucking sweet.

If I'd thought one million had been a lot for my first season... well, the number I was getting now made that literally look like change one found in the couch cushions.

I knew Rim didn't care, but I sure as hell liked knowing I could take of her the way I wanted to.

Dad lined up a meeting with an accountant and financial advisor, and we were meeting with him next week so I could set up some accounts and shit to make sure I had everything in place the way it needed to be. Dad was also drafting up a will for me to make sure everything went into Rim's name if anything ever happened to me.

I didn't like thinking like an adult. It seemed like a foreign concept. I'd rather goof off with B and play ball. But I was an adult now. It wasn't just age that made me one either. It was experience. Everything we'd been through.

I had a wife to think about.

No, technically, Rimmel and I weren't married yet, but the second I put that ring on her finger, she became my wife to me. It wasn't a feeling I planned on fighting. She was it. My heart knew it. That's all that mattered.

The amount of money coming at me was insane. I needed some help on how to handle it all. Sure, my family had always been well off. I'd never wanted for anything, but even my parents didn't have the kind of money I did now.

I wasn't about to blow it all on stupid shit. If we were smart, we could live on what I was making for the rest of our lives. Thinking about the future was something I'd been doing a lot of lately. I had everything I wanted right now. It was all pretty fucking perfect.

I knew how easily that could change.

It hadn't been an easy road to get to this point, and as basically the head of this family, it was my responsibility to make sure if shit went south, we'd all be taken care of.

But for right now, everything was good.

The stuff that mattered anyway. Sure, there might be some drama brewing with the Knights. Nothing I couldn't handle. I wasn't about to participate in it, but I'd keep an eye on it.

Just another reason to maybe put a little pressure on Gamble to sign B already. It was in the works; we had a meeting with Dad later today.

We = me + B.

It'd be nice to have my best friend on the field with me again. And even better to have someone I trusted completely to watch my back.

Not that I felt threatened.

Yet.

If the past had taught me anything, though, it was just because something didn't appear threatening at first, it didn't mean it wasn't.

*Cough, cough, *Zach* cough, cough.*

I bumped up the speed on the treadmill a bit to go harder, pushed the thoughts out of my head, and focused on the run. When that was done, I hit the weights until the back of my neck prickled with awareness and I knew I wasn't alone.

She was turning away to scurry off when I caught her out of the corner of my eye. I went on alert immediately because I knew if she was hovering this early in the door where only I was, she needed me.

I thought back to the shout I heard early this morning, but then it was followed by silence.

I had a sinking feeling whatever she was about to tell me was going to threaten the "good" that our family was finally getting back to.

CHAPTER FOUR

#Quote

"We do not fear the unknown.
We fear what we think we
know about the uknown."
-Teal Swan

#BuzzBoss

BRAEDEN

I reached for her.

She wasn't there.

All traces of sleep and comfort burst like a balloon hit with a dart. I jerked up, blinking, trying to assimilate my surroundings. The room was dim, but daylight pushed at the edges of the blinds. Ivy's pajamas (my shirt) were draped over the corner of the bed, and her scent lingered in the room.

I glanced at the clock, noting I had a couple hours before classes. I learned a long time ago not to take classes too early in the morning.

That shit was for people who didn't value sleep.

The blankets were tangled around me like I'd been tossing and turning, and it took a second to get out of bed without falling over and busting my ass. Once I was free, I grabbed some clothes from the dresser and walked across the hall stark naked.

On my way, I heard Prada barking at Ivy downstairs, and her light laugh filtered up the stairwell. The corner of my mouth tipped up as I continued on into the shower.

I stood under the hot spray for long minutes, just letting the water pelt me as I tried to erase the worst of the exhaustion from my brain.

I hadn't been sleeping well.

Not lately.

A guy would think a couple months after the shit hit the fan and finally calmed back down, he'd be sleeping better than ever. That wasn't the case.

If anything, a good night's sleep seemed harder and harder to achieve.

Before, it had been about Ivy. About making sure she was healing. All the injuries she sustained during that accident with *him* had taken weeks and weeks to heal. Her mental state was precarious as well. I was damn proud when she announced she was going to therapy and then lifted her chin as if she'd challenge whatever joke I made about a head shrink.

Hell. I didn't make any joke. If anything, I fell for her a little more because she was willing to admit she needed some help dealing.

Turns out talking to a professional—and dare I say someone who didn't want to punch a window every time she needed to work through what that fucker put her through—really helped her.

So time went on. Rome and Rim got engaged. His first NFL season ended, and he came home for the off-season. A new semester began at Alpha U, and Drew moved into the guest room permanently.

And the best part about it all was Zach wasn't out there lurking and plotting to hurt someone I loved. He was gone. Dead. Burned to death.

He couldn't hurt my family anymore.

But he was haunting me.

That entire night haunted me.

I couldn't shake the fear of almost losing Ivy forever. I was a different guy since, like a switch inside me flipped and there was no way to flip it back.

I grabbed the soap and scrubbed myself clean, then let the suds rinse away while I washed my hair.

The nightmare last night had been the worst one. Even though some of it was hazy, I remembered the mind-numbing fear of Ivy being dead. I'd never been a fearful guy. I wasn't afraid of life or anything it threw at me.

But now... now I was afraid of something.

Of death.

Of loss.

Of what I'd done.

I stuck my head under the spray and rubbed at it vigorously. The hot water felt good, loosening up my tense muscles.

I wanted Ivy. I wanted to see her face and feel the softness of her hair. It made me feel weak to need another person so much, but I couldn't help it. I did need her. It seemed like I needed her now more than ever.

Not that I would say it out loud.

She already knows...

The thought drew me up short. Last night replayed through my mind like a movie. A fucking hot, erotic movie.

Of me waking up, feeling desperate and lost. She was on top of me, offering warmth and comfort. If anyone could bring me back from the edge, it was her.

She offered herself up to me, and I'd taken it all.

Fuck.

I hadn't been gentle. If anything, I'd been an asshole.

Was that why she wasn't in bed this morning?

Had I hurt her without realizing it?

I shut off the water abruptly and grabbed a towel. The way I behaved last night was un-fucking-acceptable. I knew better than that shit. Ivy deserved better.

I had to make it right.

CHAPTER FIVE

#BuzzBoss

#UpsideDownNotification

If you can read this then you're pretty fucking awesome.

#ThisIsATest

IVY

I couldn't sleep.

Even though it was a couple hours before I needed to be awake and the pull of Braeden's warm, solid body beside mine was intoxicating, sleep was illusive.

I lay there for a while, content just to be next to him—that is until I realized there might be a reason I couldn't sleep. Once I allowed that thought space in my head, I knew there would be no use.

The sound of Romeo working out in the gym down the hall was like a beacon. I didn't even realize what I was doing until I was hovering in the partially open doorway while he punished a set of barbells with his muscle.

Want a bit of stark honesty?

Romeo intimidated me.

There. I said it.

Yes. Yes, Romeo and I had grown closer, and yes, there was this unspoken understanding between us. He even called me his sister, he and B were practically brothers, and I thought of him as my family.

But still.

Romeo and I were a lot alike in some ways. More so than anyone else in this house. Aside from the fact we were both blond bombshells (ha-ha, I had to get that in there), we both knew what it was like to be caught up in a social circle—a status quo, if you will.

At one point, both Romeo and I had been willing victims (dare I say participants) in what was the social hierarchy of Alpha U. Romeo was laidback, charming, and everyone's golden boy. He acted like it came natural, and I knew a lot of it did. But not all of it. There was no way. A guy like him (with a solid family background and values) didn't literally rise to fame on campus overnight and become the king of everything without feeling the pressure.

He had to live up to it all. He had to be the player everyone cheered for. The charmer every girl swooned for. And the bad guy still good enough that he could still play on the team.

Romeo might not know it, but I understood the balancing act he likely juggled for the last several years.

Sure, it wasn't so prevalent in his life now, not since Rimmel tripped (literally) into his life and changed everything. He didn't care about status as much—but it was still there—I knew he still felt the pressure. Maybe more now that his life was so changed.

Hence, one of the reasons he was punishing the weights right this moment.

And me? Just like him, I came to Alpha U free for the first time in my entire life. Free of my overprotective brothers. Free of the watchful eyes of my parents, grandparents, and large extended family. I hadn't realized it then, but my freedom didn't last long because I became a slave to the status race.

I became the girl everyone thought I was. The one people seemed to want me to be.

It got me hurt, violated, and betrayed.

Just like Romeo.

I watched him for a second longer. He wasn't wearing a shirt, and his smooth skin was shiny with sweat from the punishing workout he was inflicting on himself.

Damn. It made me feel bad for thinking about a donut for breakfast.

I worked out, but what he was doing made what I usually did look like a freaking kindergarten nap.

His muscles rippled as he lifted. His biceps bulged with every curl he completed. But beyond the curls, he was doing squats while standing on some half-circle bubble that made it hard to balance.

I knew he'd already been on the treadmill. I'd heard the steady of hum of it just a little while ago.

The waistband of his gym shorts was damp, the red color darker around the top than the rest of the fabric. I knew it was because he'd been dripping so much sweat, and as he moved, I couldn't help but notice the muscles in his back.

Suddenly, I wondered why I was here. What had possessed me to step into the doorway while he was training?

I turned to hurry back to my room, but his voice stopped me.

"You gonna come in or just stand there and watch?"

I froze like I'd been caught doing something illegal. How had he known I was there? His back was to me.

I swung back around with a sheepish grin on my lips. "Sorry, I—"

He looked over his shoulder, pausing in the squats and lifts, and winked. Straightening, he swung toward the rack of weights and set the ones down he'd been holding. I was still in the doorway when he snagged up a water and poured half of it down his throat.

"What's the matter, Ivy?" he asked, his tone knowing.

"I'm worried about Braeden," I rushed out. I felt my eyes widen, surprised even by my own words, though I didn't know why.

I was worried. So worried I couldn't sleep.

"And I was just thinking… and I ended up here," I added, a little bewildered.

Romeo's eyes, which had narrowed when I first spoke, softened now and a small smile played on his lips. "You can talk to me anytime."

I nodded and walked farther into the room. Now that I admitted out loud (and to myself) that I needed to talk, it seemed only natural it was Romeo I came to. It seemed completely normal the very strength that intimidated me was what drew me this morning.

He snagged a nearby towel and used it to mop up some of the sweat on his face and chest. Before I'd fallen for Braeden, it would have been natural to check out Romeo, especially when he was standing in front of me half dressed. I mean, honestly, I used to check him out all the time when he was fully clothed and walking around campus.

Now that just seemed wrong.

Sure, Romeo had an awesome body. But he was family, and he wasn't Braeden.

"What's going on with B?" he asked when I said nothing.

I hesitated, wondering how much to say, wondering if B would be upset when he found out I'd gone to Romeo about his dreams.

"Are you scared of me, Ivy?" Romeo's question cut into my inner debate.

"What?" I gasped.

He gave me a knowing look. "You seem kinda scared to be in here right now."

I felt my shoulders slump. I was acting ridiculous. Why did I feel so afraid to talk to him? Why was I so intimidated by him? Romeo had been nothing but good to me. Great, even. Clearly, deep down, I knew I could go to him because I was standing here… so why was I having such a hard time opening up?

"Braeden's gonna be really mad if he finds out I've come to you."

Romeo seemed to think about my words. Then he dropped down on a nearby weight bench. "I don't think this is about B."

I started to tell him this was exactly about B, but he held up his hand. "I don't mean what you want to talk about. I mean the reason for it. *You* need to talk to someone about B and about whatever's going on inside *you*. And I think you know I'm the guy for that talk."

I nodded. "It's just… we've never really talked like this…" My words faded away.

He tilted his head to the side. "Maybe not. But I think you and I have had a lot of conversations without saying anything."

I thought back to the times he would make sure I was okay to drive home from a party, about how he would measure me with his stare, and I would let him see I was really more sober than most realized. I thought about the night he came into my room and held me after a nightmare, how he barely said two words to me, but his presence was more than enough. I remembered how he sat beside me in the hospital after that car crash that killed Zach. We'd been the only two in the room, Romeo finally having persuaded B to take a shower. We hadn't talked about what happened that night. But he'd held my hand, and I'd cried silent tears.

I'd felt better after that cry.

In a way, words from Romeo weren't necessary. He knew how to be there for a girl without them.

He was right. This was about me. About me needing to say what was going on, because this time he wouldn't be able to see it.

"He's been having nightmares," I whispered.

"Is that the sound I heard coming from down the hall this morning?" he asked, concerned.

My eyes snapped up to his. What had he heard? Oh God, had he heard us having sex? Braeden was rough, and we probably hadn't been quiet. "He did yell out in his sleep." I hedged.

Romeo nodded. "Yeah, must be what I heard, but then it got quiet so I figured it was nothing."

So he hadn't heard. Thank God.

"He's been having them a lot actually. This morning's... it was the worst one yet. I almost yelled for you."

I felt his attention sharpen. Concern darkened his eyes. "But you didn't."

I shook my head. "No. I was able to bring him out of it."

"What's he dreaming about?"

"That night," I said, a small shudder making my shoulders quake. Romeo scooted just an inch or two closer. I glanced up. "He never wants to talk about it the next day. But it's haunting him."

"Zach?" he asked.

"Honestly? I know Zach dying weighs on him, but I'm pretty sure the nightmares are about me... In them I die that night."

Romeo muttered a soft curse and ran a hand over the back of his head.

"This morning, he—" My voice broke as I remembered. "He asked me not to leave him."

Romeo made a low sound, and I looked away, caught up in the pain I felt radiating from our bed this morning. The fear.

"What else, Ivy?" Romeo pushed. He reached for my hand.

My voice broke. "He cried," I burst out. "I've never seen him cry."

"*Fuck*," Romeo whispered and released my hand so he could pull me into his side. I buried my face in his chest and took a shuddering breath. I wasn't sure I'd ever get over how broken I felt when I wiped the wetness off Braeden's face this morning.

He hugged me tight while I fought back my own tears. Now wasn't the time to cry. I had to be stronger than that. For so, so long, Braeden was the strong one. Braeden literally held me up when I was down.

It was my turn to do it for him.

I pulled back to look up at Romeo's face. "Zach might be dead, the worst of what we went through over, but it isn't finished. He's struggling inside, Romeo. He won't talk about it. Maybe he doesn't even understand it himself. But the dreams are getting worse. He's getting harder to calm down."

"Calm down?"

I nodded. "He starts thrashing around in bed. Like he's fighting something. Or someone."

"Did he hurt you?" Romeo demanded.

I sat up straight at the steel in his tone. I tucked my hands beneath my thighs, sitting on them. "Of course not."

His hand shot out and grabbed my arm, pulling it from beneath my legs. Even though he moved fast, he was gentle, like he understood his own strength and the lack of mine.

"Where'd you get these bruises?"

I felt my face pale. I looked down at the purple marks on my wrist. I knew I had matching marks on my other one, but I kept it tucked into my side, hidden.

They were from this morning, when Braeden grabbed me.

"He didn't know what he was doing," I explained. "He was dreaming, and I... I was trying to wake him up."

"You should have yelled for me," he said, frustrated, and released my arm. He pushed off the bench and started pacing the small gym.

"That would have just made it worse," I said, no give in my voice.

Romeo looked at me over his shoulder.

"He's already beating himself up enough, but to have you break into our room to stop him from hurting me in bed?" I shook my head. "He'd never forgive himself, and you know it."

"Fuck!" Romeo spat.

"Besides, I was the one who climbed on him, to calm him down."

I felt Romeo's eyes burn my skin. "You have bruises anywhere else?"

"No!" I hurried to say. "The second he woke up, he calmed down."

Okay, that was kind of a lie. But Braeden hadn't hurt me, and I wasn't about to tell Romeo about our sexual encounter.

My reply didn't seem good enough for him. He pinned me with a solid, unblinking stare. "Are you scared of him, Ivy? This bringing up stuff for you?"

I wasn't offended he would ask. It was kind of an expected question after what I just told him. In fact, I was a little touched he'd ask. Almost like he'd stand between B and me if he needed to, until this was worked out.

Suddenly, everything didn't seem as bad as it had this morning.

"I'm fine." I promised. "Sure, I still think about what happened... but it's not like it used to be. I haven't had a panic attack in a while. Therapy helped. Braeden helped."

He glanced down at my wrist again.

I lifted my chin. "I'm not scared of him. Not even a little."

The corner of Romeo's mouth tilted up. "I like you, princess."

"Princess." I felt my nose wrinkle.

He grinned widely. "Yep. Princess. With your designer clothes, fancy dog, and air of confidence. You're the closest thing to royalty I've ever met."

"Why does that feel like an insult?" I wondered sarcastically.

"It's not." Romeo laughed. "But you're definitely stubborn. Especially when it comes to B."

"I won't let anything else hurt him," I intoned, ignoring the ridiculous nickname. "I mean it. He's protected me, shielded me, and literally saved my life. He's there for all of us, *always*. He never once has asked for anything. He's done more for all of us than you will ever know."

Romeo's amusement seemed to lift and his eyes narrowed. But I plowed on before he could question what I implied.

"It's time we protected him. It's time we get him through."

"Is that a royal decree, your highness?" Romeo's lips twitched.

My eyes narrowed and I threw out my arm to smack him. He laughed and caught my wrist, looking down and gentling his hold. "You should put on something to cover these. He'll go crazy if he sees them and realizes it was him."

I nodded. "Okay."

He brushed his thumb over the darkest mark before releasing me, as if for a second, he disappeared inside his own head, lost in thought. "Next time, call for me. I'd rather he be pissed I yanked him out of bed than see another mark on your body."

"It wasn't intentional," I said, pulling my wrist back.

"I know that. You don't ever have to defend B to me. I'll always be on his side, no matter what."

"You will?" It seemed really important to me in that moment to hear him say that.

"I swear. No matter what."

I let out a breath and nodded. "Thank you, Romeo."

He hugged me against his sweaty chest. At first, I was surprised, but then I softened and hugged him back. "I'll always be on your side too, Ivy," he added softly.

My arms tightened around him.

He chuckled. "Pretty good grip for a princess."

I groaned and pulled away. "That's gonna stick, isn't it?" I knew he'd wanted something to call me (because, you know, brothers don't call their sisters by their names), but princess?

"Oh yeah." He laughed and his eyes twinkled with amusement because he knew I hated it.

I sighed, accepting my nickname fate, and left him there, laughing behind me.

I felt better having talked to him. The reassurance he was going to be there for Braeden no matter what was exactly what I needed to hear.

Because something deep down inside me whispered that Braeden was really going to need it.

CHAPTER SIX

#CaffeineEmergency
No coffee. No wakey.
If I tell you who I am, will
you bring me a cup?
#DesperateButNotThatDesperate
#BuzzBoss

BRAEDEN

Ivy was the only one in the kitchen when I went downstairs. It was still kinda early, so I hoped we'd have a little time alone before everyone else came down for coffee.

From the doorway, I watched her quietly. She was dressed in a pair of jeans that made her legs look like they went on for miles. They weren't the normally tight kind she favored, the kind she could wear with boots. These were faded and the bottoms flared out with a wide hemline that covered her feet completely.

It made me smile because it made her look like she was floating right there above the floor.

Like an angel.

My angel.

The way the worn fabric cupped her round ass was mouthwatering. Ivy was all woman. All curves and softness. I fucking loved that about her. She wasn't too thin or so small it scared me, though she'd gotten thinner the past few months. Something I wasn't too happy about but refused to comment on. Hell, it was no wonder she lost weight after everything she'd been through. Now that she'd been in therapy a while and life was finally calming down, I knew she'd likely gain it back. I'd make sure of it.

Just like I'd make sure our life stayed calm.

Note to self: put an end to the nightmares.

If only it were that easy.

The top she was wearing was white, some relaxed material that floated over her body and moved in gentle swaying motions as she moved. It billowed out around her upper arms and then the fabric gathered around her elbows and became tighter, hugging her forearms all the way down past her wrists.

She drew the coffee down from the cabinet and tossed her long, straight hair over her shoulders. I'd always been an ass man, but lately, those long, blond strands had been equally claiming my eye. There was something about the silkiness that calmed me. Something about the way I felt when I wound my hands around the length and held on.

She's my anchor.

Once the coffee was brewing, she turned to put away the container and noticed me hovering nearby.

Her smile was immediate, and the tightness I'd had in my chest since the shower relaxed some. She didn't look upset with me; she didn't appear hurt.

I pushed off the doorway and strolled into the room. Ivy abandoned what she was doing and met me halfway. I picked her up and sat her on the counter, stepping between her legs.

"My bed was empty this morning," I growled. "I didn't like it."

A shadow passed behind her blue eyes. "I couldn't sleep. I didn't want to wake you."

I grunted, not sure what to make of that. My lips parted, about to ask the question I wasn't sure I wanted her to answer.

Ivy's hands cupped my jaw and rubbed. "You didn't shave," she purred.

My body responded to her touch, to the sound of her voice, and I pushed my jaw farther into her palms. "Too interested in finding you," I murmured.

A slight smile lifted the corners of her full mouth, and she leaned forward, rubbing her lips and jaw over the scruff. Her teeth scrapped at the underside of my chin and then went up to nip at my lower lip. "I like this. Soft and scratchy at the same time," she whispered.

"I'll keep that in mind," I murmured and kissed her softly.

Ivy drew back slightly, her hands falling into her lap and concern darkening her gaze. "Are you okay?"

I flashed her a fast smile. She'd expected me to jump her right here in the kitchen. I would have any other morning, but not right now. Right now, I had more important things to think about besides burying myself deep in my woman's body.

I said nothing, shifting to reach between us and cup her hands in mine. Slowly, gently, I slid my palms down toward her wrists, hooking my thumbs in hems of her sleeves.

Ivy stiffened and started to pull back. Mentally, I cursed myself. That one action told me everything I needed to know. I knew then I'd see marks I didn't want to see.

"What are you doing?" she demanded, her voice worried.

Backing off a little, I lifted her left hand and met her eyes. I held her gaze as I pressed a kiss to the center of her palm. The worry in her gaze turned hazy. Swiftly but gently, I pushed up the sleeve to reveal her slender wrist.

The wrist that bore my fingerprints.

A sick feeling clawed at my gut. My stomach clenched and anger burned my chest. I'd put marks on her. I'd done the one thing I was most against.

"Braeden." Ivy tried to pull her wrist away, to cover it back up.

I motioned with my chin to her other hand. "That one the same?"

Her silence was my confirmation.

"You were dreaming again," she whispered. "You didn't realize—"

"Don't you dare make excuses for me," I snapped, harsh.

She pulled her arm out of my hold and pulled down the sleeve. "I'm not."

"You fucking are, and I won't have it," I growled.

She opened her mouth, a stubborn glint in her eye, and I held up my hand. "Where else did I hurt you?"

"Nowhere."

I gave her a sour look.

Her eyes narrowed. "Are you accusing me of lying?" she intoned.

"I was too rough." My voice was hoarse. A few curse words fell from my lips as I thought about the way I'd pounded into her this morning. God, it had felt so fucking good. It made me feel like a bastard.

"Braeden James," she commanded and took my face in her hands. "Listen to me right now. Yes, you were rough. Yes, I have bruises on my wrists. But they aren't from the sex. It was because *I* climbed on top of you when you were having a nightmare. *Me.* I did that. Not you."

Anger slapped me all over again, and I felt the protest work its way up the back of my throat. Ivy must have seen it in my eyes.

"You did not hurt me. I swear," she vowed. Then in a softer, more confiding tone, she said, "I liked it."

My eyes flashed up to hers.

She nodded. "I came so hard..." Her voice trailed away. "It was like you were finally giving me all of you."

"Baby..." My voice broke. "You have all of me already."

She shook her head. "No, B. There's this piece of you, this place deep down you keep from everyone. Even from yourself."

I made a rude sound. "I know it's there. I hate it."

"I don't." God, the honest vulnerability in her voice was going to be my undoing. It was like every word she spoke was a secret she was revealing for the very first time. "I love it. I love every single part of you, Braeden James."

Those words broke me. Broke the anger I felt, the self-loathing I was allowing to swallow me whole. How was I supposed to hate any piece of myself if she saw value? How was I supposed to hold on to the fear of that piece of me when Ivy clearly glimpsed it and still sat here, unflinching?

"I can take it." She continued. "I *want* it. You try to conceal it, but I see. You feel things more deeply than anyone realizes. You keep things so tightly caged that when you finally let go, it's like a wild animal breaking loose. Stop holding back. Stop being scared. Trust yourself as much as I trust you."

She made it sound so simple.

"Bruises, Ivy." I reminded her, picking up her wrist again.

She made a sound in her throat and grabbed the hem of my T-shirt and lifted.

"Stop trying to look at me naked," I protested. "This is a serious conversation."

She laughed and stripped the shirt over my head. A sound of satisfaction filled the air.

What can I say? I was damn fine.

"Guess I should apologize, too."

"What?" Her words snapped me out of distraction.

Her index finger smoothed across my shoulder and then traced a spot that was suddenly tender to the touch. I glanced down.

"I bit you this morning. Left a mark."

Indeed. There were teeth marks on my shoulder.

Images of us in bed together, the memory of the sounds she made as she splintered apart so hard beneath me, and the feel of her teeth sinking into my flesh as I emptied my release into her buzzed through my head. "Baby, I liked it."

I covered her hand with mine, and we stood there cupping my shoulder.

"Then is it so hard to believe I liked it, too?"

I felt myself giving in. The sex was fucking level ten this morning. So fucking deep, and I'm not just talking about how far I was inside her body.

(But I totally was balls deep.)

I groaned.

Her smile was smug, like she'd somehow won a war.

"Blondie," I growled.

"B," she growled back, but it sounded like a baby kitten yawning.

I made a rude sound. "That is not intimidating."

"Yes, huh." She argued.

What the fuck kind of argument was that?

I chuckled but then turned serious again and wrapped one of my palms around her silky hair. "I shouldn't have grabbed you like that. Asleep or not. It won't happen again, I swear. I'll sleep in another room if I have to."

She gasped. "You will not!"

"I fucking will," I ground out. "I *will not* put marks on your body."

"What if I promise not to try and force you awake?" She reasoned.

"I don't know." I hedged. It was enticing. I didn't want to sleep anywhere but beside her. Just the thought of it made me anxious.

"I swear I won't," she vowed. Her voice turned pleading. "Please, B. I feel safe with you, protected. I need that."

The irony that she felt safe with me yet I put bruises on her wasn't lost on me. I was going to have to do better.

The look in her eyes is what did it. The worry I saw at the idea of her sleeping alone.

"No place I'd rather be." I relented.

She exhaled and leaned forward, pressing a cheek to my shoulder and releasing a sigh of relief.

"But, baby, you gotta promise. If I start thrashing around, get out of bed. Don't try and stop it."

She nodded against me. I tucked her a little closer, enjoying the way she felt in my arms, marveling in the fact she was mine.

I'd come so close to losing her.

So close it tormented me still.

I needed to let go of that night, but I wasn't sure I knew how.

I love every single part of you, Braeden James.

Jesus, she had no clue how much I needed to hear that. I hadn't known either.

It should have paved the way for some self-acceptance.

But something was still standing in my way.

There was still a part of me Ivy didn't know. A part no one knew but me. A part no one could ever find out about, because I knew for certain when they did...

My life would be just like the nightmares that stalked me in sleep.

CHAPTER SEVEN

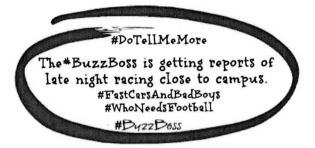

#DoTellMeMore

The #BuzzBoss is getting reports of
late night racing close to campus.
#FastCarsAndBadBoys
#WhoNeedsFootball

#BuzzBoss

IVY

It was almost too easy.

Too easy to talk B down after he saw the bruises.
Especially coming off the heels of what it took to pull
him from his nightmare last night.

'Course, maybe that's why this was an easier battle.
He was already tired.

My heart hurt for him. It ached. He was so
incredibly hard on himself in every aspect. When we
first met during freshman year, I never in a million
years would have guessed a guy like him would expect
so much from himself.

It explained a lot really, now that I stood here and
thought about it.

He never got too close, he was a *just for fun* guy for
a reason. Yeah, he said it was because he was a wild
stallion and liked to roam free. But I knew better now.

He was protecting himself.

He knew if he allowed himself to fall, to get close
to someone, it wouldn't be just for fun. He was too
guarded for that. He was too protective, too cautious

that something would take away everything he cherished.

The car accident had only made it worse. He'd been faced with his worst fear, literally thought I was dead until he pulled me out of the wreckage.

I was reluctant to tug out of his embrace because his smooth shoulder felt so good beneath my cheek and because the steady rhythm of his heartbeat was like music to my soul. But I pulled back anyway, my eyes searching for his.

Braeden's arms loosened and slid down around my hips, his fingers brushing casually over the white fabric of my shirt. His eyes were the color of milk chocolate and rimmed with thick, short lashes that looked more like dark chocolate. Without thought, I hooked my index finger into the waistband of his jeans and dipped it down past the waistband of his boxers.

"B?" I asked tentatively. He seemed relaxed and unperturbed. Still, I wanted to be sure. It was important to me to know he wasn't just shoving the anger with himself down where I couldn't see it.

"Hmm?" The sound rumbled in his throat, his eyes never leaving mine. My finger rubbed lightly across his skin. The milk chocolate of his irises deepened in color just a bit, looking more like coffee without any cream.

"Aww, come on!" a voice groaned from the doorway. "You can't just entice a guy down here with the scent of brewing coffee and then punch him in the guts with the image of his baby sister on the island— *where we eat*—and her half-naked boyfriend."

I rolled my eyes, pulled my hand free of B's waistband, and looked over my shoulder all at the same time.

Drew was standing there with rumpled, uncombed caramel-colored hair and a pair of gray sweatpants hanging low off his hips to reveal more of his lean waist than any sister cared to see. His feet were bare, which made me shiver because even though the heat was on inside, it was winter outside and there was snow on the ground. His mouth twisted into a grimace as he looked between Braeden and me. Like he'd caught us having sex or something.

"Please," I retorted. "Braeden has on more clothes than you do."

He grunted and came farther into the room, grabbed a barstool, and plunked himself on it. "Tell me the coffee's done."

"You look hung-over," Braeden observed, sounding rather amused. I frowned as he grasped me around the waist to lift me off the counter.

He set me on my feet but didn't move back, his warm body pressed close, and I relished in the feel. Even with my brother in the room, it was easy to forget we weren't alone. He reached behind me and snagged his shirt off the counter and pulled it between us.

I sighed and smoothed my palms out over his chest muscles, getting in one last caress before he covered back up.

He pushed my chin up with one finger, and a smile played on his lips. "Later." He promised quietly, dropping a quick kiss to my lips.

Behind us, Drew groaned again, and I stepped away from B to pull some mugs down out of the cabinet and fill one with black coffee. I carried it over to Drew and set it in front of him.

"You're my favorite sister," he said.

"I'm your only sister." I reminded him.

His smile was lopsided and totally endearing as he lifted the cup to his lips to take a sip. "Well, I like you better than Cam, too."

I laughed. "I'll be sure to tell him that." Camden (aka Cam) was our other brother, the middle child in our family.

"Traitor," Drew muttered as he sipped more of the coffee.

I scrutinized his face. He looked tired. Braeden said he looked hung-over, and yeah, I could totally see why. But it was the middle of the week. Surely, my brother hadn't gone out last night and gotten drunk...

Arms wrapped around me from behind, and B's chin rested on my shoulder beside my ear. I leaned back into his body, momentarily giving him my weight. It kinda felt like a relief, like I was more tired than I realized and the moment of rest was welcome. "Left my phone upstairs. I'm gonna go grab it."

I covered his hand with mine, and he caressed my wrist with his free hand, lightly skimming his fingers over the bruises my shirt covered. The action told me a lot.

Like maybe he hadn't quite forgiven himself.

I leaned back to glance up. "I love you."

He nuzzled his face in my hair, and I felt his chest fill with air when he inhaled. He was totally smelling me.

That's okay. I liked it. I liked knowing that simply the way I smelled gave B some kind of high.

"Times two," he whispered before leaving me alone with Drew.

The absence of his warm, solid body behind me made me feel slightly off balance. A little fuzzy headed.

"Why do you look so tired?" Drew asked, scrutinizing my face.

"Because it's super early and I haven't had my coffee yet," I retorted like the bratty little sister I was. I pushed away from the island and went to the pot on the counter behind me.

A wave of dizziness came over me, and I pushed it aside and reached for a mug. My hand was slightly unsteady as I poured the rich-smelling liquid into my cup. Clearly, I needed this caffeine a lot more than usual this a.m.

"Ives," Drew said from close by.

I jumped. The hot brew sloshed around in the pot but thankfully didn't spill over. I looked at Drew in surprise. I hadn't even noticed him approach.

"Geez! For someone so hung-over you sure move quietly."

Drew frowned and took the pot out of my hand, returning it to the machine. "You okay?"

"I'm fine." I reached for the mug, wanting to wrap my hands around its heat.

Drew caught my hand and cupped it in his, pulling me around so I was facing him. He was taller than me, close to six feet. He had a long body. It wasn't as bulked up as Braeden and Romeo. He didn't train the way they did. He didn't have to. He definitely had muscle definition, but it was leaner.

"You'd tell me if you weren't, right?" He pushed.

I looked into his blue eyes. They were lighter than mine, more of a sky blue to my ocean. "I'd tell you."

He nodded. "I guess I feel kinda shitty." He began. "I moved here to spend more time with you, but I feel like we haven't seen each other much."

"Are you kidding? You've been so busy. Driving *and* working," I said. "And I've had school and work."

"And the YouTube stuff." He reminded me.

I nodded. I was in the process of setting up my own YouTube channel for fashion and styling. I loved watching tutorials on makeup and videos on fashion, so much so that I decided to start my own. It was something I'd wanted to do for a while, but I was just getting around to setting up everything I needed.

I'd needed some time after everything with Zach...

And now that I was finally feeling better, I knew it would go a little faster.

"About that," I said and batted my eyes at my brother. "Will you help me set up some programs on the computer? Video editing, sound, stuff like that? And maybe show me how to optimize the channel once it's all set up?"

He nodded. "When I'm done with you, everyone on the internet is going to know who you are."

Excitement curled in my middle, and I gave a happy squeal and threw my arms around him. He chuckled and hugged me back. "You're my favorite brother," I told him.

"I'm your only brother who knows his way around a computer." His voice was dry.

I pulled back. "I really like having you here, Drew. It means a lot to me."

Now why the hell was I suddenly feeling all sentimental?

I reached for the coffee. I needed this. STAT.

"I like it here, too," he said. "Feels right. You know?"

I nodded. It was because he belonged here. He was family.

"So…" I began, taking my mug toward the fridge to grab the creamer. "Why are you hung-over in the middle of the week?"

He wasn't the only one that could be concerned.

"Who's hung-over?" A new voice joined the conversation. I peeked around the open fridge door as Trent strode into the room.

"Dude!" Drew greeted him from his casual position against the counter.

Trent poked me in the ribs on the way past. "Ivy," he greeted and then took up residence right beside Drew, mirroring his pose, his back to the island and one foot crossed over the other.

'Course, Trent had on more clothes and didn't look like he swallowed a case of beer the night before. In fact, he looked the most alert out of everyone, in a pair of loose-fitting jeans and a red hoodie with a big silver Nike check across the front.

His hair, which was actually almost the same color as my brother's (Trent's was slightly darker), was short but still styled neatly. As opposed to my brother, who likely hadn't had a haircut in months so it was all grown out and flopping around his head like he had a family of rats living in it.

The pair fist-bumped and Drew said, "How'd you get in?"

"I let him in," Braeden replied, stepping into the room. Prada was running along beside him, and I smiled and called her name.

She raced over to me and put her front paws on my legs. I abandoned the fridge and bent to give her some love. I picked her up, and she licked my chin, which made me laugh. "I wondered where you were," I told her.

"She was under the bed," B said. "Came out when I went to get my phone."

I knew it was because his dream had scared her, but I didn't tell him that.

"I'd hide too if I could," I told her. "It's too cold to get up today."

She licked me again, then wiggled around until I put her down. I reached in the fridge for her dog food and then stood there pondering the contents, looking for something other than creamer. When I didn't find it, I sighed and grabbed the caramel-flavored kind and shut the door. After it was added, I took a sip of the coffee and frowned.

For a girl who seriously needed a cup to jumpstart her morning, it just wasn't what I wanted.

Braeden was pulling down a box of cereal, and I stepped to his side and handed him the coffee. "Here, made this for you."

He grabbed it and took a sip. "That's some good shit, baby."

"So…" I began and went to grab the milk for B and a paper plate for Prada's food. "Are you going to tell me where you were last night that you came home with a hangover?" I asked Drew.

"You went out last night?" Trent said, mild surprise in his voice.

I glanced over at them, surprised myself. Drew and Trent were attached at the hip. I would have thought if one had gone out, then the other had, too.

"I'm not hung-over," Drew muttered. "I'm just tired." To punctuate his point, he added more coffee to his cup.

"I heard you come in late," Braeden said, sitting down to eat.

I put Prada's food in the microwave for a few seconds to warm it up before giving it another stir and placing it on the floor for her to attack.

"There was a big race across town. I went."

"You went to Lorhaven's turf alone?" The tightness in Trent's voice along with the underlying tone of dislike drew my attention away from the open fridge, where I was standing once more.

Drew went to races all the time. For months now, he worked during the day and then spent the rest of his time racing and building a name for himself in the driving circles here in Maryland.

So the fact that he was out late racing last night wasn't anything new. But Trent's reaction was.

"Yeah, got a last-minute call with an invite, so I went."

"Why didn't you call me?" Trent swore.

I glanced at B and our eyes met. What was this about?

"Because it was late. You have class this morning. Figured I could handle it."

Trent pushed off the island. "After all the shit we've heard, you go in there alone, without anyone to watch your back?"

Whoa. What?

"Wait, are you saying where you went last night was dangerous?" I shut the fridge door and turned.

"No," Drew answered, but at the same time, Trent said, "Yes."

Drew's eyes narrowed and he gave Trent a clear warning look. He straightened from the island, set aside his coffee, and looked at me. "Everything's fine, sis. Don't get all worked up about nothing."

"Trent doesn't seem to think it's nothing." I crossed my arms over my chest.

"Trent's just pissed he didn't get to see me leave all the other drivers in my dust last night." Drew's face turned cocky.

"You won?" Trent asked, shifting a little closer, interest in his tone.

"Smoked em'," Drew drawled.

"You should've called, man," Trent said low.

Why did he not seem as happy as Drew about this win? Usually, the pair were goofing off and talking shit about my brother's mad skills.

"I can handle myself," Drew said tight. Then he looked back at me and smiled. "Don't you worry about me, Ives. Trent's just acting like a damn woman."

Trent either didn't hear the remark or ignored it as he helped himself to the coffee and cream. Braeden was inhaling his bowl of cereal, no doubt just absorbing the currents running through the room, and Prada was dancing at the back door.

Once she was out, I went back to the fridge and looked around some more.

Romeo and Rimmel came into the kitchen, both of them heading straight for the coffee. Seconds later, Romeo was in front of the fridge, reaching past me for the cream. Before stepping away, he leaned in and pressed a kiss to my hairline.

"How ya doing, princess?"

"I was fine 'til ya called me princess," I muttered and looked up at him.

His showed me his teeth with an ornery smile. Then his face turned serious. His voice was low. "All good?"

He was checking in after our talk this morning. And if I was guessing right, he wanted to make sure I knew he was here and he was keeping an eye on me in case I needed anything.

It was really sweet, and I appreciated it.

"Yeah," I replied quietly. "All good."

He nodded, satisfied, and then glanced up. His body reacted slightly, and I noticed we'd been standing so close together.

Everyone was staring at us.

Including Braeden.

I felt my cheeks heat, embarrassed for some unknown reason. It was like I got caught doing something I shouldn't have.

"What?" I said to everyone and no one.

"Did he just call you princess?" Drew cracked.

I groaned. "Don't even think about it, Drew. I will sneak in your room and shave your eyebrows."

"Harsh," he muttered and went to sit by Braeden. "You better sleep with one eye open. Shaving eyebrows is just a gateway into more disturbing behavior. You could wake up with no hair at all, or worse." He leaned over and whispered loudly, "Missing parts!"

Braeden's eyes had been bouncing between Romeo and me, but his lips curved up at Drew's horrific words. He glanced at my brother and drawled, "I think she likes my parts where they are."

"Dude!" Drew groaned. "I can't unhear that!"

Braeden smirked and put his dishes in the sink. Prada was at the door, so he let her in and then made his way to my side. "What are you looking for in there?" he asked in my ear.

I shivered at the feel of his warm breath against my ear. "I want some orange juice," I announced.

It was so random it made even me pause. I hadn't even realized that's what I'd been looking for until I said it.

Braeden shifted around so he could look at me. "You never drink orange juice."

I shrugged. "I want some. We don't have any," I said, forlorn.

He laughed. In fact, most everyone in the room did.

Why it was so funny, I didn't know. I was sort of irritated we didn't have any.

"Sorry, princess. I drank the last of it the other day. Didn't know you'd want some," Romeo said, amused.

I felt Braeden react to Romeo's nickname for me. It wasn't so much a physical reaction, but a shift in the energy between us.

I glanced up at him, worried he was upset.

"I got time before class. C'mon, I'll take you to the store." He brushed his thumb across my cheek.

"Really?" The eagerness in my voice was apparent.

B was clearly amused. His mouth lifted in half a smile even if his eyes seemed a little bewildered. "Anything for you, Blondie."

I rushed to get my coat, the promise of OJ just too good to deny. I was pulling it on and wrapping a dark-blue scarf around my neck when B appeared at the front door, wearing his Alpha U jacket with his keys in hand.

I thought for a moment he was going to ask me about Romeo. About the way we seemed maybe a little bit closer this morning.

But he didn't ask.

And I wondered why.

CHAPTER EIGHT

#Spotted

#13 was working out hard and living up
to his #HulkStatus today at the gym.
Think he's looking to get drafted?
#NFLHopeful

#BuzzBoss

BRAEDEN

After classes, I went to the team's gym on campus
and worked out hard. I thought I didn't have the energy
for a workout like that today. I'd been fucking tired
lately, but the tension in my body needed an outlet.

So I gave it one.

After I showered and changed, I realized I was
running late for the meeting I had with Anthony. I
drove straight from campus to Rome's place (he might
not live there anymore, but it would always be his place
to me) and parked the truck right beside the Hellcat. It
had been running shitty lately. I knew it was because of
the sugar Zach poured in the gas tank. It didn't matter
that I'd taken all the lines out and flushed them, made
sure everything was clean. It just wasn't the same.

I curled my lip in disgust. The guy was dead, yet he
was still causing trouble.

The slamming of a nearby car door caught my attention, and I looked up. Romeo had been sitting in the Cat, waiting.

"What the hell you doing out here?" I walked to the back of his car where he met me on the pavement.

"Waiting for you."

"You couldn't do that in the house?"

The tension between us was palpable. The easy way we always had with each other was there, but it was overshadowed by a conversation we'd yet to have.

"I wanted to talk to you. Alone," Romeo replied.

"Yeah," I said, feeling my hackles rise. "I want to talk to you, too."

Romeo's eyes narrowed. "You got an issue?"

"Apparently, we both do."

The door to the house opened, and Rome's mom stuck her head outside. "What are you boys doing out here in the cold?" she called.

Whatever was bothering Romeo seemed to drain right out of him. The air around us seemed to clear some, aside from the irritation I was projecting.

"Coming!" Romeo yelled.

He turned back to me. "Look, let's do this first," he said, motioning toward the house. "We can talk after."

I shrugged and started past him.

"B."

I stopped but didn't turn around.

"I didn't mean to make it seem like I was sitting out here just waiting for a fight. I'm not. I just wanted to talk."

"You want to tell me why you kissed my girl this morning in the kitchen?" I asked, swinging around to face him.

Fucker actually suppressed a smile. "Someone's jealous."

"Fuck you," I spat.

A chuckle slipped from between his lips, and he crossed his arms over his chest. "Frankly, I'm offended," he said mildly. "You know I'm engaged."

"You and I both know if I thought that little kiss and nickname you pulled on my girl this morning was anything other than brotherly love, I'd be pounding your ass right now." I couldn't stop the half smile from forcing the corners of my mouth upward.

"Now you know how I feel when I see you with Rim."

I felt my eyes narrow. "That was some kind of payback? A lesson? You're my bro, man, but not even you can treat Ivy like some weapon."

Romeo rubbed a hand over his head and swore. "Fuck, you're prickly today."

I just stared him down. Yeah. Maybe I was being an asshole. I didn't much feel like being any other way right now.

He sighed. "I just thought Ivy could use a little extra... support this morning. That's what family's for."

Concern delivered a swift uppercut to my asshole nature. "Why? Something wrong with her?" I pulled my phone out of my jeans, thinking about calling her.

Romeo stepped forward and put his hand over my phone, pushing the screen down. "She's fine. I talked to her early this morning."

And then I understood. She wasn't in bed when I woke up. She'd been with him. "She told you." The words sounded hollow to my own ears. Shame burned the back of my neck.

"She didn't tell me anything." Rome corrected, his voice a little harder, like he really wanted me to listen. "We just had a conversation."

"Roman Anderson, Braeden James!" Moms yelled across the yard. "Your father is waiting!"

"Aww, shit," I drawled, smiling. "She's pulling out middle names. She means business."

Romeo laughed. "Come on. If we don't listen, you know she'll find some way to punish us."

"Grown-ass men and we're still being bossed by our mothers," I said, forlorn.

We walked toward the house, side by side. I definitely didn't feel as on guard as I did just minutes ago. If anything, I felt a little relieved.

Maybe some time with my best friend was exactly what I needed.

CHAPTER NINE

#FYI

Don't like me? Good. I don't wake up every day to impress you.

#NotEveryoneLikesTheBoss

#BuzzBoss

IVY

The warm, rich sent of coffee was welcome as I stepped into LOTUS and out of the cold. The coffee shop wasn't busy, but it wasn't empty either. It was afternoon, the time when a lot of people were finishing up classes and would start filtering in to get an afternoon pick-me-up.

I could use one. I stepped up in the line and perused the menu, even though I already knew everything they served. The line moved up, and I went with it. When the door opened behind me, I glanced around, thinking it might be Rimmel, but it wasn't.

She was probably running a little late. I decided to just order for her; that way she wouldn't have to stand in line when she arrived. Then we could get right down to girl talk.

Rimmel and I lived together, but we didn't get as much talk in as we used to in the dorm. Living with three guys made it hard to get exclusive girl time. Not that I was complaining. I liked living in a full house. I hadn't realized how much I missed it until I moved into the place Romeo rented us all and was suddenly surrounded again.

It was funny because when I first came to Alpha U, I was intent on getting some independence and space from my large family.

But once I had it, I realized it wasn't all it was cracked up to be. I realized I was a family kind of girl. Even though Rim and I were sorely outnumbered by testosterone, I still loved it.

Once I ordered, I moved down to the pick-up counter to wait. Rimmel bustled in, looking like a miniature snowman in a puffy white coat and a scarf around half her head. I giggled and waved when I saw her. She pointed to a table by the window, and I nodded, so she went over and snagged it before it was taken.

The drinks appeared, and I grabbed them up, tucking one of my selections beneath my arm, and went over to the table.

"Hey," I said as Rimmel untangled herself from her scarf.

"I think I'm trapped," she said, dropping her arms and turning to me.

I laughed. The scarf was somehow twisted around her neck and in her hair. I set everything on the table, came to her rescue, and straightened out the situation, handing her the scarf so she could pile it on top of her coat.

"A girl tries to wear her hair down and this is what happens. If you hadn't been here, I'd be in the back, begging for a stick of butter to get myself out of that contraption!" Rim gestured toward the scarf.

I didn't even bother to hide my enjoyment of her clear fashion handicap. "Hmm, I think you just gave me an idea for my style channel."

"Butter as hair detangler?" Rimmel flashed a smile.

"How to properly wear a scarf." I corrected.

"Better include a segment on how to get the hell out of one if you can't put it on right," she muttered.

I laughed some more and pushed a cup toward her. "Got you a cider."

She made a sound of appreciation and gripped the cup. "Thank you."

I pulled my mocha in front of me, along with the small bottle of orange juice I'd grabbed out of the cooler near the register.

Rimmel gestured at the juice. "Couldn't make up your mind?"

"It's a girl's prerogative to want more than one thing at once." I uncapped the juice and took a sip. The slightly tart but sweet orange flavor burst over my tongue and slid down my throat. *So good.*

I reached for the mocha and wrapped my hands around it, letting the heat from the coffee seep into my chilled fingers.

"You've never been one to drink juice," Rimmel said, sipping her drink.

I shrugged. "I think I need the sugar. I've been tired lately."

"How's things going?" she asked, lowering her voice a little, as if she were keeping our conversation private.

I was used to talking about my feelings, used to being asked about them, too. It seemed like that's all I'd done since discovering Zach raped me and then tried to kill Braeden and me. The thing was I didn't mind talking about how I was doing. It would have been perfectly natural to never want to talk about it. I think a lot of people go through that.

And yeah, at first it had been hard. But it helped. And I think by just getting it out there, by not holding it in, it made me stronger.

Rimmel and I had talked a lot in the weeks following the car accident and Zach dying. I hadn't been the one to tell her about being raped. Romeo told her. I was glad he had so I didn't have to. Sure, talking about it now wasn't as hard as it used to be, but having to tell someone you were raped... especially a friend who cared about you...

I hated watching the horror and then the pity that always flashed in their eyes. By the time Rim and I were able to talk, Zach was already dead and I was just out of the hospital.

She was a good friend.

A *best* friend.

She never judged me. She never tried to tell me whatever I was feeling in a particular moment was wrong. It was like she knew emotions, even some feelings were fleeting, and experiencing them was all part of the process of healing.

Having a girl to talk to about what happened... well, it was easier talking to her about it than Braeden or Drew. They were too hotheaded for that. They got too upset.

Rimmel never wanted to punch things when I got teary eyed about being forced into sex. She just held my hand and let me cry.

"I'm good," I answered, leaning in a little. "Therapy really helps." I reached out and laid my hand over hers. "Having good friends—family—really helps, too. I finally feel like I'm getting back to normal, you know?"

She squeezed my hand supportively. "Minus the exhaustion inspiring the OJ consumption?" she asked, a teasing note in her voice.

I tilted my head to the side. "I think all the mental turmoil I had to work through is finally catching up to me physically, if that makes sense?"

Rimmel nodded. "Totally. It's hard to focus on everything at once. For you, dealing with the inner stuff was way more important than the physical stuff. So now that you're stronger mentally, it's easier to notice how you are physically."

Of course she understood. She might not have been raped, but she'd been attacked by Zach. She'd been through a lot with her family, too. Rimmel knew what it was to try and heal.

"I think..." I began and paused. Just because I was able to talk about what was inside didn't mean it was always easy. Rimmel sensed my hesitation and gave my hand another squeeze. "I know rape is a physical violation." I paused again to pull my hand away and wrap them both around my coffee. "But I think the bigger violation is emotional. The scars he left inside are so much larger than anything he ever left on me physically."

Just coming to terms with being used in the way I was, in being treated like something other than human was something I might always struggle with.

"I'm really proud of you," Rimmel said.

I glanced up, surprised. That was the last response I expected.

She smiled, noting the shock on my face. "You've changed a lot since we first met back at the beginning of sophomore year."

I grimaced, and she shook her head.

"There was nothing wrong with the way you were back then," she clarified, then went on. "You were always nice to me, even when I tried to be invisible to you. You've always been fun and carefree in ways I never will be. I always admired that about you. But you're so much more than that. Instead of being a victim, you became a fighter. Instead of letting the pain of what happened eat you up inside—something I've done—you let it out so you could heal. You're so strong, Ivy. Strong for being the person you are, for facing everything you've faced. I wanted to tell you that you really inspire me. I might not have been through the same things you have, but even so, I've learned a lot about having grace from you."

Tears welled up in the backs of my eyes, and I blinked furiously. "I'm not wearing waterproof mascara," I hissed low. "Now I'm gonna look a mess!"

Rimmel laughed. "I'm sure you have an arsenal of products in your bag to fix yourself."

"Of course." I sniffled and waved away the silly makeup talk. "I've definitely had a lot of support the past few months, a lot of it from you. You've taught me a lot about self-acceptance and how to be the real version of me. Thanks for always being a real friend."

Rimmel pushed at her glasses and sniffled. "I'd been wanting to ask you something. I think now is a really good time."

"Of course," I said and dabbed under my eyes.

"Will you be my maid of honor?"

Well, there went what was left of my mascara. "Really?" I said, my voice wobbly.

Rimmel nodded. "There is honestly no one else I'd rather have standing there with me when I marry Romeo."

"What about B?"

Rimmel laughed. "I think he'll look better in a tux on Romeo's side than on mine in a gown."

"Seriously, though." I deadpanned. "You should totally ask him to stand on your side. Can't you just see his face?"

Both of us dissolved into a bucket of giggles.

"And the best part is he'd totally say yes because he'd never tell you no!" I added and laughed some more.

We laughed so hard people started to glance our way, but I didn't care. It felt so good to laugh.

Once the laughter subsided, Rimmel groaned. "Speaking of. I haven't even thought of dresses. Or flowers. Or anything."

"I've got this," I said, sitting up. "I can totally help you with everything."

"Would you?" Rimmel's eyes were hopeful. "Because Romeo's mom is totally on me about everything. What do I want for this? What do I want for that...? That woman is like in total wedding mode."

"Things any better between you two?" I asked.

Rimmel made a face. "I'm trying. But you know..."

I nodded enthusiastically. "I get it."

"I really would appreciate your help. With my mom not here..." Her voice trailed away, and sadness squeezed my heart. I hadn't even thought about what it must be like for her to plan a wedding without her mother. "And my grandma is so far away. I've kind of been on my own with it."

"You're never on your own," I insisted. "I'm always here. And so is B. And Drew. Trent, too."

Her eyes grew soft and she smiled. "Thanks."

We launched into a full-fledged wedding planning conversation. From the look on Rimmel's face every time I brought up another detail, she looked more and more overwhelmed.

Finally, I sat back and said, "Are you sure you want a big wedding?"

"Honestly? I'd go to Vegas in a heartbeat. But Romeo wants me to have the fairy tale, and I think his mother would be heartbroken if we didn't include her."

I nodded. I understood that. My mother would be heartbroken if I went off and got married without her. Especially since I'm her only daughter and my brothers are boneheads who will likely never find women to put up with them. But I didn't say that out loud because I didn't want to make her feel worse about her own mother not being there. And on that note, I was going to have to come up with some way to make Rimmel's mother a part of her day. It would mean so much to her.

"Well, let's keep it simple, then. We'll give his mom some things she can control and you can pick out the rest."

"Really?"

"Simple can be very elegant." I smiled. "I can't wait to go dress shopping!"

She grimaced. "Oh, and don't forget the engagement party his mother insisted on throwing us is next week. I need to come to the boutique and get something to wear. I know she's gonna have press there. I think she invited the entire NFL."

She said the last part with trepidation, and I laughed. "Sounds very formal."

Rimmel put her head in her hands.

"You know what?" I said.

She glanced up.

"What you guys need is a real engagement party. One for you and Romeo, not for his mother's society friends."

"It's been a long time since all of us went out to have fun."

Months. It had been months and months. Christmas passed quietly, with B and me splitting our time here and at my parents'. Romeo and Rim were spread thin while he finished up his first season. Drew had been MIA a lot because of his job and racing.

And now here it was midwinter with spring coming fast. Things changed so fast. Pretty soon, it would be our senior year and then we'd be all be pulled in different directions. We needed to celebrate now.

We needed to be together now.

"What are you thinking?" Rimmel asked.

My lips curved up. "Smurf Balls."

Rimmel grinned. "You want to have an engagement party at Screamerz?"

"Why not? We better do it now before we're all too old and married to still think it's fun."

Rimmel snorted. "I don't think Braeden will ever be too old for that place."

I could totally picture him at the age of eighty, still trying to dance and telling everyone he still had it. What a goofball.

The endearing, fun thought made me realize that was a side of him that hadn't been out very often lately.

"What is it?" Rimmel asked, practically reading my thoughts.

I grabbed the OJ and took a fortifying sip, wondering if Rimmel had noticed the changes in him as well.

Once I recapped the juice, I looked up to ask, but Rimmel was no longer looking at me.

And thank goodness, because the look on her face was fierce.

Very rarely did I ever see Rimmel look that way. The only times I'd seen her wear a similar expression was when someone was threatening her family.

Family = Romeo and B.

I rotated in my seat, wondering what in the world was causing such a momma bear look to come out of her.

And then I saw.

Standing right there behind me was a familiar face.

A familiar *unwelcome* face.

Missy.

CHAPTER TEN

Life is always in motion.
Everything is fleeting.
Even happiness.

#BuzzBoss

BRAEDEN

The second I entered Anthony's office, all thoughts of whatever I had going on at home, in my head, and between me and Rome were tucked away for later.

This meeting was about my future, my hopeful NFL career.

It had been a long few months. Hell, when the idea that I could actually become a pro football player became a reality, I was excited as hell. Who wouldn't be?

It was full throttle ahead.

But then my excitement was dimmed.

With everything else going on around me, it had been hard to keep up with the level of training I needed to keep myself viable. The truth was being a professional athlete took *a lot* of discipline. It took a lot of determination. This career isn't something someone just woke up and was good enough to do. Even for people like Rome, who were born with raw talent, it still took a hell of a lot of work.

It wasn't that I still didn't want to be in the NFL. I wanted to play with Romeo again almost more than anything. The thing was sometimes it felt like I had to choose between Ivy and the game.

I was committed to Ivy one hundred and ten percent. I loved her. I loved her more than anything, and because of that, I wondered how I would balance a life with her and a life of football.

I knew it was possible. I watched Rome and Rimmel do it on a daily basis.

It was because of them I was here in this meeting and still actively pursuing this path. That and the fact I *did* want this and I knew the job would offer Ivy and me the financial stability we wouldn't get anywhere else.

Anthony got the ball rolling. He became my official manager and sent in the application for me to enter the draft early. I was going to find out today if that application had been accepted. I would know in just a few minutes if the NFL would even consider me for the draft.

Then the real work would begin.

As if getting here had been child's play.

Anthony was sitting behind his desk, his dark hair combed neatly and his white dress shirt unbuttoned at the collar, his tie long discarded. Over the back of the chair he sat in was his suit jacket and on his wrist was a gold watch that probably cost a shit ton of money.

"What's all the hollering I heard out there from your mother?" he asked when Romeo and I stepped inside.

"We were shooting the shit in the driveway. Mom didn't like it," Romeo answered.

Anthony smiled. "Yes, well, your mother hates it when people are late."

"Sorry about that," I spoke up. "I was at the gym training."

Anthony waved away my words. "It's fine. I'll be working from home the rest of the day. Besides, training is more important than sitting in meetings with me. Especially now."

Romeo made a sound and slapped me on the back.

I held back my reaction to what those words might mean.

Anthony noted my reaction and smiled. "They accepted the application, Braeden. You are officially in the draft for the NFL."

"Hells yeah!" Romeo shouted.

I laughed, feeling a little shell-shocked. I mean, I knew the possibility of it being accepted was really good, but still. I guess I hung on to the fact it might be a no because I didn't want to get my hopes up.

Anthony stood up and offered me his hand, a genuine smile on his lips. I reached across the desk and shook it.

The door to the office opened, and Valerie stuck her head in. "I heard happy yelling!" she said.

"B's in the draft!" Romeo told her.

Valerie hurried into the room with a large white bag in her hand. She set it down and rushed over and pulled me into a hug. "We're so proud of you," she said.

My chest tightened. Romeo's parents had been in my life for a long time. They'd always treated me like a second son. Having them here and knowing I had their support was something that could never be replaced.

I hugged her back, and when she pulled away, she reached into the bag and pulled out a big purple hoodie. It had the Knights symbol on the chest.

I laughed.

"I got you this," she said excitedly. "And I got one for Ivy, too." She pulled out another one that wasn't quite as large. I didn't have the heart to tell her Ivy wouldn't wear hers. She'd only wear mine after I wore it and it smelled like me.

"And what would you have done if my application had been denied?" I asked.

"Nonsense. Ron Gamble isn't a dumb man."

"Gamble doesn't approve the applications, Mom," Romeo told her.

"Oh," she said and waved away the knowledge. "Well, it doesn't matter anyway, because it was approved."

I took the hoodies and laughed. "Thanks, Moms."

"You're welcome, honey. It's going to be so good to have both my boys on the same team again."

The sound of a ringing phone drifted in the room from down the hall.

"Oh, that's my cell. It's probably the caterer about the engagement party. I need to get that." She rushed from the room.

I lifted a brow at Romeo. "Engagement party?"

"Don't ask," he groaned.

Anthony laughed. "Any reason to throw a party."

I draped the purple shirts over a nearby chair and then sat down. I was freaking pumped about my application being accepted. I was one step closer to playing pro.

I glanced between Rome and his dad. "She does know I might not end up with the Knights, right?"

"That's not going to happen," Romeo said. There was no room for argument in his voice.

"Unless you got a genie in a bottle somewhere in this house," I quipped. "You and I both know the odds."

Romeo made a face like the truth pissed him off. I knew he wanted me on his team. Hell, I wanted it, too. But I had to be realistic here. I couldn't get my head or heart set on the outcome I wanted, because it would only make it harder if I got drafted on some team that wasn't the Knights.

"Obviously, the possibility of that happening is there," Anthony said. "We all know how this organization works. It's all in who picks you up first."

And if two teams tried to pick me up at the same time, I would go to the highest bidder.

In a way, it was kind of like a cattle auction.

Except it was for men.

"Gamble wants you. Head Coach Westfall wants you. They're gonna draft you." Romeo had so much confidence it was hard not to hope.

"How much did you have to do with it?" I asked point blank.

Romeo sat nearby and looked me in the eye. "You know damn well I went to bat for you. I made it no secret I want you on the field with me. But it wasn't me who convinced them, B. It was your stats from last season. I might have brought you some attention, but your record speaks for itself."

Anthony nodded. "It's true. Your stats are in line with some of the most anticipated players in the draft this year. You definitely belong."

"Any other teams interested?" I asked Anthony.

"I haven't heard much, but I know you're being looked at."

Romeo stiffened. I glanced at him and his jaw was hard. I knew it was killing him that this wasn't a done deal. It was clear just by looking at him that he hadn't even considered I'd be drafted to another team, one in another state away from him and our family.

"How many teams are ahead of the Knights in the draft order?" Romeo asked his father.

"A few." He hedged. "The Knights are somewhere in the midrange for draft picks, which is good. At least they aren't in the bottom."

If they were in the bottom, then the higher the chance I'd be picked up by another team.

Both Romeo and I fell silent, digesting the news.

"Gamble's doing everything he can to get you, Braeden. He's a determined man. This isn't something you really have any control over. We're going to have to wait and see. Until then, you need to be training every day. You need to keep your nose clean, keep your reputation clean. Press is good, but only good press."

I nodded, and Romeo glanced at me. I knew he was thinking all the good press we planned on generating had been put on hold because of Ivy's accident. I hadn't wanted to go very far while she was recovering. I'd missed all his final games of the season last year. The plan was to be in the stands, to be seen with Romeo and the team out in public.

That never happened.

I couldn't help but wonder if that was going to hurt me.

"When are we going to know?" I asked, already dreading the wait.

"Draft picks are at the end of April this year."

So I had almost two months to wait.

Fuck me.

"And until then?" I asked. Technically, I knew all this, but I just needed to hear him say it. It made it more real.

"Until then, train your ass off. The player personnel staff is going to be watching you. They'll be in contact with the head coach of the Wolves, with Alpha University, and with me since I'm your agent. Personnel will likely come and watch you train. They're going to want to see you play, maybe even how you interact with your teammates."

"Technically, they aren't my teammates anymore," I said, the realization hitting me hard. Those guys had been my extended family for over three years. I glanced at Romeo. He nodded, and I saw the understanding in his eyes.

I was getting a little taste of how he'd felt last year.

"Yes, technically, you've ended your college career, but since the Wolves are where you're coming from, I wouldn't be surprised if that's where the personnel starts."

I nodded, trying to wrap my head around it all.

You knew you were growing up when your first reaction to something as epic as being drafted by the NFL wasn't to go get wasted and party, but to plan, train, and go home and tell your girl.

"It's a lot. I know," Anthony said. "Since things with Roman happened a little differently, this is sort of my first go with some of this as well. But I want you to know, son, I'm going to do everything in my power to make sure you go to a good team, the right team. And I'm going to make damn sure they pay you well. You might be a rookie, but you're a damn good one."

"And you don't have any broken bones," Romeo cracked.

"Guess that means I'll get more money," I taunted.

Romeo laughed. "A rookie three-year contract? Yeah, you'll make more than my one season *let's see if you can play* paycheck." Then he smirked and his eyes turned cocky. "But my new four-year contract with the Knights? No way in hell you'll get what I am."

I looked at Anthony and lifted a brow. He chuckled. "I negotiate very well."

I knew Romeo had a newly signed four-year contract, but I never asked him how much he was making. Sure, I could probably look it up online, but I didn't care. We'd never been about money and we never would be.

But I had to admit now I was curious just how much he was getting paid.

"I'm going to keep on this. Just because you're draft eligible now doesn't mean I sit back and wait," Anthony said, drawing my thoughts away. "I'm going to work just as hard for you as I do for Roman."

I swallowed. "I really appreciate that. Thank you for doing this for me."

"You know we think of you like a son. We only want the best for you."

Usually, I would make a funny comment or a joke at a time like this. Something to take the edge off the feelings flooding my chest. But my sarcastic side failed me in that moment. I just couldn't bring myself to say anything that might take away from the genuineness in his words.

Anthony Anderson had been more a father to me my entire life than my actual father had been, so to hear him say those things…

Well...

Yeah.

Thankfully, Romeo was there and he knew what needed to be said.

"Geez, Dad, you don't have to kiss his ass. You already have season tickets."

Anthony threw back his head and laughed. The hand gripping my heart let go, and I let out a shaky laugh.

"Don't be getting a big head over there." Rome continued and got up to knock me on the shoulder. "I still make more money than you."

I gave him the finger.

"So is that it for the meeting?" he asked.

Anthony nodded. "I'll be in touch very soon, Braeden, let you know what's coming next." He stood and handed me a sheet of paper, the front page of my early draft application (a copy), and stapled to the front was an approval letter from the NFL.

"Thought you might want to keep this. Show your mother."

I wanted to show Ivy.

On impulse, I hugged Romeo's father. It was a quick, tight hug, and even though it was spur of the moment, he hugged me back like he wasn't surprised.

Before I pulled away, he whispered, "Proud of you," in my ear.

"C'mon," Romeo said impatiently from the door. "If we don't get out of here now, Mom's gonna come in here and make pick out napkin colors or some shit." He looked horrified.

Anthony and I laughed.

"We'll see you both next week at the party," Anthony said and shooed us away.

I tossed the sweatshirts over my shoulder and wandered to the door. Romeo pressed a finger to his lips, telling me to be quiet before he opened it.

I thought about making a bunch of noise on purpose just to draw his mother's attention. But then I realized she'd probably make me help pick shit out, too.

Oh, hells no.

That shit was for girls.

We crept through the house in a way we hadn't since we were sixteen and late for curfew. 'Course, back then we always got caught. His mom had like super-human hearing, caught us every time. She'd sit us down in the kitchen and give us a stern lecture. Then we'd charm our way out of the punishment by promising to never do it again.

Man, those were the days.

Outside, Romeo let out a huge sigh of relief and then charged me.

Before I knew what the hell he was doing, he grabbed me around the hips and lifted me up in a victory hold like I'd scored a winning touchdown. He gave a happy shout and then set me back down and punched me in the shoulder. "Fuck yeah!"

His excitement was contagious, and I grinned like a fool.

"We're going to the Superbowl this year. You and me."

"Rome…" I started. He heard the hesitation in my voice.

"Don't start that shit with me, man. It's gonna happen. Gamble will come through."

I hoped so, but I didn't have as much faith in the guy as Romeo did. I didn't bother to say that out loud, though.

"I'm gonna train with you. I know what Westfall and the coaches like to see. I know the ins and outs of the team. It's an advantage you have, and we're going to use it."

I nodded, looking at the hoodies and acceptance letter filling my hands.

"It's a good day, B. It's okay to be happy."

"You been listening to motivational CDs in your car?" I cracked.

Romeo guffawed. "Yeah, I got 'em out of your glove box."

"The fuck you did."

"C'mon, let's go have a beer and celebrate. It's on me." He glanced over his shoulder at the house like he expected his mom to come rushing out after us.

"Well, if you're paying…" I said. "And you can tell me about this party next week."

"Don't sound so thrilled about my torture. As best man, you have to be there, too. Hell, she's probably going to corner you and try and give you instructions on your speech."

"Best man," I echoed.

"Like you didn't know." Romeo scoffed.

"Well, I mean when you didn't ask…" I pretended to wipe my tears with the sleeve of the hoodie.

"There you go acting like a woman. When I stop to get beer, I'll get you some douche so you can clean out your lady parts."

"Dude, that's nasty."

"There's no one else I'd rather have standing up there with me," he said, turning serious.

"There's no one else I'd let marry my sister."

Romeo rolled his eyes.

"Of course I'll be there, man. I'll even write a speech." Truth was I was looking forward to their wedding, and yeah, I'd known I'd be the one standing up there beside them.

Just like when I get married, it would be him beside me.

The mood I was in when I showed up here seemed so far away. It seemed so insignificant in the grand scheme of life.

Yeah, nothing was perfect, but damn if we didn't have a lot.

I was on my way to the NFL. Our family was happy and intact.

No threats hung over our heads.

Romeo and Rimmel were getting married.

For right now, everything was great.

CHAPTER ELEVEN

Once best friends.
Now strangers with memories.
#Regrets

#BuzzBoss

IVY

Our eyes met, and my stomach clenched.

Ew.

I totally did not have the stomach for someone as awful as Missy today.

I turned back around abruptly without saying a word. I had nothing to say to her. I truly wanted to wash my hands of that girl and pretend our "friendship" had been nothing but a bad dream.

Rimmel's eyes remained trained on Missy like she wasn't going to let her out of her sight until she was gone. And that fierce, almost snarling look on her face stayed in place.

I had a moment to realize the look I'd only ever seen her bring out on behalf of Braeden and Romeo was now a look she used for me as well. She was warning Missy off, trying to keep her away from me, because Rimmel understood how much her betrayal had hurt.

Sure, Missy hadn't done the things Zach did, but that didn't make her any better than him. In some ways, Missy was worse than him. At least Zach never really masqueraded as my friend. He didn't hang out with me under the guise that he liked me so he could syphon information from me and my friends to blast it all over the school gossip line.

With Zach, a girl knew what she was getting.

A girl like Missy?

Well, she was sort of like a piñata.

After so many hits, she cracked open and the real contents of her nasty soul spilled out.

My stomach churned and I pressed a hand to it.

Rimmel turned away from her and toward me. "You okay?"

"I'm fine," I said, taking a breath. "I think the combination of being tired and stressed and…" I motioned over my shoulder with my head. "Has been quite enough for me today."

"You going home before work?" she asked.

I nodded.

She pulled out her cell and her fingers flew over the screen. "Romeo was going to come get me, but I'll just ride with you. Come on. Let's go."

I stood and reached for the juice. I had no desire to drink the latte I had yet to sip.

I tossed it in a nearby trashcan and pulled on my coat. Rimmel already had her coat on and was carrying the scarf she couldn't wear in her hand. It made me laugh beneath my breath.

I made it to the door before Rim, so I held it open and let her go ahead of me. Outside, my attention went directly to the fat, white flakes of snow that fell haphazardly from the sky. The wind was bitter and it made me long for a pair of my Uggs.

"Can't you take a hint?" Rimmel's voice brought me up short.

As the door swung closed behind us, Missy stepped into the walkway blocking our path. She glanced at me warily before turning her full gray gaze on Rimmel.

"I hear congratulations are in order on your engagement," she said.

"I'm pretty sure you already gave them. You know, when you posted about it for the entire school," Rim said without missing a beat.

Missy glanced around, making sure no one heard and would realize who she really was.

"So you're having an engagement party next week?" she asked.

Okay, clearly she was digging around for information. Would this girl ever stop?

"Yep. And you're not invited," Rimmel said. "If you'll excuse us, I hate the cold."

Rimmel and I started forward at once, and Missy had no choice but to back away.

When we were past, Missy called out my name. I stopped and looked over my shoulder. Our eyes met, and I made sure she saw exactly how much this little conversation meant to me.

Which was nothing.

Her eyes widened just a fraction, and I thought she might turn away.

She didn't.

In just a few quick steps, she was in front of us again. The white snow coated her dark hair like a hat, and it made me mad to realize I thought she looked pretty standing out here in it.

"Look, I've wanted to come by. I tried to come to the hospital."

"You aren't welcome at our home," I said, matter-of-fact.

She nodded. "Yeah, I know... and Braeden..." Her voice faltered. Just hearing her say his name made me dizzy with anger.

Braeden was mine.

The end.

Clearly, my inner cavewoman was making sure she was heard because the thoughts I was having were downright possessive.

B would be proud.

"I just wanted to apologize to you. Like, for real. I'm so sorry for the part I played in what happened."

Something inside me snapped (it was probably that bitchy cavewoman I had living in there). I guess all that nothing I felt for her had its limits.

"Which part was that?" I growled. "The part you played in me being *raped*? Or the part when you covered it up, then used it to slut shame me in front of the entire school?"

Missy's face paled.

I held up my hand. "Oh, maybe it was when you went to a psych ward and got a caged, sick animal all riled up so he could come after me and try to *kill* me."

I felt my hands shake as I stared at her. How I ever thought she was my friend was such a mystery to me.

"So tell me, Missy. Which one of those things are you most sorry for?"

Tears welled in her eyes, and I laughed. "Your tears, your very existence stopped affecting me the day

I stared down the nose of a gun and listened to a psycho lay out plans for how he was going to murder me and then go back for the man I love."

She gasped like I'd shocked her.

I gasped back, mocking her. "Oh." I pressed a hand to my chest. "Could it be? Something little miss-know-it-all doesn't know?"

I glanced at Rimmel, and she shrugged dramatically.

"That's right. Your little pit bull was going to kill Braeden. You know, the guy you claimed to love?"

"Ivy," Missy said, her voice hollow and raw.

"Save it, okay?" There isn't anything on this earth that would ever make me listen to what she had to say. I was done.

Beyond done.

I'd thought I'd washed my hands of her before. The nothing I felt when I thought of her had been finite.

But I guess deep down, I'd needed to rage at her, if only a little.

I had, and now I just felt drained.

"Let's go," I said to Rimmel. We turned and walked away together, leaving Missy standing there alone.

I never looked back to see if she followed us. I knew she wouldn't. She wouldn't dare.

"You were a real badass back there," I said to Rimmel, trying to lighten the mood.

"Me?" she said innocently.

I laughed. "If looks could kill…"

"If looks could kill, that one would have been gone a long time ago," Rimmel said bitterly.

I glanced at her out of the corner of my eye as we walked up the sidewalk toward my car. "I didn't realize you despised her so much."

Rimmel stopped and stared at me slack jawed. "You thought I wouldn't?"

"Of course I knew you were mad and hurt by her. But I guess I never realized she would bring out the lioness in you."

Rimmel started walking again and hooked her arm through mine. "She hurt all of us. You most of all. I guess Romeo and B have rubbed off on me a bit, because in my book, someone who hurts my family— *my sister*—like Missy has, I have no mercy for her."

I leaned my head against hers and smiled. "Don't tell them I said this, but I think a little bit of B and Romeo rubbing off on us might be a good thing."

"Oh, I won't tell them. We'd never hear the end of it."

Our laughter filled the air as we steeped up to my car. Rimmel pulled her arm from beneath mine. I searched my bag for the car keys and pulled them out. When I straightened, a wave of dizziness swept over me and I wobbled on my feet.

"Ivy?" Rimmel's voice was full of concern, and she stepped closer.

"I'm fine," I assured her. "I missed lunch, and seeing Missy made me sick."

"How about I drive home?"

"Yeah, okay," I said and surrendered the keys.

I sank into the passenger side, grateful for the seat. Once Rimmel was in and had the car on, I turned to her. "Hey, how come you didn't drive to campus today?"

Rimmel snorted. "Are you kidding? Me drive that 'death trap' in the snow?" She made air quotes as she referred to her car. "Romeo would blow a gasket. You know how he is about my car."

I laughed. "Yeah. I know."

Rimmel sighed and pulled out onto the street. "Besides, I like when he drives me around. In no time, he'll be back with the Knights and we won't see each other much."

"Time sure has been flying lately," I murmured and glanced out the windshield at the snowflakes rushing toward the car as we drove.

"I know it seems like just yesterday we got engaged, but it's already been two months."

Two months?

Had it really been that long? With the car accident, therapy, school, my job at the boutique, and everything else going on, keeping track of the calendar was just not something I'd been doing.

"I assume you're going to want to get married before Romeo leaves for training camp?" I asked, calling up the calendar app on my phone.

"Definitely."

"No date yet?"

She sighed. "No, we just keep saying soon as possible."

"Well, girl, you gotta pick a date so we can make it happen." I flipped around the calendar to look at weekend dates while keeping the weather in mind.

"Okay, I'll talk to him tonight and we'll pick one."

I made a non-committal sound and nodded. I wasn't really paying attention to what she said. I was too busy staring down at the calendar.

CHAPTER TWELVE

BRAEDEN

The heated exchange between Rome and I that was brewing got lost somewhere between football and beer.

I didn't bring it up because I didn't really want to talk about it.

I was hoping he'd forgotten, but I knew better. Rome didn't forget shit he thought was important. My guess? He was biding his time, waiting for a good time to bring it up.

Now wasn't a good time. We were too busy with the pizza and beer we'd stopped off for on the way home.

I was gonna have to do a second workout tonight because of this shit.

But whatever. It would be worth it.

The sound of the garage door opening hummed through the house, and Romeo took a sip of his beer and stood. "Girls are here."

I couldn't wait to tell Ivy about the draft.

We stepped out into the garage just as the door finished sliding up. The sound of Ivy's engine cut off, and we stood there and watched as the girls climbed out.

Rim was in the driver's seat.

What the fuck was that about?

The pair didn't see us at first. They were laughing about something as they came around the hood of the car toward the door. Ivy was the first to realize we were watching them. She glanced up, and our eyes aligned almost instantly.

But then her gaze slid away. Almost like she was upset. Or nervous.

That wasn't our usual greeting.

"'Bout time you got here," Romeo called over, and Rimmel's face cracked into a large smile.

There. That was what I was used to seeing.

Rim hurried across the snow-slick driveway and lost her balance. Rome and I both rushed forward to try and catch her, but she managed to right herself and not fall.

"And you wonder why I don't want you driving in the snow," Romeo muttered. "Damn, Smalls. You can't even walk in it."

Rimmel gave Ivy a knowing look, and they laughed.

I liked the sound of Ivy's laugh. It was familiar and comfortable. Like home.

Romeo picked Rim up and tossed her over his shoulder, heading into the house. She squealed the whole way.

I met Ivy in the center of the driveway, snowflakes gathering in her hair and clinging to the tips of her dark eyelashes. "You look like a cupcake," I announced.

That got me a smile.

I liked it.

I wanted another one.

"A cupcake?" she repeated, amused.

I nodded. "And all these snowflakes fighting for a place on you look like sprinkles. You know how much I love sprinkles."

That got me a light giggle and another smile.

Damn, I loved her.

"You ever kiss in the snow?" I murmured, slipping an arm around her waist.

"If I have, I certainly can't remember," she replied, leaning into my chest.

"Good answer," I murmured and took my time leaning down toward her. I enjoyed the way her eyelashes fluttered as if my mere closeness was too enticing for her eyes to stay open. The tip of her nose was pink from the cold, and as I leaned in slightly closer, her teeth sank into her lower lip.

She was anticipating me.

Waiting.

For me. For my lips. For a taste of only me.

I allowed my lips to brush ever so lightly over hers, and she leaned up, trying to deepen the contact. I pulled back, depriving her of a full-on kiss. "I love you," I breathed against her, my lips caressing hers with each word I whispered.

Her hands came up and clutched at the front of my shirt, and I brought us fully together. She parted immediately, already knowing what she wanted. I took my time once again, slipping my tongue against hers before curling it around completely and sucking it gently into my mouth.

The grip on my shirt slackened, and most of her weight shifted toward me.

I tightened my arms and held her up, all the while continuing the slow fuck I was giving her mouth.

I don't know how long we kissed, but I was in no hurry. We stood out there in the cold, snow falling around us in a silent curtain. I pulled back just as slowly as I began, teasing her with more before finally lifting my head.

Ivy collapsed against my chest and buried her face in the crook of my neck. Her cold nose pressed against the spot where my pulse thumped just beneath the skin. It was a shocking contrast to the way my blood boiled.

"Hey." I rubbed a hand up her back. "What's going on?"

She made a sound and snuggled closer.

I don't know why, but it scared me. Ivy was a lot of things, but clingy wasn't one of them. It wasn't that the way she clung to me now was annoying.

It was quite the opposite.

I reveled in it. In being the one she found solace in.

It was the fact she needed solace at all that concerned me.

"Blondie," I said a little firmer this time and peeled her off my chest. "What's the matter with you?"

Her lower lip stuck out in a pout and then wobbled.

It wrecked me.

The vulnerability she was projecting fucking took me down.

She reached for me again, and I let her in, drawing her close and allowing her to burrow in as close to me as she could.

* * *

I rocked us both back and forth, a slight movement but a comforting one. Clearly, she needed comfort. Maybe that's the reason Rim had been driving.

"Did something happen today?" I asked, hoarse.

Whose ass do I need to beat? the possessive bastard in me demanded.

"Promise me something," she said suddenly, pulling back and blinking the snow from her face.

"Anything."

Her eyes cleared and she shook her head. "No. No promises. Just tell me I'll never lose you."

Relief filled my limbs and made them heavy. I wanted to laugh.

I must have smiled because she scowled. "Why is that funny?"

"It's not funny. It's just the easiest promise I'll ever make."

"It's not easy. It won't be."

What the fuck was she talking about?

"Ivy." A hard note crept into my tone. "Listen to me and listen good."

Her eyes bounced between mine, like she was searching for something... but I didn't know what. I'd give it to her. Fuck, I'd give her anything if I only knew what it was she needed.

"You listening?" I demanded.

Really, I was stalling for time. I had to pull out some words right now. We all know how very little I liked words.

She nodded.

"I don't know what's gotten into that beautiful head of yours today, and honestly, it doesn't really matter. Not for this. I'm not going anywhere. Never.

Hell, I should be the one asking you to make that promise."

She snorted. Clearly, she'd spent the afternoon with my sister.

"It's ridiculous, right?" I asked.

She nodded, but then I saw the doubt creep into her eyes.

I took her face in my hands, noting how cold her skin felt. "It's just as easy for me to make that promise as it is for you. You have to trust me, baby. You have to trust that I mean it when I say I'm yours and it's not going to change."

Why, why was she suddenly being so... so... chick-like?

Hell, we made it through Missy, our mutual attempt to push each other away, rape, Zach... The list went on. Why did she suddenly need to hear I wasn't going to leave her?

"I trust you." There was no doubt in her voice. "More than anyone."

It didn't really matter, the reason. If she needed to hear it, then I'd say it.

I tucked her into my side to shelter her from the cold and turned us toward the house. "Come on, Blondie. Your sexy ass is gonna freeze."

Inside the garage, we passed the Hellcat and Ivy looked up. "I'm sorry. You totally don't need my emotional baggage right now. Today isn't about me. It's about you, and I'm dying to know how the meeting went with Anthony."

I hit the button on the wall so the door could lower. As it moved, the garage dimmed with the lost sunlight. I stopped short of opening the door leading into the house and leaned back against the wood.

She fit between my legs perfectly, and I clutched the lapels of her red coat and tugged her close. "My very existence is about you, baby. Everything else is just details."

Her face softened. "I think that might be my favorite thing you've ever said. Besides, of course, I love you."

Words for the win!

"Give me some sugar," I ordered.

She obliged.

"Tell me you like my cock," I added when she pulled back.

"Braeden James Walker!" She gasped. "What is it with you and trying to make me say that!"

"A man's mini needs to know he's appreciated," I told her.

She dropped her head back and laughed, revealing the smooth skin of her neck. "He is."

"Say it," I urged.

"No!" She laughed.

I dug my fingers into her middle and tickled her. She squirmed away with a squeal. But then she swayed on her feet.

"Whoa." My hands shot out to grab her. "Easy,"

Her fingers dug into my arm as she steadied herself.

"Ivy?"

She sighed. "I'm just a little lightheaded. I didn't eat lunch."

"Is that why Rim was driving?"

She nodded reluctantly.

I bit down on the urge to lecture her. Clearly, she wasn't feeling well, and while it was her own fault, I didn't hurt my baby when she was down. No wonder she'd been so emo when she showed. She was starved and had low blood sugar.

"We have pizza and beer inside." I smiled.

Her eyes lit up. "Is it celebratory pizza and beer?"

I grinned widely. "I'm in the draft."

Ivy gave a shout and launched herself at me. "I knew it!" she squealed. "I knew they'd accept your application! I'm so proud of you!"

She was bouncing around so much in my arms that we were both gonna end up on the floor. I chuckled and scooped her off her feet.

"Easy, woman. You trying to take us down?"

She cupped my jaw. "You deserve this, B. I'm so happy for you."

"Thanks, baby."

She grinned some more and bounced excitedly.

"Come on. You need some food. And I need some beer."

"I need details," she demanded as I kicked open the door.

"You eat. I talk. Deal?" I compromised.

"Hells yeah."

Whatever had been bothering her when she got here was clearly no longer an issue.

Crisis averted.

CHAPTER THIRTEEN

#LateNightMusings

What if one day you wake up as a baby and realize your whole life was just a dream?

#WouldYouMakeTheSameMistakesTwice

#BuzzBoss

IVY

I came awake instantly, a gasp rocked my body, and I sprang up, pushing at the hair hanging in my face and trying to focus my sleepy gaze on the source of the loud, intimidating sounds filling our bedroom.

What on earth?

Prada was in front of the closed bedroom door, her hair standing on end as she growled and barked insistently. It wasn't a *hey, I have to pee* kind of bark either.

It was a *someone is trying to hurt us* bark.

Her wails and snarls were so insistent she was going to wake the entire house. It scared me because Prada very rarely acted this way, and my heart started racing. I pressed a hand to my chest as if the action would slow it down.

She put her front paws up on the door like someone was there. A stranger. Someone she didn't like.

It made me feel vulnerable.

Braeden groaned, her noise finally breaking into his deep sleep, and I flung out a hand to grip his shoulder. "Something's wrong."

He stiffened and sat up, automatically angling his body in front of mine.

Always my shield.

"Giz!" Braeden demanded. "No!"

The sound of the doorbell going off repeatedly filtered upstairs, and Prada started going crazy all over again.

"Someone's here," I said. The hand over my heart moved up to rest at my throat, and I swallowed. It was so early. Why would anyone be here this early?

Braeden cursed and tossed the covers back and got out of bed, reaching for the first pair of basketball shorts he found. I clutched at the covers, anxiety pummeling me.

Braeden flung open the bedroom door, and Prada raced down the steps toward the front door, behaving as if she were going to eat whoever it was alive. He stepped into the hall to follow her, but a quick glance at me had him retreating to my side of the bed.

"It's okay, baby. It's probably just a neighbor." His words were soft and so was his touch as he stroked down the length of my hair.

I nodded. He was totally right. It was probably nothing. I swallowed past the lump in my throat and gave him a weak smile.

Fear was kind of a new emotion for me. So was distrust. I didn't like either, but it seemed they were born out of necessity. I couldn't get hurt again like I had by people in the past.

I supposed fear was a natural defense mechanism. It sucked I had to defend myself that way.

Our room was the first one at the top of the stairs. So the sounds from downstairs were the easiest to hear where we were.

"Coming!" Rimmel called as she moved around downstairs. The doorbell kept ringing. I heard the lock being turned and the sound of the door being opened.

Prada was still barking and growling, and Rimmel fussed at her to hush.

Then there was an odd sort of silence. The charged kind.

"What are you doing here?" Rimmel's voice was high pitched and it carried up to us.

"What the fuck?" Braeden swore and strode out of the room and disappeared down the stairs.

The front door slammed, and I heard a deeper, unfamiliar voice. "Where the hell is he?"

"You shouldn't be here," Rimmel said. I swear there was a note of fear in her voice. It didn't make what I was feeling any easier to push aside.

"Where is he!" the man yelled.

The entire house probably heard that.

I stumbled out of bed and hurried to grab a pair of shorts and pull them on beneath Braeden's Wolfpack T-shirt.

"You looking for me?" Braeden said from the bottom of the stairs. His voice was hard and almost cold.

This wasn't good. Whatever this was, it was not good.

I ran from the room, my hair trailing along behind me as I flew down the hallway. I lifted my fist to beat on the closed door, and it swung open.

Romeo's eyes widened when he saw me.

"Someone's downstairs. Rimmel sounds worried, and Braeden... He sounds upset."

"You!" the man yelled from downstairs. "Did you think I wouldn't come?"

"What the fuck is he doing here?" Romeo muttered and rushed past me.

"Romeo?" I called after him.

"It's okay, princess." He tossed the words out as he rushed down the stairs.

Call me crazy, but I wasn't comforted.

I went and banged on Drew's door. "Get up!" I yelled, then turned the handle and opened the door.

His head popped up from the pillows. "Huh?"

"Downstairs!" I hissed.

I didn't wait for him, but I rushed away and down the steps.

Romeo was still standing on the bottom step, his back muscles tense and all his attention focused on the man standing in the entryway.

He was wearing a pair of gray trousers that were wrinkled and looked like he'd been wearing them for a long time. His shoes were wet from the snow outside and his white dress shirt was untucked, rumpled, and unbuttoned at the neck.

His gray hair was disheveled and his face was craggy and lacked any kind of energy. The way he swayed on his feet made me assume he was drunk, or at the very least, coming off a drinking binge and suffering from a massive hangover.

He looked like a beaten man. A man who'd hit rock bottom and had nowhere else to go.

He was glaring at Braeden with such open hostility that I squeezed past Romeo and rushed into the room.

B was standing in front of Rimmel like she needed protecting, and Prada was standing near his feet, watching the man with her ears down.

The sound I made rushing across the wood floor barefoot caused the man to tear his boiling eyes from B. His head twisted around, and his stare zeroed in on me.

Offended, Prada started barking again and rushed over to stand in front of me.

I stopped short, and a shiver literally shook me. I felt the blood drain from my head as I stared at the man. There was something about him... something I didn't like.

He reminded me of Zach.

"Ivy, go back upstairs," Braeden said, his voice hard.

The man who reminded me of Zach curled his upper lip and looked at me with hostility, then glanced back at B. "What's the matter? Afraid she might hear what I came here to say?"

"I have no idea why the hell you're beating on our door at the fucking crack of dawn, but I can assure you I'm not afraid of you," B replied. I knew that tone. He was getting angry. He was feeling threatened.

Braeden threatened was not a good thing.

He'd been hurt too many times. He'd been backed into a corner, helpless and unable to do anything far too many times.

"Oh?" the man said with a sense of calm. "Why's that? You plan to kill me just like you did my son?"

The hush that fell over the room was so definite you could have heard a pin drop the next state over. It was something I'd never experienced before. It was as if time stood still, as if his words were some weird spell that cast a momentary freeze over everyone who stood there.

It clicked.

The reason he reminded me of Zach. This was his father.

Braeden's face was shuttered; it betrayed not one emotion. It was impressive the way he could control what others saw, but what he couldn't control was the ghostly color his skin took on.

No.

Nope.

Hell no to the tenth power.

I was the first to shake off the eerie spell. A few steps carried me across the floor, and I stepped up in front of Braeden.

It was my turn to be his shield.

"Leave," I ordered, my voice calm yet commanding. Braeden didn't need this. He didn't deserve it. He was already silently suffering enough. There was no way in hell I'd let this man come here and take any sense of peace B had.

Zach's father raised an eyebrow. "And who do you think you are to tell me what to do?"

Ugh, the smugness in his tone would take me days to wash off in the shower. God, was it a family trait to be skin-crawlingly horrible?

I lifted my chin. I felt Braeden behind me as I watched Zach's father dismiss me without another thought and refocus on my boyfriend.

Don't look at him. Leave him alone. It wasn't just a thought, but a feeling, and it gave me courage.

"I'm the girl your son raped."

He jerked like he'd been shot. All focus on B went out the window.

Good.

Everyone looked at me like they were shocked I'd just out and said it. I admit it wasn't something I went around saying or even bringing up in normal conversation. But this wasn't normal. And this guy was out for Braeden's blood.

Over my cold and dead body.

I pressed a hand to my stomach and waited for a reaction. It didn't take long to get one.

"How dare you make such an accusation, taint my son's memory with your ugly lies!" he yelled.

Behind me, Braeden stepped up, so close I felt his heat against my back. I held up my hand, a silent gesture to make him back off. This was one time I wasn't going to allow him to shield me.

"I'm not accusing. I'm stating a fact. And your son's memory was already charred and crumbling all through fault of his own."

"*Charred?*" He gasped. "So not only do you make heinous statements about my son, but then have the nerve to stand there and make cruel and unsightly jokes about the way he suffered in the last moments of his life."

I blanched.

Clearly, that hadn't been a good choice of words.

"You need to leave." Romeo spoke up when words failed me. He came off the steps and walked toward Zach's father.

"I have to say I'm surprised at you, Roman," he said, disappointment in his tone. "I knew you and my son had your difficulties, but to be a party in covering up his murder—"

"Zach and I had a lot more than difficulties," Romeo replied calmly. "And I think if you were sober, you'd realize that."

"I am sober!" he insisted.

Romeo acted like he hadn't spoken. "And I would think as a lawyer, you would know better than to come to my private residence and throw around hefty accusations like murder."

How was he so calm right now? I wanted to pull my hair and scream.

"It's not just an accusation. I have proof."

Behind me, Braeden sucked in a breath. I felt the tension radiating from him. I also felt a degree of fear.

My stomach lurched. Why couldn't we just be happy? Why couldn't everything just go back to the way it was?

It's never going to be the same again. The thought was taunting and cruel.

"There's no way you have proof," I spat, anger hitting me after my own tortured thoughts. "I was there that night. I know what happened. Braeden didn't kill Zach. Zach kidnapped me, pulled out a gun, went on in great detail about how he was going to kill me and then come back for Braeden. So I forced the car off the road. Zach didn't get out in time. He died. It was no one's fault but his own."

"Ivy…" Braeden's voice was shocked, his hand clutching at the back of my shirt.

"You had time to pull him out of that car." Zach's dad ignored almost all of my words. I guess it was easier to not hear the terrible things his son did than to try and deny them. He moved to the left for a clear path to glare at B. "I read the police reports. You pulled that girl out of the car, carried her away, then had time to call 9-1-1 and give them a location and details about the accident. All that time, my son was still sitting in the car. You didn't even try to go back for him. You left him there to die."

"Are you suggesting he should have put his own life in danger to attempt to save your son in a wreck he created? They both could have died!" I yelled. I was starting to feel slightly hysterical.

Drew had been silently watching the scene from the stairs, but upon my outburst, he came down and made his way toward me, silently taking a solid stance at my side.

"You just said yourself that my son isn't the one who created that wreck. You admitted to running that car off the road. Maybe it's you I should be looking at for murder."

The room spun, but I held my ground and stared at him levelly.

"Motherfucker!" Braeden roared and started forward.

I made an alarmed sound, and Drew grabbed him and held him back.

"How dare you say that shit to her? You have no idea what she's been through!" Braeden raged, struggling against Drew's hold.

My brother's jaw clenched and he maneuvered so he was between B and me like he was afraid he wouldn't be able to hold him back.

Zach's father gazed at Braeden, a hint of satisfaction in his eyes. "There he is. The man capable of murder."

A cold chill slivered down my spine.

"That's enough." Romeo cut in and stepped in front of us all. The calm yet commanding tone in his voice was final. "This is *my* house and you are not welcome here. Get the hell out or I'm going to call the police and have you arrested for trespassing and harassment."

"My entire life," Zach's father spat at Romeo. "They've taken my entire life from me!"

If Zach had been his entire life, then I felt sorry for him.

"Out," Romeo rumbled and shifted his stance to that of one ready to use physical force if needed. And he had the muscle to back it up. Romeo wasn't someone a person messed with. He was too levelheaded, too calm, and far too capable for someone to challenge him and win.

It struck me how we all stood there. B in front of Rim, me in front of B, Drew beside us, and Romeo in front of us all.

We were all protecting each other, a family bound together by love and loyalty.

It made this entire situation seem so much less scary.

"This isn't the last you'll see of me!" Zach's father cried, and Romeo grabbed him by the back of his neck and literally hauled him to the door.

The man didn't fight against Romeo. He just allowed himself to be dragged away.

"I'm building a case against you. Both of you!"

I stiffened.

Romeo flung open the door and shoved him out into the snow.

"You haven't heard the last of—"

The sharp slam of the door cut off the rest of his threat.

"What the fuck was that?" Romeo spat, pinning B with an incredulous stare.

"My God, he's lost it!" Rimmel said. "He's turning into Zach."

I shuddered, and Drew reached for me, pulling me into his side.

Braeden's silence wasn't something I was accustomed to, and I turned my head to look at him.

He and Romeo were standing there staring at each other like they were the only two in the room.

It wasn't odd; it happened a lot.

The bromance and all.

The look on B's face… the all-encumbering bleakness, the way he looked as though he were truly afraid he might lose it all.

"I think…" He began.

I gasped. I knew exactly what he was thinking, what he was going to say. The nightmares hadn't just been about me after all.

I hadn't been the only one involved in the crash that night.

"Braeden," I said, trying to convey my understanding, my absolute support in that one word.

He his eyes softened on me and the love I knew he had for me shone through.

But then he looked back at his best friend. "I think we should probably talk."

Romeo held up under the weight of the words, the practical admission from his best friend. Hell, if anything, Romeo seemed to draw himself up tighter, as if he were preparing for some kind of fight.

I think maybe he was.

But the fight wasn't just going to be his.

It was going to be all of ours.

Our family was being threatened. Our future.

I stepped away from Drew and slid my hand into B's. The way his fingers tightened around mine was an answer that Braeden felt it, too.

Romeo nodded once, then declared, "Family meeting."

MEETINGS, PARTIES... & MURDER? (AKA PART TWO)

CHAPTER FOURTEEN

#FriendlyReminder

Your hair might be a problem if things get lost in it. Or trapped.

#CombThatShit
#TheresNoExcuseForBadHair
#BuzzBoss

RIMMEL

Well, this was new.

Romeo just announced a family meeting like we were all in trouble and about to get our punishments doled out.

I might have laughed if this morning hadn't been so horrifying.

There I was just hanging out in my too-big sweats, enjoying my uncombed messy hair, and making coffee for everyone when all hell broke loose in the form of a man beating on the door!

Okay, he rang the doorbell.

But it was still super insistent.

I'd know Zach's father anywhere. Even the little I'd seen of him at the hospital after my attack and then again at the closed court hearing was enough to burn this man's face into my memory for life.

I'd almost felt sorry for him when I first opened the door. He looked terrible. A far cry from the put together, strong attorney I'd come to recognize. He was in shabby condition, and to be honest, he kinda smelled.

It turned my stomach.

It reminded me of the day Romeo met my father. How we'd walked into the house and he'd been a mess and drunk.

But the pity I felt for him didn't last long.

The things he'd said this morning, the accusations he so violently hurled at the people in the room.

Wow.

And Braeden, my BBFL, the guy I loved almost as fiercely as Romeo (okay, just as fiercely but in a sisterly way), how he looked standing there, shocked, caught... almost like a deer in headlights when Robert accused him of murdering Zach, pierced my heart.

My goodness, he looked as if he couldn't even defend himself.

That B didn't stick around long, though, at least not completely. The way he leapt forward when Robert accused Ivy of murder was the B I knew.

And umm, what kind of man accused a woman who almost died and was Zach's victim more than once of murder?

It was far, far too early in the morning for this.

"Call Trent," Romeo barked at Drew like he was a drill sergeant. "Tell him to get his ass over here."

Drew blinked in surprise. Surely he was used to Romeo's bossy ways by now.

Romeo, who had gone back to studying B, must have felt Drew's reaction and turned back. "He's family, ain't he?"

Drew nodded.

Okay then, Romeo gestured by lifting his arms as if to invite any more comments.

I bit my lip and suppressed a smile. Romeo being all bossy was kind of hot. Well, when it wasn't me he was bossing. I didn't like being bossed.

"Smalls, get over here!" he demanded.

I sighed loudly. So much for not being bossed. His hotness just went down a notch.

"Don't you talk to me like that, Roman Anderson!" I demanded back.

He started muttering something about stubborn women and stalked over in front of me. I expected some kind of lecture or order like he gave Drew, but instead, I found myself firmly against his chest.

His hand delved in my hair and his fingers massaged my scalp in the best way. I forgot to be annoyed and relaxed into his bare chest. He leaned down against my ear. "You okay? Did he say or do something to you before I got down here?"

He was worried.

And this was the power of Romeo.

No one else could be so pigheaded, so bossy, and so protective all at once and then totally make up for it by being heart-meltingly thoughtful.

My arms couldn't resist slipping around him and hugging close. "I'm fine," I whispered against his chest.

His muscles constricted where my breath hit his skin.

"Are you sure?" He pulled back to look down at me.

I nodded. "Braeden was down here almost the minute I opened the door." I glanced in his direction. "You know how he is. I barely got a good look at Robert before Braeden was in front of me."

Braeden gave me a look that said he wasn't sorry, and I smiled. "I'm not mad at you, B." I teased.

He grunted and a small smile played on his lips. "No one messes with my sister." He said it lightly, in his usual way, but I saw the shadows dance in his eyes.

Romeo seemed satisfied and his face softened. "I think my hand is caught in your hair." He pulled his arm like he was trying to get out of a trap. "Seriously, baby, what the hell did you do to yourself?"

I poked him in the ribs and gasped. "You're terrible!"

"Aww, baby, don't be like that," he drawled, dripping with charm. "I love your hair. Except when it tries to eat my hand. I need it for football."

I stomped on his foot (not hard enough to hurt him) and stepped back. "I can't believe I agreed to marry you!"

Ivy laughed, and Romeo pretended I offended him.

Please. It would take a lot more than that to offend him.

"You can't change your mind now, woman. We set a date." He grabbed me back and kissed me. I let him 'cause I liked his kisses.

Braeden made a sound, a cross between a growl and a gasp. "What the fuck is this!"

Everyone turned to stare at him.

"Where the hell are your pants!" He gestured toward Ivy and her bare legs.

Clearly, he'd snapped out of wherever he'd gone.

Ivy lifted up the oversized shirt, and Braeden about had heart failure. "Don't be showing your lady bits to everyone!" He gasped and moved to shield her.

Ivy rolled her eyes. "I'm wearing shorts, bonehead. See?" She pointed at the shorts she definitely was wearing. "You just can't see them because your shirt is so long."

"Accused of murder *and* my girl is trying to show off her goods. I need to go back to bed," B muttered and wiped a hand over his face.

Romeo laughed.

Drew turned back to the group and held up his phone. "Trent's on his way."

"Why don't we all take five? Rim can comb her hair, Ivy can put on pants—"

"I'm wearing pants!" she yelled.

Romeo chuckled. "Put on pants we can see, princess."

"I need orange juice for this," she declared and went off to the kitchen.

Braeden looked at me. "Why the fuck is she so into orange juice lately?"

I shrugged and followed Ivy into the kitchen.

I poured a mug of coffee while Ivy poured a glass half full of juice. We both leaned against the counter and took a healthy sip of our drinks and sighed.

She looked pale, and I pointed it out.

"It's not every day the father of the guy who raped you barges into your house and accuses you of murder."

I bit my lower lip. I couldn't imagine how she must feel right now. And just after yesterday when she told me she was finally feeling stronger emotionally. I felt angry with Robert for coming here and trying to rip apart Braeden and Ivy's life.

"I'm worried about him," Ivy confided, her voice dipping low. I knew she was talking about Braeden; there was no one else that would put that look of concern on her face.

I opened my mouth to say something and then stopped. I didn't like the thoughts and words bubbling up inside me.

"B's going to be fine. We'll all take care of him," I assured her and stepped to her side. She was gripping the juice like it was her lifeline.

"Come on. I need help brushing my hair."

She smiled.

"Maybe I'll put on some pants. Maybe I won't." Her voice was devious.

"Well, if the boys don't have to wear shirts to the family meeting, why should you have to wear pants?" I mused.

"You know you wanna see my muscles, Blondie," Braeden quipped, overhearing our words as we walked through the family room.

"Oh, is that what you're calling them these days?" She batted her eyelashes innocently.

"Burned," Drew drawled.

"Better run, sis. Don't want you to get caught in the crossfire," Braeden said and rushed at us.

Ivy held the glass in front of her. "Don't spill my juice!"

"For the love of God, woman," Braeden muttered, but he backed off and slung an arm around her shoulder gently. "Come on. Let's me you... and your juice go get dressed."

I forgot about combing my hair and dropped into Romeo's lap. He took my coffee and drank some of it.

"He seems better," I said about Braeden. "A little less... freaked."

Romeo's mouth turned grim. "Oh, he's freaked. He's trying to hold it together for Ivy." His voice lowered. "This isn't good, Smalls."

"I know."

But just how bad this really was remained to be seen.

CHAPTER FIFTEEN

#Uh-oh
The walk of shame isn't exclusive to ho's anymore. Trent Mask was seen rushing out of his frat and rushing somewhere else.
#HisLoyaltyIsDivided
#OmegaNeedsANewPrez
#BuzzBoss

ROMEO

The doorbell rang.

Rimmel's entire body changed from relaxed to anxious in about three seconds flat. She was sitting in my lap, drinking her coffee, and petting Murphy, who was sitting below us looking like he was desperate for a treat.

She tried to get up and get him one, but I wasn't willing to let her go.

I liked her where she was just fine.

The second her body stiffened, mine reacted without thought. I was so attuned to her I didn't even have to try anymore. It just was.

I pulled her in a little tighter against me, offering her shelter, and kissed her hairline. "It's Trent, baby."

Drew was already up and heading for the door to pull it open.

Rim looked a little sheepish when she relaxed back against me. "Sorry."

"Better go get Murphy a snack or he's gonna stalk us the whole time we're in here having our meeting." I patted her hip.

She climbed out of my lap and held out her hand for the mug. The coffee was almost gone since both of us had been drinking it. "I'll get more. You want some, too?"

"I'll just share with you again. Tastes better when I know your lips have been on there." I added a wink at the end.

Her cheeks turned pink, and I reveled in the sight. Fuck, I loved that I still was able to make her blush.

"'Kay," she said and turned away.

"Hurry back," I said softly so only she could hear.

"Dude," Drew said as Trent came into the room. "You look like hell."

"Not everyone wakes up looking like Romeo," Trent quipped and flashed me a grin.

I shrugged. "I woke up like this." I gestured to myself and flashed a smile.

"I didn't know someone with such short hair could mess it up." Drew guffawed.

"Like you ever comb your hair." Trent scoffed. "Besides, this is what you get when you call me at the fucking butt crack of dawn and tell me to get my ass over here."

"I didn't comb my hair either!" Rim said cheerfully as she walked by.

Trent looked at her and laughed. "Bedheads unite!"

Rimmel backtracked and held her fist out to him. Both Drew and Trent pounded theirs on hers, creating a triple pound.

It was like a meeting of some '80's hair band.

"Coffee's in the kitchen!" she called and then disappeared. Murphy went after her with a loud meow.

Trent divided his gaze between Drew and me. "Thought I'd show up to a fire or some serious emergency. You seriously didn't call me over here for coffee, did you?"

"Family meeting," I grunted.

Trent's eyes widened a bit. I rubbed a hand over my face. "Why do you two keep acting like someone stole your lunchbox when I say Trent's family? It's not new."

They were acting like a bunch of women.

Trent cleared his throat. "Well, yeah, I mean... We've been friends a while. I guess I just thought..."

I cocked my head to the side and waited.

He glanced at Drew, then back. "I guess I've always felt like kinda the third wheel."

"There's six of us," I pointed out blandly.

Trent shrugged.

"You want to be part of this family?" I asked, blunt. "You loyal to us? All of us?"

How fast he answered would tell me a lot.

He didn't even think about it. "Hells yeah. You know I got your back. I was even loyal to you over my frat, and you know how they are about that shit."

I nodded. I did know. Trent went against his fraternity more than once to help me out with Zach, and even when I'd been rushing, he looked out for me. As far as I knew, he never got any shit for it, because him getting rid of Zach wasn't just good for me, but for everyone.

"You wanna move in?" I asked, blunt yet again.

I didn't have time to dance around. We had shit to talk about. Rim appeared, and I sat back so she could avail herself of my lap. It was a freaking distraction the way she wiggled her little ass against me as she got comfortable.

My cock started to stiffen, and I palmed her hip to make her go still. She must have felt what was happening because she looked at me wide-eyed.

"Be careful, baby. That's hot," I said and took the coffee from her to have some.

We both knew I wasn't talking about the coffee.

She wiggled again, right against *the spot*. I practically choked. Rim giggled.

She was so going to pay for that later.

"Move in?" Trent said, surprise in his voice.

"B!" I yelled. "Get your ass down here!"

I looked back at Trent and shrugged. "The rest of us live here. Maybe that's why you feel so separate from us. You aren't here all the time."

Rimmel nodded. She hadn't even heard the whole conversation, but she agreed. It just proved Trent was family. She'd take him in even without knowing the reason.

Trent gave her a smile, like he, too, noticed her acceptance, and then turned back. "I—"

"'Course we're outta bedrooms. You'd have to bunk with Drew."

Drew choked on the coffee he was drinking and it dribbled down his chin. Since he wasn't wearing a shirt, he used the back of his hand to mop it off his face.

Trent laughed. "Dude, your face."

Drew gave him the finger.

B sounded like an elephant coming down the stairs, while Ivy came down a lot more gracefully. He was dressed in a pair of beat-up jeans and a hoodie. He didn't look too thrown off by this morning, but he was.

I knew without looking at him at all. Ivy looked tired as she stepped off the last step, dressed more causally than usual in a pair of leggings, tall knee socks, a T-shirt, and an oversized cardigan.

I was worried about them.

But I was getting off track. I turned back to Trent and lifted an eyebrow.

"As tempting as that sounds…" He began, and Drew hacked and coughed some more.

"Why do I even bother trying to drink this!" he demanded.

Ivy made a face at the mess he was making and rushed into the kitchen and came back with a towel, throwing it at him. He started wiping up the coffee he managed to get everywhere.

"I meant living here with you guys, not freaking sharing a room," Trent ground out, then muttered, "Perv."

B and I grinned.

"But I can't. Frat prez remember? I have to live at Omega."

I knew that, but I wanted him to know he was welcome here anyway.

"But thanks, means a lot to me," he added and settled back against the cushions.

Ivy sat on the couch beside him. She still had the now almost empty glass of juice in one hand.

He held out his fist to her. "Ives, looking good."

She pounded it out and smiled. "Thanks, Trent."

Braeden sat down beside Ivy and pulled her into his side. I suppressed a smile. He was so freaking possessive of her it was borderline ridiculous.

I liked seeing my best friend whipped. Amused the hell outta me.

"So what's this family meeting all about?" Trent asked. "Don't we have those like every Sunday when we eat pancakes?"

"No, that's family time," Rimmel said. "This is a meeting."

I didn't bother telling her that we men didn't really see the difference.

"We got shit to discuss that stays in this room," I said. "Seems we got a situation." I quickly explained to Trent about our unwelcome visitor.

He shook his head. "Can't say I'm surprised after the shit I've been hearing."

"What shit?" Braeden went on defense immediately. "And why the fuck haven't you said anything?"

"Because it's just stupid talk around the frat house." He glanced at Ivy a little apprehensively. "And I didn't think Zach was a welcome name in this house."

"What have you heard?" I asked, wanting him to go on.

"Apparently, Zach's dad has hit rock bottom. After Zach died, he started drinking, his clients started looking somewhere else for representation, and just the other day, I heard his wife left him. Filed for divorce."

Rimmel nodded. "He looked like he hit rock bottom."

I knew she was thinking about her father and the way he looked before he was carted off to rehab for his gambling after having lost literally all his possessions.

"Accusing Ivy of murder isn't hitting rock bottom. It's being a vindictive asshole," B ground out.

I gave him a glance, wondering if I was going to have to haul his ass outside and throw him in the snow to cool him off. I knew he was pissed about the things

Robert said to Ivy. Hell, I'd be too in his position, but B had a temper and he couldn't afford to lose it right now. He was already skating on a fine line.

I was thinking now I understood why.

"Whoa," Trent said, sitting back. "I haven't heard anything about that. I would have said something."

Ivy slid her hand over onto B's thigh and used her thumb to trace slow circles there. Then she rested her head against his shoulder. Some of the hair in her high ponytail rubbed against his cheek.

Braeden seemed to calm down.

Ivy was good for him.

"Robert Bettinger seems to think he'll be able to build some kind of case against Braeden and possibly Ivy." I began.

"He'll leave her the fuck out of this, so help me God," B growled.

I shot him a warning look. "Cool it, man."

"For what?" Trent asked.

"For Zach's murder." Drew finished.

Trent was dumbstruck.

I'd been too at first. But it didn't take me long to start wondering if this was part of the issues B was having lately with sleep, the reason Ivy seemed to be so concerned I wouldn't stand by him.

Did she know more about that night than she let on?

What was it Braeden never said?

"B, you didn't deny it while he was here," I said.

Everyone grew quiet and glanced his way. Ivy straightened and lifted her chin like she dared anyone to say a word to him.

Have I mentioned I thought she was good for him? B did good picking her out.

"You accusing me of something, Rome?" B's voice was dead calm.

"Hell no," I replied. "I couldn't care less if you locked the fucker in the car and made him burn."

Rimmel gasped, and I realized I probably shouldn't have said that out loud, but it was too late to take it back. Besides, it was the way I felt.

Braeden needed to know I was on his side.

I locked eyes with Ivy, and she gave me a grateful yet guarded stare.

"But I need to know what the hell we're dealing with. We all do. We need to be prepared." I glanced around at everyone, gauging their reactions.

"You really mean that?" B asked. It was like the conversation no longer involved everyone else in the room. It was my best friend asking me and only me if I still had his back.

I stared at him, unflinching. "No truer words have been spoken."

I got your back. Forever.

He relaxed. A new calm washed over him. Then he glanced down at Ivy, some of his guard sliding back up.

He's worried what her reaction will be if he admits to something.

"It's okay, B. Just say whatever you need to say," she said quietly, squeezing his thigh.

He looked up, stared at no one, and spoke to everyone.

"I let Zach die."

CHAPTER SIXTEEN

I'm hearing whispers of some very juicy info.

#MoreToCome

#BuzzBoss

RIMMEL

I couldn't sit still.

How was I supposed to sit here and listen to Braeden basically tell us he was a murderer?

I couldn't.

I wouldn't.

I had to.

Anxious, I unfolded from Romeo's lap and paced the living room, stopping to stare in front of the fireplace.

I should light it. It was cold in here.

"So, yeah, basically, Robert was right. I killed Zach." Braeden went on. His voice was hollow.

I felt the words like a knife to my chest. I don't know why. I wished I didn't. I didn't want to be affected by this. But how could I not be?

My brother was sitting in the living room, confessing to murder.

My mother was murdered.

Her life robbed when I was just a little girl. I hated the men who killed her. Part of me was still angry my father was the reason those men came for her. I was angry he didn't protect her. He should have.

I just don't know how anyone could justify killing another person.

Even a sick and twisted one like Zach.

I set my coffee on the mantle and bent down to light the pilot light at the base of the fireplace. It was gas, and as soon as the pilot was lit, I could flip the switch and the fire would ignite.

Only the dumb thing wouldn't catch.

I pushed the button frantically, becoming frustrated that it wouldn't light.

Why wouldn't it light?

A warm presence surrounded me and gentle hands pushed mine out of the way. "You trying to blow up the house, Smalls?"

"It's cold in here," I said.

Romeo pushed the button, and the blue flame flickered to life. Of course it did what he wanted on the first try.

"There you go," he said and stood, taking me with him.

With our backs to the room and his arms still around me, he whispered so softly in my ear I had to strain to hear him, "I know it's hard, sweetheart. Give him a chance to explain."

They say you're often drawn to people who possess the qualities you yourself wish you had. I was a living, breathing example of that.

I wished I could be as calm, as accepting, of this as Romeo. I loved Braeden. Next to Romeo, he was arguably the most important person in my life. I didn't want to be upset right now. I didn't want to look at B and have him see I was struggling.

Romeo pulled away, hit the switch, and left me to stand there.

With a great whoosh, I watched the fire burst to life. The flames danced for long minutes.

I'm not going to do this. I wasn't going to be angry with my brother for a choice he made in an extreme situation. Besides that, he was probably taking on way more guilt than he even deserved.

I thought about all the times he'd been there for me. The night he jumped into the pool in the middle of winter to help fish me out and then dove back in later for my glasses. The night at the hospital when he came and held me as I cried gut-wrenching sobs into his chest. The time he flew to Florida so he could be there to protect me in case things with my dad went bad. All the times I needed a hug, he just knew and hugged me.

There were so many more times that Braeden proved he was my family.

It was my turn to prove it to him.

Abruptly, I turned from the fire and strode across the room, weaved around the coffee table, and headed directly for him.

He looked at me reluctantly, a wary light in his eye.

I already hurt him by my reaction.

I climbed in his lap and tucked my arms around his neck.

I glanced at Ivy from under my lashes to make sure she wasn't upset. The look on her face could only be described as grateful. Her body slid back a little, making more room for me.

I leaned up to whisper in his ear, "Big brother *for life.*"

Braeden hugged me close, wrapping his arms around me and sighing into my hair.

"Thanks, Rim," he murmured.

I tucked my head in the crook of his neck and waited for him to tell us everything.

Ivy spoke up first. "Braeden didn't kill Zach. The car explosion killed him."

"Robert seemed to think you had time to get him out," Romeo said.

He didn't seem upset at all. He didn't sound accusatory. He just sounded like he wanted answers. I knew Romeo would stand by Braeden. There wasn't a single doubt in my mind. I never really thought he was a man who would murder someone.

Capable?

Oh yes, Romeo was capable of anything; that much I knew.

But he was also controlled in a way Braeden never had been. The words he'd said to Braeden just moments ago, how he didn't care if B locked Zach down and made him burn…

I didn't like that.

I didn't like feeling like Romeo was volatile in anyway.

I wanted stable. I wanted steady.

I pressed my face a little farther into B's neck, suddenly needing comfort.

Braeden noticed and shifted me a little closer but ducked his head down to whisper, "If this is too hard for you… if you don't want to hear this, I understand. You can leave."

I felt Romeo's stare even though my back was to him.

"I want to hear," I said. "I'm just cold."

It was a lame lie. An excuse for the way I was clinging to him all of the sudden.

B rubbed his palm up my arm briskly, as if to generate some heat. I felt him lean forward and snag the blanket off the back of the couch, then spread it over me.

"You want Rome?" he murmured.

"I want you right now," I said.

He seemed a little surprised at that but didn't say anything, just tucked his arm around me and then reached for Ivy's hand with his other.

"I never wanted to talk about this." He spoke to everyone in the room. "But I guess now I don't really have a choice."

No one said a word. They just waited as if they too were unsure if they wanted to hear.

"I watched that BMW flip over three times." His voice turned throaty, like he was battling a bad case of laryngitis. "God, we were both driving so fucking fast. I couldn't back off. He had Ivy, for Christ's sake. But me being there seemed to push him to the edge, and the next thing I knew, he was pointing a gun at her."

Drew made a sound, but I didn't look up. I just listened.

"I'll never forget what it was like to hear that gunshot, see the car swerve, and then watch it get mangled as it literally bounced and rolled through the field. When I finally made it to the wreckage, I was out of my mind. I called out to Ivy and she didn't answer..." I felt his throat work as he swallowed. "I thought she was dead."

"I wasn't," Ivy said.

Braeden shook his head and continued. "No, you weren't, but you were in bad shape. I honestly thought pulling her out of the car was going to kill her. And the gas was leaking. I saw it the minute I ran up to the car. I knew the car was going to blow up. After seeing it take such a beating and then smelling the gas, I knew it would light up."

"But you pulled her out anyway," Drew said.

"Of course I did. I'd have died trying to get her out of that car," Braeden said. "I carried her pretty far away, closer to the road. I didn't want her to get hurt when it did blow. She was in and out of consciousness, so yeah, I stayed with her a few minutes, trying to make sure she was still breathing."

"And you called 9-1-1," Ivy added.

"Yeah, and gave them a location. I thought Zach was dead. But honestly, I didn't even care. I was too worried about Ivy. A few minutes later, I heard him yelling."

Ivy nodded, and B jerked. "You heard him call out?"

"Yes, I heard him," she replied.

"Did you go back to the car?" Trent asked.

"Yeah, I went back. Zach was trapped by the seat belt or something in the driver's seat. He was struggling to get free," Braeden said, his voice taking on a new tone. A rougher sound. "He asked me to help him. Said he didn't want to die."

"You tried to help him?" Drew asked.

I felt Braeden's intake of breath. The way he steeled himself for his response. "No, I didn't. I stood there and hated him. All I saw when I looked at him was all the shit he'd done to us over the past year. The way he tortured Rimmel, how he broke Rome's arm. He fucking raped Ivy and let her think she'd just made a drunken mistake. I'd just seen him hit her. Pull a gun on her. And now she was lying feet away, barely alive."

His words brought a sullen, heavy blanket over the entire room. Zach had been a terrible person. He'd hurt so many people.

"Zach knew before I did I wasn't going to pull him out. He told me it was murder."

Romeo sucked in a breath behind me.

"I told him he deserved it. And so help me God, to this day, I still think he did. If I had pulled him out of that car, he'd be somewhere right now plotting revenge, thinking up new ways to hurt us. We'd all be looking over our shoulder, and Ivy… she'd have to look at the man who violated her in the worst possible way."

"B," Romeo said, responding to the despair in his best friend's voice.

I looked at Ivy. Her face was pale and her hand was pressed over her stomach. "We wouldn't have been safe," she said.

The way she was holding her middle…

"The car was on fire already." Braeden went on. "I knew it was going to blow. So I walked away. I barely made it to Ivy before it exploded."

So that was it. That was the entire truth of that night.

"And now you know," Braeden said. "I'm a murderer."

Cambria Hebert

CHAPTER SEVENTEEN

#LifeLesson

Life is not like a box of chocolates. It's like a jar of jalapenos. Be careful what you do today. It could burn your ass tomorrow!

#BuzzBoss

ROMEO

My best friend just announced he was a murderer.

And my girl was cuddled up in his lap. She was upset with me. I failed to see how that made any kind of sense.

Honestly, though, that was the least of my worries right now. I'd make whatever it was with Rim right. And if she needed comfort from Braeden, then she could have it. Besides, I think he needed it just as badly.

"You said the car was on fire when you went back for Zach," Trent said.

"So?" Braeden replied.

"So even if you tried to pull him out, it could have blown up and then both of you would be dead," Ivy surmised.

Braeden started shaking his head like they were making excuses for him.

"You're not a murderer, man," I said.

He looked at me sharply. "You were pissed off. You hated Zach. Fuck, we all hated him. So you stood there until it was too late to pull him out."

"It was a conscious decision." Braeden cut in.

"Who the fuck cares?" I said.

Rimmel's body tightened. Ah. That was the problem. She didn't like this cold, immoral side of mine.

"Seriously, man," Drew said. "I'm glad you let him burn. After what he did to my sister?" He shook his head. "I'd have done the same thing."

"Me, too," Trent echoed.

"I just remember feeling so relieved when I knew he was gone," Ivy admitted. She wasn't as bold as us guys with her truth, but I knew she meant it.

Braeden looked at her. "You knew this whole time?"

"Knew what?"

"That I left him there?"

Her eyes softened. "Yeah, I knew. I was out of it that night, like you said, but I heard Zach screaming, and I saw you walk away from the car."

"You never said a word." His voice held a note of awe.

"Because I never cared. It's not like you killed him in cold blood, B. It was basically self-defense. And besides, as Robert was so quick to point out, I'm just as responsible as you."

"Don't you fucking say that." His voice was vehement.

"It's true, though."

"He was going to shoot you."

"He was going to shoot you, too," she fired back. Ivy glanced at me. "Zach told me so. And he hated you, Romeo." Her eyes filled with tears. "He probably would have come for you next."

"It was him or us, B. You chose us. Your family," I said.

"I'd do it again," Braeden admitted. "I can't say I'm proud of that, but it's the truth."

What a fucking nightmare of a position he'd been in. Would I have done the same? Probably, but I wasn't sure. I hadn't killed him the night he strung up Rimmel and broke my arm even though I'd been tempted. The truth was—

Braeden cut off my inner thoughts. "Not everyone can be as controlled as you, Rome. Some of us are human."

How the fuck did he know what I was thinking? And where did he get off implying I wasn't human?

I bolted up out of my chair, kinda offended. "I never passed judgment on you," I growled.

"No. But I know you wouldn't have done what I did. I'm not made like you. I got a dark side."

This wasn't a conversation I wanted to have in front of everyone. Especially Rimmel. I shook my head and looked up at the ceiling.

"Robert's a good lawyer. He knows how to build a case. He's gonna try and pin this on you, B." I glanced at Ivy, and her mouth flattened. She knew Robert would come for her, too. I didn't say it out loud. I was afraid it would push B over the edge.

"We gotta make sure it doesn't stick," Trent said.

"None of this goes beyond these walls," Drew said. "As far as all of us know, there was no time for B to get Zach out."

"There wasn't," Ivy spoke up. "Braeden would have died trying."

Drew nodded. "Exactly. No one else needs to know anything else."

Braeden made a sound. "None of you care?"

I rolled my eyes. "Did you think we would turn our backs on you?"

"No," he said decisively. "But this isn't like the time I broke the coffee pot and pretended it wasn't me and no one said anything."

"That was you!" Rimmel gasped and sat up to glare at him. "I thought I was the one who broke it!"

"Baby..." I was amused. "We all knew it was B. You didn't?"

"No!" she declared. "I felt horrible about that for days!"

Braeden laughed. "Sorry, tutor girl."

"Why would you think you broke it?" I tried to hide my grin. Goddamn, she was so innocent.

"Because I'm clumsy! And because you gave me money to go buy a new one. I thought you were just trying to make me feel better."

Everyone laughed. Rimmel scowled. "I just wanted some coffee," I said.

Braeden patted her shoulder. "Sorry, sis. Next time I'll come clean when I break something."

Rimmel growled under her breath, and I wanted to snatch her out of B's lap and kiss her. I was starting to get irritated she was still sitting there. B had a girl.

Maybe I'd just give him a taste of his own medicine.

"Look. Point is. Breaking a coffee pot and not pulling a guy out of a burning car is a lot different," Braeden said, his voice a lot more normal. Like the weight of that night wasn't so heavy anymore.

"We're with you," Ivy said and glanced at everyone.

We all nodded.

Braeden looked down at Rim. She nodded as well.

He blew out a shaky breath. "Yeah, okay." His eyes found mine. "So what do I do?"

"Robert isn't going to go away." Trent spoke up. "I'll see what else I can find out about him at the frat. Zach's old buddies still talk about him and the drama. We can use all the upheaval in his life to discredit his accusations."

I nodded. "Yeah. That's good."

"But what if he finds some kind of proof?" B wondered.

"He's not going to," Ivy said. "There isn't any."

"I'll call my dad. He'll know how to handle Robert," I added.

Everyone nodded.

"Everyone keep your mouth shut. Trent, do some digging on campus," I ordered. "Meeting adjourned."

I went over to the couch and grinned down at Ivy. "I'm suddenly in the mood for a drink. Care to share your juice, princess?"

"Hit me." She held up her glass.

I pulled her off the couch, and she swayed on her feet. "Whoa." I anchored my arm around her, and she leaned in to me.

"Okay?"

She nodded swiftly.

Braeden's eyes were narrowed and watching us. I wasn't sure if it was concern 'cause she was unsteady or jealousy because I was touching his girl.

I smiled and decided to find out.

"Come on, princess. Your chariot awaits." I bent down and gave her my back.

She looked at me like I had three heads.

"Not getting any younger here," I intoned.

She leapt on my back, and I straightened, hooking my arms beneath her legs to give her a piggyback ride into the kitchen.

"What the fuck is this shit?" Braeden growled, setting Rim aside.

I gave him a smug, toothy grin and started off with Ivy.

"I know what you're doing!" he yelled after us.

"Getting juice?" I called back.

Ivy giggled. "Pissed you off, did he?"

I grunted. "Just a little payback."

In the kitchen, I turned so my back was against the island, and I lowered Ivy a bit so she could sit on the counter. Once I had the juice, I poured her some and then took a large gulp out of the container.

"Roman Anderson!" Rimmel said, and I lowered the jug and wiped my mouth with the back of my hand.

"Future Mrs. Anderson?"

She forgot about me drinking out of the carton and smiled. "I'm going to take a shower."

"Want some company?" I asked.

"Dude, you're an ass," B said, coming into the kitchen.

I handed him the OJ carton. "Peace offering?"

He shrugged and took a drink.

"I give up," Rimmel muttered and turned to leave.

"Now I need a new a new juice," Ivy complained.

Braeden lowered the half-gallon and belched. Loudly.

I high-fived him. "Way to make it quake."

Drew and Trent shuffled in the room to the coffee. "That was a ten-point-O on the Richter scale!" Trent called out, then went back to talking about car parts with Drew.

"I have to go," Ivy groaned and held out her arms. "I need down."

Feeling devious, I stepped forward to help her, and B slapped his hand on my chest. "Don't push me," he uttered.

I chuckled.

Braeden lifted Ivy off the counter and set her on her feet, tugging on the end of her ponytail. "Where do you think you're going?"

"I have a doctor appointment."

All eyes shifted to her.

Braeden frowned. "What's the matter?" I watched him reach for her wrist, and his eyes widened. So he knew about the bruises. I figured she couldn't hide them forever.

"Is your wrist bothering you? Hasn't been that long since you got the cast off. Was it—"

"No!" Ivy hurried to say before he could finish. "I'm fine. It's just my last follow-up from all the appointments I had after the accident."

"I thought you were done with those," Drew said, a frown in his voice.

"After today I will be," she chirped.

"I was gonna workout, but I'll drive you. Workout later," B said.

"No, I can drive myself. I have to go to class afterward."

"Sure?" he asked.

"Mm-hmm." She agreed. "I gotta go get my boots."

Braeden watched her go, and I slapped him on the shoulder. "I'll workout with ya, B."

He nodded.

"You guys wanna hit the gym?" I asked Trent and Drew.

"Can't. Gotta get to the day job." He sounded so un-thrilled I laughed.

"I have class." Trent sounded equally as horrified.

"How's the driving going?" I asked Drew.

He shrugged. "It's a tough crowd. The indie circle is pretty tight. But I'm holding my own."

"Never any doubt," I said.

Trent shifted, and I thought I sensed a little tension there. I wondered what that was about. I didn't ask, though. All my focus was on B right now.

"I'm gonna go change, bug Rim, and then we'll go."

"You drive. My truck's running like shit."

Another byproduct of Zach, I thought.

Even dead, the guy was causing everyone problems.

CHAPTER EIGHTEEN

Some love can't be denied.
#LoversGonnaLove

#BuzzBoss

RIMMEL

He was standing against the bathroom counter. Hip aligned with the edge of the granite, foot propped up over the other, arms crossed over his chest.

He still wasn't wearing a shirt, and at this point, I was convinced he did it on purpose. He knew the effect he had on me, and he was totally using it to his advantage.

Blue eyes watched me like I was the main attraction at some in-demand show. They watched me with azure fire, like the hottest part of a flame.

I opened the glass shower door and stepped out, clutching the white towel around my body and holding it closed at my chest. My hair was wet and dripping. I had to condition it twice just to be sure I could comb it. I'd already towel-dried the ends before I stepped out of the shower, but they still dripped down my back.

I wasn't wearing my glasses, so the room was slightly blurry. But I didn't mind. It gave me an excuse not to focus on the man watching me.

Instead, I grabbed my wet-to-dry brush and started at the ends of my hair. It was difficult to brush it out and hold the towel around me at the same time. Normally, I'd just drop the fabric, but I couldn't just then.

It wasn't that I was uncomfortable. Romeo had seen me naked so many times it was almost normal by now. He knew my body almost as well as I did. After all, he spent a lot of time exploring it.

It was the intimacy, the vulnerability.

I didn't feel like I could handle that right this second. I was still feeling a little raw and kinda confused.

Romeo didn't say a word, and neither did I.

For long seconds, he watched me awkwardly hold on to the towel and the brush until a grunt forced its way out the back of his throat. He unfolded his arms and pushed off the counter. His body was warm when he moved behind me and gently took the brush from my grasp.

I gave it to him and clutched at the towel around me with both hands.

He started at the bottom. Wet, it reached a little farther than halfway down my back. I probably should have gotten it cut—it was way too much to deal with—but I hadn't wanted to bother.

And now with the wedding coming up, I thought the length might be nice.

He was a lot kinder to my hair than I was. Either that or the long, tangled strands were just as affected by the sight of him without a shirt. The brush slid through easily, gliding through the length like it wouldn't dare give Romeo a hard time.

Traitor.

I watched him through the mirror. I studied the way his large, muscular body looked just behind mine. I was so much smaller, so much paler, and so much... less.

Romeo was everything.

His blond hair was a shade you couldn't get out of a bottle, the perfect tone, the perfect amount of gold and light. He'd been running his fingers through it all morning. I knew because of the way it stuck out in odd places, curling out and waving around the tops of his ears. A strand of it fell over his forehead, and it only served to make him look more attractive.

He hadn't shaved in a couple days, so the scruffy stubble that covered his lower jaw was thick and soft. It was blond, too. I had a sudden longing to feel its prickly softness between my thighs.

Even though I stood in front of him, he was so broad I could see both his shoulders behind me. They were well defined, wide, and smooth.

He'd actually leaned up just slightly since starting with the NFL. All the training and constant travel had trimmed him down, but it only served to cut out the sharp contours of his body. I could count his abs individually.

And the way his hips narrowed down into a V below his waistband...

Yeah. Like I said, Romeo was my vice.

I never thought a girl like me would have one. But there was no denying the command he had over my heart.

"You're staring," he rasped, continuing his slow, methodic strokes.

I clutched the towel tighter against me. I had no idea why. There was nothing that could keep him out. Not when he was already permanently part of me.

He finished brushing and set aside the brush. He caught my stare and held it while picking up the shirt lying on the counter in front of me.

It was his shirt, one of the Knight ones. I'd brought it in here to wear as I dried my hair and got ready for class.

He didn't say anything, just kept his gaze on mine as he pulled it over my head and gestured for me to put my arms through.

Once the shirt was on, he tugged the end of the towel and I let go. It fell to the floor, and he kicked it away.

I still stared at him. I couldn't help it.

His large hands came to rest on the edge of the counter on either side of me. "I look different now?" he asked, holding my stare.

"Now?" I tilted my head.

"Now that you heard me tell B I approve of what he did."

I sucked in a breath. So he did know that's what was eating me.

His full lips tilted up. "Oh yes, I know, baby."

"Romeo..." I began and turned to face him.

He made a sound and his hands caught my hips to stop me. "Stay there. Look." He gestured with his chin to the mirror. "You know what I see?" he asked.

I shook my head.

"I see a #jock who fell in love with a #nerd. But I'm not really a #jock, and you definitely aren't really a #nerd. Yeah, I play football and am sexy as hell."

I snorted.

He grasped my chin and pulled my face back down so I could look at us once more.

"You like books and get perfect grades. But those are a quarter of the things that make up who we are. Your messy hair and sweatpants? My excessive use of the word fuck and bossy nature? That stuff makes up another quarter."

He gathered my hair in his fist and pushed it to one side. Bending, keeping his eyes pinned on mine, he scraped his teeth across the side of my neck. I shivered.

"You know what's one hundred percent me?"

"Hmm?" I hummed soft.

"My love for you." He pressed a kiss to the exact spot his teeth had just been. My eyes drifted closed. He pulled back. "Look at me, Rimmel."

I forced my eyes open, trying not to succumb to his words and lips. But it wasn't those things that were the biggest threat. It was his eyes and the ability they had to make me feel like I was the only thing they ever saw.

"I love you with one hundred percent of who I am. That's a lot of pieces of me. So yeah, I can understand why Braeden did what he did. That guy who walked away from Zach that night, that's just a quarter of who B is. The one hundred percent of him that loves Ivy took over. The one hundred percent of his loyalty to this family won out."

He paused.

"And honestly?"

I nodded.

"One quarter of me admires that piece of Braeden, because I don't know if I would have been able to do what he did. Not because I hated Zach any less, but because I know exactly what it would do to you."

I opened my mouth to speak, but he shook his head.

My word, he had a lot to say today.

"I'm sorry the things I said downstairs hurt you, baby. I know you know what it's like to have someone taken from you. I'm sorry I made you doubt who I am deep down, because I won't condemn Braeden for a split-second choice a part of him made. But there is one thing I'm not sorry for."

"What?"

"I'm not sorry he's dead." His eyes flashed, like a lightning storm at the beach. "After what he did to you and to Ivy, there's no way in hell I could ever mourn for someone as twisted as Zach."

"I know who you are." I silenced his apology with those five words.

"I might not know every single piece that makes up all of you. That's one of the reasons I'm so excited to marry you. I want to know every single quarter. I want to spend the rest of my life learning every single thing. Even the things that might sometimes shock me. And it doesn't matter what little pieces I have yet to discover. I know the most important ones. And the more I think about it, the more I realize one of the most important is what I learned this morning."

"Rim." His voice was gruff, regretful.

"You had your turn, Roman. Now it's mine."

He let out a nervous laugh.

"Look at me." I reminded him. If he made me look, he made me see he meant every word. Then I was going to do the same to him.

"I always knew how important family was to you. It was obvious to me the day I saw you and Braeden together, even when I saw you with your parents. But I guess I never quite understood just how strong that bond was. Your loyalty amazes me. It inspires me. You're so fearless." He started to scoff, but I reached out and grabbed his hand, squeezing it. "Look."

Azure eyes snapped back to mine.

"You're so fearless in the way you support us. You don't care if one of your own made a mistake or even made a choice they might not make again. In that regard, your life is black and white. Family or not family. Loyalty doesn't have conditions with you. It's why you're an alpha, because you aren't just strong for yourself, but for everyone you love."

His front was pressed almost against my back, and I stretched my arm up, reached behind me, and cupped the back of his neck, pulling him fully against me.

He was hard. Rock solid. His length pressed into my back and was most distracting.

"I could never doubt who you are, Romeo. *Never.*"

"Smalls," he murmured and nuzzled my neck.

Our eye contact broken, I let my lips slip closed. Goodness, the way he felt behind me.

"You still wanna marry me?" he whispered in my ear.

"I should ask you that question," I breathed as chills raced along my arms.

His hips rocked into me, bringing my ass right up against his groin. "My answer would be hells yes."

"Romeo," I said with just enough command our eyes met in the mirror again. "I'm sorry. I know my reaction downstairs wasn't good. It's just my mother—"

"Shh, baby. I know."

I shook my head, trying to find the words, but it was so hard. How do you describe something in words when it was already so hard to feel?

And how the hell did a girl string together any sentence when there was a man slowly grinding his swollen and needy cock against your backside?

"Stop that," I said, reaching around to grab his hips. "I'm trying to apologize. I can't think."

I felt the laugh rumble his chest, and I leaned back more, wanting to feel it all.

"You don't need to apologize. I understand."

"I think I hurt Braeden's feelings."

"B's fine." He stopped rocking against me, but now his fingers were sliding up the backs of my thighs, dipping beneath the T-shirt and coming dangerously close to my bare bottom.

"T-there's something I want you t-to know," I stuttered, trying to concentrate.

His palm was cupping my ass cheek. His fingers were delving between my legs, seeking out my core.

"What's that?" he asked, shifting, spreading his legs so he could sink a little lower, bring his fingers closer to my entrance.

Two fingers slipped into my folds. I was wet, aching.

Against my bare cheek, his cock jerked. Without thought, I pushed myself farther against him.

"Rim."

"Hmm?" I replied, arching my back to give him better access.

"You wanted to tell me something?"

My head dropped down as his finger slid inside me. His free hand came around and lifted my chin so he could stare at me in the mirror.

"Tell me."

"Tell you what?" I mumbled and rocked into his fingers.

His eyes deepened and he growled. "Watch," he instructed and released my chin, lifting the shirt so it was right beneath my breasts.

I kept my eyes trained on his as he swiftly yanked down his shorts. His swollen, silky head pressed against me, and I moaned. Gently, he slid his finger out and palmed either side of my hips, adjusting me so my ass was on full display.

Poised at my entrance, he stopped, linked both our hands, and then put them on the counter.

"Don't look away," he ground out.

I watched his face when he joined our bodies. From this angle, he went deep and I arched my back even more to take him deeper.

We clung to each other's hands as we watched each other. He moved inside me, spearing me over and over again. My walls clutched around his length, and the feel of his hips fitting against my ass was near perfection.

The unfocused way he stared at me was addictive. Even though my vision was slightly blurry, it didn't matter. His desire and love was clear.

"Fuck, baby," he ground out as he pushed deep. "I can't hold it."

I wiggled my ass closer, just like I'd done to him this morning when I sat in his lap. I felt his cock start to spasm, and his jaw clenched. His eyes turned to glittering diamonds, and he shoved one hand between my legs and found my swollen and sensitive clit.

I ground against his groin, and he ground against my ass.

In seconds, his hot seed was filling me up, and the sensation pushed me over the edge. I cried out, and he watched right there in the mirror.

I might have been embarrassed if I'd been able to think.

The orgasm ripped through me and went on and on. At one point, I started to sink onto the counter, but he wrapped an arm around me and held me up, without once breaking eye contact.

When the bliss finally drained, I felt weak and my knees were shaking. He pulled out and eased back, only to sweep me up in his arms and carry me out of the bathroom and lay me across the bed.

He took up residence beside me, and I tucked myself close, breathing in the scent that only he wore.

"I love you," I told him.

"I love you, too," he echoed.

A few minutes later, when I could actually use my brain, I realized we'd never actually finished our conversation.

"I'm glad he's dead, too," I whispered, horrified at my own feelings.

"That doesn't make you a bad person, sweetheart. It makes you human."

That was it. The words, the *feelings* I was trying to explain but couldn't. Romeo did it in one word.

Human.

For years and years, I lived on autopilot, going from day to day without any change. I was cold, sterile. I was protecting myself.

But that protection turned me into a robot.

Then Romeo walked into the library.

He restarted my heart. He made me human again.

CHAPTER NINETEEN

#WolvesForever

The more things change, the more they
stay the same.

#Romeo&BraedenBackOnTheFieldTogether

#BuzzBoss

ROMEO

There was always one place B and I could come back to that made life seem somehow simpler than it was.

The field.

B and I became friends on a playground, but we bonded, we became brothers on a football field. Hell, back when we barely knew how to tie our shoes, it was as simple as a patch of grass. We didn't need white painted lines, stadium-quality green, or even premium leather balls.

All we needed was each other and space to run around.

We had all the bells and whistles now, basically the best kind of playing fields money could buy, but just like when we were seven, all we needed was each other.

Coach O'Connor let us into the stadium at Alpha U. It was the first time I'd been back in months. Hell, it felt like forever.

But the more things change, the more they stay the same.

The lights shone crisply on the immaculate turf. The white lines were impeccable, even though it was the off-season. The air lingered with a mixture of gasoline and freshly cut grass. Even the scent of stale sweat still clung to the stadium, haunting the open space of games past.

The only sound other than B and my footfalls on the ground was the low hum of the high-powered lights that gave this indoor arena lighting brighter than the sun at noon. But even though there was no game being played, no team rushing out through the tunnel to conquer the field, the sounds of football still reverberated through the place.

The echoes of helmets hitting together, the familiar sound of pads being slapped into place, and the faint whisper of whistles blowing erratically gave this place life, even after the games ended.

The Wolves might just scrimmage and practice on this field, but it didn't matter. The love of the game didn't come from the game itself; it came from the passion and drive inside the players. It came from the people who sat in the stands and cheered like there was no tomorrow. It came from the brotherhood that formed between teammates.

Technically, neither B nor I belonged to this team anymore, but it would likely always feel like home.

"Seems like just yesterday you two wet-behind-the-ears showoffs showed up on my field," Coach said, stopping behind us as we took it all in. "Anderson, I always knew you'd make it. You were born to play this game."

People said that to me all the time. But they weren't a coach that spent countless hours training me and conditioning me, even on the days I hated him for it. So when he said it, it meant something.

"Walker, you on the other hand..." Coach went on, and Braeden swung around to face him. "You always did have the talent. I just thought you were too big of a fuck-up to get your head on straight enough to make it."

"You trying to give me a compliment or send me to therapy?" B cracked.

"There ain't a therapist in this entire state with enough degrees or time to fix you, Walker," Coach muttered, but he was smiling, pride evident in his eyes. "I'm really proud of you, son. The draft is lucky to have you."

"Thanks, Coach," Braeden said and averted his gaze.

Aww, B-man was getting all sentimental and shit.

"Thanks for letting us use the field, Coach," I told him, giving B a minute to untwist his panties. "Wanted to get in some extra field time before the draft."

"This stadium will always be open to you boys as long as I'm around. Besides, it's the Wolves's job to make sure Walker gets in all the fine tuning he can before the NFL starts sending people to watch him practice and play.

"Make sure you're getting two workouts a day," he ordered Braeden before turning away. "If you don't manage one of the top draft picks this season, I'm gonna kick your fool ass."

"No pressure or anything!" Braeden yelled after him.

Coach held up his arm as he walked away, giving us the finger.

"Dude, he just flipped us the bird." Braeden guffawed. "What would the dean say!" He gasped after Coach.

"Screw you!" he hollered and then disappeared in the tunnel.

B and I looked at each other and burst out laughing.

I glanced out across the field again, taking in a great big breath of the football-smelling air.

Braeden dumped his duffle on the ground and stripped off his shirt. "We gonna do this shit or what?"

My shirt landed on the ground beside his, and like the pair of boys we once were, we took off, racing out into the center of the field, the grass dense underfoot. We lost ourselves in the game for hours.

We stayed so long that when we looked at the clock, Braeden swore because he'd missed his morning classes.

"YOLO!" he announced and tossed me the football for another round of passes.

"You sound like you belong in some fruity granola bar commercial," I told him. "YOLO," I muttered darkly. "Stupidest shit I ever heard."

The ball hit me in the center of my back. I spun around and looked at it now lying at my feet.

"All right, Walker." I smirked. "You wanna be a smartass. Give me ten laps," I said in a dead-on impression of Coach O'Connor.

B started for the track that circled the field. When I didn't follow, he glanced back. "You too good to run?"

"Hells no. But I'm supposed to take it easy, remember? I'm the pro. It's my offseason."

"Shit, Rome. I hope to hell Gamble makes sure I get on your team. Your candy ass is getting soft and comfy in that cushy spot of yours. You're gonna need me to watch your entitled ass this season."

"I'm not entitled," I snapped, the jab hitting me in a spot I hadn't realized *was* soft.

B stopped completely and swung around. "Hit a nerve, did I?"

My jaw clenched. "You're supposed to be running."

"What's going on, Rome?" He pressed, walking backward toward the track. "And don't try and say nothing, because that chilled interior of yours don't usually boil so fast."

I grunted. "Come on. I'll jog with you."

We fell into step beside each other, our pace automatically synced, because as I said before, football was our bonding point. We could play or train with each other blind and deaf, and we'd still be a solid unit.

We kept the stride sedate. I really meant it when I said I was supposed to be in recovery mode, and we'd already worked out hard for a long time. This would have to serve as our cool down. I was going to have to figure out how to be with him during his daily training and not end up doing all the shit he was doing.

It was hard to sit still and watch, though.

This shit was in my blood. It wasn't just a job. It was a way of life.

"So you get a front row seat to all my problems, but when it comes to yours, I get locked out?" he said, barely breathing hard as we jogged.

I gave him a sidelong glance. "Don't you think you have enough shit to be worried about right now?"

"You're my best friend, Rome. If something's going down, I'm entitled to know about it."

"Thought I was the entitled one," I drawled.

A dark look crossed his face, and he swiped the sweat off his brow with the back of his hand. "Don't fuck with me. You're not the only one who worries about his family."

"You don't need to worry about me. It's not a big deal."

He barked a laugh. "Yeah, 'cause you always act like I yanked your tighty whities up your crack when I make a joke."

"Dude, tighty whities are for dweebs."

Our snickers trailed behind us as we curved around the track.

Once we fell silent and B said nothing, I knew he wasn't going to let this go. "There's some, ah, hard feelings on the team."

"Ah, Gamble's new golden boy's making people jealous. Damn, Rome. I thought you wouldn't have that problem for at least a couple years."

I glanced at him, surprised.

He barked out a laugh. "You can't honestly tell me you didn't know this was going to happen."

I felt kinda naive in that moment. I didn't fucking like it.

"I guess I thought a bunch of grown-ass men in a national football league were better than that shit."

"Do you still believe in the Tooth Fairy, too?"

Shit. Now that I said it out loud, it did sound goddam ridiculous. In a profession where star power is rewarded with money, where touchdowns and titles earn you prestige, and you're only as hot as the media and others perceive you to be, I knew better.

In football, emotions run high; careers can literally be made or broken in a single game. Top picks and positions get paid obscene amounts of money that would keep small countries flush for years.

"I just wanna play the game," I said. "Politics and passion don't mix in my gut too well."

"How much money was your contract for, Rome?"

I wasn't offended he asked. Hell, Braeden could ask me anything, literally anything, and I'd tell him. I might have been reluctant to tell him about this, but it wasn't because I didn't trust him. I was surprised he was asking, though.

We never talked money because money didn't factor into any part of our relationship.

"Thirty million," I replied, point blank. "Plus a signing bonus that was over ten mil."

He whistled between his teeth. "Yo, Rome. Can I borrow twenty dollars? My pocket's feeling a little light."

I laughed. "I tell you I just made over forty mil on a four-year contract, and you only ask me for twenty dollars?"

"What do you think I am, a gold digger?"

I laughed again and veered off the track toward my duffle and water. Braeden followed behind and snagged his water off the floor, too.

"Money like that, you must be the starting quarterback. The front man for the team."

"It's looking that way. Final decisions won't come down 'til after the draft."

"Bet the guy you're knocking out of the top spot is pretty fucking pissed his meal ticket just got smaller."

Braeden was a lot of things. Sarcastic. Hotheaded. Dark.

But there was one thing my best friend was not. Stupid.

I lowered the water. "Yeah, Blanchard isn't too happy with me right now."

Blanchard was the starting quarterback for the Knights. Had been for the past three years. In those three years, the team had never been to the Superbowl. They'd only been in the playoffs once.

It wasn't that he was a bad player. He was the opposite. He was good.

But I was better.

I was also younger, more driven, and the media liked my smile.

Who could blame them? It was a fucking brilliant smile.

"He gonna be number two on the roster, then?" B rubbed a towel over his sweaty head.

"Yeah, but he's only got one year left on his contract, and the third quarterback on the team is performing well. I wouldn't be surprised if he takes number two."

"Rowan, right?" B asked.

I nodded, unsurprised he knew who all the quarterbacks were.

"I met him when I was at one of your games. Good guy."

I agreed. "There was some tension at the end of last season and post season before I came home. Blanchard hasn't exactly kept it hidden that he isn't happy I basically walked in and took his job."

"You worked for that spot," Braeden growled. "'Specially after everything you went through and almost didn't get to play at all."

I felt my mouth tilt up. Everyone always called me the alpha. But B was just as much one as I was.

"I'm not giving it up. The team's good, B. With a little bit of fine tuning, a few adjustments to the roster, and you on the field with me, I know we could get to the Bowl."

"And we will."

I held out my fist and we pounded it out. Braeden dropped onto the ground to stretch out his legs and back. "So how bad is it with Blanchard? Is he someone I'm gonna have to deal with?"

My mouth flattened. "Blanchard's my problem. Not yours."

"Your problems *are* my problems."

"This is exactly why I didn't say anything. You can't afford any trouble right now. You gotta be squeaky clean for the draft. No team's gonna draft a PR liability. And with—" I slammed my teeth together, not finishing the rest of my sentence.

"And with Robert Bettinger running around yelling murder, my career might be over before it begins."

Fuck! I remembered thinking the exact same thing when I broke my arm. That it was over before it began.

That was all Zach's fault, too.

Okay, to be fair, Braeden's situation wasn't all Zach's fault.

Only like 99.5% of it.

"That's not going to happen," I vowed. Which reminded me... "Get you're shit. We gotta go to my dad's office."

He needed to be made aware of this situation before rumors started flying.

Braeden began tossing his stuff in the bag.

"You're beating yourself up over this." I nudged his shoulder.

"It's my career. You of all people know the stakes."

"You know I'm not talking about football right now."

His shoulders slumped enough that I noticed.

"Ivy's worried, man. I am, too."

"She came to you?" His voice was somber.

"To talk, but she never said anything to me about that night. About Zach."

I could hear the bewilderment in his words when he said, "I didn't know she'd seen that night. She was so in and out. I honestly didn't think she knew."

"Have you talked to her at all?"

"We talked... after the bruises..."

"Today?" I pressed. "After Robert was at the house?"

He shook his head once. "No. She ran out of the house so fast this morning I barely had time to tell her good-bye."

"You're scared to talk to her." I observed.

He scoffed.

"All this time you've been feeling shitty for the choice you made that night. You've been haunted by Zach and by seeing Ivy so broken."

He looked up at me like he was surprised I knew.

"I've been there with Rim. Seeing them hurt at Zach's hands. It's the worst fucking thing in the world."

"That's the thing, Rome. I don't feel bad for the choice I made. In all honesty, I'd make the same choice again. That's what haunts me the most. I don't feel guilty." His voice dropped to a rough whisper. "I let him die, and I don't even feel bad. What the fuck does that say about me?"

I stood there silent, digesting his words.

"Jesus," he muttered. "Coach was right. I am a fuck-up."

"You were a fuck-up long before Zach died," I mused and gazed off down the field at the goal post.

The. Goal. Post.

The one I found Rimmel dangling from. The one I was yanked off and broke my arm. I hadn't been back to this stadium since that night.

"This doesn't make you like him."

Braeden had a deep-rooted fear that on some level, he was just like his abusive father.

"I know."

I must have looked shocked, because he smiled. "I let the hold he had on me go."

"Princess is good for you."

"Dude, why the fuck do you keep calling my girl princess?"

"Drives her nuts." I laughed.

His teeth flashed, bright white against the dark stubble lining his jaws. "Then by all means, carry on."

"Talk to her. I'd bet my forty mil that Ivy will stand by you. And shit, maybe if you talk to her, she won't wake up with bruises anymore."

"I put another bruise on that girl—even by accident—and I want you to kick my ass. Like a serious ass whooping," he intoned.

"With pleasure." I slung my bag over my shoulder and turned toward the exit. I knew damn well Braeden hadn't meant to leave those bruises on Ivy. I also knew he'd sleep with toothpicks holding his lids open before he ever did it again.

"I'll talk to her," he said as we left the stadium.

"B?" I called across the roof of the Hellcat before he got in.

"Yeah?"

"It's gonna be the bomb having you with the Knights."

It wasn't a done deal, Braeden and me on the same team, but it would be. I knew it just the same as I knew Rim and I belonged together.

I just hoped to God my brother didn't walk into the middle of a turf war when he finally made it to the team.

CHAPTER TWENTY

#FunFact
Women who read romance
novels have twice as many
lovers as those who don't.
#UseYourLibraryCard
#BuzzBoss

BRAEDEN

She was late.

I'd barely heard from her all day.

She was late.

My foot bounced against the floor as I tried not to panic.

The last time I couldn't get ahold of her, she'd been kidnapped.

I started to get up but then sat back down.

Ivy wasn't missing or kidnapped. I knew this. She texted, said she had to stop in at the boutique after classes. I knew where she was.

It didn't matter. I would worry until she walked in the door.

Damn, being paranoid sucked donkey balls.

Seconds but what felt like hours later, she walked in.

I leapt up over the back of the couch and went into the entryway.

"Hey," she said, smiling.

I caught her around the waist and pulled her close. She hugged me back and didn't try to pull away. When I finally let her go, she stripped off her coat, and I hung it on a nearby hook.

"Where is everyone?" she asked, bending down to pick up Prada and snuggle her.

I shrugged. "Busy."

"We're alone?"

Now why did that sound like something she didn't seem thrilled about?

"Just me and you."

"I'm starving," she announced as the dog licked her face and she giggled.

"You miss lunch again?" I frowned.

She shook her head. "No, but I haven't eaten dinner. You eat yet?"

I felt like an ass for saying yes. I probably should have asked her if she wanted to go out tonight, since everyone else was busy. Would have given us a chance to get out for a while.

My mom always said you should never stop dating your girl, even after technically you were past the dating stage.

I used to roll my eyes and wonder why the hell she thought I cared, but now as I remembered the advice, I knew she was trying to teach me how to treat a woman right.

"C'mon," I said and reached for her coat again. "I'll take you out to dinner. You pick."

"Didn't you just tell me you already ate?" She gave me a funny look.

"A man can't eat twice?" I retorted. Technically, I couldn't. I was on a strict plan until after my fate for the NFL was sealed. Twice daily workouts and a serious diet of protein, more protein, and healthy fats was pretty much my entire life.

But fuck that.

If my girl was hungry, I was gonna feed her.

"I kinda wanna stay in. I'm exhausted." Her face turned sheepish.

She looked worn out, slightly pale with faint rings beneath her eyes.

"Wanna watch a movie?"

"Sure." She smiled.

I took her hand and led her toward the kitchen. "What're you in the mood for?"

"Grilled cheese."

What the...? I glanced over my shoulder and gave her a look. The response was immediate, like she hadn't even needed to think about it. Ivy never ate grilled cheese. Too many carbs and fat she'd say.

Made me wonder if she had a really bad day and what the hell happened.

She must have noticed my surprise, because she shrugged. "I like grilled cheese."

"You're in luck." I guided her to the barstool and motioned for her to sit down. "Grilled cheese is my specialty."

"You're going to make it?"

"Hells yeah."

She settled in like she was getting ready for some show, and I was offended. "I can cook." I scoffed.

"You do make a mean protein shake, and ordering pizza is a real skill." She nodded sagely.

I grabbed the bread and slammed it on the counter. "Blondie, this is gonna be the best damn grilled cheese you ever had."

She grinned real toothy-like and put her chin in her hands.

I chuckled and got to work.

A few minutes later, I presented her a gooey, perfectly toasted, and melty sandwich on a paper plate.

I might cook, but I sure as hell didn't do dishes.

"Behold the work of a genius," I proclaimed.

She lifted one dark-blond brow I knew was perfectly arched (she told me all about how to get the right brow shape… *Yes,* that was a *long* conversation I hoped to never repeat) and said nothing as she picked up half the sandwich.

Orange-colored cheese stretched between the center, and she took a bite.

A groan rumbled from her throat as she chewed, and it was fucking hot. Damn, sounded like she was having an orgasm in her mouth. It turned me the hell on.

Ivy said nothing as she took another bite.

And another.

I watched her totally bemused as she basically destroyed the first half of my artwork.

When there was literally one bite left to the piece in her hand, she noticed my silence and looked up. Her eyes widened like she forgot I was even there, and she winced. "What?" the vulnerability in her voice amused me.

"My sandwich just blew up your world." I grinned, then leaned across the counter, pushing my face close to hers. "Boom." I motioned with my hands like a bomb just went off.

She rolled her eyes but shoved the rest into her mouth.

I chuckled and turned away to pull a glass out of cabinet and fill it with some orange juice. She was reaching for the second half of the sandwich when I set it at her elbow.

She groaned again. "How'd you know?" Completely abandoning the food, she went for the glass.

"Grilled cheese and OJ is like the perfect pair." I teased. "If you're a fa-reak."

I really thought she'd sling a comeback at me with perfect precision. She always did. It was one of the things I loved most about her. Ivy never held back. She gave as good as she got.

But she didn't. Instead, she pulled the glass away from her lips and averted her gaze, like she was suddenly embarrassed… or apprehensive.

What the shit was this?

I pushed off the island and went around to where she was sitting and slid onto the stool beside her. With one easy movement, I slid her off her seat and into my lap. Her legs wrapped around my waist, her ankles hooked around my back. I spun so she could lean her back against the counter edge and got a sudden flashback of the night we'd sat in the kitchen and she fed me ice cream.

I'd needed her that night.

She needed me right now.

"What's going on in that pretty head of yours?" I asked.

She shook her head, the high ponytail she wore swinging with the movement.

I snagged the plate and held the corner of the sandwich up to her lips. "Eat your dinner, baby."

"It really is the best grilled cheese I've ever had."

"The secret is to use extra cheese," I told her and winked.

We sat there in the silence until the rest of the food was eaten, and when it was, I leaned forward and brushed a kiss across her lips. "This morning upset you."

Her eyes shot up to mine. "How'd you know?"

"Because it isn't every day someone accuses you of murder."

"Oh, right."

Why did it seem like that wasn't what she thought I was talking about?

"He reminded me of Zach," she whispered, eradicating my train of thought.

"I'm sorry he came here. I wish you didn't ever have to think about that guy ever again."

"It was hard at first, you know? When I saw him, it was like a punch in the gut. Memories came flooding back. But then as he went on, the panic did, too. Sure, it was upsetting to see him and to hear the awful accusations. But Robert isn't Zach, and what happened to me… I'm handling it."

I rubbed a hand down her arm. She was so strong, and I was so incredibly proud of her.

"I don't want you to worry about Robert. There's no way in hell he'll ever be able to convince anyone that you had any part in Zach's death. You were his victim."

Her eyes widened, the ocean-blue darkening. "I'm not worried about me. I'm worried about what he's going to try to do to you."

My heart turned over with those words. She worried about me above herself.

"Ivy," I said, stern. "What I heard this morning pissed me off."

She opened her mouth, but I shook my head. "I'm not talking about being accused of murder. You said you ran the car off the road because Zach was going to shoot *me*."

Her eyes suddenly filled with tears.

Damn.

I knew this conversation wasn't going to be a good one, but I really didn't expect her to cry.

"He said he was going to shoot me and push my body out of the car, and when you stopped to try and help me, he was going to come back and shoot you. He was going to kill you, Braeden."

"And running the car off the road was the only way you knew how to stop him." I surmised. My heart was thumping unevenly and hard beneath my ribs.

Nightmares. I had nightmares almost every time I went to sleep, reliving the way the car turned over and skidded through the field. The horror of possibly finding her dead would likely torment me forever.

It was the same for her.

The thought of anyone possibly killing me was enough to make her risk her own life to protect me.

"I thought you knew that's why I did what I did," she added when I was unable to speak.

I shook my head. "I just thought you were struggling over the gun."

"I'd never let him hurt you," she whispered.

Emotion took me over, and I surged forward, taking her face in my hands and crushing my mouth to hers. I couldn't speak. But I could fucking kiss the shit out of her.

I kept the pressure light even though I wanted to grind my mouth into hers. She tasted like cheese and butter.

And my life.

I didn't know until that moment my life could have a flavor, but now I knew it did.

And God, it was like a drug.

Ivy clutched at the shirt stretching across my chest and bunched the fabric in her hands. Her tongue delved deep, and I opened up farther, letting her explore as deep as she wanted.

The little mewling sounds she made had my stomach muscles contracting and need hammering through my veins.

When my lungs felt like they might burst, I yanked my mouth free and sucked in a great gulp of air. Her eyes were far away and unfocused. Her cheeks were pink and her lips swollen.

"I fucking love that you did that for me. But dammit, Ivy, don't ever do that again. Don't ever risk your own life for mine *ever again*."

"You'd do it for me." Her voice was raspy.

"In a heartbeat."

She acted like that statement somehow settled an argument.

I was about to inform little Miss Know-it-all that she was wrong, but she spoke first. "Do you feel better now that everyone knows what happened that night?"

Another revelation from this morning that knocked me on my ass.

"You knew I left him there."

"I heard him yelling for you. I knew he was alive and wasn't able to get out."

I shook my head. "I don't understand. If you knew I walked away from him, how could you—"

"Still love you?" She finished.

I was going to say trust me, but it was basically the same thing.

"Are you sure you would have been able to get him out in time?"

I hedged.

A knowing look came to her eyes.

"It's definitely possible."

"But it's also possible that whatever was jamming his seatbelt or keeping him in that car would have taken a few tries to undo. You said the car was already on fire; the gas was already everywhere. You could have died trying to get him out."

I couldn't disagree with her. Not really. She was right.

Still didn't make what I did any less harsh.

"The way I see it, you had to make a choice that night. Him or me. You chose me. I could never fault you for that."

"But you were already out, safe," I argued.

"You don't get it." She shook her head and took my hand. "If you had died that night, I would have died with you. I might have lived physically, but the girl you see right now would have been gone. I don't want any life without you, Braeden. Keeping yourself alive that night wasn't just for you. It was a choice for me."

"Maybe you should skip the fashion and become a lawyer. You actually just convinced me that what I did was heroic." I smiled.

She shuddered. "I'd have to wear god-awful suits every day of my life!"

I laughed.

She sat forward and her thighs tightened around my middle.

"No more blaming yourself. It was a terrible situation, but you are not responsible for Zach's death. In a way, we all had a part in it, even Robert. If Zach had gotten help when he first needed it, maybe things would have turned out differently for everyone."

"He's not going to just drop this." I warned her. "You have to know he might go to the media. He might try to ruin our names."

"Your career," she murmured, her eyes turning into saucers like she was just realizing my NFL career could very well be taken away.

"Please." I scoffed. "You know the NFL won't pass up this big hunk of awesome."

"The timing for this could not have been worse." It sounded like she was speaking to herself.

True, the timing for Robert to start making noise about Zach's death could have been better.

But something in the back of my mind told me Robert wasn't what she was talking about.

CHAPTER TWENTY-ONE

Do you ever think about life after Alpha U?

#FourYearsGoesFast

#BuzzBoss

RIMMEL

The new animal shelter—the sister to the one I'd been volunteering in for years—was almost finished.

It was beautiful.

Never in a million years had I thought the fundraiser Valerie helped put together would be so successful that it would lead to a brand new shelter with brand new opportunities to help even more animals in need.

It was literally a dream come true.

And what was even more exciting? I was a part of creating and planning the new place. I'd learned so much about myself in the past two years. I'd grown as a person by leaps and bounds. When I came to Alpha U, I was shy, insecure, and yeah... scared.

I had no friends. I didn't want any.

All I cared about was school and animals.

And now?

Now my life was overfull. I had friends that turned into family. A family that was intensely coveted. My insecurities were barely thought of, and being scared was only a feeling I got when I watched a scary movie or took the trash out in the dark.

Please, you know you get scared when you take it out, too.

I still cared about school and animals, but they weren't the only things in my life now.

Plus, there was Romeo. He was the biggest, most welcome change of all.

My soon-to-be husband. I glanced down at the giant ring on my finger and a giddy feeling rose up inside me.

Planning a wedding wasn't something I really wanted to do, but marrying him was.

I pulled my little white hatchback up to the curb by the animal shelter and cut the engine. Romeo was parked just a few cars up, and he was leaning against the side, looking down at his phone.

The military-style leather jacket he wore hugged his broad shoulders, and the winter wind tugged at the blond strands on his head.

When he saw me pull up, the phone disappeared into his jeans, and he pushed off the Hellcat to come toward me.

Oh my, could that boy wear a pair of jeans.

"You're late," he growled and grabbed me around the waist to pull me in.

I laughed. "Sorry! I had to run over to the new shelter to check on the progress. The contractor was there, and we ended up discussing a lot of details."

"My girl, the businesswoman," he mused.

"Hardly." I scoffed. "The reason it took so long was because the poor guy had to explain things to me three times before I finally decided what I wanted. I think by the time I left, he was ready to go to the bar."

Romeo snickered, and I poked him in the ribs. He tucked an arm over my shoulders and led me toward the sidewalk.

"So how's it going over there?" he asked.

"Oh my gosh," I gushed. "It's so amazing. It's twice as big as the shelter here. And it has more storage and more room for the animals. I can't believe how wonderful it all is."

Romeo kissed the side of my head. "That's good, baby."

He held open the door, and I went ahead of him. Michelle was behind the desk, and when I came in, she hurried to get off the phone and jumped up.

"Well! How is it over there? I haven't been by in a couple days. Are they making progress? When's it going to be done?"

I laughed and held up my hands. "Slow down!"

But I was just as excited as her, so I launched into great detail about everything. Then I went off on a long-winded list of things I thought would be good to implement and a few other ideas I'd been thinking about for the past few weeks.

When I was finished, Michelle was grinning at Romeo and he was chuckling.

"What!" I demanded.

Michelle smiled. "I think you might be more excited than I am."

I blushed. "Well, this is just an amazing opportunity. I wanted to thank you, Michelle, for letting me be such a big part of the expansion. It's been so amazing to learn about this side of things and really be able to see how much of a difference we can make in these animals' lives."

She crossed her arms over her chest and beamed. "Are you kidding? Without you, we never would have been able to do this. That fundraiser you and Mrs. Anderson put together was nothing short of fantastic. People still talk about it."

"I think we should make it an annual thing, do it again next year," I said.

"After football season." Romeo cut in.

Michelle laughed. "Well, yes, you two are definitely busy enough right now, what with the wedding, school, the NFL… And isn't the engagement party this weekend?"

I suppressed a groan and nodded. Oh yes, the engagement party was just around the corner.

"Well, I'm looking forward to it. Your mother sure knows how to host a party," Michelle said to Romeo.

"That she does." He agreed.

Michelle didn't seem to notice my lack of exuberance for the party, and I wasn't about to bring it up.

"I think that's everything for the day," I said, heading toward the back to grab my things. "But I'll stop in tomorrow—"

"Rimmel? There was something else I'd like to talk to you about," she said, stopping me.

I turned back. Her brown eyes were excited and there was a small smile on her lips.

"Sure…" I started, wondering what it was.

Michelle glanced at Romeo and then back at me. "I know just how much you guys have on your plate right now, but I have an offer for you."

"For me?" I asked.

She nodded. "Remember back when the fundraiser had just concluded and we were all so thrilled with the plans and opportunity to open another shelter?"

I nodded.

"We spoke briefly about you taking on a bigger role in the running of it."

Realization dawned, and my eyes widened. "Well, yes, but then we all got busy with the plans and construction site…"

"I never forgot. We still need someone to run it, and while I could do it, I think both shelters would suffer with me trying to split my time between them. I'd always be back and forth, and I feel like the animals that will be there and the ones already here would benefit from having someone more full time."

I nodded. "What about Jen?" I asked, thinking of Michelle's right hand here at the shelter. She'd been here the longest out of everyone who worked and volunteered here. I'd always just assumed she'd be put in charge.

"Jen would be a great choice. She definitely has the experience."

I nodded, totally agreeing.

"But you have the passion. The way your eyes light up and your cheeks flush when you start talking about all the changes and additions you think we should make to the new building. It's so clear to me that there's no one better to run our sister shelter."

I didn't know what to say.

"You can't honestly be this surprised I would offer you the job."

"The job," I echoed.

"Well, yes." She laughed. "Rimmel, I'd like you to come on staff—not just be a volunteer or intern—and I'd like you to take on the role of managing the new shelter."

"But I'm too young," I burst out, like shock had somehow made me say the dumbest thing I could.

Behind me, Romeo laughed.

"You're almost a college graduate. You're getting married. And you're old enough to manage a wildly successful fundraiser."

A lot of that had been Valerie. She was the one with the social connections. She was the one who secured the venue and got people in the building. "If you think you somehow owe me this job because of the work Romeo's mother did, you don't. I didn't do that to get anything in return. I did it for the animals."

"That's exactly why you're the perfect person for the job."

I glanced at Romeo. It sort of felt like I was standing in the center of a dream. He smiled. "You definitely deserve this, babe."

"I don't know what to say."

"Say yes." Michelle urged.

How could I say yes?

"If you're wondering about the pay…" She filled the silence. "It's definitely more than what you get now, but it is a modest salary."

Technically, I didn't get anything now, but sometimes when there was extra money left over, Michelle would give me a "bonus."

"I don't care about the money," I said quickly. "But I'm still in school."

Michelle nodded. "I know. We can work around your school schedule for the next year. It will also give me a chance to really mentor you, make sure you learn everything there is to know about running a shelter. By the time you graduate and can take on full-time hours, you'll be overqualified for the job."

"I was going to go to vet school."

"I know, and I realize you might not want this job because of your dream to become a veterinarian, but I wanted to offer you this job before I did anyone else. It would be a pleasure to work with you on a permanent basis."

Romeo's warm hand settled on the small of my back, anchoring me in the moment and reminding me to breathe. What an amazing chance.

"Can I think about it?" I asked.

"Of course. We still have a while before the shelter is done. Just let me know soon. That way if you say no, I can find someone else."

"Of course," I murmured, deep in thought.

"Good. Now you two get out of here. Go do something romantic."

"My mother called. She wants us at the house to go over last-minute party stuff," Romeo informed us.

I groaned.

He laughed.

Out on the sidewalk, Romeo picked me up and spun us both in a circle.

"You're going to fall on the ice!" I gasped.

"No, baby, you're the only clumsy one in this relationship."

I pulled his hair. Not really because he insulted me, but because I couldn't resist the messy blond strands another minute.

"Ow!" he hollered, and the next thing I knew, I was pinned against the side of the Hellcat and he was kissing me.

As far as retaliation goes, this was the best.

"Congratulations on the job offer," he said when he pulled back and let my feet touch the ground.

"I can't believe she offered it to me."

"You're not a dumb woman, Rim, and that was a dumb thing to say. You earned that job. Hell, you work circles around everyone in that place and you don't even get paid."

"Sometimes she pays me," I muttered.

"You gonna take it?" he asked and stepped back to open the passenger door.

I gave him a puzzled look. "My car's over there. I can just meet you at your parents'."

He stepped forward and glowered down over me.

"Roman Anderson, are you trying to use your insane height advantage over me as intimidation?" I crossed my arms over my chest and glared up at him.

"Rimmel Hudson," he mocked. "Are you trying to tell me you'd rather ride in that bucket of bolts alone than with me in this dream wagon?"

I burst out laughing. "Dream wagon?"

"I'd call it a sex wagon, but we've never actually had sex in it..." He frowned. "Why the fuck haven't we had sex in it?"

I tilted my head and regarded him. "'Cause you're too big?"

"Get in," he demanded. "You're riding with me, and after my mother tortures us, we're having sex in the backseat."

"What if I don't want to?" My eyes narrowed.

"Please, woman." He scoffed and grabbed the hem of his shirt, lifting it to reveal a sizzling set of sculpted abs. "You know you can't say no to all this."

"You've been spending too much time with Braeden," I muttered and got into the car.

Once I was totally in, I reached for the seatbelt, but he snatched it out of my grip and fastened it for me. When he was done, he pulled back only enough to pull my earlobe into his mouth and suck.

"You're going to look so fucking hot riding me in the backseat," he whispered.

Damn him. I shivered.

His throaty laugh made my thighs clench together. He might be totally arrogant, but he was right. There was no way in hell I could ever say no to anything with him.

Once he pulled out onto the street in the direction of his parents' house, he grabbed my hand and put it beneath his on the stick shift. I was such a sucker for the way his much larger hand directed mine.

He glanced at me. "Think Michelle will be upset when you turn down the job?"

"Who said I was turning it down?"

He shrugged. "Your dream has always been to go to vet school—has been since the day we met. When you didn't say yes right away to the job, I figured that's why."

"You really think I should turn it down?"

His hand tightened around mine, and he downshifted. "Honestly, I don't care what you do. Whatever makes you happy is fine with me. But I do think if you wanted the job as much as you want to go to vet school, you would have jumped at the chance."

Was he right? Was my hesitation to take the job and decision to think it over basically just me putting off what would eventually be a no?

I wasn't so sure.

To me, it just didn't seem that simple.

CHAPTER TWENTY-TWO

#WeddingTalk
Girls everywhere are weeping
because the most eligible bachelor in
Maryland is getting hitched.
#WillTheyLast #TakingBets

#BuzzBoss

ROMEO

My mother had taken over.

I was starting to think she missed her calling as a hostage negotiator, because her powers of persuasion were unmatched.

Especially when it came to Rimmel.

Things between Mom and Rim had gone from bad to better, then all the way down the toilet, and then settling somewhere in the middle.

The middle = Rimmel avoiding her at all costs but being polite when she couldn't + my mother trying to make up for all the poor choices she'd made when it came to my girl.

Our engagement, though... that was a whole new field to navigate with Mom. From almost the second I'd proposed, she tried to sweep in and plan the wedding of the century.

I put the kibosh on that shit real fast. I skipped a quickie wedding in Vegas so Rim could have the wedding she wanted—*not* the one my mom wanted.

She of course acted like her life was over, in a mom sort of way, and Rim caved.

Rim always caved when she played the mom card.

Mom insisted on throwing us an engagement party, some big, lavish thing that everyone would talk about for weeks. I saw on Rimmel's face she didn't want an engagement party, but she graciously accepted and told my mother to plan it however she wanted.

I saw the genius behind this even if it did drive me mad.

By giving my mother something to focus on, like the engagement party, she kept my mother too busy to obsess over the actual wedding.

Good for you, Rimmel. Good. For. You.

Still, it was a temporary win. One that was speeding to an end. Like right now.

"So as you can see…" Mom was going on, with folders and charts in front of us. "Everything is all planned out and taken care of."

My eyes were starting to glaze over. This shit was for girls. Who the hell cared where people sat and what color the balloons were? Why did we even need balloons?

All I needed was one chair, a beer, and Rim on my lap.

My mother probably would have died right then and there if I said that, though. So instead, I just sat there looking like my handsome self and kept my mouth shut.

"It's all just so stunning," Rimmel said. She was totally overwhelmed, but Mom didn't notice. "I can't believe you went to all this trouble and expense. It really wasn't necessary."

"This is my only son's wedding! Of course it was necessary," she insisted, then turned her brown eyes toward me. "Roman, I took the liberty of getting you a new suit. It's hanging upstairs. I'll get it for you before you leave. It's tailored to your measurements."

How the hell did she get my measurements?

I probably didn't want to know.

"Rimmel, make sure he hangs it up as soon as you get home. It's already been steamed and is ready to wear."

"Of course." Rimmel agreed.

"Do you have your dress yet?" she asked.

Rimmel tensed slightly. "Uh, no. But it's being delivered to the boutique tomorrow. Ivy ordered me something."

"Well, good. That girl has good style. I hope she got white. You are a bride after all."

Rimmel glanced at me, and I made a face. She started laughing.

"Roman, honestly." Mom chastised me, but then she laughed, too. "I'm well aware this planning is boring you to bits."

"It's great, Mom," I said. "I appreciate you doing all this for us."

"I just can't believe you're getting married," she mused, and I was afraid she might cry. But then her face cleared and she refocused on her plans. "Everyone, and I mean *everyone*, will be there. Including the media. The second I started planning, word got out. I think the staff at the club I rented out tipped them off. I figured it would be more peaceful to have them invited than to be fighting them all off all night."

"Probably a good call." I agreed.

The media had been relentless. Since I proposed on the field and basically in front of the world (on TV), everyone and their mother thought it was their wedding, too.

Had I known what a media circus it would become, I probably wouldn't have asked her that way.

We were the front page on the sports section in the *Maryland Tribune* right after the game, and then the same paper ran a big engagement announcement in the social section a few weeks later. Several other local papers ran articles, and a couple national magazines picked up the story. Most women probably would have been pissing themselves at the fact they were on the cover of *People* magazine, but not Rim.

Ivy bought like every copy she found the day it hit stands and brought them all home. Rimmel just glanced at it and said it was nice and then went on about her day.

So far, the vultures had stayed off our property and away from our house, but I was starting to worry once the next season began and I was a full-time starting quarterback that we would never get any peace.

I was seriously considering buying a house on some land and putting up a gate so no one could get on the property without our consent.

Rimmel wouldn't like it, but it might become necessary.

"You two should also know that magazines are calling. There are several clamoring for exclusive wedding pictures. They want all the details, the venue, and they want to do the spread." Mom glanced at Rimmel. "I have to say, however, you and Ivy keeping the plans quiet is genius. It's got everyone salivating.

Some of these publications are offering big money to be the first to break the story."

"They're calling here?" Rimmel asked, mystified.

"That's why we didn't get a landline at home," I said, nudging her softly. "They would have had our number in minutes. I used to live here, and my parents' number is public record. Plus, with Dad being my agent, it's part of his job to field calls."

"I'm so sorry," Rimmel said. "That has to be annoying."

I thought it was cute the way she didn't think of this shit. She had no idea how interested people really were in us. So far, I'd managed to protect her from most of it, but I was worried about the day I wasn't going to be able to.

"It's fine." Mom waved it away. "We'll get the number changed if it gets too bad. They'll all stop calling once the wedding information leaks out."

Her eyes zeroed back in on Rim, and I saw the look in them. She wanted information, and she was going to get it. I gave her a warning look to back off my girl, but she wasn't looking at me.

"Now that the engagement party is completely planned, I'd be more than happy to assist you with the wedding."

Rimmel opened her mouth, probably to tell her no, but Mom just kept on talking.

"I haven't wanted to seem like one of *those* mothers." She began. "You know, the kind who stick their nose in everything,"

I laughed out loud. She was totally one of those mothers.

"Honestly, Roman," Mom scolded, but then went on. "I've barely asked for any details. I keep waiting for the invitation, and it never comes. People ask me about the date and the plans, and I never know what to say. It's really quite embarrassing. What kind of mother doesn't know about her own son's wedding?"

"That must be very embarrassing." Rimmel agreed.

How the hell was she keeping a straight face?

"I'm very sorry you feel left out, Mrs. Anderson—"

"Valerie." Mom corrected. She'd been trying to get Rim to call her by her first name for months. I told Mom when she talked to me about it that if she wanted Rim to see her as more than just my mother, she was going to have to treat her better.

I sighed and rubbed a hand over my head. In her own way, that's exactly what she'd been doing. She never made one snide comment about our relationship when we got engaged. She never implied she was anything but happy for us. There were no calls from a private investigator, no news bombs dropped in our laps, and no accusations that Rim was only hanging around for the money. Hell, they insisted on paying for the lavish engagement party and the wedding.

Yes, it was traditional for the bride's parents to pay, but well… that wasn't an option here. Rimmel's dad literally had nothing.

"Valerie." Rimmel agreed. "I haven't told you anything because there hasn't been anything to tell. Romeo and I just set a date."

Mom tried not to fall out of her seat. "Only just now?"

"We've only been engaged a few months, Mom." I reminded her.

"I thought you wanted to get married right away, before the start of the new season and training camps."

"We do," Rimmel said. "We just thought it was better to wait a little bit before we started planning, give Braeden and Ivy a little more time to heal."

I watched Mom's dark eyes fill with understanding. She was a lot of things, but she understood family and the commitment a person had to it. "Of course," she murmured. "They've been through a lot. I'm sure Ivy's had a lot to deal with, and since she is maid of honor... How is she doing?"

"She's doing better." Rimmel smiled. "I'll tell her you asked about her."

"Oh, yes, please do. She's a lovely girl. I never thought any girl would manage to calm Braeden down, but she did."

"But we do want to get married before the off-season is over and he leaves for training camps this summer. We picked a date, but it's so soon. I'm not sure how big of a wedding we'll be able to plan."

"Oh, we'll get it done," Mom said and sipped at her tea like she was fortifying herself for battle.

I smiled.

"When's the date?"

"We were thinking April third," Rim replied.

Mom gasped. "That's barely a month away!"

It seemed like forever to me.

"Well, it's a little more than a month." Rimmel hedged.

"Have you managed to find a venue on such short notice? All the best places book up months in advance."

Rimmel frowned. Then her teeth cut into her lower lip. "I haven't looked yet."

Mom launched into some detailed plan and pulled out some folder she'd been hiding under all the others, and surprise, surprise, it was filled with wedding information and potential plans.

I should have known she had an arsenal just waiting to pull out.

Rimmel's eyes widened when Mom starting telling her all her ideas—how she knew someone over at the best hotel in this part of the state and she could make a call to get us the date.

It was elegant and ritzy, expensive and stuffy.

In other words, it was everything Rim was not.

"Mom," I said, stern, cutting her off. "This is all great, but I think Rimmel should get to choose what she wants."

"What do you want, Rimmel?"

All eyes turned to her.

"I don't know." She turned to me. "Vegas sounded good."

Mom gasped so loud I thought she was having a heart attack. Rim and I both jumped up to help her as she pressed a hand to her chest.

"My son and future daughter-in-law will not get married in some cheap drive-up chapel! I won't have it."

"Geez, Mom. Take a chill pill." I sat back down and nudged for Rimmel to do the same.

My dad chose that moment to walk into the kitchen. When he saw us all there, he smiled widely. "I didn't know you guys were here. I've been holed up in my office all day, working."

"Let me get you some coffee, Anthony. I'm sure you could use it." Mom jumped up to pour him a cup of the fresh brew she made when we first started going over all her papers.

"It's been a long day." He sighed.

"Have you talked to Robert?" I asked.

He blanched. "Yes, I'm afraid I have." Dad shook his head sadly. "He's not doing well at all. He's adamant that Braeden is responsible for Zach dying in that crash."

"That's just ridiculous," Mom said, handing over the mug. "Braeden would never do such a thing. He's a good boy."

I don't know if I would use the words "good boy" to describe B, but I wasn't about to argue. Mom thought I was a good boy, too.

Ha.

"Does he have a case?" I asked, worried. If this got out, Braeden's entire future could be ruined, and for what?

For making sure our family wasn't tormented any further by someone who should never have been granted leave from the mental ward.

"He has enough to likely press charges. But the charges won't stick. I'll get them thrown out."

"But that would drag him and Ivy both through the mud!" Rimmel said, getting visibly upset. "They've been through so much already. I don't want to see them hurt anymore."

I pressed my hand to her back and rubbed in slow circles, trying to calm her down.

Dad sighed, and I noticed how tired he looked. It was clear he'd been working around the clock since B and I met with him and told him about the situation. "No charges have been filed yet. There's still time. If I could only make the man see reason, but I'm afraid he's past that. Zach died, he let his practice fall into the gutter, and then his wife left him."

"She couldn't stand the public shame," Mom whispered. "The fact that her son had conned his way out of a facility, stalked a poor woman, and then tried to kill her. Not to mention the fact that Robert would never just admit that Zach was wrong. He was going around the country club telling everyone that Zach was just as much a victim as the people he hurt." Mom glanced at me. "You know she's not even his mother."

"What?" Rimmel gasped.

Mom nodded. "She was his stepmother. His real mother, Robert's first wife, killed herself years ago."

I hadn't known that. Come to think of it, I didn't know much about Zach at all. All he ever was to me was an asshole.

"That's terrible." Rimmel sympathized. "I hope he's found some peace in death. He certainly never had it while I knew him."

There was that soft heart of hers again. It was specifically soft for the lost and damaged. It's why she loved the shelter so much. There were so many animals there that needed her care.

Had Zach been lost and damaged? Is that why he did all the terrible things he did?

I guess we'd never know.

I don't think it really mattered. What mattered to me was that Braeden's life wasn't destroyed because Zach's father was mad at the world for the shitty hand he was dealt.

"How close is he to having charges pressed?" I asked Dad.

"I managed to put him off today, but I really don't know if I'll be able to stop him."

"He knows the case will be a losing battle?" I pressed.

"I told him as much. Ivy was there. She was a witness. Her testimony along with the findings of the investigation would be enough to prove probable cause. That car blowing like it did was inevitable. I read the forensics report. Frankly, Braeden's lucky he got Ivy out in time before the whole thing went up."

"He just wants to take Braeden's life away like his son's was taken," Rimmel whispered, a catch in her voice.

I wrapped my arm around her and pulled her into my chest. She sniffled and wiped her face on my T-shirt.

"I'll keep working on it," Dad said. "I'm not going to give up that easily."

"Thank you," Rimmel said fiercely and got up to hug him spontaneously. A look of surprise flickered over both my mother's and father's faces.

Dad recovered first and hugged her back with the arm not holding his coffee and cleared his throat. "Of course, sweetheart," he said.

Ahh, she'd gotten to him.

She'd penetrated the impenetrable Anthony Anderson, take-no-prisoners lawyer. I'd seen very few people get a place inside my father's heart throughout my life (besides me and Mom of course), Braeden being one. And now there was my soon-to-be wife.

"Now don't you worry about this. You just focus on marrying my son."

Rimmel returned to my side and wiped her face on my shirt again. I kinda liked being her human tissue.

"Anthony," Mom said with a wise look in her eye, "please tell these two they cannot elope to Vegas."

"What?" Dad said and shook his head. "No, no, no." He set down his cup and patted Rimmel's hand.

"That's not good enough for my kids. You make sure you do up something nice for them, Valerie, and, Rimmel honey, you send me the bill."

"Oh, no," Rimmel said for like the millionth time when my parents brought up the bill.

"Yes. It will give me something to look forward to in between all these football contracts and dealings with Robert Bettinger. It'll do my heart good."

Rimmel bit down on her lower lip and nodded. If there was one person my girl had yet to learn how to say no to, it was my father. She had a soft spot for him. She told me once it was because he was an older version of me. Clearly, my mother had figured this out all on her own.

Well played, Mom. Well played.

Not too long later, we were outside in the whipping wind, hurrying toward the Hellcat.

"That was brutal," Rim moaned when I opened the door for her to get in. The heat was already toasty thanks to the remote start.

I ran around and shut myself in the driver's seat.

"You better figure out what kind of wedding you want and fast, baby. 'Cause if you don't, you're going to end up with something that will make the society pages green with envy."

"All I want is you," she whined.

"You got me." I picked up her hand and kissed the back of it. "How about me and two hundred and fifty of our most personal friends?" I joked.

"There's one person who won't be there," she said softly and looked out the window, avoiding my eyes.

Damn.

I should have seen that one coming.

"Is that why you've been a little hesitant to plan anything?" I asked.

She nodded, and I watched her throat work as she swallowed. "How does a girl plan her wedding without her mother?"

What the fuck did a guy say to that?

Sure, my mom was dramatic, all up in our business, and totally controlling, but she was here. Rimmel wouldn't ever get to say that.

I could tell her that her mom would be there in spirit. I could tell her she was looking down on our wedding from heaven. I could even tell Rimmel that her mom would be proud.

She knew all of that.

She'd heard it likely half her life.

It still didn't make it suck any less.

"So we won't plan a wedding," I said instead.

Rimmel looked at me, surprise in her tearful eyes. "What?"

"I should have taken you to Vegas the night I put that ring on your finger and you said yes. I was trying to be a good guy by giving you a wedding with our family and the shit girls are always going on about. But I forgot you aren't like most girls. You don't need dresses and flowers. So fuck this shit. Let's fly to Vegas tonight."

She laughed. It was a good sound. "You heard your parents in there. They want to be part of this."

"But this isn't about them. It's about you and me."

"If there's one thing I learned in the past couple months, it's that weddings are definitely not just about the bride and groom. If they were, we wouldn't need a venue, centerpieces, and favors. And we definitely wouldn't need to invite every person your mother sits on charitable boards with."

She was right.

Almost from the moment I proposed, it became about everyone else. We spent one night in a gorgeous hotel and then flew out early to be with our family. We'd been at home and focused on making sure everyone was okay. We'd been careful not to make too many flashy plans in fear we'd draw more media. We didn't want to celebrate too much or be too excited because it felt wrong to be so happy when B and Ivy were still trying to heal. And my mother, dear Lord, we had to give her an extravagant party just so she'd not kill us with plans and charts.

Somehow, I'd let the one thing I'd taken for myself become about everything else.

"I'm not sharing you," I growled and threw the car in gear.

"Where are we going?" she asked as I sped out of the drive. When I didn't answer, she said, "We can't go to Vegas today, as much as I want to. I have classes in the morning, a dress fitting with Ivy, and Braeden needs you…"

Yeah, everyone else.

But the most important person is you.

"Romeo?"

"I'm not going to Vegas, baby." I promised.

"Then where are you going?"

"I'm making it about me and you again."

"How are you going to do that?" She wondered.

I smiled.

CHAPTER TWENTY-THREE

#BuzzTip
How many secrets are in a phone is
directly related to how fast the owner
snatches it back.

#BuzzBoss

RIMMEL

He drove us downtown.

Even though it wasn't quite yet five o'clock, the sun was already beginning to set. Not that it had been very bright to begin with. The winter sky was gray and full of clouds, giving everything an overcast hue.

When he pulled up in front of a large stone building with great wide concrete steps, my brow furrowed. Then he parked at the curb.

How he always managed to find the best parking spot on a street was something I could only chalk up to Romeo magic.

This wasn't a part of town I was very familiar with. I'd only been downtown once before when Romeo and I had tried some restaurant a few streets over. Mostly, we stuck around campus and in the neighborhood we lived in now.

So it took me a minute to realize where he'd brought us.

Okay, fine. I saw the sign.

"The county courthouse?" I asked.

He didn't answer, only flung open his door and came around to mine. When he reached his hand into the open doorway, I didn't hesitate to give him mine. I allowed him to tug me out onto the sidewalk and pull me into his arms.

"Marry me. Marry me right the fuck now."

My heart skipped a beat and butterflies erupted in my belly. Excitement sizzled along every nerve inside my body because I knew he was being one hundred percent sincere.

"Right now?" I asked.

"Right the fuck now."

I giggled. "What about the wedding? Your parents?"

His arms shifted when he shrugged. "We'll have the wedding."

"You want to get married twice?" I laughed.

He put his forehead against mine and stared into my eyes. "I'd marry you a thousand times if I could."

"Oh, Romeo," I whispered.

"But this first time. The official time. This time is for us and only us. No reporters, no waiters with trays of appetizers, no cameras going off, and no speeches to listen to. Just me. Just you."

"Just us." My voice was wistful, totally captivated by the picture he painted.

This was the way we were meant to get married.

"You in your yoga pants and Alpha U hoodie, me in my jeans and snotty T-shirt." I laughed, and he grinned. "Us exactly as we always are together and nothing else. As far as everyone else will know, we got married on the day of our wedding. But we'll know. And every time I look at you, there will be an unspoken secret between us, a bond of how we really vowed to be together."

A tear slipped out of the corner of my eye, and he kissed it away. "It's perfect."

"Say yes, Rimmel." He urged.

"Yes."

After a quick kiss to my lips, he pulled back to take my hand, and we ran up the courthouse steps and into the huge, historic building.

Of course, we had to go through security, and he became impatient. But my lips danced with laughter, and even though I couldn't see them, I knew my eyes held a note of promise. I didn't mind the wait.

It just added to the anticipation.

The anticipation of the moment when he would become mine completely.

When we were finally cleared to travel deeper into the building, Romeo tugged me along behind him as he followed the signs toward where we needed to go. When we finally stepped into the small office, it was five minutes until five.

It was almost closing time.

There was an older woman sitting behind a very long counter on the far side of the room. Her hair was graying and styled. She smiled when Romeo approached the counter.

"We need a marriage license, please."

My heart burst with joy, and my fingers tightened around his. I suddenly wanted to scream that this beautiful man was going to marry me.

But I didn't. I somehow managed to contain my joy.

The woman chuckled like his impatience was evident to more than just me and pulled out a clipboard with an application on it. "Fill this out. Pay the fee. In Maryland, there is a standard two-day waiting period. Once it's up, you can come back in and we'll marry you."

"Two days," I intoned. Suddenly, two days seemed unbearable. It seemed like a lifetime. I was ready now.

Romeo untangled our hands and leaned on the counter to deliver a devastating smile. "Here's the thing, Kathy," he said, reading her name off the badge pinned to her shirt. "We're having a big wedding, for our family and a million of my mother's closest friends."

As he spoke, he drew the attention of the other two women in the room. Like gravity, he pulled them all in with his deep, smooth voice, charming smile, and movie star good looks.

"But I don't care about any of that stuff. I only care about her." He leaned back to wrap an arm around me and draw me into the conversation. "We don't want to wait two days. Hell, I've been waiting since the minute she shoved a wrinkled piece of paper in my face and forced me to study with her."

"I did not force you," I demanded.

He kissed my forehead like he was humoring me, and the woman off to my left sighed.

"Well, I guess I could see if the justice of the peace has left for the day," Kathy said.

"I'll go get him!" one of the other women yelled and raced off.

"It's closing time," Kathy said, her gaze bouncing between us. "A secret wedding, huh?"

"You good at keeping secrets, Kathy?" Romeo asked and then winked.

She blushed. Good Lord, she was blushing.

Seconds later, the woman who ran off returned with a man in a suit and a scowl on his face. "Here they are," she said, pointing at us.

The man looked up, and the bothered look fell away, replaced by recognition. "Roman Anderson?"

Romeo smiled. "How you doing?" He pushed his arm across the counter and held his hand out to the justice of the peace.

"I'm good," he said, shaking Romeo's hand and then glancing at me. "You want to get married?"

"Right now if we can," he replied, nodding.

"Coming in at the end of the day was pretty smart," the man said. "No one would suspect you'd be here."

"That's the idea," he said.

"I take it you don't want the media to know about this?"

"No. It's a secret," I said, thrilled at the idea of Romeo and me having a secret no one else knew.

"Do it, Abe." The woman who ran off to find him encouraged him.

"I can waive the two-day waiting period as long as you both can attest to the fact that no one is forcing you to be here. This is not a union under duress."

"The only duress I feel right now is the possibility that you're going to say no," I said.

Romeo laughed. "What she said."

"All right, then. It'd be my pleasure to marry you and your lady, Mr. Anderson."

"Romeo," he said and grinned. "And thank you."

"You can thank me by signing your autograph after you're married."

"Sure thing."

The justice of the peace turned to the three women standing there taking it all in. "I'm going to need a witness."

All three of them raised their hands and then scowled at each other for daring to take the position.

"Three witnesses should make it extra official, don't you think, Romeo?" I asked.

"I like extra official." He agreed.

The women all looked at Abe with hope in their eyes. He chuckled. "Everybody in my office."

Kathy, the woman standing just behind the counter, pointed to the papers. "Fill these out and then we'll get you two lovebirds married."

Romeo picked up a pen and started writing furiously.

Married.

Romeo and I were getting married.

CHAPTER TWENTY-FOUR

Be all in or get all out.
Life's too short to be half-assed.

#BuzzBoss

ROMEO

We filled out the papers.

We signed our names.

And now here Rim and I stood in a tiny office in the back of the courthouse with Abe, the justice of the peace, Kathy, and her two friends, about to be married.

Ever since I met her, I'd been finding ways to get my name on her. After today, she'd wear it forever.

"Shall I begin?" Abe asked.

"Please," Rimmel answered, her eyes never leaving mine.

She was standing right here before me, her head barely reaching my shoulder, my dark-blue sweatshirt hanging past her thighs, and the hem of her black yoga pants dragging the floor. Her hair was pulled up in a messy knot on her head, and the black-framed glasses she'd been wearing since the first moment I laid eyes on her were perched on her face.

She was exactly who I wanted and nothing less.

Her hands felt small and slightly cold in mine as I held them between us. Automatically, I folded mine around them, giving her the warmth my skin was offering.

"We are gathered here today, *in secret...*" Abe began, and I flashed him a smile. "To join this man and this woman in marriage."

Rimmel smiled brightly, so bright I saw it in her eyes.

"No one in this room has any objections." Abe went on. "So we can move right on."

I barely heard what Abe was saying. I got lost so deep in her eyes. I don't know how I ever got here, but my God, I was grateful.

"Do you Roman William Anderson take Rimmel Anne Hudson to be your lawfully wedded wife, for—"

"Hells yeah," I said, cutting him off. I didn't need to hear everything he was going to list. It didn't matter. I'd agree to anything to make her mine.

One of the women standing as witness giggled, but I didn't dare tear my eyes away from my love.

"Alrighty then," Abe said and turned to Rimmel.

"Do you Rimmel Anne Hudson take Roman William Anderson to be your lawfully wedded husband—"

"Yes," she said, just as impatient.

"Do you have rings?" Abe asked.

Shit! In my rush to make it official, I hadn't even thought about rings.

"We don't need them," Rimmel said smoothly. "I don't need anything but this."

I love you, I mouthed.

I love you, she mouthed back.

"Okay, then. Repeat after me." Abe looked at me.

I cleared my throat. "I got this."

Abe gestured with his hand that I should continue.

Rimmel was watching me, eyes shimmering with unshed tears, and my chest expanded.

"A lot of people say you stole my heart. You managed somehow to get the heart of a player who would never settle down. But that's not the truth. The truth is you never had to steal my heart, baby, because I gave it to you. I'd give you anything you ask for, but you ask for nothing. You, with your gentle touch and fierce love of animals. I promise to love you even when you drag home fifty cats and fifty dogs because you couldn't bear to leave them at the shelter for one more day. I promise to love you even when your hair tries to eat my hand and when my car cries because you're a terrible driver. I never knew I needed you, Rim, until I saw you that night, soaking wet from the rain, sitting on the floor of the shelter, with a one-eyed cat in your lap. But I do need you. I need you so fucking much. I don't know how or why you let me in, but thank you. Thank you for making me the luckiest bastard on the face of this earth. I'll never take you for granted. I'll love you long after I'm gone. I vow to you here and now, in front of all these strangers..."

She laughed. Then she sniffled and a few tears slid behind her glasses.

"We're a team now, and as long as I'm breathing, you'll never be alone in life, not ever."

Rimmel pulled her hands free of mine and reached for the hem of my shirt, bent, and used it to wipe the tears falling freely down her face.

"You have a shirt of your own," I pointed out, a smile in my voice.

"I like yours better," she said, her voice raspy with tears.

"Can't say that I blame her," Kathy said, and the two women standing beside her made sounds of agreement.

Abe cleared his throat and turned to Rimmel. "And now you may repeat after me."

Rimmel straightened and shook her head. "I got this."

"I thought you might," he said and gestured for her to take the floor.

CHAPTER TWENTY-FIVE

#BroTip

When your girl says "do whatever you want to do," do NOT do whatever you want.

#BuzzBoss

RIMMEL

I was crying like a baby.

There was just no stopping the tears.

We might be standing in a tiny office with an audience of people we didn't even know, but it didn't matter.

This was perfect.

It was exactly what I needed. It was everything I wanted.

And Romeo, oh my word, Romeo. I think one of my ovaries burst when he said his vows. He knew exactly what to say and how to say it. There was no way on earth I would ever say anything so eloquent and soul-shattering.

But I could try.

"I've spent a lot of time reading in my life. You know I like my books. I always read nonfiction. I never had time for fairy tales. But what no one ever knew was sometimes I would sit in the back of a library, in a place where no one would ever see, and I'd read a love story. They were always so epic and so maddeningly impossible, but it didn't stop a little piece inside of me from wishing for something like that of my own. And then I met you. You were impossible, rude, and way out of my league. You drew attention wherever you went, and I'd spent most my life trying to hide. But there was no hiding from you. I don't need to read love stories ever again, and not because they're impossible, but because our love story is the greatest one I'll ever know. Even when you try to boss me around and insult my driving, my love for you will always win. I promise to love you even when the reporters follow our every move and your mother drives me crazy. I promise to love every quarter of you I unearth, and I vow that nothing and no one could ever make me doubt the man you are. Thank you for turning my life upside down, for not running when I tried to push you away. I swear I'll never take you for granted, and I'll give you every piece of me that exists. You'll never be alone, and you'll always know you're loved as long as I walk this earth."

My voice fell away, and there was a long stretch of silence in the space all around us.

I'd never seen Romeo cry, not ever. But in this moment, I watched the way his eyes glittered and knew the reason they glistened so intensely was because unshed tears were in his gaze.

He tore his eyes from mine only for a second to glance at Abe. "Wrap it up, my man," he said.

I giggled.

He said a few more things I never heard and then, "With the full authority and power vested in me by the state of Maryland, I now pronounce you husband and wife."

I jumped up and down a little, unable to contain my happiness.

"Mr. Anderson, you can kiss your bride."

"About time," he drawled.

But he didn't plant one on me right away, not like I thought he would. Instead, he slowly slid the glasses up onto my head, taking away the small barrier between us.

The butterflies were still fluttering furiously in my stomach, so much so that my entire middle vibrated and my fingers shook.

Romeo stepped up, so close that our feet bumped together, and his face turned down, his blue, blue eyes swept over my face. He cupped my jaw in both his palms, spreading his fingers wide. Even without my glasses, he stood so close I could see him clearly.

His gaze divided itself between my lips and my eyes as he literally stripped me bare just with his stare.

"Romeo," I whispered, reaching up to grab his wrists. I was desperate for our first kiss, desperate to seal in all the beautiful words we'd just exchanged.

"You're perfect," he murmured, then brought his lips to mine.

I sighed on contact. Everything inside me fell silent, the butterflies stopped fluttering, my fingers stopped shaking, and for one suspended moment in time, my heart stopped beating.

His lips were soft and smooth. They nibbled at my mouth gently as his thumb stroked the underside of my jaw. His tongue slipped out and met mine; they slowly moved together, stroking and caressing until the familiar pool of moisture met the fabric of my panties.

He started to pull back, but I tightened my hold on his wrists and leaned up for one last taste before letting him go.

We stood there smiling stupidly at each other until Abe cleared his throat and we remembered we weren't alone.

After that, everything moved fast but in a blur, like a dream.

A dream I never wanted to wake from.

An official marriage license was presented to us. Kathy and her friends cried. Romeo signed a lot of stuff for Abe, and then all four of them promised to never tell anyone about our secret wedding.

When we stepped outside, it was completely dark. The night was cold, but I didn't feel it. I was so drunk on Romeo that I could likely get hit by a bus and I wouldn't even feel it.

We were holding hands, but he let go and moved in front of me.

Crouching low, he offered his back.

I laughed and jumped on, looping my arms around his neck.

"There's no threshold to carry you over right now, and I sure as hell am not doing it when we get home. Ivy would call us out in seconds," he said. "Besides, since this entire wedding was untraditional and spur of the moment, then this moment should be, too."

He gave me a piggyback ride to the Hellcat, and I pressed warm, moist kisses to the back of his neck the entire ride.

"Mrs. Anderson," he said when he set me on my feet.

"Mr. Anderson," I echoed.

"How do you feel about consummating our marriage in the back of a Hellcat?"

"I feel like it would be the perfect end to this perfect night."

He pulled me close, and I dipped my head back to stare up at him.

"Oh, baby," he drawled. "This isn't the end. This is only the beginning."

Best. Beginning. Ever.

CHAPTER TWENTY-SIX

#JustSoYouKnow

Safe sex is not locking the car door.

#BuzzBoss

ROMEO

Married to the girl of my dreams?

Having her ride me in a Hellcat?

Knowing this was just the beginning of our life together?

Hells yeah.

Cambria Hebert

CHAPTER TWENTY-SEVEN

Never make eye contact while eating a banana.

#BuzzBoss

RIMMEL

I couldn't stop smiling.

I know all we did was run off to the courthouse and exchange a few vows.

Well, okay.

They weren't just a few vows. They were words I would never in my entire life forget.

It wasn't fancy. I looked like a bum, and Romeo's hair had been a mess (like I was one to judge there), but it had been the single best moment of my entire life.

Our status truly didn't matter. The status that the world held us to didn't matter. The heartache, the joy, the tears, and even the arguments that led us here were moments frozen in time, and they all brought me to this point.

All that mattered was how much we loved each other.

Maybe most people didn't feel different after they get married. I can certainly see why. After we left the courthouse last night, Romeo drove to some place where all that surrounded the road were trees and fields. We climbed into the backseat of the Hellcat and went at each other like it was our first time.

I guess in a lot of ways, it was.

Our first time making love as husband and wife.

Romeo was so big we barely fit. There were no candles, flowers, or silky sheets. It was stripped down, raw, and totally hot.

When we finally untangled ourselves from each other and the Hellcat, we drove home in the middle of the night and snuck into the house, crept through the dark, and fell into bed, where we made love all over again.

We barely got any sleep, and when morning came, it looked like every other day.

But everything inside me was totally changed.

For the first time in a very long time, I felt completely settled. I knew I was exactly where I belonged. The bond between Romeo and me would never break, and that knowledge gave me this all-encompassing confidence, like there was nothing in this entire world I couldn't handle.

It took us a while to peel ourselves from the sheets. We were too busy making out like teenagers to pay attention to the clock. When I finally did, I gasped and jumped up because usually by now, I would have been up for over an hour.

"If I don't get up, I'm going to be late for classes," I said, stumbling out of bed and falling onto the floor.

I lay there sprawled out on the hardwood floor, wearing literally nothing but the T-shirt Romeo wore last night when we got married.

It was my new favorite shirt.

Snotty and all.

Romeo's blond head appeared over the side of the mattress, the strands of his eternally rumpled hair falling over his forehead and his blue eyes dancing with amusement.

"What's ya doin' down there, Smalls?"

"We need a rug," I groaned and rubbed my hip. The action caused the shirt to ride up and display everything beneath it (no panties).

"Nice view," he growled and reached his arm over the side to caressed my inner thigh.

"I could be down here with a serious injury and all you see is my lady bits!" I demanded, trying not to laugh.

Romeo catapulted out of bed (it really wasn't fair he was so agile and I was so disastrous) and picked me up to cradle me against his chest.

"That better, wife?" he drawled.

"Better," I whispered and rubbed my hand over his stubbled jaw.

"Whenever I look at you today, all I'm gonna see is last night. Is it wrong it thrills the shit out of me that no one's going to know I already made you mine?"

"If it's wrong, then I don't want to be right."

"Damn, baby. You're starting to pick up some of my smooth lines."

I rolled my eyes. "Take me to the closet. I need clothes!"

Technically, I should have showered. But I didn't want to for two reasons:

1) I was short on time
and…

2) I couldn't bear the idea of washing off our wedding night just yet. I wanted him all over my skin today. I wanted to tingle everywhere he touched.

Usually, I would have grabbed the first thing my hand closed around and prayed it matched, but today I found myself looking through my clothes to find something nicer than what I normally threw on.

Romeo was going to be looking at me today and remembering last night. My husband was going to be looking at his *wife* for the first time today.

I wanted to look nice.

I wanted to look as beautiful as he made me feel.

I chose a pair of dark-wash skinny jeans, layered a black ribbed tank top over a plain white tank, and added a slouchy cream-colored sweater in a waffle knit texture. I added the gold cameo necklace that had been my mother's (seemed appropriate to make her part of this day) and then hollered for Romeo to come back into the closet.

"You're bossy when you're married," he appeared, toothbrush in hand and white foam from the toothpaste all around his mouth.

I laughed.

"You could have finished." I gestured to his mouth.

"The way you were yelling, I thought maybe you fell over again."

I smacked him in the bare stomach and pointed to the very top shelf to a plain brown shoebox. "I need my shoes."

"Poor Smalls, can't reach her shoes," he said around his toothbrush as he jammed it back into his mouth and then reached for the box.

It was a big box, and he set it at my feet.

"Thank you!" I chirped.

He tried to kiss me with his foamy mouth, and I screeched and jumped away. "Only married five minutes and already she's tired of my kisses. What's next, Smalls? You gonna start telling me you have a headache to get out of sex?"

"Not bloody likely!" I yelled after him as he strolled back to the sink.

I yanked off the lid to the box and smiled. Inside was a pair of boots Ivy had given me for Christmas. Did I mention she was the best gift giver ever? Yeah, that girl could shop.

They were a pair of Uggs in traditional leopard print. They were tall and cozy-looking and lined with fluffy soft fur.

I'd never had a genuine pair of Uggs before. I only ever bought myself the less expensive knockoffs, but she swore she found them at some outlet store in her hometown and they hadn't cost much at all.

They were so beautiful I hadn't even worn them yet. I'd been saving them. I didn't realize what for until now.

I pulled them out, stroking the full-on shoe gorgeousness, and pulled them on. They were the perfect accessory to my outfit and they were nice and toasty warm.

When I walked out of the closet into the bathroom, Romeo gave me an appreciative once-over. "You look hot."

As soon as we finished getting ready and he was dressed in a pair of jeans and a blue long-sleeved polo, we left the little world that was our bedroom.

Everyone was already downstairs, and when we walked into the room, an obvious sort of silence filled the space. I turned around from getting a mug and noted everyone was staring at us. I glanced at Romeo, and he winked.

"Recovering from last night?" B asked.

"Last night?" I squeaked. He couldn't possibly know, could he?

Romeo didn't seem concerned at all. He moved forward, took the mug out of my hands, and poured me some coffee.

"Your meeting with the mother of the groom." Braeden clarified like he was talking to someone who had no brain.

Right. We went to Romeo's parents' last night.

"When you weren't the first one down here this morning, I figured you were still trying to sleep off the wedding plans Moms made." He snickered into his coffee, and Ivy rolled her eyes but then gave me a sympathetic look.

I laughed and took the coffee Romeo held out. "She had an entire folder full of plans."

"She didn't!" Ivy gasped.

I nodded. "How she had time for all that and the engagement party, I'll never figure out."

Romeo settled against the counter and pulled me in front of him, anchoring my back against his front. "We're going to our own engagement party and we aren't even engaged anymore, he whispered into my ear."

I smiled and sipped at the coffee.

Drew groaned from beside Ivy. "Not you guys, too. What's a guy gotta do around here to have breakfast without walking in on make-out sessions or witnessing the whispering of sweet nothings in each other's ears?"

"Who said they were sweet nothings?" I arched a brow wickedly. "Maybe they were naughty somethings."

Braeden choked on his coffee, and the mug made a sharp sound when it hit the counter. "If I wasn't so disturbed by that thought, sis, I would tell you that was a damn good comeback.

"You better get your girl, Rome. She's turning into some kind of dirty talker." He looked at me proudly and sighed. "Baby sis is growing up. I've taught you so much."

I rolled my eyes, and Ivy told him he was an idiot.

Drew just grinned and shoveled more cereal into his mouth.

Romeo helped himself to my coffee with a low chuckle.

"You look super cute," Ivy said. "I was wondering if you were ever gonna wear those boots."

"They're almost too beautiful to wear," I mused.

"No way," she said, picking up the orange juice in front of her and taking a sip. "They're too pretty not to wear."

I tried to remember the last time I'd seen her drink a cup of coffee. It had been a while.

"Did my dress for the party come in?" I asked her. "And please tell me it's white."

Ivy scoffed. "Of course it's white. You're the bride."

Well, thank heavens she seemed to understand the rules Romeo's mother seemed to live by, because I sure as hell didn't.

"And yep, it's there. It came in late last night. I saw it when I stopped at the boutique. Meet me there later after classes, and we'll do a fitting and make some plans."

I turned to Romeo. "You left your suit at your mother's. You're going to have to go get it today, and please, for the love of God, don't wrinkle it."

He gave me a salute, and I smiled. "Braeden and Drew, you two better have suits."

They both seemed bewildered as to why they would need a suit. I rubbed at my forehead with my hand.

"I've got it covered." Ivy assured me. "Trent, too."

"Where is Trent?" I asked. I was used to him popping in most mornings to hang out.

"He texted and said he had frat house shit to deal with. He'll be over tonight for dinner," Drew answered.

"Dude, he texted you to tell you he wouldn't be here for breakfast?" B scoffed.

Drew shoved another bite into his mouth. "So?"

"Are you dating or just friends?"

Drew's spoon clattered against the bowl, and he burped loudly.

One gets used to hearing all kinds of nasty sounds when they live with three men.

"We're super bros." He clarified, but clearly, it wasn't a very good clarification

"Super bros?" Romeo asked, amused.

"It's man talk for BFFs." Ivy came to her brother's defense.

Drew dumped his dishes in the sink and turned around. "Much as I'd like to stay here and be entertained by y'all, my incredibly boring desk job is waiting."

Even though Drew stayed here to pursue a driving career, he still had to get a job in computer programing until he could actually make money off of driving.

"Bye, Drew!" Ivy called.

He stopped beside her to kiss her head. "See ya later, Ives."

When he was gone, I turned to Ivy. "Please tell me you have time to do something with this," I pointed to my hair.

"Emergency braid?" she asked.

I nodded gratefully. Seemed like a shame to ruin such a nice outfit with such bad hair.

We left the guys in the kitchen and headed into Ivy and B's bathroom, where I sat on the toilet seat so she could get to work.

"You seem really happy this morning." She observed as she brushed.

"I'm happy every morning."

"I know. I just mean a little extra happy. Like sparkly."

I laughed. "I guess I feel a little extra sparkly this morning."

"It's the boots."

"It's totally the boots." I agreed.

It wasn't the boots. But that was my secret.

"So tell me. How bad was she last night?"

I laughed. "Pretty bad. She's totally been side planning our wedding without anyone knowing."

"How'd she take it when you told her to forget it all?"

I was silent a second too long, and Ivy gasped. "You did not tell her you'd use it all?"

"No." I sighed. "I didn't. But I'm tempted to."

"What!" she exclaimed and forgot all about my hair. She rushed around and sat on the edge of the tub, facing me, while gripping the brush like she might need it to beat some sense into me. "You cannot let her plan your wedding, Rimmel. It would be everything you aren't. This is *your* day."

I'd already had my day. And it had been absolutely perfect. So now when I thought about Romeo's mother taking over the plans, when I thought about the likely five hundred guests that would be there on "my" day, it didn't bother me at all. If anything, I was kind of relieved she wanted to take over because then I wouldn't have to.

I realized now that I didn't really care what kind of wedding Romeo and I had just so long as we got to say I do.

And we did.

I shrugged. "It's kind of her day, too. And yours and Romeo's. It's a day for all of us. And since I don't really care what kind of wedding we have, why not let her plan it? We know whatever she does will be beautiful."

Ivy reached out and touched my forehead. "Are you feeling okay? You feeling nauseous, too."

I snorted. "I'm fine."

"I can't in good conscience allow this. As maid of honor, I'm putting my foot down. You are going to choose what you want for your wedding. I don't care if I have to stand over you for every decision you need to make."

I'd barely listened to her speech. "What do you me am I feeling nauseous, *too*." I looked at her with a sharpened gaze. "Are you sick?"

Ivy made a sound and got up to finish my hair. "I'm fine. Just feel a little yucky this morning."

"How did your doctor appointment go?"

"It was good," she said, sounding like she was way too focused on my hair to converse.

But I knew better than that. Ivy could braid my hair in her sleep.

"Ivy," I said.

She sighed. "I'm fine, Rim. I promise. I didn't mean to worry you. I ate a grilled cheese last night that Braeden made. Is it any wonder my stomach hurts this morning?"

"Ew." I wrinkled my nose. "You ate something he cooked?"

She giggled. "It was actually pretty good. But now I kinda regret it."

She finished up my hair and showed me in the mirror. It looked amazing, as always. "Thank you," I said and gave her a quick hug.

I could tell she was surprised by my display of affection, but she hugged me back anyway.

When I pulled back, it looked like she might have something to say. But then whatever it was disappeared. "I'll see you later at the boutique?"

"I'll be there," I said, taking in her bright-blue skinny jeans, black boots, and oversized black cowl-neck sweater. Her hair was up on the top of her head in a sleek knot, and her makeup was flawless as usual.

She didn't look like anything was wrong.

"Awesome!" Her white teeth flashed.

But I knew better than anyone that looks could sometimes be deceiving.

CHAPTER TWENTY-EIGHT

Tonight is the engagement party.
Word is big name magazines are
going to be there.
But I'll report first.

#BuzzBoss

ROMEO

Mom invited the entire Knights institution to our engagement party. That alone was a crap ton of people.

All but about ten percent of the entire staff came. The entire team was here.

I saw that as a good day for me in football.

Yeah, I know. I was at some fancy pants party, and this wasn't a football game. But every day was a day in football, whether it was a game day or not.

The way I saw my teammates' presence tonight was a show of loyalty. A show of respect for who they all knew was going to be the team leader. No, it hadn't been announced yet, but it really didn't need to be. I knew it by the deal my father got for me. I knew it by the huge amount of money they were paying me to play for them for the next four years.

Know how else I knew?

I knew by the way Blanchard looked at me. I hoped the guy never played poker, because if he did, he would suck. He had no ability to look at a person and conceal the way he felt.

And when he looked at me, I saw resentment.

Not hatred, not loathing, or anything equally as alarming.

It was just resentment. Anger with me for taking his top spot away. Anger with himself for losing it. Hell, he was probably even mad at the calendar because I was younger than him.

Football was a game of high stakes and big money. It was a tough pill to swallow when the game you excelled at suddenly turned on you.

I had no doubt if I had been any other position or a quarterback on any other team, Blanchard and I would get along. Hell, maybe we'd even go out for beers. This wasn't necessarily personal, but the sting of the cut sure made it feel like it was.

When we first locked eyes across the room, I made a choice. I could acknowledge the way I knew he felt and fuel that fire, or I could pretend I didn't notice.

I didn't do either.

Starting a fight wasn't my thing. But backing down sure as hell wasn't either.

Instead, I opted for respect.

I met his eyes, keeping my gaze as strong and steady as his. After a few beats passed, I lifted my beer to him, a sign of esteem and also an acknowledgement that I understood the undercurrents between us.

I didn't want a fight with the number two quarterback on the team.

I was tired of fighting.

We didn't have to be friends, but I didn't want to have to watch my back every time I walked through a door.

Blanchard wasn't quite as diplomatic as me. He didn't raise his glass or even smile. He lowered his chin and then turned away.

Well then, so much for not watching my back.

I made it a point to make eye contact with the guys who stood around him. His friends who had been loyal to him far longer than they'd ever known me. I hoped they wouldn't be a problem. I hoped they were smart and recognized a shift in power when they saw it.

I wasn't an asshole. But I knew how to be. And if anyone wanted to challenge me on the Knights, I'd accept the challenge and I'd win.

All but one of the players returned my look and raised their beers.

Respect.

They didn't have to like me, but the respect was mandatory.

Rimmel slid up to my side, and the familiar feel of her hand in mine made me forget about the team.

"Have I told you how absolutely beautiful you look tonight?" I asked, glancing down at what everyone assumed to be my soon-to-be wife.

Really beautiful was in understatement for the way she glowed tonight. Rimmel was a beautiful woman without even trying, but holy hell, when she tried… she was breathtaking.

And tonight, I found myself in the position of not being able to breathe an awful lot.

She looked like an angel dressed in a white lace gown. I knew Ivy was the one who picked it, so of course it was going to be a nice dress, but my new sister had outdone herself with the choice. It looked exactly like something Rimmel would wear.

As I said, it was snow white in color, made completely of lace with white silk underneath. It was long-sleeved, but the sleeves were sheer, giving me glimpses of Rimmel's creamy skin and making me ache to run my hands over her naked body.

Rimmel told me the neckline was called a sweetheart, but all I knew was it afforded me a nice view of her chest and, once again, a mouthwatering view of her smooth skin.

The dress hugged her chest, bringing her narrow form into a slight V shape at the waist, but then the dress flared out, billowing out around her hips and thighs, making her look like she was heaven sent.

Once again, I got a glimpse of skin because the gown wasn't long. The front ended mid-thigh and then gradually became longer around the back so it draped like a waterfall toward the floor. The entire uneven hemline looked as though it had been dipped in gold. But not the kind of gold that looked gaudy or even painted on. It was more of an understated golden hue that colored the lace and wasn't too shiny, like someone threw a jar of glitter at her.

Rim's thin legs stretched to the floor into the gold heels perched on her feet. How the hell Ivy got her to wear heels I would never know. Honestly, all I could think about was how they would feel wrapped around my waist.

Yes, okay. I just said she looked like a heaven-sent angel, and she did—the way she floated around the room—and yes, maybe it was wrong to think such spicy thoughts about a woman who appeared so divine.

But hell. I never said *I* was an angel.

* * *

"Once or twice." She smiled and reached up to adjust my tie. "You look like a golden statue come to life." The long length of her hair was down tonight, curled into long, loose waves and pinned up on the sides away from her face so it could cascade down her back.

"It's the tie," I said and leaned down to kiss her softly. People around us clapped, and I felt like a circus animal. "Think if I do a trick, people will throw snacks at us?" I whispered in her ear.

"Certainly would be entertaining," she mused.

A few photographers appeared in front of us, and I set my beer on a tray that was passing by. I didn't care to give the impression I was a drinker, especially not before the beginning of my first season as a starter.

Rimmel was holding a champagne flute in her hand, and the golden bubbly only accentuated the entire goddess look she was going for. So when she tried to put it down I shook my head slightly. "You're perfect the way you are."

She made a face at me and handed the glass off Ivy, who had approached me from behind. "Until all the papers decide your new wife is a drunkard and start making up headlines about rehab."

I would have laughed at the ridiculousness, but she was probably right.

We turned toward the cameras and smiled, posing for picture after picture until they all drifted away.

"My face hurts," she muttered, and Ivy stuck the champagne under her nose.

Braeden materialized right beside Ivy and handed me a fresh beer.

"I have to say," Ivy said, "Valerie did an amazing job. This place is freaking amazing."

"Moms has style." Braeden agreed.

"Be sure you tell her that," I told him. "She'll live on that for months."

"It's a done deal."

Rimmel sipped at her champagne and glanced around the huge ballroom, taking in the décor. It wasn't the first time she'd done that tonight, and I'm sure it wouldn't be the last.

"It really is beautiful." Rim agreed. "See what I mean about the wedding?" Her comment was directed at Ivy.

"Oh, I can see it." She agreed and crossed her arms. "But I'm still not convinced."

"What are you talking about?" I asked.

"Wedding stuff," Rim said.

I grunted and drank some beer.

"Where's your champagne?" Rimmel asked Ivy, and I noticed she was the only one without a drink in her hand.

Ivy shrugged one shoulder. "I'm not drinking tonight."

Didn't seem odd to me at all. There were quite a few times when we went out in the past several months that Ivy didn't drink. After everything that happened to her, I understood, and with tonight being such a large crowd and filled with so many people she didn't know, I thought it was a smart choice on her part.

Not that anything would happen to Ivy tonight. Braeden and I would make sure of that.

Rimmel didn't seem to think along the same lines, though. I felt the air around her shift, and when I glanced in her direction, she was studying Ivy with a calculating glint in her eye.

Odd.

Movement from across the room caught my attention, and I saw Ron Gamble talking with the head coach of the team. Both of them seemed relaxed and jovial with drinks in their hands.

I leaned down to Rimmel's ear. "I know it's our engagement and all, but I was wondering if you minded a little football talk?"

She glanced toward the men I'd just been looking at and then to a group of my teammates standing nearby. "Braeden?" she whispered.

I nodded. "It's a good time to introduce him around."

"Is that even allowed in the football league? Is that like fraternization or something?"

"Who the hell knows?" I said, surprised she would even think about that. My girl was wising up to the game of football. "This is a social setting. It's just uncontrollable who one might bump into at a party," I said casually.

"By all means, you and Braeden go do whatever it takes to make sure my brother gets to play with my husband."

I bent down to look directly in her eyes. Even with heels on, she was still just Smalls. "You're sure?"

Her eyes softened. "We had our night. This night is for us, but it's for our family, too. Now go take care of B. Give me a signal if you need me to step in and do some charming."

In that dress, they'd all be putty in her hands.

"I fucking love you," I growled.

"I fucking love you, too."

"Let's go find a broom closet, have a quickie."

"You have a one-track mind." She shook her head, but she was smiling.

"You know it turns me on when you say the word fuck." It totally did. Hearing that dirty word come out of her pure little mouth never ceased to make me horny.

"Later." She promised and tugged on the gold tie my mother picked to go with the suit. I didn't like it so much at first. But now I didn't mind it.

"B!" I said and straightened. "C'mon, we got shit to do."

He turned to Ivy and made a face, showing her all his pearly whites. "I got anything in my teeth?"

"No, but I sure wish you had some manners," Ivy quipped.

Braeden dived forward and kissed her. She laughed.

"Love you," he said.

"Times two," she whispered, and then I clapped him on the back so he would move his ass.

We had some schmoozing to do.

CHAPTER TWENTY-NINE

Could the Knights be courting #13?

#BuzzBoss

RIMMEL

I was in a fairy tale.

A literal fairy tale come to life.

I knew what Valerie had planned for tonight. I knew the color scheme, and I knew the location. But I hadn't known it would be this gorgeous.

The grand ballroom of the hotel was a huge open space with high ceilings that had to be at least twenty feet tall. They rose up in the center like a steeple, and running horizontally across the wide space were large wooden beams that added a rustic touch to an otherwise austere place.

In between the beams, lights hung down from the ceiling, clear glass that looked like water drops with a single bulb in the center. They sparkled and glowed around the room, and while the room itself was far too bright for the pendants to look like stars, the effect was no less dramatic.

Everything was decorated in a white and matte gold scheme. Not the kind of gold that looked brassy and plucked right out of the eighties, but a modern gold finish that seemed to play perfectly with the white.

There were round tables draped with white linens and large over-the-top centerpieces of white daisies and gold-painted baby's breath bursting out of planters that stood tall, finished with an aged white texture. Where Valerie found so many perfect white daisies in the middle of winter I would never know.

Because the planters stood on what looked like thick podiums, the space on the table beneath them was filled with clear glass votive holders and lit white candles.

The dishes on the tables were white, edged in gold, and the linens were the exact same shade of gold on everything else.

Champagne flowed freely throughout the room, going around on trays and also being poured at the two bars on opposite sides of the room.

Canapés were being served and later, there would be a sit-down meal. There wasn't a DJ. Oh no. There was a live band, and they seemed to seamlessly play a mixture of current popular songs and songs that would never go out of style.

Who the hell needed a wedding when you had an engagement party like this?

"Do you think Romeo knows all these people?" Ivy leaned in and asked.

I laughed. "Definitely not. I'd be surprised if his mother knew them all."

"Did you know someone from *People* is here?"

I shook my head. "No, but I'm not surprised. They're trying to get exclusive pictures from the wedding."

As if on cue, a stylish woman wearing what I knew had to be a designer dress approached us. "Rimmel Hudson?" she asked, and I thought, *It's Rimmel Anderson now.* "I'm Rachel Wintor, the head editor at *People.*"

"Wonderful to meet you. Thank you so much for being here tonight," I said politely and offered her my hand.

She took it and then looked between Ivy and me, then back at me. "I have to say you look more beautiful tonight than I've ever seen you look. Would it be okay if I asked who you are wearing and quote you on it?"

Even though Ivy was standing there, the picture of poise and style, I knew she was probably going to pee her pants any minute now.

"Of course." I smiled. "Please meet Ivy Forrester. She's my stylist. Every nice outfit you've ever seen me wear is courtesy of her brilliant eye."

"Ivy." Rachel turned her full attention to my friend. "It's a pleasure to meet you. You certainly seem to know your way around a closet."

I laughed lightly. "I've never met anyone better. She's currently in the process of starting up her own YouTube channel dedicated to style and teaching clueless people like me how to look their best."

"Really?" Rachel seemed interested.

"Yes, she's in high demand where we're from."

Ivy gave me a look and then turned back to Rachel and turned up the Ivy charm. She had the kind of personality that attracted people. They gravitated toward her confident air and beautiful face.

And she certainly looked beautiful tonight, with her hair straight and sleek around her shoulders, dramatic smoky eye, and retro inspired lip color. Her dress was simple and stunning, a black curve-hugging design that went all the way to the floor. It was long-sleeved and had a modest scoop neckline, but when she turned around, it was completely backless.

To finish off the look, she was wearing large square faux diamond earrings, a silver cuff bracelet, and a teardrop-shaped pendant necklace on a chain so thin you might not notice it at all except for the way it glittered beneath the light.

She finished off the look with a sky-high red heels that occasionally peeked out from beneath the hem of her gown.

"I'm not the only one who knows her way around a closet," Ivy said, her blue eyes sparkling. "Is that a gown from the spring Lager Collection?"

I had no idea, but clearly, Ivy did. Rachel smiled. "You know your designers."

Ivy looked put out. "I wouldn't call myself a stylist if I didn't. I didn't think the Lager Collection was available yet."

"It isn't. But Lager is a friend of mine."

"Well, he keeps you very well dressed." Ivy smiled.

Rachel turned back to me. "So who are you wearing, Rimmel? Your gown is stunning."

I glanced at Ivy because I had no idea who I was wearing. It could be Target for all I knew or cared.

"It's an indie designer by the name of Sophie Blanc. She's extremely talented, and I think you'll probably feature her on the pages of your style issue someday soon."

"An indie?" Rachel purred. "Bold choice."

Ivy shrugged one shoulder delicately. "I wouldn't say bold. It's clearly a beautiful gown, and it complements Rimmel's body shape perfectly. Sophie was very accommodating in tailoring it to fit her measurements, and the craftsmanship is amazing. She even added the gold trim to the hem at my request because I wanted something to make the dress really special. There's a whole lot of talent in the indie design world. People with a fresh eye and a lot of determination to make it. They just need a chance to shine."

"Well, this designer is certainly shining tonight, courtesy of Miss Hudson here." Rachel nodded. "How do you spell the designer's name?"

Ivy spelled it out while Rachel wrote it in a small notebook. When she was done, she looked up. "And who did you hair and makeup?"

"Ivy," I replied.

Rachel gave Ivy another interested glance. "You're talented yourself."

"I've been styling Rimmel for a while now. I know what works best on her," Ivy answered pragmatically.

"And who are you wearing tonight?"

"Calvin Klein. Vintage. Shoes are by Vera Wang."

"Would you ladies mind if I took a few pictures? On the record, of course."

"Of course," I said and smiled. I wished I could kick off these god-awful heels and hide in a corner for a while.

But I wasn't going to do that.

Instead, I asked Ivy how my hair was while Rachel signaled to a photographer whose job was likely to follow her around and take pictures on demand.

I rose up to my full height (which was pretty dang good with these heels!) and smiled, tipping my chin the way Ivy taught me and posing one foot slightly in front of the other.

After she got pictures of my dress from what seemed like every angle, I slyly pulled Ivy in and got a few pictures with her.

"You know Ivy's dating a former Alpha U football player who was recently accepted into the draft for the NFL," I said.

"Braeden Walker?" Rachel said.

I smiled because she already knew his name. Ivy beamed proudly. "That's him. He's around here somewhere, likely with Romeo."

"Rimmel, would you mind if we got a few pictures of you and Romeo together?"

"Of course." I lied. "I'm not real sure where he's gotten to." And like magic, he appeared.

"Ladies." His smooth voice cut into the moment. I sighed and my body relaxed. I hadn't even realized I'd been tense. "Does everyone have everything they need?"

Rachel wasn't immune to Romeo's power, and she was momentarily struck silent. I glanced at Ivy and suppressed a giggle.

"Congratulations on your engagement, Mr. Anderson." Rachel started.

"Romeo." He corrected politely.

"Romeo. And congratulations are also in order on your four-year contract with the Maryland Knights."

"Life's pretty good right now." He agreed.

"Rachel is from *People*," I explained to Romeo, and as I spoke, he leaned in closer to me and placed his hand on the small of my back. "They'd like a few pictures."

"Absolutely." He nodded. It was like he wasn't bothered at all. 'Course, he was used to cameras in his face all the time. During the season when he wasn't at home, he was photographed constantly.

Rachel pointed to an area across the room where the pendants hung low enough they would be visible in the background. Instead of taking my hand or arm and leading me over to the spot, Romeo surprised everyone by sweeping me off my feet and holding me against his chest.

Ivy hurriedly fussed around to make sure my dress was covering all the important parts, and the high-low hemline draped beautifully even in his arms.

Everyone in the place stopped what they were doing and turned toward us. Laughter and whispers moved through the crowd, and Romeo turned on the full power of his smile, directing it toward Rachel. "Rim isn't very good in heels. It's safer for everyone if she travels this way."

Rachel was charmed and then snapped out of it and started barking orders at her cameraman to not miss a second.

You'd think with all eyes on us, it would have been hard for me to smile and act like I didn't mind the attention.

But it wasn't.

All I had to do was look up at Romeo, and everyone else fell away.

"You just had to do that, didn't you?" I mused.

"The cameras love us, baby. Gotta give the people what they want."

"How's it going with B?" I asked as we stepped beneath the sparkling lights.

"Real good. I'll find him again once I've safely rescued you from the paparazzi."

"How'd you know I needed rescued?"

He grinned down at me. "I didn't. I just wanted an excuse to come over and touch you."

I cupped his face and sighed. "You never need an excuse."

He kissed me sweetly as we stood beneath the teardrop-shaped lights. Everyone started clapping, and I realized where we were.

I jerked and would have fallen out of his arms if his reflexes weren't so good. He stood me on my feet, and we posed for a couple pictures, and then Rachel started hinting around about the wedding details and exclusive photos.

I let Romeo deftly handle that, and by the time she walked away, I had no doubt that within fifteen minutes, she'd realize she'd been completely dazzled and he never actually agreed to anything.

Finally, blissfully, we were alone.

Well, as alone as two people could be in a crowded room.

For all of two seconds.

"Rimmel!" Valerie said, stepping up to us. "There's someone I would love to introduce you to."

Romeo met my eyes, and I knew exactly what he was thinking about. Our wedding. The night we stole just for us.

I smiled and turned to his mother. "Of course."

Valerie led me off toward someone she thought might be interested in donating to the animal shelters, and Romeo went off in search of B.

The next hour continued in pretty much the same pattern. We mingled, we smiled, and we posed for endless pictures. Occasionally, I would get a stolen moment with Ivy or with someone in our family, but they always seemed fleeting.

Finally, the servers announced the dinner, and everyone made their way to their seats. Romeo and I were at a huge table with his parents, Braeden, Ivy, Braeden's mom and her date, Drew, and Trent that was near the center of the room.

The Knights players were at a couple tables beside us, along with another table for Ron Gamble and all the coaches and main staff for the team.

The band still played, but it was a much softer melody that was actually kind of relaxing as I sat there and sipped at champagne.

A few cameras went off close by and their flashes blinded me. Reflexively, I lifted my hand to shield my face from the bright disruption.

"Mind giving us a break for a bit?" Romeo asked, his tone was friendly, but there was an unmistakable note of steel behind his words.

"Sorry about that, Mr. Anderson," one of them said, and Valerie jumped up to guide them away to a table she'd set up just for the vultures, providing a free meal.

On one hand, I thought it was annoying she was catering to them, but on the other, the free food would keep them away for a least a little while.

"You okay?" he asked, leaning in. His hand settled beneath the table over my thigh, and the feel of him was so welcome.

"Yes," I said, sheepish, and set down my glass. "Sorry, I dropped my guard a little with the soft music and champagne and forgot about them. They just startled me, but I'll be ready for them next time."

He frowned a little and concern deepened his crazy blue eyes. "I don't want you to have to be on guard all the time. That's not the life I want for you."

I covered my hand with his and leaned forward, pressing our foreheads together. "I'm not on guard all the time. Just at your mother's parties."

He smiled and the corners of his eyes crinkled as I stared into them.

"Our life is perfect the way it is. I wouldn't change it."

The sound of knives and forks hitting against glass created a light tinkling sound, and Romeo smiled. "They want you to kiss me."

I snorted, and the action made my head pull away from his, but I didn't like that, so I reached up and grabbed the back of his neck to anchor myself against him once more.

"They aren't gonna stop 'til you kiss me, Smalls."

The distance between us was already so minimal I barely had to move to touch my lips to his. He tasted like beer and I tasted like champagne, the two flavors melding to together to create an interesting cocktail.

We dined on braised beef tips, wide egg noodles with some kind of really good sauce, roasted vegetables, and salad. There were also baskets of freshly sliced French bread going around. For dessert, we were served chocolate cheesecake with a white chocolate drizzle.

I thought I'd be too nervous to eat, but that wasn't the case.

The first bite turned me into some kind of starved animal, and I ate almost everything they put in front of me. Thank God I managed not to spill any of it on my white gown.

I didn't feel bad about it, though, because Braeden plowed through his plate and then half of Ivy's with so much gusto he actually attracted attention.

"Hollow leg!" one of the Knights players yelled out, cupping his hands around his mouth as he hollered so it would carry over to our table.

Romeo laughed and smacked Braeden, drawing his attention from his plate.

"What?" B looked up, still chewing.

I laughed, and Ivy looked toward the sky like she was asking for help from the heavens.

Ha.

"Looks like they're already giving you nicknames," Romeo scoffed.

"What the fu—"

Ivy gasped and slapped a hand over his mouth, her blue eyes wide with horror. "Watch your mouth. We're at a formal event."

From the sparkle in B's eyes and the look on Ivy's face, I knew he licked her hand. To her credit, she didn't pull away.

"Behave," she hissed before finally removing her hand and letting him speak.

"Hollow leg got served!" said the player who was sitting next to the one who bestowed Braeden his new moniker (I was still trying to learn all their names when they weren't wearing jerseys).

Braeden made a face like he was about to spew forth a few other colorful words, but then he sighed and said, "What, pray tell, does hollow leg mean?"

Pray tell?

Where on earth did he come up with that?

I gave Romeo a look, and he snickered.

"Means you eat so much your leg must be hollow to hold it all!"

The entire table of players laughed.

Seriously. Is this how a bunch of grown men behaved together?

"Gotta get my gains on if I want to pummel you in practice," Braeden yelled and returned to eating.

"We'll see about that, rookie!"

Braeden saluted them with his fork, and everyone at the table laughed and went back to eating.

Romeo slapped B on the back. "Already part of the team." He was looking at the table where Gamble and the coaches were. They'd been watching the exchange and now were talking quietly.

"Don't jinx me, Rome." Braeden warned and pushed away the plate.

"No more business talk," Valerie leaned around me (she sat herself right beside me) and told the boys.

Then she stood up and called the entire room to attention. She surprised me by giving a short speech, thanking everyone for traveling into town for the party, announcing an open bar for the rest of the night, and then making a toast to me and Romeo.

She didn't make anyone else get up and give a speech. Maybe she realized as best man, it would have been Braeden's job, and one speech from him at the reception was more than enough.

The band started playing louder, more lively music, and couples started to migrate toward the dance floor.

I watched as Drew led a dark-haired girl out onto the floor and pulled her close for a slow song. Trent was talking to one of the Knights—I think his last name was Thomas—and from what I could hear, the topic of conversation was football. Big surprise there.

Ivy excused herself to the ladies' room, and I was just about to follow her (it's true women do go to the ladies' room in packs), when I caught the tail end of Romeo and Braeden's conversation.

"Relax, B. It's going to work out," Romeo was saying.

"I like these guys, Rome, but we gotta be realistic. The odds aren't good."

They were talking about the draft picks. I knew how badly they wanted to play on the same team, and I wished there was something I could do to help make that happen.

Rachel Wintor was standing close by, talking with a man I hadn't been introduced to. I didn't know anything about football. I didn't know anything about the world Romeo and I were venturing into, but I did know one thing.

I'd learned it last year when Romeo got a contract because he became an underdog. He became a media darling.

I concentrated on walking the way I was supposed to in these dumb heels and approached Rachel and her companion. They both turned toward me, smiling like I knew they would.

It was a party in mine and Romeo's honor after all.

"Rachel," I said warmly, trying my best to not sound awkward and my normal antisocial self. "I just wanted to thank you again for coming."

"Oh, the pleasure is all mine. This has been a wonderful party." I was about to launch into my plan, but she kept on talking. "Rimmel, have you met Paul

Carson? He's the senior chief editor over at Brindle Publishing."

I extended my hand and smiled. "Pleasure to meet you, Mr. Carson. We are glad to have you here."

"I must say, Miss Hudson, the photographs we've printed in our magazines do not do you justice."

I felt myself blush, and I tried to not look like an idiot. "Thank you. So your company publishes magazines?"

"Oh, yes," Rachel gushed. "Brindle Publishing is an umbrella house. They handle many different types of publications."

I glanced back at Paul. "Sounds very diverse. Which magazines do you print?"

"Mostly sports related. We have brands for every major sport here in the United States. Your fiancé has been quite the regular in our football themed magazine *Kick Off.*"

I gasped. "I know that magazine! It's all over our house. Romeo and Braeden read it like the Bible."

Paul laughed heartily, and I felt self-conscious. But then I remembered that's why I was over here, and I smiled. "My other brother carries around a racing magazine…" I paused to think of the title. "*GearShark*," I finally said.

Paul chuckled. "That's one of ours, too."

"Well, you're very popular at our house." I widened my eyes a bit like I just had a great idea.

Clearly, I was learning a thing or two from Romeo.

"I would love to introduce you both to my brother, Braeden Walker." I glanced at Rachel. "I told you about him before." She nodded, and I looked at Paul, trying to smile like Romeo when he wanted something. "And I have no doubt Braeden and Romeo both would love to meet the man behind their Bible."

"Who could say no to an offer like that?" Paul grinned and spread his arm out wide for me to lead the way.

If good publicity, if popularity in the media helped get them jobs, then I would bring the media to Braeden... and lucky me, I had two people with lots of connections right here following behind me.

And yes, I was innocent, but I wasn't that innocent. I wasn't about to believe if Braeden did get a spot on the Knights like we all hoped for, it would be because the media made him look good. I understood much more went into something like that.

But it wouldn't hurt.

Good publicity was good for the Knights as a whole, and the more of a crowd their players drew in, the better.

Romeo and Braeden were standing in a group with a few players and their parents when I approached. Romeo saw me first and smiled, but then his eyes went to the people behind me and he gave me a barely there quizzical look.

I winked.

"Braeden," I said, angling myself in front of Romeo so I could get his attention.

"Sis," B answered, interrupting whatever he was saying to look at me.

Quickly, I made the introductions and threw out a couple of his stats just because I knew them. If he knew what I was doing, he didn't let on. He was as skilled as Romeo in that regard. Braeden was quite charming when he wanted to be, and years of playing for the Wolves taught him how to handle press.

He took control of the conversation, and I slid back away from the three of them because I didn't want to topic to somehow turn back to me or what I was wearing.

When I turned completely away and faced Romeo, I heard Braeden say, "That's like a football Bible!"

Paul and Rachel both laughed, and I gave myself a mental high-five.

"Dance with me." Romeo caught me around the waist and towed me onto the edge of the dance floor.

"Wait!" I protested and kicked off my heels before returning to his hold.

He laughed. "I like what you did back there," he said, dipping low and talking against my ear.

I stretched up a little and pressed closer against him. The gold silk tie he was wearing brushed against my skin. "I know he's nervous about the draft."

Romeo nodded. "Yeah. He's gonna be fine, though, baby. He's a good player. He's gotten better in the last year."

"Think he'll make it to the Knights?"

"I sure as hell hope so." It sounded like a prayer. But then he gazed down at me. "You're handling the press like a pro tonight."

"It'll take some getting used to. But it's not all bad. Especially if it helps B."

"I love you," he said soft.

My fingers played with the ends of the hair brushing against the collar of his jacket. "Love you." I laid my head against his chest and let him support most of my weight. The song playing was beautiful, something I'd never heard before.

My eyes drifted closed, and I exhaled. The night would be winding down soon. We still had a few hours left. I was sure. We'd need to stay and see everyone off, but for the most part, the night was almost over.

Valerie definitely knew how to host a party, and it convinced me more I should let her handle the entire wedding. April third was coming fast, and I knew if anyone could pull off an amazing wedding, it was her.

As I melted into my husband (who everyone thought was my fiancé) the air in the room shifted and became charged with a feeling that up until now had been absent.

Tension.

A few murmurs moved through the crowd.

Romeo stiffened.

"His son was the one who attacked Romeo and Rimmel," someone whispered.

In an instant, I pulled back from Romeo's arms and craned my neck, looking around. Romeo made a sound in the back of his throat. "Oh, hells no," he growled.

"I've come to congratulate the happy couple!" a man yelled. "No thanks to them, my son will never see an occasion such as this!"

A panicked feeling slammed into my middle like I'd been punched right in the gut.

The crowd shifted, and I caught a full-on view of our uninvited, unwelcome guest.

Zach's father.

CHAPTER THIRTY

#YouKnowItsTrue
Men are like public toilets.
They are either taken...
or full of shit.
#BuzzBoss

ROMEO

She winked at me.

She. Fucking. Winked.

I'd given out lots of winks in my lifetime. They never ceased to make the ladies giggle and panties drop.

Can't say I'd ever been on the receiving end of a wink.

Until now.

Until my *wife* went and freaking mastered the sexiest wink in the history of sexy winks.

On her first try.

Day-um.

When I pulled her out onto the dance floor, all I could think about was the time at Screamerz when we'd done a little more than dancing. I had to restrain myself tonight. I mean, this wasn't a nightclub, the lights weren't near dark, and my parents were in the room somewhere.

That last thought was enough to make the boner I was starting to rock die a swift and painful death.

This wasn't my first time at an event like this. I made some appearances last year during the season, attended a few events. And I grew up with my mother. She hosted crap like this on a regular basis. That meant I was used to it. Rim wasn't.

But damn if she didn't own the room.

You'd never know by looking at her that she hated this kind of stuff. She made it look natural. There had to be five hundred people here, easy, but she outshined them all.

Even from across the room, I felt her pull. The warmth of her smile, the light sound of her laughter. More than once, the shine of her wavy hair caught my attention when she shook her head beneath the lights.

And her legs.

Damn, what a pair of stems.

I don't know what the hell kind of magic those gold heels and flirty short/long dress of hers was wielding, but I was completely under her spell.

And it wasn't just me.

I saw people looking.

Hell, I looked for people looking (a guy needed to know who was checking out his girl). Eyes went back to her again and again. I even caught a few members of the Knights totally checking her out.

It pissed me off, but I didn't say a word. This wasn't the time or place. But once we got on the field, I'd deliver some payback.

Besides, she was mine. Totally. Completely. It didn't matter if men looked at her, because she didn't want them and she never would.

I knew how to keep my girl happy, and I'd spend the rest of my life doing it.

I sensed when he walked in. I didn't know who was here, just that someone or something that wasn't supposed to be was.

* * *

The heaviness that suddenly befell the room was intense. Even in a crowd, his presence rippled through swiftly until it stopped at me.

Robert was by one of the wide archways that led out into the hall that led outside. He was in a suit, but it wasn't in any presentable shape. The color was dull gray, and it only served to make him look worse.

His hair was disheveled, his jaw unshaven. The gray in his hair seemed a lot more pronounced, like he was aging at some exponential rate. The second Rimmel saw him, she pulled out of my arms, her body went rigid, and her face went pale.

It pissed me off, and I growled something, but I didn't think about what it was because Robert started yelling.

"I've come to congratulate the happy couple! No thanks to them, my son will never see an occasion such as this!"

I moved to stand in front of Rim and at the same time sought out Braeden in the crowd. I found him immediately. He was still standing with the two reporters, and my jaw tightened. He did not need this tonight.

He was well aware of who was here. He might have only heard that voice once, but it had been enough.

A man didn't forget the sound of the voice that accused him of murder.

Drew was on the dance floor, closest to Rim and me. I turned swiftly and picked her up, her bare feet dangling over the floor as I stepped over to Drew's side. He'd been dancing with some brunette, but when he saw us, he stepped away from her and toward my girl.

"Watch her," I ordered low and plunked Rim down beside him.

"I got her," Drew replied and put his arm across her shoulders.

Rimmel opened her mouth to argue, but I gave her a hard look. "Stay with Drew."

Her mouth slammed shut. I never talked to her like that. Sure, I bossed her around, but I never really meant that shit. I only did it 'cause I thought it was cute when she got pissed off.

But I wasn't joking now.

Drew angled himself in front of her, and I turned back. She might be mad at me later, and she could be mad all she wanted. At least she'd be safe and out of the crossfire that was surely about to start.

The crowd parted as I made my way toward Robert. He was leaving. Now. Somewhere not too far away, I heard my mother summoning security.

He'd be gone before they got here. I didn't like to make a scene, but sometimes it couldn't be helped. At least I wouldn't ruin his ugly-ass suit when I threw him out on his ass.

His hollow eyes locked on me. It wasn't a look of a man bent on revenge. It wasn't even a look of hate. Zach had those looks down to a science.

No, Robert Bettinger was a man in pain. He was a lost man acting out because he didn't know what else to do.

I felt kinda sorry for him.

Kinda.

This wasn't the time or place for his issues. He could put them back in his bag and check them at the door.

"Where is he?" Robert asked, his voice loud enough to carry. Not that it mattered. He could whisper, and everyone would still hear. The place was quiet enough to hear a mouse fart. Even the band had stopped playing.

"You aren't welcome here," I answered. "Please leave."

"Not too long ago, I'd have been on the guest list."

Yeah, well, that was before your son tried to kill my family.

"I bet the bastard who killed my son is on the guest list!"

I sucked in a breath and hurried the rest of the way toward him.

A few things happened at once.

Ivy entered through the same wide archway Robert had just come through. She must have been out in the bathroom in the hall. The second she saw him, her steps faltered and she took a step back.

I gave her a look, silently telling her to get the hell out of here before he saw her.

But, of course, Robert followed my gaze and all his attention went to Ivy. "You," he spat, with more dislike in his voice than before. "Have you been filling the society elite's head with lies about how my son raped you!"

A collective gasp went through the room.

All the blood drained from Ivy's face. She turned so white, so fast it scared me.

Braeden shoved through the crowd and stopped beside me just in time to see Ivy wobble on her feet and reach out a steadying hand to catch herself on the wall.

"You son of a bitch!" B roared and lunged forward.

I caught him around the waist, barely able to restrain him. As much as Robert deserved it, Braeden attacking him in a room full of people would only hurt B. Robert could use it as ammo in the case he was trying to build, and an entire room full of people including all the important Knights staff would get a front row seat to B's temper.

That would not be good publicity.

"Man, not now," I told him quietly. "Think about your future. *Think*."

Braeden fought against me some more. I put him in a tighter grip. "Look at Ivy," I demanded. "She's going to fall over. This is too fucking much. You need to take care of *her*."

The fight left his body instantly. He went completely slack.

I let go, and he rushed past Robert and lifted Ivy into his arms and hurried out of sight.

I gave the lead singer of the band a *what the fuck* Look and motioned for him to start playing again. Hopefully, the music would drown out Robert's yapping.

Gentle would be the last word used to describe how I was when I grabbed Robert right up under his armpit as the music began. It was some upbeat, happy song, and I wanted to laugh.

I towed Robert out of the room, my father hastening after us.

"I can't believe you had the nerve to show up here," Dad told his old colleague.

"I can't believe you had the nerve to throw a party! My son is dead."

"And we're all very sorry about that, Robert, but Zach's been gone for several months, and our family has a right to move on."

Security came around the corner down the hall and rushed forward.

'Bout fucking time.

Robert opened his mouth to say something no one wanted to hear, and I slapped a hand over his face. I was well aware of the reporters and cameramen watching from inside the door. People were riveted by whatever personal drama was conspiring right here under their noses.

"If you don't shut the fuck up right now"—I leaned in close so only he could hear my words—"you won't be the only one building a lawsuit."

His eyes flared and he tried to say something, but my hand blocked the words.

Dad sighed. "You know as well as I do that Romeo would be within his legal rights to file a restraining order. Is that what you want, Robert? Another dark cloud over your family? Would you like a lawsuit for defamation of character?"

Beneath my hand, his nostrils flared. He was like a bull in a china shop, a bomb about to detonate.

"What's going on here?" one of the security members asked.

"He needs to be escorted off the property," I said. "Now."

Robert was seized by both arms and all but hauled away.

"My son was nothing but a victim!" The broken sound that ripped from his chest made the back of my neck tighten. "He was a victim his entire life. It's all my fault."

Dad and I stood there for a long time, staring after him, even after he'd disappeared.

My father turned to me. "I hate to say this, but it was a good thing he showed up tonight."

"How much beer have you had tonight, Dad?" I muttered, still watching where he'd gone. If he came running back in here, I was gonna take him out.

I didn't think of Zach as a victim. I thought of him as an aggressor. But I guess it wasn't so out of left field that the guy had been a victim of something in his life. How else would his wild behavior make any sense?

"Not near enough." Dad chuckled and shook his head. "He just set fire to his credibility, and no less than five hundred people were here to see how unstable he behaved. If he ever somehow gets charges filed against Braeden, they won't stick because he clearly can't remain objective."

After I was sure he wasn't going to come back, I looked around for B and Ivy. They hadn't come back in. "I'm going to go talk to Braeden," I told Dad.

He nodded. "I'll let Rimmel know you're okay and with Braeden."

"Thanks." Dad turned back, but I called his name. I stepped close to him and spoke quietly. "How much damage did Robert do to Braeden tonight?"

He sighed and rubbed a hand over his face. "I don't know. I would say none because he never actually accused Braeden directly, but you and I both know everyone realizes Braeden and Ivy were at the scene of the accident. Those details spread like wildfire."

"I can't believe he tried to make it sound like Ivy was lying. That was really fucking low. No one had to know she was raped."

My father's expression hardened. "I agree. That was uncalled for. I'll go inside and try and do some damage control, see what people are saying."

Yeah, maybe it was callous to be standing here talking about doing damage control for Braeden's reputation and career. But this was my brother. His life. I wouldn't let Zach take anything else from my family.

"Excuse me!" a familiar voice echoed from the crowd. Seconds later, Rimmel emerged from the gathered people and burst into the hall. Drew and Trent scrambled along behind her, and it kinda made me smile.

It was Snow White followed by two of her dwarfs.

Well, really big dwarfs.

"Is he gone?" she asked the second she saw me.

I nodded and held out my hand. She rushed forward and slid hers home. Drew and Trent hung back a little, and I hitched my chin toward the doors leading outside. "Ivy's out there."

Outside was dark and cold. Patches of snow clung to the sidewalk and the grassy area beyond. The wind wasn't blowing very hard, but there was enough of a breeze to make it feel even colder.

I stripped off the black suit jacket I was wearing over my white dress shirt and gold tie as my eyes scanned the dark for B. They weren't too far ahead, leaning against the outside of the building close to the large wooden deck, which was closed for the winter.

Rimmel started forward first, and I draped my jacket around her as she went. That dress was beautiful, but she was gonna freeze her ass off. Thank God she put her shoes back on or I'd be stripping mine off too, and she'd been walking around in boats.

She shoved her arms through the sleeves as we hurried forward, the long length of her hair trapped beneath the coat, and she made no attempt to pull it free. She likely didn't even notice, as she was too focused on our family.

"Ivy!" Rimmel fretted. "Are you okay?"

"What the hell is wrong with my sister?" Drew said, alarmed. His footsteps quickened on the pavement as he went around us all to stop right beside Braeden.

Ivy was leaning against the building, B's suit jacket pulled around her shoulders and her hands tucked up beneath the lapels, holding it in place. Braeden had both hands leaning on the building on either side of her body, as if he were worried she might fall over and he'd need to catch her.

"I'm fine," she said, her voice a little shaky. "I just wasn't expecting him to show up and tell everyone I was raped."

Rimmel's hand found mine and clutched. I glanced down at her, but she wasn't looking at me. She was looking toward Ivy with a concern on her face.

"Are you feeling all right?" she asked.

Ivy nodded, an action I knew Rim couldn't see because of B and Drew standing in front of her.

I looked at B, trying to gauge where he was with his emotions. His face was shuttered, but his shoulders were so tense it looked painful. He was fucking pissed, but he was holding on to it all for Ivy's sake.

"He's been escorted out of here. He's not getting back in. He might have said some shit in front of the reporters to stir the pot, but he lost all credibility with that stunt."

Braeden shoved off the wall and swung to face me. "You think I give a flying fuck about my career right now?" he yelled. "That motherfucker just accused Ivy of lying about what his scumbag son did to her! Acted like it was her who was in the wrong."

"He's his father," Ivy said miserably.

Braeden's eyes flared. "That's no fucking excuse! If my son did something so fucking reprehensible, I would never defend him!"

I agreed. One hundred percent.

But Braeden's words seemed to upset Ivy more.

A sob tore from her throat, and she started to cry. Drew pulled her into his chest and hugged her close, glaring at B over her head.

"Ivy..." Braeden sighed and most of his anger dissolved. He looked tired when he turned to me. "I'm gonna take her home. You cool with that?"

I nodded, wishing I could leave with them. This was my fucking party, and I had to at least go inside and smile and act like nothing was wrong. If the media smelled trouble, they'd be all over us all. Braeden might not care right now, but he would if the press was swarming outside our house.

"Get the hell out of here," I said and pulled my car keys out of my pocket. "Take the Cat. I'll have my parents drop us home." The four of us had driven together, leaving B's truck behind.

"I have my Mustang," Trent said from beside Drew. "I'll drive everyone home, and you and Rim can keep the Cat here for when you can get out."

"Thanks," B said and motioned for me to keep the keys.

"I'll go pull it around," Trent said.

"C'mon, Ives," Drew said gently and started to lead her away.

"Hells no," Braeden snapped and reached for her. "She stays with me."

She fit herself into his side with a sigh. Drew looked like he wanted to argue, but Ivy shook her head. "It's fine. Go with Trent. My feet hurt. I'll wait here."

Drew jogged after Trent, and then it was just the four of us.

"I'm really sorry about tonight, princess." I called her by the nickname she hated, hoping it would get her to smile.

It didn't.

"I should have had security at the door watching for him."

"This isn't your fault, Romeo," Ivy said, sounding a little more like herself. "I shouldn't let it get to me. It's just now everyone knows. Now, whenever they look at me, it's all they'll see. I don't want to see what I'm trying to move past in everyone's eyes when they look at me."

Braeden closed his eyes momentarily and his throat worked when he swallowed.

"We'll find a way to put a gag order on him," I vowed.

"Damage is done," B muttered. "I outta go find that—"

"Stop right there," I intoned. "You already have enough to worry about without adding Robert crying assault."

"Fucker deserves it," he muttered darkly.

"He ain't worth it," I reminded him.

A few yards away, Trent's silver Mustang slid up to the curb just on the other side of the grass.

"I left my clutch inside," Ivy said, straightening.

"I'll go grab it for you," Rimmel offered and then went rushing off inside.

Before the door behind her could swing shut, it was pushed open and a few of the Knights walked out. "There he is," Thomas said when he saw me.

I hitched my chin. "What's going on?"

"Nothing, just wanted to come offer our support to our quarterback and our rookie."

"Decent of you," I said and held out my fist to pound it out. Thomas returned the gesture as he and four other teammates stopped beside us.

Blanchard was one of them. He was hanging toward the back, just watching. I took it as a sign of good faith that he was out here supporting.

"Thanks, guys," Braeden said, tightening his arm around Ivy.

"Don't you worry about that douche, Mrs. Hollow Leg," Thomas said, focusing on her. "No one's gonna hassle you about some drunk asshole's attempt at attention."

Ivy's mouth kicked up in a smile. "Mrs. Hollow Leg?"

Crawford, the player beside Thomas, nodded. "Yeah, you're one of us now. We take care of our own."

Yeah.

This was definitely a team I was fucking proud to be on.

I might have been unsure about the Knights when I walked onto their team last season, but all my doubts were gone now. This was my new pack, and they were accepting my family as their own.

I could tell by the look on Braeden's face that he was surprised they'd rally around us that fast.

Of course, there was an asshole in every bunch that had to ruin everyone's good time.

"He's not one of us, not yet," Blanchard said from the back.

My hackles rose.

Thomas, Crawford, and Bingle all looked at him. "Technically, no," Thomas said. "But it's just details. Soon as the draft's over, he will be."

"We'll see," Blanchard droned.

"What the fuck is your problem, man?" Braeden spewed. "You got a problem with me personally, or is it just because Rome knocked you out of the top spot?"

Crawford whistled beneath his breath. So the team had noticed the undercurrents going around. I wondered if they had, but I never brought it up. That's not the kind of leader I wanted to be.

"I didn't realize I'd been replaced." Blanchard lifted an eyebrow.

"Details." Braeden scoffed.

Blanchard didn't like being challenged like this, especially in front of four of his teammates, one of which was me. He stepped around all the guys and up to Braeden. "Don't get your hopes up too high, *Rookie*. When the media starts making up headlines about the NFL hopeful's dirty past as a murderer, those *details* you seem so unconcerned about are gonna bite you in the ass."

"Chill, man," Thomas said and slapped Blanchard on the shoulder.

Blanchard shrugged him off and glared at B.

Don't do it, Braeden. Don't let him get the best of you.

"You said it yourself," Braeden retorted calmly. "Any headlines they run with will be made up."

He turned away to guide Ivy toward the Mustang. I was fucking proud of him right there. Blanchard offered him a big pile of ammo, and B walked away.

"I don't know," Blanchard called out. "You look like a murderer to me."

"Shut the fuck up," I growled.

The other players' eyes widened, and they all took a collective step back from their quarterback.

B laughed, an amused-sounding chuckle, and dropped his arm from around Ivy to glance back. "Enjoy your spot on the bench this season."

Braeden might have been in total control of his anger just then, but not everyone was.

Blanchard fucking snapped. "You son of a bitch," he ground out and leapt forward.

"No!" Ivy shouted and shoved away from Braeden to step in front of the giant football player rushing at my brother.

Blanchard's body went taut when he saw her, but it was too late. He freaking body-checked her. Rammed into her so hard she went flying backward and hit the cold, hard ground.

The jacket that had been draped over her shoulders flew off, landing in a heap behind her body.

She cried out when she hit the ground, and from inside the Mustang, I heard Drew yell. Braeden's neck bulged with anger, and I grabbed Blanchard and tossed him behind me.

"Hold him!" I demanded, and my teammates grabbed ahold of him. I might not let Braeden pummel his ass, but Blanchard wasn't going to walk away from this unharmed.

Braeden moved to push by me, and I shoved him back. He looked at me, incredulous, about to yell, but Ivy whimpered.

Both of us forgot about Blanchard and rushed toward her.

She was still on the ground, sitting up, hunched in on herself with her arm wrapped tightly around her middle.

"Ivy." Braeden dropped to his knees beside her. "Baby, are you hurt?"

She made a sound of pain and hunched around herself even more, as if she were doubling over from a cramp.

A bad feeling wormed around inside me, but I didn't know why.

"No," she moaned.

"No what?" Braeden panicked.

"The baby," she sobbed, pressing a hand to her stomach.

Everything stopped.

Braeden froze like someone hit pause on a movie.

We all stared down at Ivy, wondering if what we just heard was actually what we just heard.

"What did you just say?" Braeden whispered, his voice deadly soft as he stared.

Ivy looked at him with tears streaking down her face. "Our baby."

Braeden looked at her hand where she was cradling her stomach. His hand shot out to hover over her middle. He was completely speechless, his eyes wild.

But then Ivy whimpered again and shifted, as if she were in pain. Braeden snapped out of it, and carefully— so damn carefully—he lifted her into his arms.

"We're going to the ER." His voice was almost unrecognizable.

Before I could say anything, he started running toward the Mustang.

Holy fucking shit.

Ivy was pregnant.

HERE COMES THE BRIDE... & A BABY? (AKA PART THREE)

CHAPTER THIRTY-ONE

Zach was murdered?
His father seems to think so.
#GrievingFather OR #Truth

#BuzzBoss

IVY

I never set out to have a baby.

Hell, it was so far removed from any plan I had for my life, it never even occurred to me as a possibility when I started wrinkling my nose at the taste of coffee, feeling dizzy and exhausted, and wanting things like orange juice and grilled cheese.

I was on the pill. Getting pregnant shouldn't have happened.

But it did.

I was.

I was growing another person.

One part me and one part Braeden.

Shock was an understatement for how I felt when I looked at my calendar one day and realized I was over a month late.

Shock *and* fear.

But even though I was terrified, even though I knew my life was going to change forever and I had no earthly idea how to tell Braeden or what he would say…

I was happy.

So happy.

How could I not be? A part of Braeden was growing inside me.

I didn't know how to tell him. It seemed impossible to just walk in the door one night and announce I was pregnant and his life would never be the same, that he would be bound to me for the rest of our lives, no matter what.

I knew Braeden loved me. That was never a question. But we weren't ready for this. Our life together thus far had been tumultuous. We were still dealing with the effects from everything that happened.

Braeden was on the cusp of what I knew was going to be an amazing football career. I was trying to figure out my place in fashion. We were still navigating the world as a couple.

How then could I look him in the eye and tell him this?

What if he was angry? What if he hated me? What if he decided it was all just too much?

What if now none of that even mattered?

I'd seen that giant guy coming at Braeden after he'd turned to walk away. I'd been upset and wanting to go home, but in that moment, that hadn't mattered. All I saw was someone threatening the man I loved. The man who'd been suffering needlessly so much lately.

And there he was walking away, trying to be the bigger guy.

Okay, fine. B was far from innocent.

But he was going to let that go. He was going to get in the Mustang and drive away.

Moose Head had other ideas.

The man who knocked me down = Moose Head.

He was giant, scowling, and came charging at Braeden. Plus, he had a big head. Like a moose.

I pushed B back, not that he actually went anywhere, but I stepped between them, thinking I'd stop the situation before it got any worse. I only wanted to protect Braeden.

And now it might have cost our baby its life.

I sat there curled in on myself, arms wrapped around my middle, as unstoppable tears dripped down my face. I'd had a little time to digest this. I'd had a little time to get used to the idea of a baby, and I'd gotten to carry him around inside me.

Braeden hadn't gotten any of that.

I hadn't even told him.

God, this was not the way I wanted to tell him.

He might not get any time at all now. His baby could be gone practically before he ever knew it existed.

"I'm so sorry," I sobbed, the words hoarse and low.

"Don't say that," Braeden demanded, his voice as gravelly as mine. I was gathered in his lap in the front seat of the Mustang. His arms were all the seat belt I needed; he was so tightly wrapped around me. I could feel the hammering of his heart against his chest and feel the ragged breaths he pulled into his lungs at an uneven rate.

His hands were fisted tightly, but they lay gentle at my sides.

I wanted to sit up and explain, to tell him everything, but all that came out of me was tears.

After I dropped the bomb, he'd rushed me into the car, sat down with me in his lap, and demanded Trent drive before the door was even shut. No one said a word about him holding me in his lap while Trent drove like a wild man toward the ER.

"Braeden, you better tell me what the fuck is wrong with my sister," Drew demanded from the backseat.

He'd been just as silent as I. The only words he' spoken since demanding we get to the ER was the brief rebuff of my apology.

"Ivy's pregnant," Braeden ground out.

I couldn't tell what he was feeling from the sound of his voice.

"You asshole!" Drew swore from the backseat. "You got my sister pregnant, then let that moose body check her into the ground!"

See, he totally looked like a moose.

Braeden didn't say anything. He didn't try to defend himself. The only reaction Drew's words got was the even more frantic beating of his heart.

"Now isn't the time, Drew," Trent said. It seemed he was the only voice of reason in this car.

"You're taking his side!" Drew demanded.

I felt rather than saw Trent jerk. "I'm on Ivy's side right now. And you acting like a fucking moron is *not* helping her condition."

That shut Drew up.

Thank God.

"Ivy, are you in pain?" Braeden asked. He sounded in pain himself.

"I'm not sure," I mumbled, wiping at my face with the backs of my hands. "I don't feel good. That was a really hard fall… The baby…"

I started crying all over again.

Braeden pushed my head into his chest, and I clung to him, finally releasing my middle so I could dig my hands into his dress shirt and hang on.

"I need an anchor right now, B." I sobbed. "Please, please, don't let me drift away."

I'd never really thought much about what a piece of glass felt like when it shattered. But now I understood. Glass was deceiving in some ways. It looked thick and strong. Even though it was clear, you always knew it was there—sometimes a barrier to all sorts of things. Like rain. Snow. Wind.

Pain.

But glass wasn't always as strong as it looked. All it took was one well-placed hit to crack it. Once the slightest pressure was applied to the break, it splintered and spread, snaking across the surface and threating to break itself in two.

And sometimes, a piece of glass didn't just break.

It shattered into a million jagged pieces.

That was how I felt just then, as though I had cracked but was holding it together—only to have something hit me in just the right spot.

"I got you," Braeden whispered against my hair. "You're not going anywhere." He lifted his head and spoke over mine. "Here, just drop me."

The car stopped swiftly, but I didn't jerk forward at all. Braeden was holding me too tightly for that. The passenger door opened instantly, and Drew stood on the sidewalk. He reached in for me, and Braeden growled.

We got out of the car as one. Braeden didn't even pause. He literally just kept moving. A car door slammed behind us, but I wasn't sure if Drew had gotten in the car or stayed with us.

The swooshing of the automatic double doors was loud, and the air they pushed at me caused me to shiver. The shiver turned into the shakes, and I tried to no avail to stop my body from quaking.

I knew he had to feel it. I was too close for him not to. But he didn't say a word; he just quickly walked through the ER and right up to the desk.

"Sir?" a nurse said.

"I need a doctor," Braeden rasped. "Right now. She's pregnant and she fell. I…" The way his voice just dropped away made me hurt.

"Miss, are you bleeding?" the nurse asked.

I jerked like she shot me. I didn't want to bleed.

"What the hell kind of question is that to ask her out here in front of everyone?" Braeden demanded.

I sucked in a ragged breath and lifted my head. "Excuse him. He's just…" *Scared.* "Worried. I don't know if I'm bleeding."

The nurse looked back and forth between us. Her eyes softened. "First baby?"

Braeden made a sound.

More tears leaked from my eyes.

"Come on," she said, grabbing a clipboard full of papers and a pen. "Follow me."

She had no idea the war she'd avoided by taking me back right away. Braeden probably would have brought the roof down if she told him to sit in the waiting room.

Thank God.

I needed answers. I needed to know…

She yanked back a curtain to a tiny cubicle with a narrow bed in the center. Braeden stepped right up to it but didn't lay me down. Instead, he stood there holding me, standing over the mattress.

The curtain made a scraping sound as it was pulled back around, closing us off from prying eyes.

"You'll need to put her on the bed," the nurse said, not unkind.

Reluctantly, he laid me down, and I tried not to wince.

"How far along are you?" she asked, pen hovering above the clipboard.

I glanced at Braeden and then away. "Twelve weeks."

He sucked in a breath, and I didn't dare look at him again.

"What caused the fall?" she asked.

"What?" I echoed, barely hearing her. I was desperate to look at Braeden's face but so incredibly afraid, too.

"A ladder? Down the stairs? Off a chair?"

Oh. She wanted to know how I fell.

I licked my lips. "Someone pushed me."

The nurse's eyes snapped up. "Someone pushed you?" She looked at Braeden.

A little bit of panic left me to make room for indignation. "Don't even look at him like that," I snapped. "It was someone else. A very large football player. I hit the ground hard."

"Why do you look familiar to me?" the nurse asked, continuing to look at Braeden.

He rose to his full, impressive height. "Who the hell cares? She needs medical attention. This is not some friendly house call!"

"Date of your last period?" she asked.

I told her. Then I said, "His mother is Nurse Walker. She's a nurse here. And he was just drafted by the NFL. We aren't trying to be rude, but I'm very scared." I felt my lip wobble.

"Shit, Ivy, not the lip." Braeden swore.

I bit down on it, trying to make it stop.

"You're Caroline's son?" The nurse glanced back at B and smiled.

"My baby!" Braeden roared and pointed at me.

I didn't bother apologizing again. I wanted answers, too. And I was too busy crying again because Braeden had acknowledged his child.

The nurse pulled the top paper off the clipboard and then placed the whole thing on the bed. "I need you to fill this out as soon as possible." Then she handed me an ugly hospital gown. "Put this on and then go to the bathroom at the end of the hall"—she pointed in a direction—"and check to see if you're bleeding. If you are, I need to know immediately."

"Is that bad if I am?" I whispered.

"It all depends."

That was the shittiest answer I'd ever heard.

I nodded and picked up the gown.

"I'll get the doctor." She started to leave and then turned back. "Try not to worry too much. It's not good for you or the baby. You're early into your pregnancy, honey, and your body is built to protect that little baby. Chances are you'll be just fine."

I tried to be comforted by her words, but I wasn't. I wouldn't be until I heard a doctor tell me so.

Little baby.

Calling it little made it seem that much more fragile.

Yep. I started crying. Again.

She walked around the curtain, and Braeden did something that showed me just how freaked out he really was.

"Ma'am," he called to the nurse, poking his head outside.

I didn't hear her reply, but she must have because he spoke again.

"Page my mother."

CHAPTER THIRTY-TWO

Team rivalry?
Someone needs to learn who their
Alpha is.

#BuzzBoss

BRAEDEN

Tiny hands.

Tiny feet.

So much tiny for such a huge, life altering thing.

I stared through the wall of glass, seeing things I'd seen before, but never actually saw. There were three little carts parked behind the glass. All of them on big wheels with steel frames and legs that held the clear containers with little cards on the front. The cards had neatly typed names, identifying the babies inside.

Baby.

Ivy was pregnant.

Maybe.

As I stood there and watched the three tiny, brand new lives squirm and sleep inside those clear rolling baskets, I couldn't conjure up any of the anger that usually was so quick to come.

I should be frothing at the mouth right now for a piece of Blanchard, for what he'd done.

But all I could see were those three tiny babies and hear that one terrifying word on repeat: *Maybe.*

I was terrified she was pregnant. I was terrified she wasn't.

I didn't want a baby. *That baby is part of Ivy. Part of me.*

How the hell did this happen? How long has she known? Why didn't she tell me?

Maybe.

One of the babies, bundled up in blue, somehow got his hand free of the tightly wrapped blanket (for real, though, he looked like a burrito) and his miniature fist started waving around like he had no control over the thing whatsoever.

I stared at him, totally entranced as his fist shook and he began to fuss.

Babies were loud.

They needed lots of stuff.

Somehow he managed to stuff part of his hand into his mouth. His fussing quieted as he sucked at his fingers.

He was kinda cute.

Abruptly, I spun away from the glass and leaned my back against it instead, kicking out one of my legs and crossing my arms over my chest. The white tile floors were shiny underfoot, and people bustled around up the hall.

But for some unspoken reason, no one came down the hall where I stood. They left me here in peace to drown in thoughts and misery.

I don't know how much time passed. It likely wasn't long. Just long enough for me to freak out away from prying eyes.

A body settled next to mine, taking up almost the same stance against the glass. I didn't have to look to know who it was. There was only one person it could be.

"Figured you'd be here," Romeo said.

"I needed a minute, just some time to… ah, think."

"Ivy?" he asked.

I shook my head once. "Don't know. Kicked me out of the room for an exam." I rubbed a hand over my face and groaned.

God, she was a wreck. She couldn't stop crying, and the way she kept hunching in on herself, around our child… protecting the piece of us that was growing inside her.

She needed an anchor right now, but I felt like a boat with a hole in it.

I was taking on water, filling up slowly, and I was beginning to sink. I felt as helpless right now as I had the night I watched Zach's BMW flip over three times.

"So we're waiting…" Romeo surmised.

"Yeah." I leaned my head back against the glass, looking up at the ceiling.

We stood there in silence together for a few minutes. He didn't say anything. He was just there.

Like a brother.

"Where is everyone?" I asked.

"In the waiting room."

"Drew still gonna beat my ass?"

"He'll have to go through me."

"I don't need you to fight my battles, Rome."

"I know."

We lapsed into silence again.

"I don't know anything about being a father," I whispered.

"I don't think anyone knows anything about being a father," he whispered back.

"Mine sure as hell didn't. Fucked me up good."

"What's the one thing you always wanted from your father that you never got?"

"For him to not hit my mother?" I quipped.

Romeo gave me a look.

I sighed. "For him to love me. For him to fucking care."

"And look at you," Rome said, pushing off the wall and turning to look through the glass. "You're not even sure you want this kid yet, but you already care a whole fucking a lot."

"I want him," I said, my voice hoarse.

"What's that?" Rome looked at me.

I looked up, caught his eye. I knew he heard me. He just wanted me to say it again. "I want him."

Romeo smiled. "I know."

"How'd you know?" I pushed off the wall and turned so we were both staring through the glass.

"Because if that was Rim, I'd feel the same way."

"What if she lost it?" I hated saying it out loud. I hated the way it made me feel. Like I'd spent four days doing nothing but throwing up and my insides were empty and aching.

I'd known about this for all of five minutes—most of which I'd spent going out of my mind and practically pissing myself. But even while I was doing all of that, deep down I was petrified there would be no baby at all.

Romeo pulled in a breath like he also would be broken. "We'll deal with it. As a family."

I glanced over at him, grateful as hell he was here. His arms were crossed over his chest, and I could see part of his right hand. It was red with a few raw-looking cuts.

"What happened to your hand?"

He looked down at it, flexed his fingers against his folded arm, and grunted. "That was my nephew and sister he knocked around."

Surprise rippled through me. "You went after Blanchard?"

"Didn't have to go after him. He stayed right there for his beating."

I grunted. "So I can't ruin my career, but you can ruin yours?"

"Pretty much." He smirked.

"I'd give you the finger, but there are babies present." I motioned toward the windows.

"Already thinking like a dad," he mused.

The statement punched me in the gut. I didn't even know if I was going to be a dad.

"I really appreciate you being here, Rome. For being my family."

"I'll always be your family, man. No matter what." His voice was sincere.

I hugged him.

Right there in front of the babies. Gave the little guys a show.

He hugged me back, and for once, I wasn't worried about who might see. "I love you, Rome," I admitted.

"I love you too, B."

We pulled apart then.

"Dude, that baby in there kinda looks like a wrinkled grandpa," Romeo cracked.

I laughed. "You say that shit about my kid and I'll pound ya."

"Hopefully, he'll look like Ivy." He turned to me and smirked.

"You think it's a boy?" Earlier, he'd call him a nephew.

He shrugged one shoulder. "Sounds good to me."

It did sound good.

"Braeden," a familiar voice carried down the hall. My entire body tensed, and I jerked around.

"Mom. Ivy—" I rushed out, my inner panic skyrocketing.

"She's fine, honey. They're going to do an ultrasound, to check everything out. I told her I'd find you, see if you wanted to be in the room."

I rushed down the hall, not even glancing back at Romeo.

"Let us know." He called after me.

I lifted a hand in response. I wasn't able to find my voice to answer.

This was it.

I was about to find out my future.

CHAPTER THIRTY-THREE

Family takes care of family.

#FamilyIsntAlwaysBlood

#BuzzBoss

IVY

He wouldn't let me walk to the bathroom.

The second I changed into the dreadful gown.

(Seriously, though, why can't these gowns be attractive? Isn't it bad enough that patients have to be in here for some dreadful reason, but then to be handed a gown that's seriously depressing is just wrong. Wrong, I tell ya.)

Anyway, the second I was wearing the aforementioned heinous gown, I moved to get down off the bed. and Braeden growled.

He *growled*.

At me.

I never would have let him get away with that if I wasn't still shaking like a leaf and so scared. A few nurses and patients looked our way when he carried me down the small hallway toward the bathroom. When he walked into the small room and stood there like he expected me to check for bleeding while he was standing there, I shook my head.

"I need a minute."

His face darkened, and my eyes yet again filled with tears. "Please. I'll be fine. Just wait outside the door."

Gingerly, I was placed on my feet, and the door closed behind me.

I stared at myself in the tiny mirror beneath the god-awful lighting. I told myself that was the reason I looked so bad. It was a lie I didn't believe. I knew the truth. I looked terrible because I felt terrible.

He'd yet to say much about the baby.

I had no idea how he was feeling other than being extremely worried.

I lifted the gown, bunched it around my waist, and reached for my panties. I had a pretty good idea if I was bleeding or not, but I couldn't be sure. I felt so freaked but also out of it that I couldn't really rely on what I thought.

My feelings were all over the place. I'd never felt so wild with emotion. Not even the night I remembered that Zach raped me.

My back was aching. That couldn't be a good sign. What if I hit the ground so hard it was going to cause a miscarriage?

What if the pains in my back were the beginning of the end?

A sob broke free from my throat, and I bit down on my lip, hard, so no one outside would hear.

I'd been walking around in sort of a panic about this pregnancy since I found out. It was amazing how fast any doubts and fears I had disappeared when I was faced with not being pregnant anymore.

Taking a deep breath, I looked.

Then I used the facilities and checked again.

The sound of the flushing toilet covered up the first sob that ripped from my throat. And I managed to hold the rest in while I washed my hands.

The second I shut the water off, I caught my reflection in the mirror again, and the dam opened up again.

I gripped the sides of the white porcelain sink and cried. It didn't matter how many times I told myself to get it together, there was no way I could.

The door burst open, and Braeden filled the doorway. I glanced behind me at his stricken eyes, and it made me cry worse.

"Oh, baby," he murmured and picked me up again. I buried my face in his neck on the way back to our little cubicle.

He sat on the bed with me in his arms. I climbed closer into his lap and breathed in his scent. The tie he'd been wearing had long since been ripped away, and the buttons of the white dress shirt were undone at his neck. As I cried, my tears slid down his neck and disappeared beneath the collar of his shirt.

"Ivy." He tried to pull me back, but I clung to him. I didn't want to see the look in his eyes. "Ivy, I need to know. Was there... was there blood?"

"No." I wailed. My shoulders shook.

His whole body seemed to sag. "Isn't that a good thing?"

"My back hurts." I wailed again. "I don't feel good."

"Okay," he soothed, rubbing a warm palm up my back. He had big hands, and it made me feel a little more secure.

My sobs turned into hiccups and my eyes slid closed.

The sound of the curtain being pulled back made me stiffen, but I didn't pull away.

"Mom," Braeden said, relief in his voice.

"One of the girls on the floor called me, then Romeo did, too, but no one would say what was wrong. What in the world happened?"

I lifted my head and tried to smile. "Hi, Ms. Walker."

"Ivy, honey." Worry marred her beautiful face, and she was still dressed in the navy gown she'd worn to the party earlier. "What's happened?"

I swallowed and looked at Braeden. I couldn't say it.

"Ivy's pregnant. After we went outside at the hotel... she fell, and now she's worried—*we're* worried—about the baby."

He said he was worried about the baby.

I buried my face in his neck again.

Behind me, she gasped. "A baby?"

I felt B nod. "It was a surprise."

He didn't even act like he'd only just found out. He made it sound like we were totally in this together.

"That's wonderful!" she burst out.

I started crying more.

Braeden must have glared at her because she came rushing over. "Oh, honey. I didn't mean to upset you. What have the doctors said?"

"We're still waiting," B said shortly.

"That's not acceptable. I'll go pull some strings."

"Thank you." The gratitude in his voice was overwhelming.

I felt a tentative touch on my arm, and I glanced up. "We're gonna know something really soon, okay. Try to calm down."

I nodded.

His mom left, but I heard her out in the hall, barking orders. I'd never heard her sound that way, so authoritative and bossy.

"Oh shit," said B. "Mom's on the warpath."

"Braeden." I sat back and met his eyes. The warm chocolate color was so welcome to my cold and trembling insides.

He stroked the side of my head. "We'll talk after we hear something, okay, baby?"

I nodded and snuggled back into his chest.

Within seconds, his mother had rounded up a doctor and nurse and a lot of results.

"Braeden," she said briskly, pulling back the curtain. "We need some space in here. Ivy's going to be examined. Then I'll come find you."

"It's okay," I whispered.

He left me then to the prodding yet capable hands of the doctor and nurse. I asked Braeden's mom to stay. I liked her, and it made me feel better to have someone nearby that I trusted.

She stood up by my head while I was examined and poked and prodded. I answered a hundred questions, and the entire time, the doctor nodded and the nurse wrote down notes.

When the exam was done, he straightened and looked at me. My hands rung in the crappy paper sheet they placed over my lower half.

"I see no signs of miscarriage."

I sniffled loudly and sagged against the mattress.

"Everything appears to be as it should. Because you didn't fall from something high, the risk of really harming the fetus is slim. Your body is very prepared to protect a developing child, especially since it's still so small."

I nodded, relieved but still nervous.

He smiled. "Your first pregnancy?" He glanced at Caroline, then back at me. "An unexpected surprise?"

I felt my hackles rise. "Unexpected, yes, but that in no way means I care any less about this baby."

He smiled. "Good to know. New mothers tend to panic more quickly, so it's understandable why you were so worried. You did the right thing coming in immediately."

"Why does my back hurt?"

"Probably because you fell on it."

I know he wasn't trying to make me feel dumb, but I did. "The baby..." I murmured.

"We'll do an ultrasound just to be on the safe side and for your peace of mind." Beside me, Caroline was nodding her approval. "But as of now, I honestly see no cause for concern. There is no reason why you won't continue on with a healthy pregnancy."

I wiped away the stray tears on my cheeks.

"I'm just going to get the ultrasound machine. I'll be right back." The doctor and nurse left.

I pressed my hands to my face. Then I jerked them away. "Braeden."

"I'll go get him," his mother said and ran from the room.

By the time he pulled open the curtain and stuck his head in, the doctor and nurse were back and prepping me for the ultrasound.

"This the father?" the doctor asked.

"Yes," I said, and he slipped into the room and came to my side.

"Okay, Blondie?" he murmured and kissed my forehead.

"So far so good," I replied.

"Who's ready to see their baby?" the doctor announced.

The nurse squirted this really cold, clear gel on my lower abdomen, and the doctor pressed a wand-looking thing attached to the machine by the bed onto the area and spread it around.

"There we go," he said a few minutes later and pointed to the screen.

Braeden and I both stared over at the small black and white screen with a bunch of moving shapes and blobs.

I couldn't tell what anything was, and it honestly didn't make me feel any better.

The doctor started pointing out various parts inside me, and I wanted to scream I only cared about the baby, but I held it in. Maybe he needed to look at everything surrounding the fetus, too.

"Ahh." A minute later he smiled. "There he is."

"Where?" I asked anxiously.

"This shape right here." He outlined the area with his finger. "Everything looks great."

He glanced away from the screen at us. "Baby is happy and healthy in there."

Braeden was leaning on the side of the bed, intent on the screen. Upon hearing the news, I grabbed his arm and started crying.

"Are you sure?" Braeden asked, still staring at the screen and rubbing at his hair with his free hand. It was wild-looking already from the way he'd been raking his hands through it all night.

I blinked through my waterworks and watched him. His eyes never left the little shape that made up our child. He stared at it intently, this look of awe on his face.

"I'm sure. Everything looks as it should be." He smiled. "You said you were twelve weeks along?"

I nodded. "That's what they calculated when I went in for a pregnancy test."

"I'd put you not quite that far along," he said and clicked a few more buttons like he was double-checking a few things.

Through it all, Braeden watched the screen.

"Estimated due date is September twentieth."

I nodded. That was later than I was originally told, but it was fine with me. We were going to need all the time we could to be ready for this.

The doctor pulled away the wand and replaced it on the machine. The nurse handed me a tissue to clean off the gel on my stomach, and I started wiping it away.

Braeden's hand caught mine and he took over, gently cleaning up my stomach.

"You said him," B said.

"Figure of speech," the doctor said. "It's too early to tell what the sex of the baby is. You'll be able to find that out when she's further along."

"Thank you," I said, finally feeling like I could breathe.

My baby was okay.

He smiled. "I'll have the nurse print out a couple photos of the ultrasound so you can take them with you. I see no reason to keep you, so I'll get your discharge papers together, and you can be on your way.

Just take it easy for the next couple days. The back pain should go away on its own, but if it doesn't, call your regular OB-GYN and make an appointment."

"I will, thank you."

Braeden stepped away from the bed and held out his hand. "Doc, thank you for giving us peace of mind so quickly."

The doctor shook Braeden's hand. "My pleasure. You all have a good night."

He left, and the nurse went with him.

Braeden and I locked eyes. "You took about ten years off my life tonight, Blondie."

"I'm really sorry." I dragged in an uneven breath.

"Don't be sorry, sweetheart. I'm just glad you're okay."

But what about the baby? It was on the tip of my tongue, but I didn't ask.

"Everyone's out in the waiting room. I'm gonna go tell them what's going on."

"Tell them all I said thank you for being here."

He kissed my forehead. "I will. Be right back."

When I was alone, I lay back against the mattress and closed my eyes. Thank goodness everything was okay.

Physically, anyway.

Now all that was left was to talk to Braeden.

CHAPTER THIRTY-FOUR

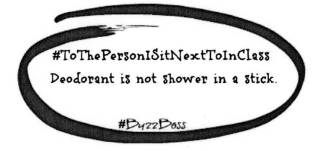

#ToThePersonISitNextToInClass
Deodorant is not shower in a stick.

#BuzzBoss

BRAEDEN

The nurse stopped me in the hallway on the way back into Ivy's room.

"I have something for you," she said and held out a small sheet.

It kind of looked like a larger version of those pictures that print out of a photo booth. But it wasn't just pictures of people making funny faces.

It was the ultrasound printouts.

"Thanks," I murmured and stared down at the three pictures of my child.

Well, right now it was sort of like a little blob, but it was still my kid.

Pressure filled my chest like it was being squeezed, so I took a breath. I already had my freak out moment. I was sure I'd have about a million more. Hell, I could feel the panic right beneath my skin.

But not right now.

Right now, I needed to be there for Ivy. I needed to talk to her. To find out how she was feeling. To find out how this even happened.

Well, I knew *how* it happened… but she was on the pill.

When I cleared the curtain, she was lying back on the bed with the blankets over her legs. She looked terrible. Her face was blotchy and red, her eyes puffy and dark all around the edges. I knew the darkness was likely from the eye makeup she'd been wearing tonight, smeared from her crying, but it was still hard to see.

I didn't like seeing Ivy in pain.

It hurt me. If I could trade places with her and be in that bed right then, I would do it, no matter the cost.

"Hey," she said when I pulled the curtain closed.

"Hey."

Her eyes zeroed in on the pictures in my hand, and I saw the spark of interest. I sat on the edge of the bed and held them out to her. She took them carefully, like they were the most important things in the world to her.

She studied the blobs on the pictures intently, her eyes taking in every last detail.

And then she smiled.

Her finger brushed lightly over the blob that was supposed be the baby.

Inside my chest, my heart rolled over like it had been kicked by a strong boot. Seeing her like this was making me come undone.

I could imagine the way she'd look with my child in her arms, how peaceful and happy she'd be. Pride swelled up within me and so did love.

I definitely wasn't the kind of guy anyone expected to become a father, not even me. Hell, I was sarcastic, sometimes selfish, and sort of immature.

I had no idea how to be a dad. My own had been a piss-poor example.

I didn't care.

It was the absolute worst timing. We weren't ready. My NFL career was just getting started. I had no money, and I drove a car that couldn't hold a car seat.

Holy shit, I need to get a car seat.

I didn't care.

As I looked at Ivy staring lovingly at a picture of the child she was carrying, I knew without a shadow of a doubt that I wanted this baby. I wanted her. I wanted the family we were creating.

"Braeden…" My name was spoken reluctantly on her lips. Finally, her tired blue eyes looked up at me, away from the images.

"The OJ and grilled cheese were cravings," I said.

Of all the words in the world I could have said, those were the ones I chose.

Dumbass.

She smiled. "I'm thinking so."

"The dizziness…" I thought back, then felt my eyes widen. "All those times you seemed worried and afraid."

She glanced down at her lap.

"Hey." I lifted her chin with my fingers so I could look at her again. "How long have you known?"

"Not very long. Remember that doctor appointment I had the other morning? My last follow-up?"

I nodded.

"It wasn't a follow-up. I'd been looking at the calendar the day before with Rimmel, and I realized I was late. Like really late. So I went in for a blood test. It was positive."

"How…?"

"All those antibiotics I took after the accident? The ones so I didn't get an infection?"

I nodded.

"The doctor says they interacted with my birth control and made it less effective."

And I'd been going at her like a bitch in heat. I'd been so freaked out after the accident, freaked that I'd almost lost her. I'd buried myself in her body (gently) every chance I got because it made me feel so close to her.

The morning I'd gone at her like a rabid animal punched me in the gut. "That morning," I rasped. "When I was so rough. Did I hurt you? Hurt the baby?"

She smiled like something I'd said made her happy. "The baby's fine."

"Why didn't you tell me, Blondie?"

That wiped the smile right off her face. Worry etched into her forehead and around her eyes. "I was scared," she admitted. "I felt so freaked out, but at the same time, I was happy, you know?"

I nodded.

"I almost felt bad for being happy. We didn't plan this. I didn't want you to think I was trying to trap you or that I was going to make a bunch of demands." Her eyes held a note of pleading when she looked up. "I don't want anything from you, I swear. And you have so much going on right now with football… and Robert Bettinger. I was supposed to be protecting you, and here I am adding to your problems."

I sucked in a breath. The fact that she felt this was absolutely unacceptable.

"You've been carrying around a piece of me inside you for ten weeks."

I don't think that's what she was expecting me to say. Her red-rimmed eyes widened and she gave me her complete attention.

"You're literally growing a hybrid of us—of me and you. I understand why you think I was going to freak out. My history of freaking out over everything doesn't give me a lot of street cred."

She giggled, and I smiled, swift.

"I won't lie to you. This is an epic shock. I wasn't expecting this. I'm not ready, and it scares me to death."

"I understand," she whispered, lowering her gaze.

"But oh my God, Ivy. You've got my baby inside you. It thrills the shit out of me."

Her eyes snapped back up, hope lighting them. "It does?"

I nodded. "When you fell tonight, I was beyond pissed, but then you held your stomach and said 'your baby.' The anger went away. It went so fast it made me dizzy. All I could think about was getting you to safety, doing everything I could to make sure that baby was okay."

"I really didn't mean for this to happen."

I chuckled. "I know that, baby. I was a more-than-willing participant in what it took to make that little critter." I gestured at her stomach.

She gasped. "Critter! That's a terrible thing to call her."

"Her?"

She nodded once. "She likes pink."

I sat there and smiled like a big stupid idiot. She was so ridiculous, but fuck, I loved her.

"Rome thinks it's a boy."

She rolled her eyes. "Of course he does."

I leaned forward and covered her stomach with my hand. Right now it was flat, but I knew soon it would begin to round. I was looking forward to it.

"We're gonna figure this out. We're gonna make it work. I'm not going to leave you, and I promise to try and be the best dad I can be."

She sighed wistfully. "You're going to be so good at it."

I wasn't so sure about that, but I wasn't about to ruin her happy thoughts.

"You aren't mad?" she asked like she had to make sure.

"Yes."

She sucked in a breath.

"I'm fucking pissed you got in the way of Blanchard and put yourself and my baby at risk."

"I only wanted to stop him. I didn't think he'd knock me down."

A rumbled started in my chest and vibrated my throat.

"Braeden." She grabbed my hand. "I'm okay and so is the baby. Promise me you won't go after him. Promise."

"I don't have to," I said, smug. "Rome already beat his ass."

She gasped. "He didn't!"

"You're damn right he did."

"You two are absolutely horrible." She shook her head like she was bewildered.

"But we love you. *I* love you."

Her eyes filled with tears.

"Please don't cry anymore, baby. I can't take it."

"I love you." She sniffled, trying to hold it back.

She looked so damn cute sitting there looking all terrible and vulnerable.

"We're getting married," I announced and stood up.

"What!" she gasped.

I nodded like it was done. "We're getting married as soon as possible."

"You can't just announce we're getting married."

"Why the hell not!" I demanded.

"You have to ask."

God, this woman was going to be the death of me. I muttered and grumbled. Then I sighed. "Ivy, will you marry me?"

"No."

"What did you just say to me?" I growled.

"I said no," she growled back, a stubborn glint in her eyes.

"You can't say no!" I hollered.

"I just did."

The nurse pulled back the curtain, carrying some papers. "Ready to go?" she chirped as if she didn't notice the storm brewing in the tiny space.

"Yes, please," Ivy said. Her voice was so weary, concern overshadowed my incredulous anger.

"I'll have everything you need at the desk. Come on out when you're changed."

When she was gone, Ivy moved to get up from the bed, and I hurried around to help her. "Here," I said, putting the gown she'd come here in beside her and gently untying the string behind her neck.

"Thank you," she said, leaning into me a little as she stripped off the hospital gown.

I dropped the argument. She'd been through enough tonight. We both had. She needed some rest and so did my baby.

But I wasn't going to let this go.

Oh, hells no.

I didn't know why Ivy said no to getting married, but she sure as hell was going to change her mind.

CHAPTER THIRTY-FIVE

#MarriageHumor

Marriage is when a man looses his bachelors degree and a woman gets her masters degree.

#BuzzBoss

IVY

Braeden was an idiot.

He thought he could order me to marry him? As if I didn't have a choice?

Bonehead.

He wanted to get married because he thought it was the right thing to do. Because he thought it was his responsibility now that I was pregnant.

As if I would marry a man because it was his *duty*.

Scoff.

I don't think so.

CHAPTER THIRTY-SIX

#WiseBuzz
"Forgivenss is a virtue of the brave."
-Gandhi
#BuzzBoss

BRAEDEN

"Braeden, help me. I can't get out."

The scent of gasoline consumed the air. It was putrid and off-putting. But I stood there anyway and just stared.

"You're not going to help me, are you?"

"No."

"That's murder."

A flame ignited. I heard the whooshing sound it made before my eyes ever saw it. Zach heard it, too. His eyes widened as if he finally understood he was going to die.

He started struggling. The sounds of him pleading for his life fell on deaf ears. I was beyond hearing him.

I watched as the flames grew, the orange and red flickering in the night. I was standing so close I could see the blue center—the hottest part of the flame. The metal groaned beneath the destructive heat.

The flames climbed higher and higher in the sky and devoured more and more of the car.

"*Help me!*" *Zach screamed.*

I just stood there and stared. The heat of the fire was intense. It actually was painful to stand so close. But I didn't move back, not even when I felt the smoke from the burning tire fill my lungs.

I was transfixed.

"*Murderer!*" *Zach accused.* "*You're nothing but a murderer! You're going to hell for this. This will haunt you forever!*"

Tendrils of fire reached through the shattered window, stretching their deathly claim toward him. The second the flame grabbed hold, his scream pierced through the air. High-pitched, tortured, and bloodcurdling.

My stomach turned as the flames consumed him. He flailed about as he burned, the scent of roasting flesh so incredibly strong.

Suddenly, he stopped screaming.

I thought he was dead.

I watched his body, still strangely intact, as if the flames were having trouble gobbling him. His mouth opened, but he didn't scream. Even through the harsh glow of the inferno, his eyes snapped open. Lucid, clear… accusing.

"*I will get you for this!*" *he keened.*

And then the blaze continued into his mouth, his eyes rolled back in his head, and he slumped forward, no longer visible.

I jerked awake, sweat coating my skin and dampening my hair. My body jolted up as I gasped and my arms flung out.

I could still smell the scent of burning flesh. It clung to my consciousness like a bad song stuck on repeat in the back of my mind.

I blinked, trying to push away the disturbing images, the sound of Zach's screams, and his accusation that I was a murderer.

I was.

I'd made a choice and walked away.

In that moment, it had been him or me. I chose me.

It hadn't been fair what I did. I understood that. Life never played by the rules, so why should I?

Was this my punishment? Was this the karma I'd taunted Zach with before I walked away? Would I be haunted by nightmares the rest of my life and walk around with the knowledge that I might someday go to hell?

"Braeden..." Ivy pushed up off the mattress into a sitting position. Her hair was mussed and around her shoulders. "Another nightmare?"

"Sorry to wake you, baby." At least this time I hadn't hurt her with my thrashing about.

Her cool hands slid around my bicep from behind. It felt good against my hot skin. She leaned forward and rested her cheek against the outside of my arm. "What was it about?"

"Zach." My voice was gruff and deep.

She pressed a kiss to my arm and then slid away, lying back against the pillows. "Come here," she said and tugged on my arm.

I went. She was just too enticing. I laid my head on her stomach and wrapped my arms around her body. She smelled good, like coconut, and it reminded me of the beach. I felt every breath she took, and her fingers started running through my hair.

It felt so good my scalp tingled with goose bumps.

"Maybe talking about it would help," she suggested quietly.

"Talking about it won't change what I did."

"No." She agreed, still dragging her fingers through my hair and along my scalp. "But it might help you come to terms with that night."

"I don't feel guilty," I told her.

"Maybe you do." She rebuffed gently, almost kindly.

Maybe she was right. If I didn't feel some kind of guilt, I wouldn't be having these dreams.

I turned my head and pressed a kiss to her stomach. "What will I tell him?" I rasped, thinking of my child and how one day he was going to ask me about that night.

"You'll tell him you made a choice, a *human* choice, and you did it to protect his mother."

"I'd do anything for you," I whispered.

"Forgive yourself."

My heart skipped a beat. She wanted the one thing I wasn't sure I could give her. "I'm not sure I can."

"I forgive you."

My eyes closed. Her words penetrated me all the way to the soul. How could she say that and actually mean it?

"He never will," I said. I never realized how much it bothered me that Zach's father was in so much pain. I was lying here right now with my head pressed against my growing child, and I already loved him fiercely. Possessively.

I knew the feelings would only intensify the first time that baby was placed in my arms.

I took that away from another man.

I wouldn't forgive me either.

"Probably not," she allowed. I loved that she never lied. "But that doesn't mean you aren't worth forgiveness. And his grief doesn't make him a better father. It just makes you both men who made mistakes."

"You sound like a fortune cookie."

"Mmm, Chinese."

I laughed. Her tastes in food had changed dramatically since getting pregnant. It was supposedly normal, but it was also amusing. "Is my little Critter hungry?"

She pulled my hair when I called our child by the nickname that totally stuck, and she hated. It didn't hurt at all. "It's the middle of the night."

"So? You want Chinese; I will get you Chinese."

"You know what I want." Her voice turned serious.

The words, *Why do you care so much?* were right there on the tip of my tongue, but I held them back. It was stupid question. I knew why she cared so much.

"I don't know how," I admitted. Forgiveness wasn't something that came easy for me. Okay, it didn't come at all.

Take my own father for example. I'd told him on his deathbed I couldn't forgive him for all the things he'd done to my mother and me. I'd let it go in my own way. He no longer haunted me. But I would never forgive him for what he did. To me, forgiving him would be like saying what he did was okay. And it wasn't.

What I did would never be okay either. Maybe that's why I didn't know how to forgive myself. Maybe I didn't deserve forgiveness, just like my father.

"Someday you will." She promised and continued playing with my hair.

"Did you tell your parents about the baby yet?" I asked, snuggling a little closer into her body.

Yes. Snuggled.

Sometimes a guy just needs to do these things.

"Not yet," she hedged. "I told Drew not to say a word either."

"Think they're going to be upset?" As I spoke, her hand drifted away from my hair and her nails lightly scraped over my back.

"I don't know. I'm sure it will be a shock like it was to us."

"I'm afraid I'm going to miss his birth," I admitted. It was something that had been gnawing away at my insides these past few days. And since I was already acting good and girly, I figured I'd just get it all out there right then.

"It's going to be a tricky time." She agreed, like she also thought about it.

She was due at the beginning of the football season. Assuming I would be drafted by the NFL, I was going to be out of town, wherever my team was. How was I supposed to give my first season with the NFL my full attention when I had Ivy and a baby to think of?

What Romeo asked me the night at the hospital really resonated with me.

What is the one thing you wanted most from your father? For him to be there. For him to love me.

I was going to fucking be there for my kid. If someone asked him or her the same question when they're my age, that was *not* going to be their answer.

I couldn't miss the birth. Not only for the baby, but for Ivy, too. She needed my support. She needed to know I would be there.

"I could talk to Anthony," I said, thinking out loud. "Maybe see if I can push back the draft, finish my senior year here at Alpha U, and then maybe—"

"No." Her voice was final.

I lifted my head and looked up. "No?" My lips twitched. It was pretty fucking cute she was bossing me.

"This is your dream. Your career. It's your opportunity. I'm not holding you back from that."

"I don't think that, Ivy," I said, sitting up and facing her. "You aren't holding me back."

"No. I'm not, because you're going to get drafted. You're going to play football, and I'm going to be right there cheering you on."

She was amazing. Fierce. Loyal. Protective.

And now she was carrying my child.

"I don't want to miss the beginning of this baby's life." I rubbed a hand over my face. But if I didn't play, I wouldn't get paid. A three-year contract with the NFL would set us up for life. It would guarantee Ivy and my child wouldn't want for anything.

"You won't." She reached out and took my hand, giving it a firm squeeze. "This is really important to you, isn't it?"

I lifted an eyebrow. "You're surprised?"

"It's just before I told you, I was so worried."

I couldn't help but chuckle. "I've always been like a free range chicken."

"A free range chicken?" she echoed blankly.

"Roaming free. It's what I did." I joked.

"Isn't that like a cell phone commercial or something?"

I laughed. "Those days are over, Ivy, and frankly, I couldn't be more glad. I hadn't realized how exhausting it was playing the field, making sure I never got too close. You're my home now. You and this baby. No one's more surprised than me, but I wouldn't trade you for anything in this entire world, including a football contract."

"I'll travel with you," she said. "Whatever city you go to, I'll go there, too. You can see me whenever you have a minute, even if it's only five minutes out of the entire day. And when I get too far along to travel, you can come back for the birth. Soon as I'm able, I'll bring the baby to wherever you are."

"You'd do that?"

"You're not the only one in the relationship who would do anything for the other."

There were still a lot of details to work out. Still so much to take into consideration, but for now, I was happy.

"You're going to be the best dad, Braeden. I can't wait to see it." Her voice was full of emotion.

Now was a good time to strike.

"I'd make a pretty good husband, too."

That earned me a sour look.

What was it with this woman?

"Most women would sell a kidney to marry this." I scoffed and gestured to my bare chest.

"I like my kidneys. Both of them."

"So you love me and will have my baby, but you won't marry me."

"Totes."

Totes? On what fucking planet did this make sense?

Ivy rolled onto her side, facing me, and slid down under the covers. The sound of her yawn filled the room. As if we were disturbing her, Her Royal Highness Prada got up from near Ivy's feet and burrowed under the covers to lie right up against her.

I lay down, too, as close to Ivy as the stinking dog would let me.

She reached out again and started dragging her fingers through my hair. It was almost as good as sprinkles.

"You're going to say yes eventually." I glowered.

"We'll see."

We'll see?

Challenge accepted.

CHAPTER THIRTY-SEVEN

#WatchOut
I'm pretty sure I'm going to be one of those senior citizens who bites everyone.
#BuzzBoss

RIMMEL

How did we all get so old?

Okay. Fine. We weren't old in the literal sense. It's not like we were all walking around with canes and Depends.

Our numerical ages were still quite young, but our family—especially me, Romeo, Braeden, and Ivy—had grown up so much. I felt like we'd all aged beyond our years.

In such a short time, too.

It was no wonder I was sitting here profoundly pondering our futures.

Or more specifically, *my* future.

I had a decision to make, and it was a big one. I was doubting myself, questioning what I wanted. I was beginning to realize I wasn't necessarily questioning the way I felt, but rather how the way I felt was changing me.

If that made any sense.

For so, so long, I'd wanted only one thing. To become a veterinarian. To help and devote myself to giving a voice to those who could not do it for themselves. I still wanted to do that. I always would. That part of me was something I knew would never go away no matter how many changes I went through in my life.

But now I didn't just want one thing.

I wanted way more.

And oddly, Ivy's pregnancy reminded me that time was fluid; it moved and flowed. It also reminded me that my life was a lot more than just animals now.

And so here I sat. The sun barely lifted off the horizon and the frigid chill of the early morning air froze my toes even though they were still buried safely under the mountain of blankets on our gigantic king-size bed.

I glanced beside me at Romeo. Even in the dark, his blond hair was light. It was a little longer now than it used to be, and when he woke up in the morning, it was wild around his head, making him look even more rakish and charming than he already was.

My husband.

The awe of knowing that's who he was to me was still as bold as the first day we got married. As I stared down at him sleeping, I thought a part of me would always be a little bit in awe of Romeo Anderson.

And it was mostly because of that—because of him—that my decision was so easy yet so very hard.

I knew what I wanted. I knew where my future lay.

But my head was battling my heart, and the tug-of-war between the two wasn't something I enjoyed.

As if he somehow sensed my inner strife, Romeo stirred. His head turned to me, blond locks of hair falling over his forehead and his piercing blue eyes slitting open and peering up at me.

"Rim?"

"Go back to sleep," I told him, reaching out and tucking the hair away from his face. His skin was so warm. It always was.

That partnered with the blond hair and warm-toned skin made me strongly suspect the man had his own personal sun inside him, and it radiated out, giving him that extra something that everyone always reacted to.

He yawned, showing me just about all his white teeth, and pushed up so he could lean against the headboard beside me.

"Why you awake at the ass crack of dawn, Smalls?" His voice was rumbly from sleep, and as he spoke, he rubbed his face with one hand.

"I was watching my husband sleep."

"You aren't planning on murdering me, are ya?"

I poked him in the ribs. "I think I'll keep you around for a while."

"I'm a pretty useful guy."

I stretched my lips into a catlike smile. "Especially when I need something off a high shelf."

"There's that," he allowed. But then the playfulness left his tone. "There's also when I know something's eating at you."

I sighed.

"You having regrets about getting married the way we did?"

"No!" I gasped. The force of my denial shot my back up away from the headboard. "That was literally the best day of my entire life."

He bestowed upon me a beautiful smile, and if I didn't already know he possessed the light of his own personal sun, it would have been confirmed just then.

"It was a damn good day," he answered, gruff, and picked up my hand to kiss the palm. "Woman, your hands are like ice."

"It's cold."

"I got ya blanket right here." He lifted his arm, and I slid myself beneath it, fitting right against his side. For good measure, I stuffed my toes between his legs and sighed at the blessed warmth. He jerked like I shot him and then muttered something about needing some meat on my bones but didn't make a move to try and get away from my freezing limbs.

"Braeden is going to make a really good dad."

He made a sound. "It sure as hell is going to be fun to watch him with a baby. Dude knows absolutely nothing about kids."

"Do you?" I asked inquisitively.

"Nope."

"Me either." I giggled. "I hope Ivy does or we're all in trouble."

"We can practice on our nephew so we don't screw up ours."

"That's a terrible thing to say!" I gasped and looked up at him. "And who says it's a boy?"

He grunted. "Damn well better be or I'm gonna have to move up my timeline for a house with a wall around it."

"What timeline? And why on earth would we need a wall around our house if they have a girl?"

"Because you know any girl born into this family is gonna be gorgeous. And you've seen how B is when anyone—including me—looks at Ivy too long. Imagine what the hell he'd be like with a daughter."

"You feel protective of her already," I said.

And yes.

I will admit this.

Only once.

Never again.

Hearing him already outline a plan to protect his new niece or nephew made me feel like one of my ovaries exploded.

I mean really. I was only human.

He shrugged. "That baby's my family. But even before I found out about him, I planned to buy us a house on a lot of land with a wall and a gate. I want to make sure you're protected. I want you safe."

Emotion clogged my throat, and it took me a few minutes to swallow past it. He was so incredibly thoughtful. Even though he seemed so carefree, he was always thinking, always keeping an eye on those he loved most, and always figuring ways to make sure he took care of them.

Maybe I teased him because the feelings he brought out in me were so intense it was almost— *almost*—too much to bear. "You can't just lock me away behind a gate, you know."

He chuckled. "I know that, and with you going away to vet school, I figured we'd have at least four years before we actually started building. But, baby, you know the press is insistent. I don't see it going away in the near future. The more I play, the worse it's going to be. I don't want them bothering you. I don't want us looking over our shoulders every time we pull up to our

* * *

home. And I especially don't want people trying to get looks of the newest member of our family. Braeden is going to be like a bear with a raging case of monkey butt when that baby's born. We'll be lucky if he lets us touch him."

A bear with a raging case of monkey butt?
Ew.

"You want us all to live together?"

He froze momentarily, like it was something he just assumed was automatic, like it never required any thought. "I thought you'd like it that way. I know you and B are close… If you'd rather have a place of our own—"

I laid a hand on his chest, reveling in the strong beat of his heart beneath my palm. "I love living with everyone. I think it's a perfect idea. They're going to need help with the baby anyway."

"Yeah," he said, like the thought never really occurred to him.

I thought it was amusing.

Leave it to Romeo to think of elaborate plans to protect us all and the baby, but not even once consider the fact that babies needed round-the-clock care.

"I don't really know how much we're going to be around." He finished, his voice concerned.

"About that…" I started, sitting up away from him and leaning back against the white upholstered headboard. "I'm not going to vet school."

His eyes widened and then his mouth flattened. I knew he wasn't going to be happy about this. "I wasn't implying that you need to stay home to help take care of their baby or that you going off to pursue your dream is disloyalty to this family."

"I know that," I said, firm.

"You're going." He said it like it was final. Like he was the be all, end all, say all to what I did.

"Don't you take that tone with me," I growled.

He grinned, a big, stupid, dopey grin.

I scowled. I wasn't trying to be funny.

"Damn. Smalls finally got the growl. Someone must be pissy."

"If you know I'm *pissy,* then why are you making it worse by taunting me?"

"'Cause you're sexy when you growl."

I rolled my eyes. It always came back to sex. Good Lord, when he was eighty, he was still gonna be making inappropriate jokes.

"It's not my dream anymore. I have a new dream now."

He seemed skeptical. There was a light in his eyes that made it clear he was wondering if I was just saying that because I thought it's what he wanted to hear.

I couldn't be mad, because that was Romeo. He just wanted me to be happy and he wouldn't let anyone get in the way of that—not even himself.

"Why don't you tell me exactly what's on your mind?" he said and picked me up, slipping me into his lap with ease.

I laid my head against his chest, and he tucked the blankets around me, even though I wasn't cold anymore. He already warmed me up.

"I want to take the job Michelle offered me, running the new shelter. I know it's not very high pay, especially considering what you make—"

"The money isn't even an issue, Rim. You could work for free and I wouldn't give a fuck as long as it made you happy."

"You only say that because you're making enough for five people." I teased.

His chin almost hit his chest beside my face when he looked down at me. "Even if I wasn't making shit, I'd still say the same thing."

"I know." I lifted my face a fraction and kissed the underside of his chin. "I've been so involved with the building of that shelter, it already feels like my place. When I think about leaving soon and letting someone else take it over, it makes my stomach hurt."

"That's just 'cause B tried to cook dinner the other night."

I dissolved in a fit of giggles. "Oh my God, I thought the kitchen would never un-smell again!"

He laughed low and it rumbled through his chest and vibrated my ear. "That shit was bad."

I honestly still didn't know what he was trying to cook. I don't think any of us knew. I wasn't even sure he did. When I got home, I thought something had died. But no. It was just Braeden making a "family" dinner.

Seems he made a "bomb" grilled cheese for Ivy (which she did say tasted really good) and then got it in his head he was gourmet.

He wasn't.

I wiped the tears out of my eyes from laughing and took a breath. "I don't want to miss any of this," I whispered.

His body went calm, and I felt him listening.

"I don't want you to go off to football and me to go off to some school where I'll be buried under lab work and exams. That's four years of our life I won't get back."

"Baby, you can't give up on your dream because it's going to be hard to be away. We'll still see each other. I'll fly to you instead of home when I have time off."

"That's not good enough," I said, my voice taking on a tone that suspiciously sounded like whining. "I don't want to live in some cold dorm with some roommate who isn't my family. I don't want to go to bed without the scent of you on my sheets and the memories of all the times we'd made love in our bed."

"I can't go off and live my dream if you don't go off and live yours," he said quietly.

"Vet school isn't my dream anymore, Romeo. You are. Our family is."

He opened his mouth. I felt the protest in the set of his shoulders.

I sat up and looked at him intently. "Animals will always be my passion. I still truly believe in being their voice. But I don't have to be a veterinarian to be that for them. I have way more to give animals than a medical degree. I have compassion and caring. I have passion and love. The shelter does so much good, Romeo. You know that. I could be a part of that. I could run it, make it a sanctuary for these animals, the ones like Murphy, the ones who started out like me."

"Ah, babe." He brushed a hand over my head and let it slide all the way down my arm.

"And you know I'm not a big fan of the press and the circles we've become a part of, but I can use that. I can use your connections, make them my connections, too, and make an even bigger difference. Maybe someday I can open a shelter of my own."

"I'll buy you one right now." He totally meant it.

"I don't want you to buy me one." I laughed. "I want to work for it. I want to make it happen because of what I can do. You and your mother opened those doors for me, but I want to be the one to step through."

"You could go to vet school, open up your own animal clinic," he said, playing devil's advocate.

I shook my head. "It's not what I want. If I graduate next year, stay here, and run the shelter I can still be your wife—a real wife. I can come to your games. I can sleep in our bed. I won't be so buried under coursework that I feel like I'm isolated without my family. I feel like I just found my family, Romeo. I don't want to lose it."

"You will never lose this family. We're all going to be together forever. I promise you that." The underlying vow of an alpha came through with those words.

I knew without a doubt, without a single question in my entire being that it was the truth. Romeo would keep this family together even if he had to do it with his bare hands.

I felt tears well behind my eyes. "Please understand. I've been thinking about this a long time. It was hard to reconcile within myself." I pressed a hand to my chest. "My heart wants to be here. My heart wants to see what I can do beyond the classroom. My intuition tells me this is where I belong. I've found my place. Yeah, my head still likes to remind me I promised to be a vet, but I'm not giving up that dream—I'm just adapting it."

"I can't say no to you." His eyes glittered like sapphires expertly cut to shine the most intensely. "I can't say no when you tell me your heart wants the life we've made."

"I want it so badly I ache inside." I'd been aching for weeks now, worrying over this decision, so afraid I'd make the wrong one.

But choosing love and family is never the wrong decision, and now that I'd said it out loud, it seemed so simple. So easy.

"Lovers gonna love," he quipped like it was something he'd been saying for all eternity.

I'd never heard him say that, ever.

But goodness, it was so true.

"What do you think?" I chewed my lower lip as I waited to hear what he would say. No, I didn't need his permission, but he did get a say.

"I think I really fucking love you."

"Does that mean you're happy I'm going to stay here and work?"

Within seconds, he had me flat on my back and was over me. "You have no idea how happy you make me. It was killing me that you were going to be that much farther away."

"You never told me that. You always acted like you were happy."

"I'd never do anything to hold you back, baby."

"Make love to me. Right now."

His teeth flashed. "I'm not sure I want to."

Please. He couldn't even pretend with me. I rocked my hips and brushed up against his already rigid cock.

His smile fell away. "Ahh." When he looked at me, desire burned in his eyes and in the rigid set of his jaw.

"I want my husband inside me," I said, bold.

"You keep making sexy demands and I'm gonna come in my shorts." He kissed me so swift I barely had time to feel it.

Romeo sprang up to his knees and shoved his boxers down. His cock stood straight out and jerked in tiny rapid movements with the force of his need.

My tongue slid over my lips as I stared at it, and a small sound escaped from his lips. I pushed up into a sitting position, and he reached down to tug my shirt up over my head and throw it away. The ends of my hair tickled my breasts, and my nipples tightened instantly. Between my legs was already growing wet, silky moisture pooling in my core, readying my body for his sweet intrusion.

He tried to push me back down, his knees already straddling my hips. I made a sound of protest and took his cock in my hand. With a firm grip, I slid down until I hit the base, where I gave it a little squeeze, and he moaned. I jacked him gently, once, twice, a third time, but then I swooped forward and took him deep into my mouth.

There was no warning. There was no teasing lick or gradual slip. One second my hand was doing all the work, and the next I felt his swollen, smooth bead near the back of my throat.

He made a garbled sound like he was choking, but I knew he wasn't. The way his cock jerked around in my mouth told me he really liked what I was doing. My lips fastened firmly around him and dragged upward, making sure I sucked every last inch on my way to his tip.

"Rimmel." He said my name like a prayer as his fingers tangled in my hair. I moaned and sucked him deep once more, this time using my free hand to gently massage his balls.

"Fuck," he rasped, and I was pretty sure I felt the fingers against my scalp tremble.

We went on like that for a few minutes, me taking him deep and fast but then releasing him slow and easy. By the time he pushed me away, his chest was slick with sweat and he was panting as if it took every ounce of will he had to not come apart right there against my tongue.

"Are you ready for me?" he asked, pushing me down into the blankets.

"So ready."

He was so impatient he slid his fingers beneath the edge of my panties to see for himself. Pure liquid met his touch and he slid even farther into my opening. My eyes closed. He groaned.

"Baby…" It was the closest thing to a whimper I'd ever heard from him.

I knew exactly what he wanted.

I reached between us and shoved the panties down. He ripped them off my legs and then pushed my thighs as wide as they would go. He loved doing that. He loved opening me up so completely, as if the sight of me so open and vulnerable made him weak.

I held my legs there even after his large hands released my thighs.

"Oh, Romeo," I beckoned and threw my arms up over my head.

He surged forward, knowing exactly where to go. He slid home at the very same time he grabbed my hands and linked them with his.

He ground into me so deeply that my body actually glided up on the bed.

I moaned, and he did it again, over and over. The pressure he created was so delicious and the weight of his pelvis against mine was like the cherry on top an already dreamy sundae.

My fingers griped his, and I held on as he literally took me for a ride.

He speared me over and over. The thick, hard cock seemed to hit every single one of my most sensitive spots.

I started to pant as well, and then I started to beg.

God, he was playing with me. Literally holding me down with his strength while he fucked me senseless.

My whimpers of need seemed to break into the haze he was in. He surged deep, tilted his head down, and looked into my eyes.

Slowly, so achingly slowly, he lowered until his lips claimed mine.

He kissed me through the orgasm. He swallowed every last sound of pleasure I yelled. The second my cries started to die, his body went rigid. I kissed him with renewed passion, pulled his tongue into my mouth, and sucked while he emptied deep inside my body.

He tried to hold himself over me, knowing his large size would be too much, but his arms were wobbling and his chest was heaving. With one last burst of strength, he rolled, placing himself beneath me and draping my body on top of his.

I snuggled into him, tucking my hands between us, and heaved a contented sigh.

"If we weren't already married, I'd marry you again," he said between deep breaths.

"That's good considering you are marrying me again."

"I can't wait to put that wedding band on your finger." He stroked my back.

"I guess we should go buy some. I want to see mine on your finger, too."

"Yeah, we're gonna need to make those wedding plans. My mother cornered me at the party and has called me every day since."

I groaned. "Okay, yes. Today. I'll start today." Thank goodness it was Saturday.

"Don't forget to get plane tickets for your dad and grandparents," he reminded me. He was insistent that we pay for them to be here. It was so incredibly sweet, because we both knew my dad would never be able to afford to come. And what was even sweeter was that even after everything my father had done, Romeo was still the first one to say we needed to invite him to the wedding.

"I wish my mom was here," I whispered.

Both his arms wrapped around me. "I do too, baby."

I clung to him for long moments, soaking in the comfort I suddenly needed before pulling back and pushing my hair out of my face. "Might as well get up. We've got wedding plans to make."

CHAPTER THIRTY-EIGHT

Size matters.

(if she says it doesn't, she's lying)

#BuzzBoss

BRAEDEN

The damn dog had to pee.

And you know what that meant?

It meant I had to haul my ass out of the warm, comfortable bed and go all the way downstairs to let her out.

With a groan, I rolled out of bed and grabbed a pair of sweatpants off the nearby chair and nearly fell over trying to put the damn things on.

Prada stood by the door and watched me struggle like she was silently amused. "What are you looking at?" I muttered.

She wagged her tail.

"You're the only dog I'd ever do this shit for," I told her and opened the door.

She ran ahead of me down the stairs, her nails making a light click-clacking sound on the wood as she pranced toward the kitchen.

The sun was up but low in the sky, which was gray. Surely spring weather was on the horizon. Hell, it was almost spring break.

Spring break would mark a year since Ivy and I first dropped the hate/hate relationship and admitted it was more like attraction/attraction, which we then denied/denied, but now it was love/love.

So much had happened in the last year. It was like a damned whirlwind.

There was a light on in the kitchen, the one over the sink. At first I thought someone had just left it on overnight, but when I stepped into the room, I saw Romeo and Rimmel standing by the coffee pot, making out.

Drew was right. This kitchen was downright sinful.

"Brother alert," I said, my voice still half asleep.

Prada was by the door, so I opened it up and let her into the backyard. The air wasn't too spring-like, and I hoped once the sun cracked through the clouds, it would warm up.

"Someone's up early," Rimmel said.

I grunted. "I'm not the only one."

It was a damned shame to be out of bed this early on a weekend.

I opened up the back door again and stuck my face in the opening. "Giz, get your ass in here!"

She ignored me.

I shut the door and muttered my way over to the island, where I sat down. A steaming cup of coffee appeared in front of me with just the right amount of creamer.

"God bless you," I told Rimmel.

She laughed.

"You look like shit," Romeo said.

I gave him the finger. "Didn't get much sleep last night."

"Is Ivy okay?" Rimmel worried.

"She's fine, sis." I assured her. Like I'd be sitting here drinking coffee if my girl wasn't anything but okay.

I drank more coffee. Clearly, I needed it.

Rimmel went around the island, carrying her own mug that seemed a lot bigger in her hands than it did in mine, and opened the door.

"Come on, Prada!" she called. The dog came prancing through the door the next second. "That's a good girl!"

"Why ya gotta do me like that, Giz?" I asked the dog. Her ear hair was all wild and crazy from whatever the hell she'd been doing in the yard.

She sat below me, looking up with hopeful brown eyes I just couldn't say no to. So I pushed off the stool and grabbed her treats. She danced around while I dug one out and handed it to her. She ran off like she'd won the lottery, and I returned to my coffee.

Seconds later, Murphy came sauntering into the kitchen and jumped up on the counter.

"This house is overrun with animals," I grumped.

Rimmel gave me a small frown, which made me feel like shit, and then gave her cat too many treats. Romeo was drinking his coffee, studying me in the way he always did when he was trying to see right through me.

I took another gulp of coffee and got up again, this time going around to Rim and pulling her into a hug. She hugged me back immediately, and it made me a little less grouchy. "Sorry, sis. I'm being an ass," I apologized next to her ear.

"I still love you," she told me.

"You still having dreams?" Romeo asked.

"What dreams?" Rim pulled back and stared between the two of us. I gave Romeo a WTF look.

"B's been having some dreams about the night Zach died."

Rimmel looked back at me with wide, sad eyes. Damn, she had some puppy dog eyes when she wanted to. First Giz and now her.

I was turning into a damn cup of Jell-O.

She hugged me again, wrapping her arms tight around my waist and holding on. I hugged her back while glaring at Rome over her head. He just shrugged.

"I'm fine. Nothing I can't handle." Okay, so maybe I wasn't handling it that good, but I was working on it. "But I need some sisterly advice."

That part got her attention, and she forgot about the dreams.

Finally. The coffee was kicking in. Jumpstarting my brain.

Rimmel grabbed my hand and towed me back to the chairs. I sat down, and she sat down right beside me, her knees bumping the side of my leg. She made a grabby motion at her coffee and Romeo picked it up, took a sip, and then gave her the mug.

When she wrapped her hands around it, the giant-ass rock Romeo put on her finger nearly blinded me.

"Ivy won't marry me," I announced, sour.

Romeo started laughing.

Rimmel choked delicately on her coffee and tried to cover it up but wasn't very successful. Setting the mug aside, she gave me all her undivided attention. "You asked Ivy to marry you?"

"Uh, yeah." I hedged.

Why the hell was everyone so damn surprised?

"When?" Rimmel asked.

"At the hospital. The night she fell."

"Did you ask her over a bedpan?" Romeo drawled.

"She didn't tell me." Rimmel frowned.

"Probably because she flat out told me no. Refused. Told me no again this morning," I muttered. And every time I asked her in between.

Talk about a kick to a guy's ego.

"She's pregnant with my kid, but she won't marry me."

Rimmel made a disapproving sound. The sound all women make when they want to tell you what you did wrong.

"What?"

"What did you say when you asked, exactly?"

I blanched. "I kinda told her we were getting married."

Romeo laughed again.

"Dude, I will come over there and drop you," I growled.

He smiled some more.

"Romeo," Rimmel admonished.

That shut him up.

I beamed at him.

"So you ordered Ivy to marry you on the night you found out she was pregnant," Rimmel surmised.

"So?"

"So you didn't *ask* her. You probably were bossy as hell—"

"I was—" I cut her off to argue.

"Braeden James," Rimmel warned. I stopped talking. "Why did you ask Ivy to marry you?"

I gave her a look that asked, *Isn't it obvious?*

* * *

363

"Is it because she's pregnant and you feel like it would be the right thing for you to do?" Rimmel prodded.

Realization started to climb up the back of my neck.

"Had you planned to ask her before you found out? Did you tell her you loved her and that's why you wanted to marry her?"

"Oh shit." I groaned and scrubbed a hand over my face. I went to drink some coffee, but my cup was empty. I held it out to Romeo. "Take pity on me."

He refilled my cup, and I drank it black.

"Lots of girls dream about the day they get engaged. They picture someone telling them how much they love them and want them. What they don't picture is being scared out of their mind and then their boyfriend ordering them to get married because he finds out he has a baby on the way."

"I would marry her even if there wasn't a baby."

"Did you tell her that?" Rimmel asked gently.

No. No, I didn't.

Ivy thought I was marrying her out of some sense of obligation. I never gave her reason to think anything else.

A cuss word fell from my lips.

Rimmel patted my arm. "Maybe you should try asking her in a more... traditional way."

"Get a rock, dude. A big one," Romeo added.

Shit. I never even thought about a ring. Here Rim was walking around with a big-ass diamond from a romantic proposal on national TV.

And what did Ivy get?

She got me yelling at her over her hospital bed.

I'd have said no, too.

"The size of the ring doesn't matter," Rimmel said.

Romeo laughed. "And a guy's dick size doesn't matter either."

"I cannot believe you just said that." Rimmel's cheeks turned pink.

I laughed and pulled her close for another hug. "I'd be lost without you, sis. Thanks."

She kissed me on the cheek before returning back to the seat beside me.

"I don't even know why I come down here in the morning," Drew intoned, coming in the room. "Why the hell are you talking about dick size?"

"We were trying to make B feel better about his," Romeo drawled.

"I will pull it out right now." I warned. "Get the measuring tape."

"Ew!" Rimmel shot up from her chair. "I'm going to go shower. Get this nasty talk out of your system before I come back."

"Aw, sis, come back. We were having a nice brother-sister moment!" I called.

"Ew!" she said again.

Drew was pouring himself some coffee, and Rimmel held hers out for a refill before she escaped. He obliged her and winked. She snorted and poured some creamer in.

On her way past Romeo, she slowed and dragged her fingertips across his bare abs. He caught her hand and leaned down to kiss her. "I'll be up in a minute, baby."

"Love you, sis!" I yelled when she was gone.

"Love you!"

"What the hell are you doing up so early?" I said, turning back to Drew.

"Couldn't sleep," he mumbled.

"Seems to be a lot of that going around," Romeo commented.

"What's going on, Rome?" I felt bad because I hadn't picked up on anything. He seemed fine.

"Nothing. Rim's just missing her mom."

I made a mental note to try and spend some extra time with her. I wasn't her mother, but I loved her and that counted for something, didn't it?

"Drew, we need to talk," I said.

"This about my sister?" His eyes narrowed.

He was still mad I got her pregnant. To him it was all on me. I wasn't upset about it. I understood. I'd be the same way about Rimmel.

"Yeah."

"Don't you need to talk to me?" Romeo said.

I rolled my eyes. "Didn't we just do that?"

"Want me to come shopping with you later?" he offered.

"Shopping?" Drew wondered. "What the hell is happening here?"

"Yeah, sure. That'd be cool."

"I'll leave you guys to it, then." Romeo pushed off the counter and slapped me on the back on his way out of the kitchen.

Drew sat a few stools down. "What the fuck was that about?"

"You and Ivy are close. She's closer to you than anyone else in her family, right?"

He nodded. "Yeah."

"Then I think it's right I ask you."

"Ask me what?"

"I want to ask Ivy to marry me." Drew's eyes widened. I cleared my throat. "I know you aren't her dad, but I think your blessing would mean a lot to her. And I'd like it, too."

"You asking because of the baby?" He scrutinized me. Clearly, he wasn't going to make this easy.

And clearly, I was the world's biggest idiot if the first thing he thought was I was doing this out of obligation and I never even realized it would look that way.

"Ivy's the only woman I've ever loved. Part of me always knew we were meant to be, even before we ever started dating. It's one of the reasons I gave her such a hard time. It was easier that way, you know?"

He nodded.

"So am I marrying her because of the baby? No. I'm marrying her because I love her and I always will. Would I have asked her this early? Probably not. She's still healing from everything he did to her. I don't want to push. But that's my kid. Either way, we're heading for the altar. Now it's just a little sooner."

Drew studied me like he was really considering what I said. It was kind of making me nervous. Drew and I got along. Hell, I liked the guy. But I was his sister's boyfriend and he was overprotective, so yeah, there was a little tension there.

"You got my blessing," Drew finally said. Just like that.

"Really?"

He nodded. "I know you'll treat her right. Her and my niece or nephew."

"I will."

Drew sat up to his full height. "But you have to know, Walker, if you hurt her in any way, I will kill you."

"Seems fair." I held out my hand.

Drew shook it. "Gotta say I'm surprised you came to me before you asked. I like that."

"I kinda already asked," I admitted. "She said no."

Drew laughed. "That's my baby sis. Making you work for it."

I didn't think it was too funny, but I refrained from imparting that little bit of information.

The sound of shuffling feet coming through the living room was familiar, and I glanced over my shoulder. Ivy was coming into the kitchen in a pair of loose pajama pants and my Wolfpack T-shirt.

Without saying a word, she crossed to the fridge pulled out the juice and poured some in a glass. Before she even put the container away, she leaned against the counter and took a sip.

Entertained, I got up and grabbed the bottle, capped it, and put it away. I looked at her fingers—specifically her ring finger—and tried to imagine what kind of ring she would want to put there.

"Ives, come over here and talk to your big bro. Let me tell you about the latest article I read in *GearShark*."

She plopped down next to Drew, and he started talking about cars and racing and how the indie racing world was getting big and soon might be just as big as NASCAR.

I listened with half an ear while the other half plotted.

My coffee cup was almost empty again when the doorbell rang. All three of us looked toward the door and then back at each other.

"Stay here," I told Ivy and strode out to the entryway and pulled open the door.

"Anthony," I said, surprised to see Romeo's dad on the porch so early in the morning. "Why do I get the feeling this isn't just a friendly visit?"

Flashes of my nightmare from just hours ago replayed in my head like some B-rated movie.

Anthony stepped inside, and I closed the door behind him.

Ivy and Drew came out of the kitchen and stopped short when they saw who it was.

"Because it isn't," he said. "I have news, and I'm afraid it isn't very good."

Cambria Hebert

CHAPTER THIRTY-NINE

We all have stories we won't ever tell.
I know most of yours.

#BuzzBoss

IVY

I missed coffee.

I never knew being pregnant could mess with your taste buds, but as I sat here and watched everyone around me drink it like I always used to, it became a harsh reality.

Even though I wanted to drink it, was tempted to snatch the cup from Drew's hand and take sip, I knew it wouldn't be the same. So odd how one day it could be something I absolutely loved, and the next day it turned to the stale taste of cigarettes across my tongue.

My only hope was once I had the baby, I could go back to my coffee-loving ways.

Until then, I'd stick to orange juice.

Yeah, I know. It had too much sugar and was too acidic. Were you going to argue with a pregnant woman's hormones?

Yeah.

Didn't think so.

I wasn't about to either.

Everyone was up early this morning. Seemed there was something in the air that was keeping us all awake. I guess we all had our own personal demons to work through.

The doorbell rang.

As usual, Braeden rushed out ahead of me like a shield, and when I stood to follow, Drew put himself in front of me as well.

This time it wasn't an unwelcomed guest with wild accusations. It was Anthony Anderson, but judging from the way he looked and the words that fell out of his mouth, I kinda wished it had been someone unwelcome.

I didn't want to hear whatever he came to say.

Perhaps we all weren't up battling our personal demons this morning. Perhaps deep down, all of us knew something was about to happen, something we all needed to be together for.

I fidgeted in the space between the living room and kitchen, watching Braeden's and Anthony's grim faces by the door.

"Can I get you some coffee, Mr. Anderson?" I asked.

"Call me Tony," he corrected. "And yes, please."

I was grateful for the brief escape, and I went into the kitchen and let out a breath. At the counter, I stood for long seconds, my back to the room, and tried to prepare myself for whatever it was he was here to say.

Obviously, this had to do with Braeden and Zach's father. Obviously, if he was here as a lawyer at this early hour of the morning, then it must be bad.

My hand trembled slightly when I lifted the pot to fill the mug with coffee, making sure to leave enough space for a bit of cream.

Once the pot was replaced, I gripped the edge of the counter and bowed my head.

"Hey," a familiar voice whispered, and a hand rubbed over my back. I turned my head and stared at my brother, letting him see the fear in my eyes.

"Drew."

"Come on." His voice was low, but it was too deep to be a whisper. I went to him willingly, and he folded me against his chest. He always hugged the tightest. Always. Ever since I was a little girl, it was Drew's hugs that were always the most solid. He wasn't afraid to squeeze me, and I loved the feeling of a big brother bear hug.

"I'm scared," I whispered against his chest.

He hugged me even tighter. "Don't be scared, Ives. I know I haven't been here as long as everyone else, but there are a few things I've learned about this family that I know as well as my own name."

"What?" I asked, still pressing close.

I felt him smile, and he kissed the top of my head. "If one of us is in trouble, we all are. You're never ever alone, and the only thing luckier than a winning lottery ticket is Braeden."

"Braeden isn't very lucky right now."

"That's where you're wrong, sis. He's the luckiest bastard I ever met. He has you. He has an entire family that's gonna fight for him."

"Even you?" My voice was small, reminding me of all the times I'd gone to him when I was young, scared, and needing him to make it better.

His chest rumbled with laughter. "Even me. I won't let someone with an axe to grind take away my sister's only, especially when she needs him around to change diapers."

He was my only.

It was the perfect way to describe what Braeden was to me.

Not the father of my child.

Not my boyfriend.

Not my one true love.

My only.

"Get the coffee," he said and released me. "I got your juice." He picked up the glass and gave me a smirk.

"Are you disappointed in me?" I blurted out.

Where did that come from?

He frowned. "What?"

I put a hand over my middle, holding my child. "I know you blame Braeden for..." My words faltered because I wasn't going to call this baby a mistake. I didn't even want to call her an accident. "I was just as much involved..."

The glass made a thudding sound when he put the juice back on the granite. "Stop right there. I know how many people it takes to make a baby."

I grimaced. I wasn't going to mention sex. Geez.

"You think I'm disappointed in you?"

I nodded and tried to hold myself together. Now was not the time for this conversation, but I couldn't stop the vulnerability from bubbling up inside me. It was like I had to get it out because the only thing I was going to have room for was whatever was waiting for me in the other room.

"I don't think I could take it if you are... You have to know how important you are to me, Drew."

He made a strangled sound, closing the distance between us. "You're just as important to me, kid. That's why I'm here. I packed my shit and moved up the East Coast to be where you are. Hell, I even told Dad I couldn't be the son he wanted for you."

"You did that for you." I corrected.

"I did it for both of us." He tugged on the ends of my hair, and I smiled.

I glanced down between us, looking at our bare feet against the tile. We had the same shaped feet. His were just bigger.

"I could never be disappointed in you, Ivy."

I looked up.

"I'm shocked as hell you even worried about that."

"Well, you haven't said much about the baby... and that night in the car, you yelled at Braeden."

He gave me a lopsided smile. "I'm gonna yell at him for the rest of our lives. That's my job as your big brother."

"But the baby," I pressed.

"Is going to be spoiled as shit." He finished. "'Cause I'm gonna love him or her as much as I love you. I'm not disappointed in you, Ives. I'm so fucking proud for everything you've come through and for the mother you already are to that little munchkin."

I needed to hear that so much. And now that I had, I felt so much lighter. "I'm so glad you came here."

He chuckled. "Me, too." He used his thumbs to wipe away the tears I hadn't realized spilled over. "This place has totally changed me."

Something about the way he said that struck me. "What do you mean?"

His blue eyes, which were usually so open, became shuttered.

"Drew?"

He shook his head. "Nothing."

I grabbed his arm. "It isn't nothing. Tell me."

"Everything okay in here?" Braeden asked from the doorway.

Drew took advantage of my distraction and removed himself from the conversation. "Get the coffee." He picked up my juice.

"We're all good," Drew told Braeden as he walked by him and into the living room.

I stared after him with a funny feeling in my stomach.

"What's the matter?" B asked.

"I don't know," I replied thoughtfully, staring after my brother. I shook off the feeling and carried the coffee to the fridge and added a bit of cream.

When I made it to B's side, his hand found a spot on the small of my back. All my attention turned to him and whatever Anthony was about to say.

"It's going to be fine." I assured him.

Everyone was gathered in the living room when I handed the coffee to Tony. He thanked me and took a sip before sitting it on the table in front of him. He looked tired, his blue eyes weary.

Romeo and Rimmel were sitting on the end of the couch, close to the chair Anthony was in. Rim looked worried, and Romeo had a stubborn set to his jaw, like whatever this was about was going to be sorry it ever came our way.

It made me feel stronger.

As if he sensed me looking, his sapphire gaze shifted to me. I caught a glimpse of the player he was on the football field. The cold determination, the steely strength behind the laidback persona. He was ready for this, and whatever it was didn't stand a chance.

I sat down near Rimmel, and Braeden sat on my other side. I braved a glance up at him, worried about what I might see.

But he looked a lot like Romeo.

Stubborn, with a hint of fire in his dark eyes. There was no laidback persona to look behind with him, though. He was just as intense as always and ready to defend what was his.

"Trent should be here," Rimmel said.

He should be, but there was no way we could wait the time it would take for him to get here. We were all too keyed up.

Drew made a sound and pulled out his cell. His fingers flew over the screen.

"We'll just have to fill him in," I said and looked at Tony, ready to start.

"Hang on," Drew said and tossed the phone in his lap.

Seconds later, the sound of feet pounding above our heads made everyone look around at the staircase.

Trent came rushing down, his movements unsteady, like he was still half asleep. "I'm here," he said, rushing into the room. His shirt was rumpled and he had pillow marks on the side of his face. His hair was mussed and eyes blurry.

Everyone turned their eyes to Drew, who actually looked a little embarrassed. "He had too much to drink to drive home."

"The hangover is real," Trent said and slid onto the floor near the chair Drew was sitting in. All the seats in the room were already taken.

"He slept in your room?" Braeden asked, totally ready to have a field day with this.

"Someone had to make sure his drunk ass didn't choke on his own puke," Drew retorted. Then he muttered, "Like you and Romeo never shared a room."

"Ocean City!" They both burst out at the same time.

Rimmel and I looked at one another and shrugged. "We probably don't want to know." I assured her. She agreed.

"Everyone is here, then?" Anthony asked, clearing his throat.

On the floor, Trent moaned at their volume and put his head in his hands. Drew rolled his eyes and held his coffee mug down in front of him. Trent took it in both hands and held it in front of him like it was some kind of holy object.

"What's going on, Dad?" Romeo asked.

"I received a call early this morning. I know some people in the department. He was actually at your engagement party," he said to his son.

Romeo nodded.

Tony looked away from him and at Braeden, regret in his eyes. "Robert Bettinger is in the process of filing criminal charges against you, Braeden. Because it's the weekend, not much is going to happen, but come Monday morning, they will likely be issuing a warrant for your arrest."

I made a sound and collapsed back into the couch. Arrested? Braeden was going to go to jail? I pressed a hand over my stomach and forced myself to breathe.

I would not cry.

Beside me, Braeden was tense but silent.

Too silent.

"On what charges?" Romeo demanded.

"Manslaughter."

"No!" I burst out and leapt to my feet. "That's insane. It was a car accident. *Zach* kidnapped me. *He* held a gun on me. *He* raped me!"

"Apparently, Robert got ahold of the 9-1-1 call that Braeden made the night of the crash. Robert claims that in the background, Zach can be heard yelling for help. He's claiming Braeden had ample time to pull Zach free of the wreckage."

"It's not true!" I demanded, not even trying anymore to stop the tears. This was a nightmare. I wished I'd never drunk that drink he gave me that night. I wished I'd been smarter, braver. If I had, maybe none of this would be happening right now.

"Ivy." Braeden appeared behind me, reaching for my hand.

I jerked away from him and sobbed. "He didn't kill him. He can't go to jail."

"Stop." Braeden wrapped around me from behind.

Everyone in the room was beyond silent. I felt their stares like one hundred-pound weights, but I couldn't stop.

How could they be so calm?

How could they just sit here and listen to the news Braeden's entire life was about to go up in flames.

"Stop," he murmured again against my ear. "Calm down. This isn't good for the baby."

"Baby?" Tony repeated, alarmed.

"Ivy's pregnant," Romeo informed him.

I clung to Braeden's forearms where they enclosed me.

Anthony looked at us with a stricken look on his face. "You're expecting?"

"Yes," I sobbed. "Please don't let them take him away."

Anthony's face fell, and I could see the regret in his eyes.

I gasped and straightened. "I'm the one who forced the car off the road. Robert knows that. I'm the reason that wreck even happened. I'll turn myself in. I'll go to the police right now. Then they'll have to leave Braeden out of it."

"No!" every man in the room yelled at the same time.

Men were stupid.

"They'll have to accept it was self-defense on my part. He was holding a gun on me. He actually fired a shot." I went on.

"The police already know that, Ivy." Tony's voice was calm. "They know the details of that night. No one lied."

"Then how can they do this?" Rimmel asked, her voice just as hoarse as mine.

"Because Robert believes he can prove something in court. You'll be charged, released on bond, and then it will go to trial."

"His entire career will be ruined," Romeo said.

"It certainly isn't going to help. I'm not sure any team will draft you with a manslaughter case hanging over your head. The press coverage is going to be negative. No team wants that stigma."

"I'll drop out of the draft," Braeden said calmly. "It will save a lot of headache."

How could he be so calm? I glanced at Romeo for help, but he was staring at the wall, his jaw clenched.

"It might be best for this season." Anthony agreed reluctantly.

"He's not going to jail!" I yelled.

Braeden picked me up and sat down with me in his lap. His arms were like vises around me, keeping me from being able to get up and pace.

"No." Anthony assured me. "I won't let that happen."

I fell back against B's chest, grateful for some kind of positive news.

"You think you can win his case?" Rimmel asked.

"I do. There's no way Robert will be able to prove beyond a shadow of a doubt that Braeden had time to pull him out of that car. Yes, it will look bad because Zach was conscious and yelling, but that doesn't mean Braeden didn't try to help him."

"I didn't." Braeden interrupted.

No one in the room said a word. We all silently united as one wall behind him and his admittance.

Tony didn't seem surprised at all. "I figured as much. After everything, I can't really say I blame you, son."

"Really?" Ah, finally, some emotion in Braeden's voice. It seemed he wasn't as stoic about this as he was pretending to be.

"I've known you since you were barely seven years old, son. I think of you like one of my own. Valerie does, too. You aren't a killer and you never will be. As far as I'm concerned, Zach died by his own fault. Not by yours. And judging from the stony silence in this room and the way I'm being measured"—he smiled a little at the comment—"I'm pretty sure everyone else sitting here agrees."

"I might have been able to get him out." Braeden pressed, pushing Anthony as far as he could.

"*Might have.* That's reasonable doubt. Not even you can sit here and say you wouldn't have died trying to get that boy out of the car."

"So then how can Robert even press these charges?" Drew asked.

"Because he knows people and he knows how to work the system," Tony answered, blunt.

"Fuck!" Romeo growled and pushed off the couch. He paced behind it, wearing a path in the floor.

"I just want you to be prepared." Tony spoke to Braeden. "When they come here for you, don't put up a fight. *Don't say anything.* Not one word unless I'm present and give you permission to speak."

Braeden nodded.

"I can tell by the look on your face you think you deserve this. I might even guess you've been waiting for it."

I sucked in a breath and pulled back to look at B over my shoulder.

"Seems like maybe I should be punished, that I shouldn't get off scot-free."

That was why he was being so calm about this right now? That was why he wasn't cussing and pacing the room like Romeo or crying and yelling like me?

He thought he deserved to be punished.

As if he wasn't punishing himself enough as it was.

"That's bullshit and you damn well know it," Romeo snapped.

"Maybe once I do my time, I'll be able to move on." His words were spoken so quietly. So matter-of-fact.

They destroyed me.

"You're not going to jail." I refused.

"No. But I'm still being punished. My biggest regret is the NFL. I'm not going to be able to take care of you the way I wanted."

"Fuck that," Romeo ground out and stopped to glower down at him.

"It was fun while it lasted, Rome," B said. "Us maybe back on the same team again. But we both know this will demolish my career. Even if they accept me into the draft after next season, the probability that the Knights will want me or, hell, even get me are gonna be a lot less."

I'm not really sure why he thought that, but the way Romeo's mouth flattened told me Braeden was right.

He was so accepting.

So willing to take this as his fate.

Where was the fighter that usually was so ready to go into battle?

He only fights for his family. Not for himself.

I jumped up with enough force Braeden had no choice but to let me go.

"You're not going to fight for yourself." I accused him, angry.

His eyes narrowed and he started to push up, likely to grab me and "subdue" me like before.

Oh, hells no.

"Don't you dare touch me!" I yelled and stumbled back beside my brother.

"I don't accept this," I ground out. "You all just sit here, so willing to let Robert take away everything. I'm so disappointed in this family." I hiccuped. "This isn't who we are."

"Ivy," Romeo intoned.

I gave him a hard look, and he shut up.

"None of you want to fight?" I looked at Braeden. Resolve filled my insides, laying thickly over the panic and fear. "Then I'll do it alone."

I rushed across the room to where my bag was hanging by the door. I snatched it off the wall and jammed my feet into a pair of Uggs.

"Ivy!" Braeden yelled and came rushing toward me.

Before he could make it to my side, I rushed out the front door and ran across the lawn to my car.

They were all acting like it was over. Like there was nothing left to do.

Silly players.

The clock might be winding down. The offense game was strong.

But the game wasn't over yet.

There was still one play left, and I knew exactly what it was.

CHAPTER FORTY

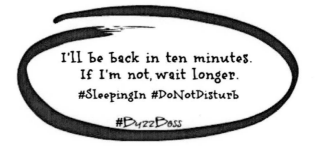

I'll be back in ten minutes.
If I'm not, wait longer.
#SleepingIn #DoNotDisturb

#BuzzBoss

BRAEDEN

I stood in the center of the yard and watched her drive away.

She shouldn't be driving like this.

What the fuck was she even thinking?

Where the hell was she going?

On impulse, I ran to the truck, intent on following her down the street.

Fuck!

The keys were in the house.

I hit the steering wheel and let out a frustrated yell.

I looked over when someone knocked on the window. Romeo glared at me through the glass. I popped the door open, and he caught the steel frame and pulled it wide.

"Let her go."

I looked at him like he had three heads. "Are you fucking insane?"

"Let her cool off. She just needs a minute," Romeo said, calm.

"Did you not see her?" I shot out. "She was talking crazy."

"Not crazy," Romeo said. Then his lips turned up. "Just a little louder than the rest of us."

I gaped at him as a cool wind blew. My muscles constricted against the chill. "Not you, too."

"You really think anyone in that house is just going to let you get dragged through the mud."

"Your dad—"

"My dad will do everything he can *legally*."

"What are you saying, Romeo?" I asked.

"Will you hang with Rim for a while?"

"What?" I shook my head. Everyone in this family was going fucking crazy.

"She's upset. She needs her BBFL. And there's somewhere I need to be."

Two things:

1) He never said BBFL because he thought it was stupid. So that was a dead giveaway he was up to something.

and...

2) He didn't have to be anywhere.

"Where you going?" I crossed my arms over my chest.

"Nowhere you need to know about."

I advanced on him, my fists tightening against my sides. "You can't fix this. I don't *want* you to fix this. Goddamn, Rome. Let me do what I need to do."

"So ruining your entire career, upsetting your soon-to-be wife, and making your kid live with the stigma that his father was charged of manslaughter is what *you* need to do? Selfish much?"

I decked him.

I punched him right in his cocky, know-it-all face.

I got sick satisfaction by the way his head snapped back and the surprise flooded his eyes. "You deserved that," I ground out, thinking about hitting him again.

He smiled.

The motherfucker smiled.

"'Bout time you showed up," he drawled.

He was goading me?

I swung at him again. This time he was ready, and he moved so my fist only grazed his shoulder. So I acted fast, shifted my weight, and buried another punch right in his midsection.

Romeo's eyes flared, and I motioned for him to bring it on.

He swung, and I moved, but he was quick and anticipated my countermove, so he brought his other fist and socked me in the jaw.

Ambidextrous asshole.

The hit was hard, and I stumbled back but gained my footing. Physically, Romeo and I were well matched. In the past year, I'd put on a little more bulk than he had, so technically, I might have had him with my weight, but Romeo didn't live by technicalities.

Rome was a born leader and he gave as good as he got.

He hit me again, and I felt the warm trickle of blood at my lip. I ignored it and let out a cry, tackling him onto the ground.

The driveway was hard and cold. Neither of us was wearing a shirt, but those things didn't penetrate my temper. All I could think about was how fucking pissed I was.

And scared.

I was scared, too.

Truth was I wanted to just accept my fate. I wanted to take my punishment. Maybe I couldn't have saved Zach. Maybe I could have. Either way, it didn't matter anymore. He was dead.

I wasn't sorry he was. That was his punishment.

Perhaps this was mine.

I swung down, and Romeo rolled, pinning me beneath him. I grabbed his arms and started grappling with him. I caught some traction with my foot, and I rolled us again, putting me back on top.

I raised my fist again, ready to take a shot. This time I wasn't going to miss.

"Stop!" a hysterical voice screamed.

I glanced up. Romeo grabbed my fist in his hand.

Rimmel was running across the yard frantically. She tripped on her sweats, and I stiffened, but she caught herself and kept on running.

"Don't you dare hit him, Braeden!" she demanded. "Trent! Drew!" she yelled behind her as she rushed.

"You're in trouble now," Romeo sang.

I shoved off him and stood. "He started it."

Rimmel stopped before us, hands on her hips. "What the hell are you two doing out here fighting in the middle of the yard? This is not the zoo!"

"Rome sure looks like an ass to me."

Rimmel gasped.

"He got me right here, baby." Romeo was good at sounding pathetic as he pointed at his jaw. Of course my sister fell for that shit. She made a distressed sound and rushed forward to take his face in her hands and look him over.

"Pansy ass," I muttered as Drew and Trent came out onto the lawn.

Rimmel turned to me with an angry look, but then it changed to one of concern. "You're bleeding!"

"Looks like he's not the only one who took a few hits." I dabbed at the corner of my lip.

"How could you!" Rimmel accused Romeo and rushed to my side to dab at my face.

"You should probably clean that up, baby," Romeo said, completely unbothered by the fact he just got yelled at by his girl. He stepped forward and kissed her on the head.

She pulled back from me, bewildered.

Romeo retreated into the house and shut the door behind him.

Rimmel turned back to me. "What in the world happened?"

"Man stuff," I said.

"Told ya brothers hit each other," Drew quipped.

I half smiled, remembering the night she'd lit into him for threatening me.

"We shouldn't be fighting now," she said sadly. "We need each other."

I felt bad. She was right. Not only had I upset Ivy, who freaking sped away, but I took shots at my best friend and now hurt my sister.

"I'm sorry, tutor girl." I draped an arm over her shoulder, hoping that coupled with the use of the nickname I sometimes called her would buy me some points.

The garage door opened and the smooth purr of the Hellcat filled the driveway. We all turned to watch as Romeo backed the car out of the garage and hit the brakes so we would all move out of his way.

I guided Rim to the grass, and he backed up a little more. She rushed to the window, and it slid down a little. "Where are you going?" she demanded.

He said something I couldn't hear.

Her shoulders slumped and she nodded, backing up to my side.

Before he rolled up the window, his eyes locked on mine. We stared at each other silently for long moments before the window slid back into place and he drove away.

Wherever he was going was for me.

CHAPTER FORTY-ONE

You don't like me.
Until you need me.
#BuzzBossKnowsThings

#BuzzBoss

IVY

I knocked on the door and waited.

My stomach was in knots, and I knew I probably looked a mess. I'd run out of the house without any makeup on and my hair just barely brushed through. I was dressed in a pair of chocolate-colored leggings and an oversized mint-colored hoodie with fur around the hood. Beneath it was Braeden's Wolfpack T-shirt—I'd slept in it and just threw on some comfy clothes when I rolled out of bed this morning because I wanted to go get some juice.

Was I wearing a bra?

I'd never tell.

I was still in shock over everything that happened this morning. The way everyone just stood around without saying a word. I couldn't just sit. I had to act.

This wasn't somewhere I wanted to be.

I *needed* to be here.

I was determined to fight for Braeden, just like he'd fought for me so many times before.

I thought back to all those nights he slept on the floor outside our bedroom door just in case I needed him. Even if I lived to be a hundred, that knowledge would always melt my heart.

And as I stood here at the door of my once-best friend, it also strengthened my resolve.

The door opened and Missy's dark head appeared. Clearly, she'd still been in bed. She was dressed in pajamas and her hair was rumpled.

"I need your help," I said without pause.

Her body jerked upright and her eyes went wide. Clearly, she hadn't been expecting to see me. Or hear those words out of my mouth.

But I didn't have time for games. The truth was I did need her, and she owed me.

She owed us all.

"Ivy."

I nodded. "Let me in."

She pulled the door wide, and I stepped inside. Her room looked like it always did. Gray and yellow with pops of white. The covers on her bed were shoved aside and the pillows were all askew, and one bore the dent of her head.

I stood in the center of the room, not really sure what to do with myself.

How far we'd come.

At one time, I would have flopped right down on her bed and made myself at home. But she was a stranger to me now.

I glanced at the bed where her roommate was lying, scrolling through her phone.

"Would you give us a minute?" Missy asked.

I smiled sweetly when the girl looked at me.

"Sure. Want a coffee?"

"Sure, thanks," Missy said.

The girl looked at me, and I wrinkled my nose. "No."

"You say no to coffee?" Missy asked when the roommate was gone.

I shrugged. I didn't come here to talk about my tastes, and I wasn't going to tell her about the baby. The way she was, it would probably send her into some wild jealous rage.

"I need your help," I said again.

"Why would I help you?"

I didn't even laugh. I just looked at her, dead calm. "Because you owe me and you know it."

"I don't know what you could possibly need me for." She sniffed.

At least she didn't try to deny she was a scallywag.

Progress? Nah. But at least it gave me hope she'd do what I wanted.

"It's for Braeden." I dropped his name like an atomic bomb.

In a way, he was.

To the friendship I once had with Missy.

Of course, it really wasn't him that blew things up. It was her. He was just who she used as an excuse.

Her gray eyes flared. Even after all these months, she still had a soft spot for him. Love? I didn't like to think about that. Besides, I wasn't really sure she was capable of loving anyone but herself.

But she definitely felt something for him, and I was going to use it.

"What's wrong with Braeden?" she asked softly.

God, I hated hearing her say his name. I swallowed down that reaction and took a steadying breath. I knew she knew what happened the night Zach died. I also knew Braeden had been here to accuse her of the panty trick. It was the reason he knew Zach was lurking around, because Missy broke down and told him.

So because the BuzzBoss knew probably a lot more than even I did, I didn't bother trying to explain.

"Robert Bettinger is filing charges on Monday morning against Braeden for manslaughter."

She gasped. "What!"

"So help me God, if I read this on the Buzzfeed," I growled.

"I won't do that," she snapped.

"You better not, or I will bury you at this school."

She glared at me, a glint coming into her eyes. I stepped forward and glared back. I had a hell of a lot more at stake here, and I meant this. I would take her down. She'd never be able to show her face in the entire state if she hurt Braeden with this information.

She must have sensed my total intent, because she nodded and then said, "But he didn't kill Zach."

"No. He didn't. But Robert is so grief stricken he can't think straight. And he seems to think ruining Braeden's entire career will make him feel better."

"His career?"

I sighed. "I know you know he was put in the draft for the NFL."

She glanced away. Yeah. Missy still kept tabs on him.

The little bitch.

"If he gets arrested, everything changes."

She nodded. "What does this have to do with me?"

I told her.

Her eyes burned with interest, and even a little satisfaction.

"You have what I need, don't you?" I asked.

She nodded.

Hope took hold inside me, and I clung to it.

"So what's in it for me?" she asked when I was done talking.

"Nothing," I deadpanned. I wasn't giving her shit. Then I relented... a little. "It's a chance to make up for some of the hurt you've caused. I know you still... have feelings for Braeden. Don't let him go down for something he doesn't deserve."

It killed me that she was the one that had the power to help him. I wished I never had to see her face again.

This wasn't about me. It was about B.

He told me he'd do anything for me. I told him the feeling was mutual.

This was me proving it.

She thought about it for a long minute, and I wanted to scream. But I didn't. I stood there and waited, holding my breath.

"Give me a second to change," she said.

"You'll do it?" I asked.

"Of course," she said, a sly smile forming on her lips. "What's good about being the BuzzBoss if you can't take advantage of the power?"

Ew, she was slimy.

But right now, slimy was just what I needed.

CHAPTER FORTY-TWO

Some love you never get over.
You just learn to live without it.

#ByzzBoss

ROMEO

Pretentious.

That's the word that came to mind when I pulled up the driveway of Robert Bettinger's estate.

It was a large white colonial-style house with a long curved driveway. Sure, I knew he made good money and was a successful lawyer, and sure, everyone liked nice things. But there was an ostentatious vibe about this place that smacked a man in the face when he arrived.

We're better than you.

I almost felt sorry for Zach because he no doubt felt the pressure from just living in a place like this. Pressure to live up to the image his father seemed to desperately want.

There was a black Mercedes and a BMW parked near the front door. Both cars looked ritzy and kind of somber. It made me a little too happy to park the lime-green muscle of my car right beside them.

After the engine was off, I got out and stretched a little. B landed a couple good hits this morning. I hoped he was feeling the ones I gave him just like I was.

It had been worth it, though. Seeing him just accept his fate, become a mere shell of the asshole I knew he was, had been scarier than anything my father was saying. He needed a good reminding of who he was. So I gave it to him.

I also gave him a chance to take some of his anger out on me.

That's what brothers were for.

In the back of my mind, I wondered about Ivy. I hadn't expected any less of a reaction from her this morning. It was pretty on point with how I felt. I just held it in.

But still. She was pregnant and scared for the father of her baby. I didn't know where she was or what she was doing, and I worried about her.

I knew Braeden was probably worried, too.

As I walked up to the front door, I shot her a quick text.

We're all worried. Me included. Call me.

I hoped I'd get an immediate reply, but none came. I sent the screen dark and shoved it back in my coat. Before I could even knock on the door, it swung open.

Robert stood there in a pair of navy-blue jogging pants with silver stripes down the sides. He was wearing a white t-shirt with a blue zip-up jacket over it that matched the pants.

Was this some eighties workout video? Or was this his further attempt at projecting an air of superiority.

"Did I interrupt your workout?" I couldn't help but ask.

The look he gave me was bewildered. "What?"

"Nothing," I said and inwardly laughed. Yep. He just thought the outfit made him look rich.

"What are you doing here, Roman?" He sniffed. His hair was combed and his face was shaven. It was quite a contrast to the last few times I'd seen him. He seemed a little more together this morning, a little less like he was falling apart.

I wasn't sure if that was a good thing or a bad thing...

Good thing = maybe he would see reason.

Bad thing = maybe he was putting himself back together so he could take Braeden apart.

"I came to talk to you," I said.

"I don't think we have anything to say to one another."

"I think we do."

He moved to shut the door in my face. I slapped my palm on the wood and pushed.

He looked at me wide-eyed.

"What's the matter, Bettinger? Afraid you might not like what I have to say?"

A man like him couldn't resist a challenge.

He let me in.

The wide foyer was spotless, just like I knew it would be. Everything was austere and in its place. My parents had a big house, but it wasn't like this. Their place was a home. This was a museum.

I followed him into a formal sitting room to the left of the wide front door. The furnishings were dark—dark wood, dark leather—and had a very traditional, masculine feel.

I didn't sit down. I preferred to stand when I wanted to tower over the people I wanted something from. Plus, there was no way in hell I'd give him the satisfaction of looking down on me.

"Say what you came to say and then get out. I have a case to prepare."

"The one against Braeden you mean?" I replied coolly.

"Your father works fast." His voice was just as cool.

"Did you think he wouldn't?"

"It's his right." He shrugged a shoulder and sat in a leather club chair.

I wandered over to some ugly-ass painting and pretended to look at it. "Is it your right to destroy someone else's life because of the way your son lived his?"

"If you came here to trash talk my son, I suggest you leave," he said hotly.

I turned and looked at him. "You knew damn well when you let me in this wasn't some visit where I was going to shit rainbows and lie to you about Zach."

"I won't listen to you disparage his memory."

"I don't have to do that. His own actions speak for themselves."

"He was sick," his father said, the first hint of anything other than steadfast denial I'd heard from him.

I'd always suspected that. "What was wrong with him?"

He glanced up at my tone. It was a lot different than the one I'd been using before—kinder, less accusatory.

"He never had an easy life, my son. That was my fault. I did all the wrong things and tried to pretend too long that everything was fine when it wasn't."

"You tried to help him at the end. You sent him to that hospital."

"I didn't know he was so far gone, so much like her, that he was able to fool the doctors into letting him out for a little while. If only I'd known. Everything would be different."

I almost felt bad for Zach.

But this guy? Zach's father?

I felt downright sorry for him.

He was clearly living in deep regret over the things he thought he should have done. I probably should have gone, just left him in peace.

I couldn't do that.

"Who was he like?" I pressed.

"His mother. She was severely bipolar. It... it wasn't a healthy environment to grow up in."

Zach was bipolar. It explained so much. How else could he be one person (the charming frat president) one minute and someone else the next (a psycho douche)?

"You blame yourself," I said, coming around and sitting in a nearby chair.

"When you become a parent someday, you'll understand. It's a father's job to protect his children, even when it's hard. I turned a blind eye for too long, and now he's dead."

"And you want to punish Braeden for your mistakes."

His eyes flared and anger gathered around him like a heavy coat. "Braeden will be punished for allowing my son to die."

I shook my head sadly. "You're a good lawyer, Mr. Bettinger. My father has always respected you, and your family name has been highly regarded in my home my entire life."

He looked up, gleaning a little satisfaction from the praise.

See? Pretentious.

"You're a smart man. You know full well my father is going to be able to prove reasonable doubt that Braeden didn't kill your son that night."

He glared at me.

Oh, yes. He knew.

I smiled. And now he knew I knew.

"So you aren't doing this to see justice served. You're doing this to ruin Braeden's life to hopefully make up for the fact that you never did right by your son."

He leapt out of his chair with flared nostrils.

I leaned back and looked up. "Maybe you think this is one way you can do right by your son. To make sure people know he wasn't the reason he died, but it was because someone else killed him. After everything," I added, soft. "You're still worried about your status."

"You need to leave." He huffed.

"Drop this. Don't file those charges on Monday. Let this go. Let your son rest in peace."

He jerked back like I punched him. "How dare you lecture me about giving my son peace! You have no idea what his life was like!"

"Which is exactly why you need to let his death have amity."

Amity. That was a fifty-dollar word. Rim was rubbing off on me.

"You don't want *amity* for my son," he spat. "You just want to save face. You're the one worried about status, about that football career."

"You're wrong," I said hard and stood. He had to look up to maintain eye contact. "I could give two shits about my status. I stopped caring about that a long time ago. And my football career is solid. I already have a contract. It's ironclad. What happens with Braeden won't affect that."

"Then why are you here?" he ground out. "Why are you pushing me?"

"Because I'm protecting my family just like you're trying to protect yours."

"Get out." He started out of the room toward the entry hall. I followed along behind him at a much less hurried pace.

"Drop the charges."

He flung open the door and turned. "I will never drop those charges, and nothing you can say will ever make me change my mind."

"You will after you hear what I have to say."

I looked past Robert and onto the front porch where Ivy stood, filling the doorway. Her eyes were determined, and her back was straight.

I smiled.

"Seems we had the same idea, princess," I drawled, fucking impressed she'd come here. To the house belonging to the father of the man who raped her. And she did it for my brother.

Her eyes flickered to mine. "I saw your car outside. What are you doing here?"

"Same thing you are."

Her blue eyes softened for a second when she smiled at me. I winked.

"Well, let me save you the trouble," Robert snapped at her. "No!"

"I think you better let us in," a new voice joined in as someone stepped up behind Ivy.

I drew back. Ivy brought Missy?

What. The. Fuck?

Ivy glanced at me. *Trust me,* she said with her eyes. I nodded once.

Robert seemed just as surprised as me that there was now not one, but two women filling the doorway. Before he could recover, Ivy marched inside with Missy hot on her heels.

"You're going to listen to what I have to say, Mr. Bettinger," Ivy intoned. "Because if you don't, the entire world is going to know exactly what kind of man your son really was."

His face blanched. Ivy stepped forward, grabbed the door from his hand, and slammed it closed.

CHAPTER FORTY-THREE

Standing in front of the biggest story of the year. #BuzzBoss knows all. Stay tuned.

#BuzzBoss

IVY

I made her ride with me.

There was no way in hell I was going to trust she would actually get into her car and follow along behind me like a loyal and faithful friend.

It made for an awkward car ride, especially since I wasn't about to make small talk or entertain any of her tries.

It wasn't hard to find his address, and once I did, it was just a matter of following the GPS on my phone. When we pulled up the driveway and I saw the unmistakable green Hellcat, I wanted to laugh out loud.

Of course he was here.

I should have known better than to underestimate my family.

"What's he doing here?" Missy worried. Her anxiety level rocketed as she stared at the car.

"Guess we'll find out."

I parked right behind his car and looked at Missy. "You're doing this."

It wasn't a question. I didn't want reassurance. I wanted her to know she wasn't getting out of this.

"Maybe once I do, it will prove to you that I really am sorry for all the stuff that happened between us."

You mean all the stuff you did to me? I thought. I didn't say it out loud because I wasn't about to antagonize her right now. I needed something from her.

"Come on," I said and got out of my Toyota.

My stomach growled and felt queasy at the same time. I'd been feeling morning sickness for a while now. At first, I just brushed it off, sometimes I ignored it, but I couldn't do that anymore, not now that I knew the cause.

I should have eaten this morning. Sick or not, my baby needed nourishment.

Not that I expected to be standing on this porch, either.

Just as I was about to knock, the door flew open, and Robert was yelling at Romeo inside. Romeo didn't seem concerned at all.

Typical Romeo.

But I didn't like the things he was saying. If Romeo hadn't been able to get through to Robert, then what hope did I have?

You have the BuzzBoss.

God help me, it was a comforting thought.

It didn't matter.

It didn't matter that Romeo was getting nowhere. It didn't matter that looking at Robert reminded me of the hell I went through with Zach. It didn't even matter my old best friend was standing behind me and I was using her as my secret weapon.

I was doing this.

I wasn't leaving here until I got what I wanted.

After I slammed the door, Robert stood staring at us like he couldn't believe I'd just invited myself into this mausoleum he called a home.

"He calls you princess?" Missy asked, gawking between Romeo and me.

To reply, Romeo walked to my side and draped his arm across my shoulders. Missy stared as he leaned down and kissed the top of my head. "I texted," he growled. "You didn't answer."

"I was busy."

"So I see."

Missy continued to openly gape. I hadn't been this close to Romeo before. It happened naturally over the course of time, time Missy was no longer a part of.

"Don't let it happen again."

I rolled my eyes and poked him in the ribs. He tightened his arm around me.

"I don't know what's going on here, but if you don't leave, I'll be calling the police."

"No, you won't," I said and pulled away from Romeo.

He let me go but stayed close.

"And how do you know that?" Robert scoffed.

"Because you've made it clear you want your son's name to not be ruined any more than it already is."

"If it's ruined at all, it's because of the lies you're spreading about him."

"I didn't have anything to do with the attack on Rimmel and Romeo," I countered.

He started to argue with me, and I held up my hand. "I'm not here to debate anything with you. Or even argue. We're never going to see eye to eye on this. It doesn't matter. The only thing that matters is that you understand what will happen if you go after Braeden."

I walked into the over-decorated formal sitting room just off the entryway and pointed to the wood coffee table and then at Missy.

Missy dropped to her knees beside the table, pulled the laptop out of her bag, and opened it up. As the laptop booted up, she laid the bag she'd brought with her beside it on the table.

"What is this?" Robert demanded, stopping in the center of the room to stare at Missy and me.

"It's the only chance you're going to get," I said, flat.

Romeo stood nearby, arms crossed, watching the unfolding scene.

"I understand you loved your son, Mr. Bettinger. No one is here to dispute that. But I know you have to be aware your son wasn't always the nicest guy. He did things. A lot of things that were unsavory."

"If this about the alleged rape—"

"It's not alleged!" I snapped. How dare he try and make it out like I was pretending? It was the single most horrible thing to ever happen to me, and I would *not* stand here and allow him to make light of it. "Your son drugged me. He used my room key and took me into my own room, into my own bed, and he *raped* me." I dragged in a breath. "He said horrible things to me that night, things I wish I could forget. I have to live with that. I have to live with his voice taunting me as he violated me."

Robert paled and took a step forward. His eyes were angry, and it scared me.

But I held my ground.

Romeo noticed him moving, and he stepped forward and dropped a hand on his shoulder. "Stay back," he warned.

It wasn't a friendly warning.

"I have proof." I kept going. "Proof that he raped me. I have an entire folder of pictures that make it very clear about what happened to me that night. Your son took pictures because he was proud of what he did. And then he sent them to the school BuzzBoss in hopes that his conquest would get out and humiliate me even more."

Robert made a strangled sound. "I don't believe you."

"Believe it," Missy said. "And those aren't the only photos he sent the BuzzBoss."

"What is a *BuzzBoss*?" he asked, his voice becoming a little nervous.

"Think of it as a direct hotline to every single student on the Alpha U campus. Kind of like a chain email but way faster and more accessible."

"I can't believe the dean would allow such a thing."

"He doesn't," Missy said. "BuzzBoss got taken down. But that's the thing about the web. Alpha U doesn't own it all."

"And how do you know what this BuzzBoss has on my son?"

Missy stood. "Because you're looking at him." As if to prove a point, she pulled out her phone, did a few things, and then slid it back into her pocket.

Seconds later, both Romeo's and my phone went off. Romeo pulled his out of his back pocket and lit up his screen.

"Well. Would you look at that?" Romeo scoffed and read the buzz out loud. "*Standing in front of the biggest story of the year. #BuzzBoss knows all. Stay tuned.*"

He held the phone out so Robert could see the notification. I dug out my phone, pulled it up, and did the same.

The challenge left his eyes, and beneath Romeo's hand, his shoulder sagged.

"What do you have on him?"

Missy made a sound and dropped in front of the laptop. Within seconds, she had file after file of photos pulled up.

"Here he is the beginning of last year, hazing one of the dropouts from the Omega fraternity."

She turned the screen around to show a picture of Zach holding down a young-looking student and pouring what looked like vodka in his mouth. You can tell by the picture the kid was already drunk and was choking on the liquid being forced on him. He also had a black eye and a bloody nose.

"Here he is shoplifting from a local business, something I have pictures from twenty different days of him doing. I would imagine he'd stolen quite a lot in twenty plus trips." Missy clocked through several images in which he was clearly stealing.

"Here he is vandalizing one of the professor's cars a few semesters ago. I heard that spray paint had been impossible to get off and the teacher had to pay to have his car entirely repainted."

Another picture.

"Here he is assaulting a girl from a campus sorority."

That image was particularly difficult to look at, but I couldn't not look. She was tied to a bed, hands and feet. She was completely naked, and Zach was, umm... doing things to her with a beer bottle.

I must have made a sound because Romeo was suddenly beside me, gently turning my face away from the screen. "Change it," he roughly ordered.

Another click brought up another. And another. And another.

Each picture seemed to get worse than the last. I was horrified that I wasn't the first and only woman he assaulted. In fact, some of them he was so horrible to, it made me feel guilty for being in so much pain about what he did to me.

I ended up burying my face in Romeo's chest as Missy went through more than a dozen photos, going over them in graphic detail. I was going to have to add an extra therapy session to my schedule for this. This whole time I'd been so ashamed, so adamant that no one know what happened to me. I was embarrassed and didn't want people to look at me as a victim.

Was that how all these girls felt, too?

Were they ashamed, afraid, and alone?

Maybe if I had said something, it would have helped another one of his victims.

I started to tremble, and Romeo swore lightly under his breath. "I think he gets the point," he said over my head to Missy.

I heard the snap of her computer lid, and I took another moment to compose myself.

"Rest assured, I have more of the same. All of those are backed up on a hard drive that only I know the location of," Missy intoned. I heard the rustling of the bag she'd brought along, and I looked up.

"About Braeden…" She began, clutching the bag. "I know for a fact that Zach had intent to kill him. He told me."

"He didn't," Robert said, his voice small and shaky.

"He was obsessed with me before he died. He thought we were going to be together." She dumped out the contents of the bag on the table. "These are gifts he sent to me. Each has a handwritten note." She picked up one small card and took it across the room, handing it to Robert. "Recognize the handwriting?"

He stared down at the card. My heart broke for him when he started to cry.

Missy snatched the card away as if she were afraid he might try to destroy it. "He stole this dress from the place where Ivy works. The night he kidnapped Ivy, he left it on my door with a note. He wanted me to wear it to celebrate the next night after he killed B and Ivy. The note makes his intentions quite clear."

Romeo sucked in a breath, and I pulled back to look at Missy gratefully.

But she wasn't done.

"You can check the log at the hospital he was in upstate. He had a visitor before he was released. It was me. I signed in under the false name Blair Brien. I'm sure if the staff were called to testify, they could identify me as that woman."

"My son." Robert's voice broke.

"Your son was very sick," Romeo said gently, kindly. Like he was talking down a man from a ledge. "You already told me that. I believe you. We all believe you. Maybe the things he did were symptoms of that illness. Right now, it isn't public knowledge the kind of things he did. Yes, the accident details and how he kidnapped Ivy are public record, but I think you and I can both agree that's nothing compared to things Missy has on him."

Robert was utterly defeated in a way I'd never seen before. He practically slinked over to the leather club chair and sank into the cushions. "You would release all that information? Use it to completely ruin my son's name."

"And your reputation," Romeo intoned.

"My wife would never agree to come back, then. Never." His voice was empty.

I'd feel bad if I wasn't doing this for Braeden.

"Oh, I would use it." Missy's voice was almost chilling and dark with promise. "The BuzzBoss doesn't hold back. It's cost me a lot." She looked at me but then back at Robert. "But it would cost you way more."

"What do you want?" he sobbed.

My stomach turned. I felt dizzy. What we were doing was disgusting. We were basically blackmailing this man.

But what choice did I have?

It was him or me.

Just like the night Braeden made a choice.

Him or Zach.

"Walk away from your vendetta against Braeden." Romeo cut in, cold and calculating. It was clear he was the son of a lawyer, because he knew exactly when to move in for the kill. "Drop your entire case, don't file charges, and stay the hell away from my entire family."

"And once I do, what's to stop you from releasing all that information anyway as revenge?"

"I give you my word," Romeo said. "I think you know my word means something."

"What about her?" Robert looked to Missy.

"She'll delete everything," Romeo answered.

Missy's eyes widened, and I thought she was going to protest.

"And if anything she showed you tonight ends up on the BuzzFeed, you can sue her for defamation of character and I'll testify against her."

She gasped. "You wouldn't."

"Fuck yes, I will," he rumbled.

"Do we have a deal?" I said, anxious to get the hell out of there. I just wanted it done.

"What choice do I have?" Robert replied miserably.

"There's always a choice," I said. "You just have to choose the one you can live with."

Robert seemed to consider my words.

"Let your son rest in peace," Romeo said softly.

"I'll drop the case. The charges will never see the light of day. Your friend is free."

I sucked in a breath, afraid to believe.

Romeo stepped forward and held out his hand. "Do I have your word?"

Robert looked between Romeo and his hand, then slowly placed his inside. "You have my word."

When he was done, he moved past me to stand in front of Missy. "I'd like your word as well."

Her word doesn't mean a thing, I thought. But I wasn't about to tell him that, not after getting what I wanted.

"Fine," she said and shook his hand.

Missy started packing up her stuff.

Robert turned to Romeo. "I'll call your father and let him know. Then I'll call my contacts and shut it all down."

"Do it today," Romeo ordered. "If Braeden gets so much as a speeding ticket on Monday, I'll start posting that shit myself."

"I'll sue you." Robert threatened.

"You'll have to prove it was me first."

"So arrogant," Robert muttered.

"I could say the same thing about you." He smiled, but it wasn't a gesture that reached his eyes.

"Now that you've gotten what you wanted, kindly get out." There was nothing kind about the way he said it.

"With pleasure," I said and started ahead. A wave of dizziness slammed into me, and I swayed on my feet.

"Whoa," Romeo rushed forward and picked me up. "The baby?" he worried.

"Baby!" Missy gasped.

I shut my eyes and winced.

"Ivy." Romeo worried and gave me a little shake.

I opened my eyes. "I'm fine. With all the excitement, I didn't eat. And I barely got my juice."

He chuckled. "Damn orange juice."

"Don't tell B. He'll only worry. He's been through enough."

Romeo's eyes narrowed.

"Please?"

"Fine, but we're going to get you food right now."

Robert walked to where we stood and looked at me with searching eyes. "You're expecting?"

"Yes." I lifted my chin and replied.

He nodded. "I understand why you fought so hard," he said. "If you'll fight that hard for the father of your child, then you'll fight even harder for the child himself."

"Yes. I will. Don't forget that." My absolute confidence in that statement made a ghostlike smile appear on Robert's face.

"It's for the best, then. I hope you do a better job with your child than I ever did with mine."

"We're going," Romeo said to Missy over his shoulder.

The three of us walked out of the house while Robert held the door. Well, I didn't walk. Romeo carried me because he refused to put me down.

He was as bad as Braeden.

When the door to the house latched behind us, Romeo continued on down the stairs.

"Wait!" Missy called after him.

He stopped and turned.

She came rushing down the stairs. "You're pregnant?" she asked. "With Braeden's baby?"

I squeezed Romeo's arm because I knew he was about to say something sarcastic and mean. I didn't like Missy, but she did just totally help keep B out of jail.

"Yes, I am."

So many emotions passed behind her eyes. One I just couldn't ignore any longer.

"You love him, don't you?" I asked.

She smiled sadly. "It doesn't matter because he loves you."

"I truly am sorry."

"So am I," she said.

Romeo didn't seem to care we were having a moment. He made a rude sound and jolted me gently. "Give her your keys, princess."

"My keys!"

"You're coming with me," he said.

"My car—"

"Missy can drive your car back to our place."

Was he on drugs? Or maybe I was a lot dizzier than I thought. I was hearing things.

"You'll meet us there, right, Missy?"

"Are you serious right now?" I asked, trying to get down from his arms. I was driving myself home.

"Serious as a heart attack. Stop trying to get down. It ain't happening."

"You're stupid!"

"That the best you got, princess?" He was totally amused.

"I can walk," I grumped.

"Last time we let you do that, you ended up here."

I wilted. Braeden was probably really upset. Romeo wasn't the only one who had texted. "Is he mad?"

"What do you think?" he asked.

I frowned.

"You know he won't stay made at you for very long. He never does." Then he pinned me with a hard look. "You never should have come here alone."

"I wasn't alone," I rebuffed.

We both looked at Missy as if just realizing she was still there. She was watching us with a shuttered look on her face. But even so, I could tell she was hurt. It was like I had the life she wanted.

The sad thing was it had been her life, too. She was the one who threw it away.

"We should go," I said, wiggling down.

"I'm not letting you out of my sight. Not after you almost face-planted in there. My nephew is starved."

"It's a boy?" Missy's voice cracked.

"It's too early to tell," I said, elbowing Romeo. "He just likes to say that."

I pulled the keys out of my bag and held them out to her. "Do you mind?"

"Sure," she said and took them.

"We'll be right behind you. I'm gonna swing through the first drive-thru we see," Romeo told her as he went to the Hellcat and managed to open the passenger door while still carrying me.

"Okay," Missy said, her voice sounding a little faraway.

"You want anything?" Romeo offered. That was awfully nice of him.

"Um, no thanks." She seemed surprised he would offer.

"Cool. See you at the house. Someone will drive you back to the dorms."

Missy drove away first because she was parked behind Romeo. When she was gone, he glanced at me. "Think we can trust her with your car?"

I grimaced. "I hope so."

He started up the engine and then leaned on the steering wheel, turning his head to look at me. "That was all you in there." He motioned toward the house.

"I had some backup." I smacked him lightly in the arm.

"How'd you know she'd help you?"

I glanced away and out the window. "Because she's in love with him."

"I'm sure going to her was hard," he said. "And then what went down in there."

I pushed away the unwanted images of the few pictures I looked at. "It was worth it," I whispered.

Anything for Braeden.

"Do me a favor, huh?" Romeo asked and pulled down the driveway.

"What?"

"Marry my bro, 'kay? Not only does he really love you, but I wanna keep you around, too."

I smiled. "I'll keep that in mind."

He grinned and held his fist in the space between us, and we pounded it out.

"He's free." The relief in his voice matched the relief I felt.

I melted back against the leather seat and let out a sigh.

He was free.

CHAPTER FORTY-FOUR

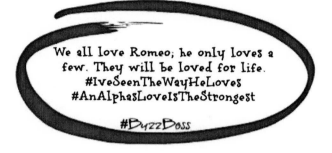

We all love Romeo; he only loves a few. They will be loved for life.
#IveSeenTheWayHeLoves
#AnAlphasLoveIsTheStrongest

#BuzzBoss

BRAEDEN

I was standing in the driveway when Ivy pulled up.

Soon as the car rolled to a stop, I rushed over and wrenched open the driver's side door. "What the hell were you think—"

I stopped short.

Missy blinked up at me in surprise.

"Two seconds, that's how long you got to explain," I growled and looked in the backseat for Ivy. The car was empty. Where the hell was my girl?

I moved back, and Missy turned off the engine and got out.

"She's on her way," she said, her eyes never once leaving me. It's like they latched on and wouldn't let go.

A long time ago, I would have liked that.

Now it just pissed me off.

"That's not good enough," I intoned.

The familiar purr of the Hellcat cut into our conversation. I craned my neck as Romeo pulled into the driveway. I peered through the windshield. Ivy waved at me from the passenger seat. He stopped the car right beside me, and I forgot about Missy to open the door.

Ivy climbed out, and I let out a string of curses. "Do you have any idea how pissed I am at you?" I swore even as I pulled her close and buried my face in her hair.

"I'm sorry," she said against my shoulder.

"You didn't answer your phone. I was worried sick."

"I'm fine. I promise."

Romeo got out carrying a Styrofoam cup with a straw sticking out of the lid. He came around the hood and held it out to Ivy. "It's not empty yet."

She groaned, and I looked between them.

"He's as bossy as you are." Ivy scowled.

"She didn't eat breakfast," he tattled.

I made a frustrated sound and grabbed what looked like a milkshake and thrust it at her. "Feed my kid."

"I ate a hamburger in the car," she muttered.

Romeo and I both stared at her until she rolled her eyes and put the straw between her lips.

Only then did I turn to him. "Thanks for finding her, man, and bringing her back." I held out my hand.

He shook it, but as he did, he said, "She found me."

I glanced over at Missy, wondering how the hell she fit into all this. "I need answers."

"Inside," Romeo said. "Everybody still here?"

I nodded. "Even your dad. Rim's been worrying."

I didn't need to say anything else. He started inside immediately. I reached for Ivy's hand to entwine our fingers together. A few steps toward the house and she glanced over her shoulder at Missy. "Come on."

I slid her a look out of the corner of my eye but didn't say anything else about her invitation for the devil.

Missy followed along behind us silently. When the three of us walked into the house, everyone looked up with surprised faces.

Missy blanched but otherwise said nothing, and her chin tipped up stubbornly.

Rimmel was already in Romeo's lap, and Anthony was still sitting in the same chair he had been when he told me I was going to get arrested.

Ever since mine and Rome's punch-fest in the driveway, I'd been thinking about what he said. Was it selfish of me to want to just take the punishment— even if the punishment wasn't exactly warranted? Even if it would mess up not just my future, but Ivy's and my baby's?

I wasn't a weak guy—hell, I was far from it. Everyone called Rome the alpha male of this family, and yeah, he was the head of us all. But that didn't mean I wasn't an alpha in my own right.

I was.

Still, I wasn't too sure how to fight these charges without making everything worse. And I was tired. So fucking tired. Giving a shit about stuff was a hell of a lot harder than just having fun.

"Ivy has news," Romeo said, drawing all the stares away from Missy and me out of my own head.

My eyes whipped to Ivy. She glanced at me and smiled. "I went to see Robert."

"What!" I ground out.

"Be quiet." She hushed me, and Drew laughed.

I gave him a narrow look. "You think it's funny your sister went to the house where her rapist grew up?" I spat.

That shut him up.

"I didn't go alone. Missy came with me, and Romeo was there when I arrived."

"You went to see Robert?" Rimmel asked Romeo.

"I wasn't about to just accept what he was doing to this family."

"Roman," Tony spoke up. "I'm not so sure that was a good idea. You both probably just gave him more ammunition to use in court."

"I brought a little ammunition of my own," Ivy said.

Romeo grinned. "You shoulda seen her, B. She owned it."

"Owned what?" I asked, frustrated.

Ivy stepped forward and sat on the coffee table in the center of the room. "When I left this morning, I went to the dorms to see Missy."

Missy came a little farther into the room and nodded.

"As the BuzzBoss, she has a whole computer full of dirty secrets on half the people on campus."

"Try all the people on campus." Missy corrected. I glanced at her, and she shrugged. "People are devious."

She would know about that.

"Anyway, Zach was so crazy I figured we weren't the only people he'd tortured over the years. Turns out I was right. Missy has files full of horrible things Zach has done."

Why did that make my skin crawl, and why did those words put shadows in her baby blues?

"What did you do, Ivy?" I asked quietly, already regretting that whatever she did in my name had somehow cost her.

"We…" She began, glancing at Rome and Missy. "Just showed Robert how it would benefit him to let all this go and let his son rest in peace."

I pinned Romeo with a hard look. "Talk."

He did. He told everyone exactly what went down at Robert Bettinger's house this morning. I was fucking blown away. Ivy sat on the table, drinking her milkshake like she hadn't just blackmailed a powerful lawyer into giving me my life back.

When Romeo was done, he turned to his father. "Think we can trust Robert to drop this like he promised."

Anthony nodded. "After hearing what kind of information you have on Zach, I know he will. Robert still has to live in this community, and he won't want to give up his good name. I've known him a long time, and when he gives his word, he's good for it."

It was over?

Just this morning, I was looking at manslaughter charges and saying good-bye to my football career, and now… just hours later, everything was handed back to me.

I looked at Rome. He smiled. I felt something inside me crack. *I was free.*

"Princess don't play," Romeo quipped.

Rimmel giggled.

I spun and sought out Ivy. She must have recognized the look in my eyes because she lowered the drink from her lips. I rushed forward and picked her up off the table and held her out in front of me.

"You fought for me."

"For us." She corrected.

"You shouldn't have gone there," I growled and crushed her against me. "It was stupid and reckless. I know it hurt you."

Her hands clutched at my back, holding me to her. It's like we weren't in a room full of people. We were alone in our own little world, a world that was now full of a bright future.

"Thank you," I rasped.

She hugged me tighter, then pulled back. "I couldn't have done it without Missy. She's the one who used the information she had on Zach to convince Robert."

I stepped up in front of Missy. Her eyes were slightly wary, but she didn't move back. I hugged her. It wasn't the kind of hug I gave Ivy, or even a friend. But it was a hug just the same. Then I pulled back to meet her surprised, gray stare. "Thanks, Miss."

"You're welcome." Her voice was hoarse.

I turned back to my family, and Rim rushed at me. I caught her, and she laughed. "I'm so happy!"

I chuckled. "That makes two of us, tutor girl."

"This calls for beers!" Drew said.

"It's not even noon!" Ivy admonished.

"I'm never drinking again," Trent groaned.

Rimmel gasped. "I forgot! Ivy, wasn't tonight the night we were all supposed to go to Screamerz for…" She glanced at Tony and grimaced.

He laughed. "An engagement party full of people your age?"

Romeo laughed.

"I completely forgot," Ivy said.

"Cancel," I told her.

"What!" Ivy gasped. "We can't just cancel. Everyone is supposed to be there!"

"Yeah, it can be an engagement slash celebration for you." Rimmel agreed.

"They're ganging up on you, B," Romeo drawled.

"Fine," I mumbled and mentally began to adjust the plans I had for the night.

Anthony stood. "I should be going. Valerie is going to want to hear the news. She's going to be so relieved." He came around the table and stood before me. "I'm happy for you, son."

"Thanks," I said, and he hugged me.

I returned the hug, and I suddenly had a strong sense of what it would have been like to have a father. Hell, maybe all this time I had. Tony never treated me as anything less than a son. He'd always been there, just like this morning, sitting in our living room for hours, trying to come up with a way to make sure I still had a future.

That was family.

Not blood.

And that was what I was going to teach my child.

I was a little choked up when he pulled back. When he looked into my eyes, he must have seen, because he nodded once. "Always going to be here for you, son."

He picked up his briefcase and car keys off the table.

"Would it be okay if I come with you?" Rimmel asked Tony.

Romeo made a choking sound. "You want to go to my parents'?"

Rimmel nodded. "I have an idea, and Valerie is the best person to help me."

"Baby, are you sure?" Romeo asked.

"Definitely." She nodded and turned to Ivy. "Wanna come? I could for sure use your help."

"Maid of honor on duty," she said and nodded.

"Well, then, it will be a pleasure to have such lovely ladies keeping me company on the way. Between this and the news about Braeden, Valerie will be on top of the world."

Rimmel grinned, and I chuckled. "Someone is starting to thaw where Moms is concerned."

"I'm just happy." Rimmel agreed.

"Call when you're done," I told Ivy. "We'll come get you."

Tony was already by the door, waiting, and after Rim said bye to Romeo, she met him over there as well. Ivy took her time practically dancing around the room, giving everyone a hug.

It was funny as hell.

"You put liquor in my girl's shake?" I asked Romeo as she hugged Drew.

Ivy bounded over to Trent and hugged his hung-over ass as well. She wrinkled her nose. "You smell. Go take a shower."

"Yes, ma'am," he muttered.

"Oh," she said when she moved toward the door and saw Missy. "Uh…"

"I'll drive her back to campus," I said. Ivy turned and looked at me, wariness in her eyes.

"I'll go with him," Romeo said.

That seemed to make her feel a little more comfortable, and she turned back to Missy. "Thanks for everything."

"It was the least I could do," she replied. Her eyes held a lot of regret, and I knew it was because of everything she could have been a part of with this family, but Missy made her choice.

Yeah, maybe what she did today made her not as despicable, but she would never be a part of this family again.

The girls left with Tony, and I turned back to the guys.

"I got a lot of shit to do before tonight," I announced. "All three of you are gonna help."

"Trent's gonna take a shower first," Drew said. "So we don't have to smell him the entire day."

Trent gave us all the finger. Times two.

"What you got in mind, B?" Romeo asked.

Something that just this morning I was uncertain of. But now? Now it was full steam ahead.

The future.

CHAPTER FORTY-FIVE

#ComePartyWithRomeo
Your #BuzzBoss has learned there
will be a second engagement party
for the campus celebs tonight @
Screamerz

#BuzzBoss

IVY

Word got out.

Really, we all should have expected it. 'Course, with everything going on and the fact we almost forgot to attend our own party, I guess it didn't seem so farfetched that none of us thought about it.

And yeah, the latest Buzz courtesy of the BuzzBoss herself certainly helped add to the crowd. Frankly, the fact that she obviously went home after everything that happened this morning and then posted a notification about the engagement party I set up at Screamerz for Romeo and Rimmel tonight didn't give me the warm and fuzzies.

It totes made me worry.

If she would use the info she overheard at our house this morning about something as silly as a party, then what would she do with all the other information she learned? The stuff that wasn't so silly?

I tried not to think about it, but as Braeden turned the truck into the way crowded parking lot and reporters swarmed and lifted their cameras, it was hard not to.

She was probably inside.

To get inside, she had to walk past the reporters. Missy was nothing if not dramatic, and I hoped she avoided the urge to perform on her way.

"Damn. I hope inside isn't like this," Braeden muttered as he looked for a spot.

Behind us, the green Hellcat purred into the lot and was closely followed by Drew and Trent in my brother's Mustang. It was like a little family parade.

Braeden insisted we take his truck tonight. It seemed silly to me for us to bring three cars to the same place, but when I pointed that out, everyone snickered.

Why that was so funny I had no idea.

They were up to something. Rimmel and I never should have left the four of them to their own devices almost the entire day while we planned what was going to be an amazing wedding.

For all the "I don't knows" and "I don't really cares," Rimmel certainly decided on what she wanted quick.

Well, okay, not so much the details, but she knew the exact location she wanted, and when Valerie said she thought it might not be possible, Rim proved her wrong.

Yep. She proved Valerie Anderson wrong.

She picked up her phone, dialed a number to a private line, and minutes later, we had a wedding location.

Score: Rimmel - 2 (1 for the location + 1 for getting Romeo), Valerie - 100

Rim was totes catching up.

After she got her way on that and announced the colors she wanted to use, everything else became just details again. Valerie sort of started to take over, but Rimmel didn't seem to care.

We were supposed to go back over to the Andersons' in a few days, because more decisions had to be made.

Braeden started laughing, and it pulled me out of my thoughts. "What?" I asked.

He motioned with his chin. "I should have known."

I glanced ahead and smiled. There was an empty parking spot near the club's entrance. Romeo always had a parking spot.

Always.

But this time there were two beside it.

One for each of us.

Braeden took the spot on the far right, Romeo pulled right beside him, and my brother took up the one on the left.

Braeden rolled his window down as the truck's engine still ran. Romeo rolled down both the passenger side and driver's side windows of his car, and as I peered around B, I saw my brother do the same.

"Hells yeah!" B hollered.

Laughter from everyone filtered into the cab but was way too quickly interrupted by the paparazzi swarming the Hellcat.

Everyone rolled up their windows, trying to get one last minute's peace before we had to make our way through it all.

"Stay close," B told me, wrapping one of the loose waves falling over my shoulder around his finger.

"With pleasure," I replied.

He popped his door open and held it wide, using it as sort of a barricade against the people calling out Romeo's and Rimmel's names.

But the second he was on the pavement, people started calling his name, too.

He smiled and waved for the cameras but then came back inside the cab and held out his hand. "Come on."

I gave him my hand and slid across the seat. He lifted me out of the elevated red truck and quickly put me on my feet. I was a little disappointed he didn't slide me down his body like always.

"You just had to wear a dress, didn't ya, Blondie?" he muttered, smoothing his hand over the flirty skirt.

He was worried I was going to flash someone.

I gave him a cheeky smile. "Good thing I'm wearing underwear."

He groaned and reached behind him to open the passenger door of the Hellcat. "Come on, tutor girl."

Rimmel climbed out of the car, looking photo ready, thanks to me, and smiled. "Thanks," she murmured to B and then smiled for the cameras.

She was dressed in a pair of white skinny jeans, black bootie wedges with black bows on the sides, and a loose yellow chiffon top with fluttery cap sleeves. Over that, she was wearing a black leather jacket that she would never have picked out if I hadn't literally handed it to her and told her to put it on.

It might not be her preferred hoodie, but she looked really awesome in it.

To top off her outfit, I pulled her long hair up into a high ponytail that I flat-ironed so it would fall sleekly down her back. Her black-rimmed glasses only enhanced the look. She was totally rocking the whole "sexy nerd" look.

Romeo came around the back of the Hellcat and pulled Rimmel into his side. They were stopped immediately for pictures, and instead of trying to rush away, they stopped and smiled, looking every bit the football royalty they had become.

Braeden finally slammed the door to his truck, and a few reporters called his name from behind. He linked our hands and turned. We smiled for a couple photos as reporters yelled out questions to him about the draft, the rumors that the Knights wanted him, and about his history with Romeo.

I heard Romeo answering similar questions, and of course, they were also being asked about their wedding, the location, and all those details.

It was chilly out, and my choice to wear a skirt only served in delivering me a nice draft up my legs. I shivered lightly, and Braeden paused for a split second in answering a question to anchor me at his side with his arm.

"Is there a wedding in the works for you two as well?" someone beside me asked.

"That's for me to know and you to find out," Braeden replied smoothly. He leaned into my ear to whisper, "Come on," and then we pivoted around again to join Romeo and Rimmel.

"Do you have a comment on the rumors you had time to pull out the man who died in the car accident with your girlfriend, but you left him in the vehicle to die?" a rather loud and rather rude reporter yelled.

Braeden stopped. The set of his jaw was hard. Of course the media was going to be all over this. How could they not conjure up all kinds of scenarios after what happened at the party the other night when Robert showed up?

"I don't comment on gossip," Braeden said, hard, and then started walking again.

Romeo had heard the exchange and was standing there with a look on his face that matched B's. The second we reached them, he took Rimmel's hand and both guys positioned themselves so they were on the outside of us and Rim and I were shielded.

Drew and Trent were right beside the Mustang, and the second we approached, Trent took up residence in front of me and Rim, and Drew did the same from behind.

They were closing us in, making it so Rim and I were completely inaccessible to the press.

The bouncer at the door saw us coming and opened it swiftly, nodding at the guys. "No press!" he yelled when a few reporters tried to slip in with us.

"Thank Christ," Braeden muttered.

I took a chance to look around, and of course, the place was packed. The second we walked in, people started cheering and howling. This was the Wolfpack country, and to the people of Alpha U, Romeo and B would always be Wolves first.

After that, drinks appeared, music pumped through the entire warehouse-looking building, and it was an all-around typical college night.

In other words, it was the best.

Rimmel's tongue was blue from the Smurf Balls, Drew and Trent were surrounded by so many women on the dance floor they were scarcely visible, and Missy sat at a table with a group of people I didn't know. I couldn't help but notice how she watched my friends and me half the night.

I danced as much as B would let me. He kept telling me to sit down because of the baby. All the guys were extra watchful of me, worried someone might body check me like before.

It was going to be a long nine months, and this poor baby… God help her if she was a girl. With three very large, very protective uncles right in her home, plus a daddy who tackled men for a living… well, she was going to need a lot of patience.

Ooh! Patience was a nice name.

A slow song came over the speakers, and Braeden's familiar arms wrapped around me from behind. "Time to go, Blondie."

I craned my neck so I could look back at him. "Go?"

"We got somewhere we need to be."

"Where?" I questioned, narrowing my eyes.

"Somewhere." He kissed the tip of my nose.

"'Kay." I sighed. I was such a sucker.

Braeden went over and said something in Romeo's ear, and he nodded. I watched them pound it out, and Rimmel gave me a *what's going on* look, and I shrugged.

But then she smiled. A secret-like smile.

She knew, too.

Once the good-byes were said, B led me to the door. On the way, we passed right by Missy's table.

I couldn't help it. I stopped in front of her. She looked up at me, mild surprise in her eyes. "Twice in one day? Be careful, Ivy. People might think we're friends again."

File that under things that will never happen.

"How can we be sure you won't talk?" I cut right to the chase.

"How little faith you have."

I lifted a perfectly sculpted brow at her. "Big crowd tonight. The BuzzBoss made sure everyone knew where the party was." It was an innocent statement, but she knew damn well what I meant.

Missy shrugged one of her delicate shoulders. "That's what the BuzzBoss does. Keeps people in the know on important social events."

"Just social?"

She stood up from the table then, giving her new friends a smile (the poor suckers), and leaned in. "I'm not going to say anything. Parties are one thing; real life is different."

I believed her. Maybe I shouldn't, but I did.

"I won't hurt you like that." She lowered her voice. "Not again. Not especially now that other people are involved." She glanced pointedly at my waist.

So it was the baby that convinced her to let all this go?

"Good luck, Ivy," Missy said, the note of finality in her voice clear.

My stomach dropped a little. I'd written Missy off a long time ago. I stopped thinking of her as my friend.

But I never really said good-bye to her.

In a way, it had never really been finished.

She just said good-bye. This was it. The complete and total end of my relationship with her.

"Thank you," I said sincerely. "I hope you find a good life and keep it."

I hope you don't screw it up like you did with us.

"Me, too." Her eyes slid to Braeden, who was standing there silently listening to our entire exchange.

"See ya, Missy," was all he said.

"Bye, Braeden," she echoed.

We stood there awkwardly for a few seconds more, and then she sat back down at her table and turned toward her friends.

It hurt a little. Missy and I hadn't drifted apart naturally, but after everything, the result was just the same.

Braeden's palm settled against my back, reminding me that even though that part of my life was over the best part was just beginning.

Out in the parking lot we hurried through the crowd of reporters still camped out. There were less than when we first arrived but still enough to be annoying.

After the question about Zach's death, it was completely unspoken that we not talk to any more press. At least not until the rumors died down.

Inside the truck, I sat close to B, his large hand on my thigh, scooting up beneath my skirt.

"Maybe this whole dress thing isn't so bad." He smiled wickedly.

Of course it wasn't bad. I looked cute as hell with the full hot-pink skirt, navy heels, and navy baby tee with white polka dots. Since it was cold, I added a military-style fitted jacket in white with dark-colored buttons.

"Where are we going?" I asked.

He put the truck in reverse and backed out of the spot. As he drove through the parking lot, he tossed me an impressive smile. "You issued a challenge, baby. I had to rise to the occasion."

I recalled no such challenge, but I had to admit I was excited to find out what so-called occasion he was rising to.

CHAPTER FORTY-SIX

The worst kind of good bye is the one when you know you won't ever say hello again.

#TimeToMoveOn

#BuzzBoss

BRAEDEN

I was nervous.

I didn't like it.

Confidence wasn't something I usually had to work for, but Ivy always had been. She deserved a lot more than I ever thought I could give a woman, but that wasn't going to stop me. They say the best things in life come from pushing out of your comfort zone, and I was learning whoever the hell said that was right.

It was probably some smart guy like Albert Einstein or some shit.

I went out of my comfort zone when I turned her dorm room into a beach, when I promised Ivy it was our beginning, and that from then on it was only her.

I didn't regret it.

Not even a little.

I never thought I was a relationship kind of guy. I always ran away when the feels got real.

I was done running.

I was in so deep with Ivy, it would kill me if I ever had to go back.

I pulled onto the familiar one-lane back road that she and I had driven down quite a few times before. She didn't say anything, but her cheek found its way to my shoulder, and as I drove, we sat silently, so close together, as the wide landscape opened up before us.

This was it. This was the best I had.

If she said no tonight…

I wasn't taking no for an answer.

Oh, hells no.

We rounded a bend in the road, and off to my left the ground gently fell away, revealing a sweeping view of mountaintops and trees. I knew in the morning, a dewy fog would rise up between the bare tree branches and create an eerily beautiful sunrise.

My eyes abandoned the would-be view and glanced off to the right—toward the other side of the road. In this section of the mountain, there used to be an apple orchard. Many of the trees were long gone and tall grasses grew in their place, but there were still a few old, twisty apple trees that still grew here, jutting out of the earth like they owned the place.

Hell, they'd been here long enough. Maybe they did.

I looked for one particular grouping of trees that still stood not far away from the road. It was easy to find, and I smiled.

It was lit up just like it was supposed to be. Soft golden light shone against the otherwise dark background.

I knew when Ivy noticed the glow. Her head lifted from my shoulder, and she leaned forward a bit to stare out the windshield. "What is that?" she asked.

"Not sure." I hedged as we drove closer at an unhurried pace. I wanted her to take it all in, let her wonder, and frankly, I needed a minute to calm my shit.

God, you'd think I was a virgin and it was my first time getting some.

"Are those lights?" she asked as we approached. Her voice was slightly wondrous. She leaned a little closer to the windshield and then patted me on the arm excitedly. "Those are lights. Someone wrapped those old trees in lights!"

"You don't say?" I drawled.

"You did this!" She gasped. "Oh my word, it's gorgeous."

Yep. It turned out a lot better than I thought it would. I mean, really, four guys with a bunch of lights and shit, a ladder, and a truck? The entire time I caught shit for it, too. They all voted me "closest thing to a living book boyfriend."

Like they even knew what the hell that was.

I was never going to live it down.

Naturally, I had to remind Rome of his grand proposal on national TV. That at least shut him up. The other two, though... they ribbed us endlessly.

Their days were coming. Hell, if a guy like me could get taken down by love, then so the hell could they.

At least we were alone tonight. Just me, Ivy, and the stars.

As we drew closer, the details came into sight. Three twisty, bare apple trees created a small, enclosed space in the wide-open land. We'd wrapped the trunks starting at the ground with yards of white lights and carried them up along some of the lowest-hanging branches. The trees hadn't been pruned in a long time, so the branches were uneven and crooked, but as I looked at the way they illuminated the night, I realized it only added to the charm.

We didn't take the lights up into the upper branches, because on those, I'd hung jars from long white cord and put battery-powered candles in them that we'd turned on before we left. I hadn't been able to tell how bright the light would be when we were here in daylight, but seeing it now, it looked pretty damn good.

The jars hung at different heights, some lower and some higher. There was a gentle breeze tonight, and they swayed gently beneath the canopy of branches.

"Braeden," Ivy whispered, her eyes never leaving the illuminated space when I stopped in front of the sight. "There are stars, too!" She gasped and gripped my arm again.

You ever sit around and cut out a million stars out of white paper?

It sucked.

Gave my hand a damn cramp and a crick in my neck.

And threading the little fuckers onto long strings, one after the other, without ripping them?

Sucked even worse.

But I had to admit the way the lights cast a golden glow over the plain white paper and the way they seemed to rain down from the trees was pretty cool.

What was better?

The way Ivy was staring out the window at it all like she'd never seen anything so beautiful.

I pulled forward a little more and slid the truck in reverse. Ivy craned her neck around so she could stare out the back window at the decorations as if she were too impatient to lose the view for even a second. I backed off the road, into the grass, and steered the bed of the truck so it slid right under the trees. Once it was in park, I jumped out and leapt up into the bed.

I used the same blankets and pillows we used before, tossing them around the back to make for a comfortable place to sit. Since it was colder out (technically, it was still winter) than all the other times we'd come here, I added a few extra blankets and made sure to layer a few thick sleeping bags I'd rummaged out of my mom's garage on the bed so we had some cushion to sit on.

When that was done, I lifted Ivy out of the cab, and she raced around to the tailgate, where she spun in a circle in the grass and looked up at the lights. She looked beautiful. Her nose was already pink from the cold, her eyes were sparkling with happiness, and the golden waves of her hair practically shone like a halo beneath the lights.

When I stood rooted in place, just watching her, she laughed and blew me a kiss.

Owned.

There wasn't a single solitary part of me Ivy didn't own.

Every star I cut, every light I strung, and every single stupid joke the guys made at my expense today suddenly became nothing compared to seeing her standing here beneath it all.

"Come over here!" She grinned and beckoned me with her hands.

I grabbed her up the second she was within reach and kissed her until my lungs burned from lack of air.

"I can't believe you did all this," she whispered, looking up into the trees once more.

"Figured I owed you since I screwed up so royally before."

Her nose wrinkled and her eyes found mine. "What do you mean?"

Instead of answering, I picked her up and deposited her in the bed of the truck. I jumped in after her, and we both kicked off our shoes and dove into the blankets.

"You cold?" I asked, tucking a second blanket around her shoulders.

"No way," she murmured, still staring up at the trees. Some of the jars and stars hung down close to us, and she reached up and fingered one of the paper stars.

"Did you cut these?"

"Got the blister to prove it."

"Let me see," she instructed, and her slim hand appeared from beneath a pile of covers. I held mine out and turned it so she could see the proof of my hard labor.

(Hey, a guy's gotta get all the credit he can when he does something like this.)

"Poor thing," she crooned and lifted my hand to kiss it.

"I got one right here, too." I showed her my other hand.

Her lips brushed over it in a cool caress.

"Here, too." I pointed to my lips.

"Hmm," she mused. "I'm not seeing that one."

"Woman, get over here!" I wrapped both arms around her, and we toppled over, with her on my chest.

Her hair fell like a curtain around us, blocking out everything but the closeness of her lips, the love in her eyes, and the feel of her body right against mine.

I used my tongue to coax her mouth open, gently tracing the contours of her lips until they parted on a contented sigh. I swept inside her mouth, using my tongue lazily to kiss her in a languid caress that made my head feel fuzzy.

With a sigh, she rolled off me and onto her back. We lay there, our heads touching and our fingers entwined, and stared up at the lights and stars.

"I love it here," she whispered.

"Make a wish," I whispered back. The nerves I felt when we first got here returned, no longer subdued by the heat of our kiss.

"There's lots of stars to pick from," she mused, and it played right into my hands.

Meant to be.

I untangled myself from the blanket and stood.

"What are you doing?" she asked.

"I have just the star for you to wish on."

Please don't let her think this is cheesy, I silently prayed.

"Show me," Ivy said, still snuggled in a mountain of blankets.

I walked toward the tailgate and stretched up to one star that was different from the rest. "This one," I said, catching it between my fingers as it moved in the night air.

"It's different." She abandoned the warmth she'd been lying in and came over to stand beside me. "Oh, it's like it's 3-D. Is it hollow inside?"

"I think I want to wish on this one. You mind?"

Her eyes were curious when they turned on me, away from the star. "Sure."

It took a second to tug it down, but when I did, the star filled my palm. It was simple and crudely cut, but it got the job done.

"I wish I may, I wish I might," I murmured as I slowly opened the star, taking it apart, *"have this wish I wish tonight."*

When I was done, the star lay open on my palm, each point slightly curled in from being folded. In the center, tied to the string it had been hanging from, was a diamond ring.

Ivy made a sound and pressed her hand to her mouth. Her eyes were twice the size they normally were as she divided her gaze between me and the ring.

"I wish for you, Blondie," I said. "I wish to spend the rest of my life loving the shit out of you."

Her eyes glittered more than any of the lights I'd strung up tonight, and she stared down at the ring, her eyes never once straying.

"Hey," I murmured and tipped her chin up with my free hand. "I know I asked before, and I know it totally sucked. It's hard for me to… to tell you just how much I want you. I demanded you marry me, not because you're pregnant, but because there's no going back. I'm like a golden retriever, baby. Loyal 'til the very end."

She laughed. It was muffled against her hand, which was still pressed to her mouth.

"Marry me, Ivy. Not because of the baby. Not because without you, I might literally drift away. Marry me because I fucking love you. And you fucking love me. Marry me because it doesn't matter if I ask you now or in three years. The result is still the same. We're inevitable, just like the stars in a cloudless night sky."

Her hand fell away from her mouth and tears rolled down her cheeks. She looked back at the ring still lying in the center of my palm.

"And if I say no?" she asked.

My gut clenched, but I tried not to show her how bad it would be if she turned me down tonight. "I'll ask you again tomorrow. And the day after that."

"Ask me again right now." The wistful tone in which she asked was definitely not demanding.

I grasped the ring between my thumb and index finger, lifted it out of the star, and held it so the emerald-cut solitaire winked up at her, courtesy of the candles hanging nearby.

"I wish for you. For us. Marry me, Ivy. Say you'll marry me."

A few heartbeats passed of nothing but the winter wind. She lifted her hand as if she wanted to touch the ring but then dropped it and looked up into my face.

"Oh yes." Her voice was breathless.

"Yes?" I wanted to make sure I heard what she actually said and not what I'd been desperately wanting to hear.

"I'll marry you."

I gave a shout and sank low to wrap my arms around her waist and lift, spinning her in a circle. She laughed, and I set her back on her feet and she pushed her hand between us.

I slid the ring onto her finger, sighing in relief that it fit. I had a pretty good idea it would, considering I snooped around in her jewelry box before Romeo and I went to the jewelry store.

"This is the most beautiful ring I've ever seen." Ivy pulled her hand back and thrust it underneath a few low-hanging lights. She turned her hand this way and that, watching it catch the light with brilliance.

"Cushion cut?" she asked, glancing at me.

I nodded. Figured she'd know what it was. The lady at the counter had to tell me.

When I first looked at it, all I saw was a large, sparkly rectangle on a shiny band.

It was a two and a half-carat emerald style, cushion-cut diamond solitaire in a traditional four-prong setting. Each corner of the diamond had a small ball of white gold where the diamond was fastened.

The band was simple white gold, thin in comparison to the size of the stone.

It was simple, but it was classy, and it was the kind of ring that would hopefully never go out of style. I'd been nervous making this final decision, because Ivy was so trendy and into fashion, but the woman said when choosing something like this, classic was best.

"I figured I could get you a wedding band of all diamonds, add a little more sparkle to your finger." I rubbed the back of my neck as I spoke.

Why was she being so quiet? Did she not like it? Was it too simple?

"It doesn't need any extra sparkle. I absolutely love it."

"Yeah?" Damn, I felt like a man just given a second chance at life.

"Are you kidding? It's stunning. And it's huge!" She gasped and looked over her shoulder at me. "How the hell did you pay for this?"

I chuckled. "Don't worry about it."

It was on credit. After I signed a contract with the NFL, I'd just pay it off.

She started to twist it off her finger, shaking her head. "It's way too much. I don't need something this fancy."

I caught her hand and shoved it back down her finger. "The hell you don't," I growled. "That doesn't come off. Ever."

"I'd be just as happy with something a quarter of this size."

"I wouldn't." Like I'd freaking hand my girl anything less.

She should know better.

Her teeth sank into her bottom lip and she looked down at it again. It was just a ring, the thing all women loved to wear. It seemed dumb to me before, to stake your claim with a piece of stone.

But seeing it sitting there, circling her finger, it wasn't dumb. It was perfect. It was just one more way I could claim her as mine.

"I really do love it." She seemed to feel guilty.

"Look at me," I said and grasped her face. "The price of this ring is small compared to the way I feel about you."

Her lower lip wobbled.

Oh shit.

I pulled it into my mouth and sucked it gently. She grabbed my wrists and clung to me to deepen the kiss.

A forceful blast of air came out of nowhere, and she shivered. I led her back to the blankets and piled them on top us both. "I know it's cold out. We can go."

"No way!" she protested. "All we need is some Boone's Farm." She giggled.

I groaned. That shit was nasty.

I reached into the corner of the bed and pulled out a bag. Inside were two red solo cups and a clear container of orange juice.

When she saw it, she laughed.

"No Boone's for you," I said and poured her some juice, and she sipped it, making a sound of pleasure in the back of her throat. It made me horny.

"You promise this isn't because of the baby?"

"It's not because of the baby," I vowed. "I was always going to marry you, Blondie. I just asked a little faster is all."

"You make me so happy." The sincerity in her voice was honest and real.

"Times two."

We lay down in the blankets and stared up at the stars, both paper and real. Ivy's hand began to wander, caressing my chest and abs, teasing me with her trailing fingertips beneath my shirt. When her hand unfastened the button on my jeans, my breath caught in my throat.

She delved beneath the waistband of my boxers and wrapped a hand around my already throbbing cock. She didn't say anything as she slowly jacked me until my tip was moistened with precum and my balls drew taut.

The tips of her fingers were damp from my need, and she delved deeper into my boxers so she could gently massage my tightened sack with the small amount of silky wetness.

My moan floated up into the sky, and I felt her smile against my shoulder.

"I'd have a lot better access if you were wearing less," she whispered in my ear, punctuating the words with a scrape of teeth across my earlobe.

Needless to say, every article of clothing I was wearing disappeared.

She made a sound of appreciation when I leaned back against the blankets. Her tongue flicked out over my nipple, and it hardened instantly. Using her teeth, she drew the tiny pebble up and into her mouth, where she lavished it with her tongue and suckled deeply.

My cock was practically weeping now. I could feel the moisture on my lower belly. I was so fucking turned on I was afraid I'd blow the second she touched me again.

Ivy left my nipple and moved the other one. After she sucked and teased it as well, I was subconsciously thrusting my hips into the space beneath the blankets. She purred, kissing down the center of my chest, stopping to delve her tongue into my belly button and then circle around. She drew up onto her knees, knelt beside me, and continued downward.

I moaned again when she buried her face in the short nest of springy curls just above my cock. She nuzzled them with her nose and lips while her fingertips lightly dragged over my inner thigh.

I spread my legs, giving her more access. Her fingers explored the sensitive flesh just behind my sack. She dragged a finger across it, applying just the right amount of pressure. At the exact same moment, she lifted her head slightly and caught my eye.

I felt drunk when I stared down my body at her. Her freaking teasing was making me useless.

Lightly, she drummed her fingers against my balls and then dragged her fingers back down that line of sensitized skin. Her tongue shot out and she lapped at all the moisture my cock had leaked on my lower abs.

She made a sound like it was delicious as she laved it up and continued to play below my cock.

* * *

I jerked up and a curse fell from my lips. She laughed and sucked one of my balls into her mouth. Then she moved to the other.

"Ivy," I groaned. "I'm gonna fucking come before we even have sex."

In response, she jerked my cock up, holding it straight up from my body and slid her lips down over the shaft.

The warm moisture of her mouth, the just-right pressure of her lips, and the way her tongue seemed to wrap around the head of my cock like it was looking for more juice to swallow was my undoing.

My hips surged up; I bucked like a fucking wild bull. Ivy went with me, and I grabbed her hair, holding her against my crotch as an orgasm ripped out of me and poured against her tongue.

She rocked into me, her entire body thrusting with pleasure as she drank me down. I closed my eyes because I couldn't see and feel something so powerful at the same time.

Too soon, I was empty and lying back against the blankets.

I felt bereft.

Sad.

I wanted more. I wanted so much more.

Ivy released my cock, and it fell against my stomach. Then she giggled and nipped at my head, making me hiss out a breath.

"You're still hard," she observed.

"That's because you're the fucking cock whisperer," I moaned.

She licked up my length like I was a giant lollipop and she was addicted to sugar. My still-hard length jumped in response to her touch.

Abruptly, she left me, standing up in the center of the blankets. I watched her through half-closed eyes, and she reached beneath the skirt she was wearing and slid her panties down her thighs.

I had a sudden burst of energy and I sat up, wrapped my hands around her ankles, and then slid my palms up, grazing the backs of her calves, behind her knees, and then finally to her inner thighs.

I climbed up beneath her skirt and pushed her thighs apart. Her legs were trembling when I dove into her wet and ready center. She was dripping for me, and I drank her in the same way she'd done me. I slipped the tip of my tongue in her slit, penetrating her core just enough that she could feel it.

Her knees buckled, and she grabbed onto my shoulders. She fell forward, over my head, and I eased her down onto the blankets, face first.

The bare cheeks of her ass peeked out from the skirt, and I growled. She had a nice fucking ass. I shoved the fabric up to reveal it all and reached between her thighs again.

"Oh," she said when I slipped two fingers in her from behind.

She tilted up her round ass to give me better access, and I nipped at her flesh with my teeth as I moved my fingers inside her.

Unable to take the separation any longer, I positioned myself behind her. My still rock-hard cock slid along her ass cheeks and down to her drenched center.

I pushed into her opening and buried myself so far that her ass hit my hips.

"This okay, baby?" My voice was gruff with pleasure, but even so, I wanted to be sure it was just as good for her.

"More," she whimpered and bore down on my cock. The walls of her core flexed around me, and I started to move. I slid in and out of her, holding on to her hips and taking in the sweet view of her behind.

When I felt the first stirring of another orgasm, I let out a moan.

She moaned too and wiggled onto me a little farther.

"That's it," I murmured and bent at the waist, bringing my front against her back. I kept thrusting into her even as I reached around her and found the bud between her folds.

She was so swollen and sensitized she cried out the second my thumb brushed over it. I increased the pressure on the area and rubbed and teased until she began shuddering around me. Her cries of release were the sweetest sounds I'd ever heard.

A few more thrusts inside her and I came again. Bright spots exploded behind my eyes, and I pulled out so I could collapse beside her.

She was still lying on her stomach, and she turned her head to look at me. "Sex under the stars is my favorite."

I grinned. "Tell me you like my cock."

"I think me moaning in ecstasy a few seconds ago was pretty much the same thing."

I brushed the hair away from her face. "I can't wait to call you my wife."

"Thank you, Braeden."

My brow wrinkled. "For what?"

"For picking me. For being everything I always used to think you weren't."

I laughed. "Thank you for making me work for it. And for sticking around when I didn't get it right on the first try."

She lifted her hand and stared at the ring and sighed. I grabbed her hand and kissed it.

She said yes.

Finally.

I was getting married.

CHAPTER FORTY-SEVEN

#BlindedByBling

Anyone else notice the giant rock on the finger of our #ResidentHulks lady?

#AnotherWedding

#BuzzBoss

RIMMEL

Maybe a wedding wasn't just about two people.

Or even four in my case.

Maybe it was a celebration for an entire family, and this whole time I had been going about it all wrong.

Or maybe I was just really happy I was already married and Romeo and I had the best ceremony any girl like me could ask for.

I knew before Braeden and Ivy even left our party at Screamerz the next time I saw them, they would be engaged. Ivy couldn't resist Braeden when he brought out his charm, and according to Romeo, he had it out in full force the night he proposed.

It had taken me months to figure out what I wanted for our wedding despite being asked almost on a daily basis. But then one day, it became so crystal clear, and it happened not because of just Romeo and me, but because of our family.

It was quite clear to me the night of our engagement that the press was important to Romeo's career. After all, football depended on fans just like books depended on readers. What better way to inspire fans than by giving them something to root for, something to identify with, something to love?

It got me to thinking.

And then the morning Braeden was basically set free from Robert's warpath, his career inadvertently became tenuous.

No, no one else realized this, except maybe Anthony, but like me, Anthony wasn't about to rain on the good news parade.

Early on, I seemed to understand what it took the others longer to figure out, perhaps because I knew what the press was like—how they could turn on you over something as silly and minimal as an outfit choice.

Murder was a lot more serious than clothes.

After the scene Robert made at the party, it was only a matter of time before the paparazzi came snooping.

What they needed was something else to focus on. Something positive that would help my family and the Knights at the same time.

And so our wedding plans were born.

Valerie was skeptical at first, until I whipped out my phone and made a few calls.

To Ron Gamble to be exact.

He'd given me his private number once, but I'd never used it. Until now.

Ron knew a good idea when he heard one, so he was quick to agree to what I wanted.

That's all it took to get Valerie on board, and I knew without a doubt we would have the best football-themed wedding the entire state of Maryland had ever seen.

When B and Ivy got engaged immediately after, it was pretty much fate. It was only natural for Romeo and me to include them. They were family, and as I discovered, that's what weddings were about.

What had originally began as a wedding for two became a wedding for four.

Romeo and me. Braeden and Ivy.

A double wedding to be held at the Knights football stadium right in the center of the field. It would be a huge affair, yet Valerie would make sure it remained exclusive. After all, the most sought-after things were always exclusive.

Not only would this event make a splash in the media, but also in the football world. It would give the press something to ask about besides the rumors surrounding Braeden.

But above everything else, it would truly be a day for our entire family to remember.

There was also a side bonus for me. Since Valerie and now Ivy were deeply involved in the planning, I didn't have to do much of it.

Score.

We chose the Knights colors for our theme, and then Ivy decided instead of sending traditional invitations, we would send tickets to the "game."

It became quite the thing to be one of the lucky ones to get a "ticket" in the mail.

Magazines and publications became more aggressive about exclusive rights to the wedding photos. And while Valerie and Ivy were busy planning menus and centerpieces, I made a side deal of my own.

I offered Rachel Wintor at *People* the exclusive.

But I didn't want money.

I wanted a full-page article about Braeden. All positive press. All about the rising star being drafted this year.

She agreed like I knew she would.

The entire month of March passed in a blur. I accepted the job running the animal shelter, kept up with my course load, and in every spare moment we had, we prepped for the wedding.

My grandparents and dad were coming, and Ivy's entire family (which was huge) was also on the guest list.

Her mother came to help us shop for wedding gowns—a moment I found to be insanely bittersweet.

I sat in the dress shop and watched them together, mother and daughter, as close as I knew my mother and I would be if she'd been alive. I kept the pain I felt at her absence inside; I didn't want to dampen anyone's spirit during this happy time.

April came, and the day of the wedding arrived.

We were all staying at the same gorgeous hotel Romeo and I stayed the night we got engaged. Romeo somehow managed to get us the same exact suite we'd had that night.

Ivy was adamant that the guys not see us until the ceremony because it was bad luck. The thought of not spending the night in Romeo's arms almost had me telling her we were already married so it didn't matter... but I kept my mouth shut.

It was easy to get caught up in the wedding spirit, and I kind of liked the idea of torturing Romeo with a night alone.

It would make our "wedding night" that much sweeter.

So the night before, Ivy came up to our suite and Romeo went to Ivy and B's. Since my room was the biggest, it made sense the brides would use it to get ready for the wedding the morning of.

The ceremony wasn't until the early afternoon, so I thought we'd have a relaxing morning around the room, but when Ivy plopped down on my bed way early, my daydreams were thwarted.

I groaned, opening one eye. "It's too early." I begged for five more minutes.

"We're getting married!" Ivy said. "We don't have time for sleep!"

"How do you—a pregnant woman with morning sickness—have more energy than me?" I groaned.

"I brought you a present!"

"Well, why didn't you say so!" I said and rolled to the center of the big bed and patted the side I'd just been lying in.

Ivy laughed and climbed in next to me. In her hands, she had a large white box with a white satin bow.

After I slid my glasses on, she put it in my lap.

"You didn't have to do this," I told her, touched that she did.

"Are you kidding? What kind of maid of honor would I be if I didn't?"

I grinned and tore into the paper to reveal a white box. I pulled off the lid and brushed aside the tissue paper.

"Ivy!" I shrieked. "Oh my gosh, these are so amazing!"

"I know!" She agreed with just as much excitement.

It was a pair of white Converse sneakers. In place of the laces were white satin ribbons, and the toes were studded with sparkling clear crystals. I lifted them reverently and held them in my hands.

I turned them sideways and gasped again.

There along the side, it said Mrs. Anderson in the same crystals as the toes.

"Look at the bottom!" She insisted.

I flipped one over and laughed. There on the sole was a decal that read #Bride in blue.

"So this gift totally covers something new and something blue." She nodded.

I started crying.

For so long, I lived in a world where my family was small, my friends were none, and love was just something I read about in books.

But now, all those things were my life, and it was so amazing.

"Aww!" Ivy threw her arms around me and hugged me close.

"I knew you were dreading the heels you were supposed to wear today, so I figured it would be totes appropriate for you to have a pair of wedding sneakers. They're not really anything to cry over."

"I love the shoes so much, but it's not them. It's you. You're like the sister I always wanted. I can't tell you how happy I am you're marrying my brother and we get to be family. I'm so looking forward to when my niece or nephew arrives. I'm so thankful for all of you."

Ivy wiped at her eyes. "Great. Now you're going to make me cry."

"I got you something, too," I confessed. "But it's not nearly as epic as bride Converse!"

I fished a small box out of the nightstand and handed it to her. It was also wrapped all in white. When she opened the box and peered inside, she smiled. "How did you know!"

"I listen. And sometimes Braeden talks a lot, especially when he's had a few beers."

Ivy lifted the garter out of the box. I'd had it made. It was a deep-blue lace band with a large white anchor on the side. The anchor was material that looked like a pearl.

"He's my anchor," she whispered, fingering the anchor.

"You're his," I added. "And it's blue!"

She nodded. "Thank you."

"There's something else in there." I pointed.

She went back to the tissue paper and found the bracelet. It was a Pandora, the kind made of cord. I'd chosen white because of the occasion. On the bracelet were two charms. A silver anchor, representing her marriage to B, and a round pendant with the word *sisters* engraved in the center.

She looked down at it, rubbing the sister charm in her fingers.

"I thought I could get you a charm for every milestone you have. The next one we add will be for the baby."

We proceeded to cry like a bunch of girls and proclaim our sisterly love for each other.

It was kinda awesome.

But then Ivy pulled back and set aside the box. "I actually have something else for you, too. I was going to show you when we were getting dressed at the stadium, but since we're already crying, might as well get the rest of the tears out now, too."

Before I could say anything, she jumped out of the bed with a, "Stay there!" and raced out of the room. Seconds later, she returned carrying a familiar garment bag.

"Is that my gown?" I asked.

Ivy nodded. "I didn't ask you before I had it altered, so I really hope you like it."

"You had my dress altered?" I asked, sort of alarmed. It had been perfect before, so even though I trusted Ivy implicitly, I was nervous. I mean, it was my *wedding gown*.

Ivy hung the bag on the top of the door and then unzipped the front. She glanced at me before slipping her hands inside and pulling out the fabric to drape over the open sides.

I caught a flash of yellow.

But my dress was all white...

"I know how hard this entire wedding has been for you." She started, a little nervous. "Because your mom can't be here."

My chest tightened.

"And I didn't say anything at the time, but I noticed the way you watched me and my mom when we were shopping that day."

"Ivy, I—"

She held up her hand. "Let me get this out," she said, her voice already teary.

"It gave me an idea. So I called your grandmother in Florida—Romeo gave me the number—and I asked her if there was anything left of your mom's that she had. I was hoping for her actual wedding gown, but your Gran didn't know where that was. But she did have something. A yellow dress that she wore the day they brought you home from the hospital."

I nodded. I could picture the dress in my head perfectly. Yellow had been my mother's favorite color because it reminded her of the sunshine. I had pictures of her carrying me inside the house the day I was born. I still could hear her voice telling me it was the best day of her life.

I brushed a tear off my cheek. "I know the dress."

"She mailed it to me," Ivy said. "And I had a piece of the dress cut out and sewed onto your gown."

I sucked in a breath as Ivy turned the gown so I could see.

Right there on the waist, off to the side, was a yellow heart the size of my palm, the color of sunshine.

"So now that dress and your mother can be a part of the day you came home *and* the day you get married."

I couldn't say or do anything. I just sat there in the center of bed and stared at the yellow heart that was now a part of my gown.

"Rimmel?" Ivy said, wary, after a few moments. "Did I do the wrong thing? Are you upset I had this cut out of her dress?"

You know what happened, right?

I burst into tears.

Not the delicate, *let me dab the corners of my eyes on a single tissue* kind, either.

The ugly kind.

The kind that snotted up your whole face, made your eyes red and your chest heave. I fell over and buried my face in Romeo's pillow. Even after only one night in this bed with him, it smelled like him.

I cried harder.

I cried so hard it hurt my chest.

Poor Ivy was so horrified she started crying, too.

Drew burst into the room seconds later to find us both. "What the hell is going on in here?" he bellowed.

Neither one of us thought it was strange he was in my hotel room without being let in. Maybe I'd have asked him if I hadn't been bawling like a baby.

"I cut up Rimmel's mom's dress and put in on her other dress, and she hates it and I'm a terrible friend!" Ivy sobbed. "And she gave me a garter with an anchor on it!"

Drew's eyes widened like he had no idea what the hell was happening.

"I don't hate it!" I sobbed. "It's the most thoughtful thing anyone's ever done for me!"

Ivy cried some more, and Drew frowned. "Ives, stop it. That can't be good for the baby."

When she didn't stop, he went forward and hugged her. "Stop," he said and rubbed her back.

"I'm sorry." I climbed out of the bed and went across the room to hug them both.

Then we were all standing there in a three-way hug while we used Drew as a human tissue. Trent appeared, and I heard his feet halt at the door. "What the fuck is going on in here?"

"Dude, they won't stop crying." Drew sounded horrified.

I held out my arm to Trent, and he laughed and joined the hug. "Aww, family times," he quipped.

Ivy sniffled.

"Both of you better quit it or I'm gonna call Romeo and B. They sent us up here to check on you." Trent went on.

Ah, so that was how they got in here.

His threat worked wonders in shutting off the waterworks. Once we were both under control, the two guys backed out of the room warily, like they expected us to explode again. Before Drew went, he rubbed his hand over Ivy's softly rounding belly and smiled.

"Is the baby okay?" I stressed.

"She's fine." Ivy promised and wiped her eyes. Then she rested her hand over her belly. She wasn't showing much except for her stomach, where the belly was softly rounding out. I thought she looked adorable, and by the way B watched her around the house, he thought so, too.

"I'm sorry I lost it." I sniffled and walked over to see the gown up close and personal. "I really have been missing her." I fingered the yellow fabric. It was silky to the touch. "And this really makes me feel like she's here with me today."

"She is." Ivy smiled and hugged me. "Oh," she added, "and just so you're prepared, there will be an empty seat in the front row today, with a yellow rose bundle on the seat."

"For her?" I asked, getting emotional again.

"Yeah. In memory of her."

I hugged her for a long time. She didn't seem to mind.

"Thank you," I whispered finally.

She took a shuddering breath and pulled back. "I'm going to take a shower. Hair and makeup people will be here in an hour, and I want to be ready."

I groaned.

"It won't be so bad." She laughed and headed for the door. "But don't forget. My mom, your grandmother, and Romeo's mom will all be invading soon as well."

Double groan.

* * *

Everyone was staying here at the hotel and we would all be riding over to the stadium in limos.

Yep. A line of limos going down the road like some royal parade.

I was kind of embarrassed.

"There's a bottle of champagne chilling, so maybe you should have a glass, relax a little," Ivy suggested.

She knew me too well.

"Thanks. I will after I shower, too." I agreed.

When I stepped out of the bathroom a short while later, I wrapped myself in one of Romeo's button-ups (that way I could take it off easily once my hair was done) and a pair of black leggings and headed out into the bedroom.

Romeo was sitting in the center of the bed.

I gasped and pressed a hand to my chest. "You scared me!"

He chuckled. "After one night alone, you already forget what I look like in our bed?"

I rolled my eyes. "You're not supposed to be here." My eyes widened. "She didn't see you, did she?"

He laughed and held out his hand. "Hell no. I don't want that pregnant bridezilla's wrath."

I climbed into the bed and onto his lap. "I was hoping you'd sneak in," I whispered.

"Woulda come through the window, but it's kinda hard when we're on the top floor."

"Like that night at the dorms," I mused, thinking back to the beginning of our relationship.

He chuckled.

"That your dress over there?" he asked, and I gasped and slapped my hands over his eyes.

"You can't see that!"

I felt rather than saw him roll his eyes. "It's not bad luck if we're already married."

"I'm so glad we had that night," I confided and lowered my fingers.

He smiled and gazed into me with blue eyes like no one else's. "I am, too."

He made a growling sound and rolled us over, pressing me into the mattress with his weight. His palm explored beneath the hem of my shirt, and he groaned when he felt I wasn't wearing a bra.

I filled my hands with his hair and tugged him just a little closer, exploring his mouth with my tongue as if it were the first time. I knew we were already married, but the anticipation of today still made my body hum.

I tugged his hair so he lifted his head slightly, and he gave me a lazy smile.

"I can't wait to see a wedding ring on your finger tonight," I confided. "And that way everyone will know you're taken, and not just me."

"Baby, I've been taken since the day we met."

My heart skipped a beat.

He dipped his head again and thrust against me. We made out like teenagers, fully clothed and afraid if we went any further, we'd get caught.

"One night without you, Smalls, and I'm already desperate." His voice was hoarse, and he leaned in to kiss the side of my neck.

"Tonight." I promised, reaching between us and stroking his hard length.

"Rimmel!" Ivy called from outside the door. "They're here!"

I used Romeo's shoulder to muffle my laughter. "Coming!" I yelled. "I have to go," I told him.

* * *

He groaned. "Don't make me go back out there. My mother keeps asking me about last-minute details. And trying to make me put on my suit… What the hell am I going to do in a suit a million hours before the ceremony? Then she'd be all over me not to wrinkle it."

I giggled. "She just wants to take your picture."

He moaned. "You're killing me, Smalls."

"I love you."

He pressed his forehead against mine. "I love you, too."

He helped me off the bed, and we straightened each other's clothes. "Distract the herd of women so I can slip out the front door."

I saluted him.

He gave me one last swift kiss before holding the door for me to go ahead of him. "I'll see you at the altar, Mrs. Anderson."

My stomach danced with butterflies.

"See you there."

CHAPTER FORTY-EIGHT

#YouMightBe
You might be football royalty when
you are allowed to get married
directly on the fifty yard line.
#BiggestWeddingOfTheYear
#BuzzBoss

IVY

As a girl, when I dreamed of my wedding, I thought of fairy tales. Of castles on hills or beaches with pristine sand and crashing waves. I even used to daydream about a southern wedding in the mountains of North Carolina in a rustic barn with bare feet.

I never dreamed I'd get married on a football field. With my very best friends right beside me. I never thought I'd have a growing child in my belly when I pledged my love to someone forever.

I never dreamed of any of those things, because not even in my dreams could I conjure something so perfect.

It was everything I never knew I wanted, and in just a few short minutes, it wouldn't be a dream anymore... It would be reality.

The guests were here, all six hundred of them. Even though I was still in the back, I could picture them sitting in the rows and rows of pristine white chairs that were perfectly placed near the end zone of the Knights home field.

Down the center of the chairs was the aisle Rim and I would walk down, the path that led to the rest of our lives. It was lined with white and silver lanterns filled with flickering candles, and white rose petals fell like snow across the deep green of the turf.

Right on the touchdown line began a large white platform that would lift the brides and grooms off the field enough for all the guests to see. It wasn't a terribly large platform because we didn't have a large bridal party.

There was no reason to.

Rimmel and I would stand with Romeo and Braeden, and my brother would stand on Braeden's side, and Trent would stand on Romeo's.

The rectangular platform was lined with more of the white and silver-painted lanterns in various shapes and sizes. They too would flicker and dance with light as we said our vows.

The goal post, which stood close behind, was draped with a thick garland of white flowers that dripped off the pole into long strands of more white blooms that were lit from within with white lights.

I had no idea how Valerie got such an elegant, large display of flowers made, but it was absolutely gorgeous.

Right on the fifty yard line was a massive white tent. There was no time to go inside to see how everything came together for the reception. Valerie caught Rimmel and me snooping around the field when we were supposed to be getting dressed and chased us back in the locker rooms before we could get a peek.

I had an idea what it would look like, of course, but Valerie was in charge of the setup and a lot of the details, so I knew it would be a surprise even to me.

The morning passed by in a flurry of activity. Once Rimmel and I had our moment together, we spent several hours getting our hair and makeup done. Everyone but me sipped champagne, and I sipped orange juice.

Out of a champagne glass, of course.

Now here we were, standing in a locker room in wedding gowns.

Everyone but the photographer had gone to find their seats. My father and Rimmel's father were waiting outside to escort us onto the field.

We could hear the soft playing of music over the loud speakers even in here, and I wondered for like the millionth time what Braeden was doing right that minute.

"I can't believe I'm getting married," I said and walked over to the large floor-to-ceiling mirror hanging on the wall.

I think for the first time ever, I was more nervous than Rimmel. Usually, I was the calm one, but today, it was the other way around. Maybe it was because she had liquor and I didn't.

I stood in front of the mirror and took in my appearance, scrutinizing every last detail. My hair was up in a simple bun with a thick braid wound around the perimeter. A few loose wisps of hair framed my face and lay against the back of my neck. The style wasn't slicked back and sleek, it was more casual elegant, which I thought fit the whole football field theme.

I went classic with my makeup because making trendy, bold choices on a girl's wedding day wasn't the best idea. So we concentrated on achieving glowing, luminous skin, neutral yet dramatic eyes (with gorgeous fluffy false lashes), peachy cheeks with golden highlights, and pale pink lips.

I'd exfoliated and moisturized my skin almost to death leading up to today, so my bare arms and chest would look soft and touchable in Braeden's eyes.

What I considered the most dramatic statement of my wedding look was my gown. I'd been worried how much of a baby bump I'd be sporting for my walk down the aisle, and while I was happy to be pregnant, no woman wants her baby bump to been seen before she is on her wedding day.

So I chose something that would help conceal it but still flatter my shape.

The gown was snow white with thin straps and a neckline that plunged low between my breasts (which were slightly fuller thanks to the baby). The waistline was defined right below my breasts with a thick white band of the same white fabric that made up the top. It was a backless dress, except for the thin white straps that went all the way down to the waistband.

Basically, the top was simple and beautiful. It was tailored to fit me perfectly, so I didn't have to worry about some kind of wardrobe malfunction and one of my girls falling out.

Nobody wanted to see that.

The bottom half of the gown was more dramatic and honestly made me feel like a princess. It was a long, full skirt that blossomed right out from the fitted waistband. Layers of tulle floated over the satin under layer with a slightly sheer quality. What made the fact that the tulle was slightly sheer so special was there was color beneath it. A deep blush pink started just beneath the waist, and it faded out to a soft muted shade that gave way to pure white right above my knees.

It was a soft effect overall, and between the accent of the color and the fullness of the skirt, my baby bump wasn't even noticeable.

To top it off, I added a pair of glittery pink heels.

Because a girl always needed a little glitter.

And a little pink.

The only jewelry I was wearing was my engagement ring (on my French-manicured hands) and a pair of diamonds in my ears that I borrowed from my mother. The blue garter with the anchor from Rimmel was wrapped around my thigh.

"You're the most beautiful bride I've ever seen," Rimmel said, coming up behind me.

I smiled and turned so she could see her reflection.

"I don't know. I think you have me beat." I smiled.

She snorted.

But then she smiled, her voice soft. "I've never looked this beautiful before."

"You're beautiful every day," I corrected. "But a hair and makeup team plus a gorgeous gown sure goes a long way for a girl."

We both laughed.

Rimmel's long hair was down, curled loosely to give it a tousled feel and then the sides were gathered toward the back of her head in some kind of artistic knot with baby's breath adorning the style. It looked gorgeous against her dark, shiny hair.

Her makeup was also classic, but her lips weren't pale pink like mine. They were a deeper berry shade. It looked gorgeous on her full lips. I was surprised she agreed to wear it, but when the makeup artist suggested it, she agreed.

* * *

Again, maybe it was the champagne.

Or maybe she was just happy to be getting married.

She did refuse to wear contacts, even though the makeup artist went on and on about it. It kind of made me mad because Rimmel should be exactly who she was on her wedding day, and glasses were totally Rim.

So to end the argument, I pulled out a pair of white-framed glasses I had hidden away.

Yeah, maybe I'd seen this coming.

Rimmel declared they were quite bride-ly and shoved them on her face.

I gave the makeup artist an *I dare you* look to say one word and wisely, she shut up.

Her gown wasn't as full as mine. She was so small that something with a full skirt would have swallowed her whole. Instead, her dress was more A-line, fitted at the top and gently flared at the waist to float down and swirl around her Converse.

I just hoped she didn't trip on the hem, which was a little too long now that she wasn't wearing heels.

The top of the gown was lace lined with a fabric that matched her skin. It had a wide boat neckline that accented her collarbones and tops of her shoulders and sheer three-quarter lace sleeves. The back of the gown had white buttons up the back, and the waistline was defined by a thin white band. It was right beneath the white band that I had the yellow heart sewed from her mother's dress. When she stood in the ceremony with her back to the crowd, everyone would be able to see it.

She wasn't wearing any jewelry except for her engagement ring and a bracelet her grandmother had worn on her own wedding day.

"I'm glad we're doing this together," she said and turned to me.

"Me, too." I sniffled. "No crying! Save our makeup."

She smiled. "I'm sure they're waiting."

I picked up the bouquet of sterling silver and dark-purple roses bound together with a dark-purple satin bow and handed them to her. Then I picked up my own bouquet of light and dark-pink roses.

"Ready?" she asked, offering me her arm.

I was so ready.

We walked down the aisle together. Sure, we could have gone separately with our dads. But it made it more special to go together.

Rimmel and I were arm and arm, and our fathers took up our sides.

I knew the decorations looked gorgeous. Thank goodness we'd come and taken a peek before the ceremony, because the second we stepped at the end of the aisle, I saw nothing but the man waiting for me.

I knew by the way Rimmel's arm tightened around mine as we walked that it was the exact same for her.

Braeden in a suit was what dreams were made of.

His broad shoulders and tapered waist were practically made to pull off the clean lines of a classic tailored suit jacket. The suit was ink blank, not a crease in sight, and beneath the jacket was a crisp white dress shirt, black buttoned-up vest, and a wide black silk tie that was knotted perfectly at his throat and disappeared elegantly beneath the vest.

There was a pocket on the left breast of the jacket, and just the edge of a crisp white cloth could be seen. His shoes were the same inky black, and they made his strong legs go all the way to the platform where he stood waiting.

But beyond the way he owned that suit, it was his eyes that owned me. His dark-chocolate gaze never left mine, and the smile on his lips was sexy and held a note of promise for when we were alone. My hands trembled as I gripped my flowers and tried to focus on not falling over.

Speaking of…

The too-long hemline of Rimmel's gown proved to be a worthy opponent.

The toe of her Converse caught on the gown, and she went stumbling forward. I gasped and snapped out of the trance I'd been in with B, locking my arm and tugging to keep her from falling.

Her father, who was on her other side, acted fast and also pulled her up. Between the two of us, we managed to keep her off the ground, but her bouquet hadn't been as lucky.

A few gasps went through the crowd and then a bit of applause when she was righted and didn't face plant.

The four of us had halted in the center of the aisle, and she glanced at me sheepishly. "Maybe for once I should have worn the heels."

A giggle bubbled up out of me, and then she joined in.

"Ladies." A smooth voice cut in, and Rimmel gasped.

Romeo was standing there before us in the middle of the aisle, an amused glint in his eyes.

"Romeo!" Rimmel said. "Sorry to keep you waiting,"

His eyes went right to her, and oh my word, the way his blue eyes looked at her intently… It was like he'd forgotten we were in the middle of a wedding.

Romeo looked just as good as Braeden in a suit, but instead of black, he was wearing a deep blue. It only served to make his eyes stand out that much more. He left his jacket unbuttoned to reveal the same colored button-up vest and a wide blue tie over a classic white dress shirt. The pocket on his left breast was adorned with the same color handkerchief... and something else.

A tiny pair of gold glasses were pinned to the breast.

I knew immediately it was his way of representing Rimmel.

I glanced between the two, totally captivated by the chemistry that sizzled around them. Rimmel's cheeks were pink, and Romeo's smile was rueful. "You shouldn't have worn heels, Smalls."

She snorted and lifted her gown to reveal the Converse. People around us chuckled, and Romeo threw back his head and laughed. He glanced at Brock and offered his hand. "Mind if I take it from here?"

Rimmel's father chuckled and then kissed his daughter on the cheek.

"Thanks, Dad," she whispered.

Romeo bent to pick up her forgotten bouquet and hand it to his bride-to-be. A few purple rose petals fluttered to the ground, but otherwise, it looked the same.

The second she took it, Romeo swept her up into his arms. She made a surprised sound and squealed. "I'm supposed to walk down the aisle to you!"

"But, baby," he drawled, not even bothering to lower his voice, "if I let you walk to me, you might take out half the guests and light the place on fire with all these candles."

She gasped.

He glanced at me and winked. "Looking like a bona fide princess, princess."

I smiled back.

Everyone clapped when Romeo leapt up on the platform with Rimmel in his arms and then set her on her feet before him.

From close by, Braeden cleared his throat. "Get your ass down here, Blondie!" he called to me.

I froze for a second, thinking my father was going to have an issue for Braeden's choice of words. When I glanced at him, he chuckled. "Clearly, he's impatient. Can't say I blame him."

My eyes filled, and we began walking again.

After my father kissed my cheek, B took my hand and helped me up onto the platform.

The ceremony itself was traditional. The four of us chose to not write our own vows, mostly for the sake of time and consideration for the six hundred people in attendance.

But also because Braeden said he wasn't good with words and didn't want to embarrass himself.

I begged to differ. I had a whole memory full of swoon-worthy things he'd said to me.

When the man officiating the ceremony asked us all if we had anything more to add before he pronounced us man and wife, I raised my hand. "I have something to say."

He inclined his head.

I blushed. "It's private." Then I beckoned Braeden with my finger.

He looked at me oddly but leaned forward, and I put my lips right up to his ear. "I like your cock."

"I knew it!" He chortled and burst out laughing.

I pulled back, pleased with myself, and we were all pronounced man and wife.

Everyone cheered as we kissed.

And kissed some more.

Braeden gently rubbed his palm over the front of my belly as if not only in this moment was he thinking of me, but also of our child.

When the four of us ran down the aisle, hand in hand, guests threw multicolored sprinkles at us that looked like little rainbows filling the sky.

When the guests were walking across the field to the reception tent, we posed for picture upon picture.

At one point, Braeden pulled me into an entrance for one of the tunnels and leaned against the wall, pulling me between his legs and wrapping his arms around me.

"You finally said it." He grinned.

I rolled my eyes. "We just got married in the most beautiful ceremony ever, and that's the one thing you remember?"

"I remember lots of things," he murmured, sweeping his thumb across my lower lip. "Like how lost I was without you and how fucking lucky I am to have you by my side."

"You make me so happy," I whispered, leaning into his chest and wrapping my arms around his neck.

"Times two, baby." He brushed his lips over mine. "Times two."

"Do you think we'll always be this happy?" I asked, blinking back happy tears.

Once again, he caressed my baby bump, letting his palm lie directly over our baby. "No," he answered softly. "We're gonna be even happier."

He was right.

CHAPTER FORTY-NINE

#OneFamilyUnited
Heard the wedding was like a
fairy tale. With fireworks.
#WishingYouALifetimeofHappy
#BuzzBoss

RIMMEL

I was right.

The sight of Romeo with a wedding band on his left hand was so worth everything we'd been through to get here.

It'd only been a little while since I put it there, but already, I felt a change.

Not a change anyone else would notice, but for me, it was profound. For a lot of my life, I'd felt alone. I'd been alone. Some of it was my own doing and some of it was out of my control.

I wasn't alone anymore, and I never would be again.

Seeing that ring was a visual reminder of it.

"In a way, I feel sorry for them," Romeo said, wrapping his arms around me from behind and whispering in my ear.

I glanced up to see B and Ivy coming across the field toward us from wherever they'd gone for a stolen moment.

"Why?" I asked, leaning back to look into my husband's eyes.

"Because they have to smile for pictures, spend time with guests. Right after we got married, the only thing we had to do was be together."

I agreed. We definitely had a better deal.

I lifted his hand and kissed the titanium band on his finger. "I'm starting to understand why you always wanted a piece of you on me. This is totally doing it for me."

He arched an eyebrow. "Oh yeah?"

I nodded.

His lips curved into a sexy smile. "I'm liking this, too." He lifted my hand and showed me the thin diamond band resting against my engagement ring.

"I'm so glad you were failing all your classes and needed a tutor." I wrapped my arms around his waist.

He laughed. "I'm so glad you weren't a lesbian."

I rolled my eyes, but he didn't see because he kissed me.

"Think anyone would miss us if we skipped out and started the honeymoon early?" Braeden said, coming up behind us.

"We can't leave our reception!" Ivy gasped.

Romeo lifted his head and grinned.

Valerie poked her head out of the tent and pinned the four of us with a stare. "Do you not hear the band announcing you?"

"Uh, no," I said, embarrassed. We'd been too busy kissing.

"Sorry, Mom," Romeo said sheepishly, and Valerie's face softened.

"Come on, then. People are waiting."

The folds of the tent drew back, and my breath caught.

"Oh my God," Ivy breathed. "It's stunning."

"Better than stunning." I nodded.

"All I see is lights and flowers," B said.

"I hope there's cake," Romeo added.

I snorted. They were such boneheads.

"Come on," Ivy said and pulled Braeden ahead of us.

They made their entrance first, and people clapped and cheered. I didn't really hear any of it. I was too entranced by the beauty the tent held.

It was like a whole other world. I never would have guessed, standing outside, that such a simple white tent could house something so wonderful.

Inside, the lights were dim, creating an intimate feel. The ceiling was draped in tulle, but between that and the ceiling of the tent were thousands and thousands of twinkling lights. Because of the dark lighting, they looked like millions of vibrant stars floating overhead.

Right at the entrance was a huge archway of white flowers with cascading greenery and crystals that sparkled against the lights.

The tables inside were round, draped in white, and surrounded by white chairs with dark-purple velvet cushions. The centerpieces were these hugely elaborate bouquets that stood up off the table on tall clear cylinders, making the round, full white tops appear to float. Around the bottom were clusters of white candles with beautifully flickering wicks. The centerpieces weren't the only drama on the table. Each place setting was set impeccably with china, polished silverware, cloth napkins, and large wine glasses.

Everything was white with pops of silver and gold. Occasionally, as I looked around, I saw some of the purple the Knights wore, but I didn't see much of the orange.

It didn't matter.

This was so beyond gorgeous, and Valerie could have not used any of the colors I wanted and it would still be beautiful.

"They're waiting for us, baby," Romeo said and anchored his arm around my waist.

We walked fully into the tent while people clapped, and I marveled at how closely the ceiling resembled a night sky.

There was so much white it almost felt like we were in some elegant winter wonderland. In the center of the tent was the dance floor. It was constructed of floating wood painted with wide distressed stripes of white and gold.

Romeo led me to the head table at the front of the room. It was rectangular with the same centerpieces (we had two), candles, and settings. At the front of the table, sitting on the floor, were more lanterns like we had out at the ceremony, and there was a huge golden bow fixed to the front of the tablecloth.

B and Ivy were already there, and the second we joined them, champagne started being passed around the room.

The entire night was magical, filled with friends and family.

More than once, I caught myself getting lost in Romeo's blue gaze, and more than once, I found myself thanking God this was my life.

Right before we were set to cut our cake (some elaborate affair with purple roses cascading down the side), Romeo caught my hand and pulled me outside.

Lights from inside spilled out and stretched across the football field.

Even though there were a ton of people inside, they felt like a world away. Down the field, the lanterns from the ceremony still flickered. Romeo drew me farther away from the tent. My shoes sank into the turf, and the night enveloped us.

"Where are we going?" I asked.

"Something I wanted to show you," Romeo said, withdrawing from my hand and pulling out his cell. After he spent a few seconds tapping on the screen, he slid it back into his trousers.

We walked a little more, about halfway between the tent and the ceremony location, and he stopped. "Right here should be good."

"For what?" I wondered.

He pulled me in front of him and wrapped his arms around my waist. His chin rested on my shoulder, and his voice filled my ear. "Look up."

Just as he said it, the sound of something shooting into the sky cut through the night. I looked up and so did he.

Bright, brilliant fireworks cut through the sky, glittering and flashing before our eyes.

I laughed. "You did this?"

"Just for you," he replied in my ear.

People gathered outside the tent to watch, but we were far enough away that we were alone.

• • •

Once the spectacular light show stopped exploding in the night, I sighed and turned to look up at him. "It was beautiful."

He kissed the tip of my nose. "One more." His eyes went up, and I followed his gaze.

One last firework exploded right above us.

It wasn't an ordinary firework. This one was different.

It was a red heart with a hashtag in front of it.

Like a montage in a movie, all our best moments replayed in my mind. The first moment we met, the night he came to the shelter with me in the rain. Climbing through my dorm window, and the night of our first kiss.

It was the most beautiful movie I'd ever seen.

But it wasn't a movie. It was my life.

Our life.

I turned in his hold as a tear slid down my cheek. My arms looped around his neck, and he gazed down. "There I was, Romeo, going along with my boring and ordinary life. Then you came along and gave me a fairy tale."

"No one will ever love you like I do, Smalls," he vowed.

"I know." I smiled. "But I'm gonna love you more."

We met each other halfway and kissed in the center of the football field. His lips were familiar to me now but no less devastating than the first time they ever touched mine.

I might only be one girl.

I might only have one life.

But there was only one Romeo.

And he was mine.

"Get a room!" Braeden yelled down the field.

We broke apart and laughed.

"Come on!" he yelled at us again. "You can make out later. It's party time!"

Romeo held out his hand between us, his wedding band catching my eye. "What say you, Mrs. Anderson? Can I have this dance?"

I slipped my hand into his. "You can have all of them."

"Hells yeah." His lips broke out in that sexy smile I loved so much.

Hand in hand, we ran across the field toward where Braeden and Ivy waited.

We were one family united.

HAPPILY EVER AFTER...
TIMES TWO

(AKA EPILOGUE)

The tiniest feet make the biggest
footprints in our hearts.

#BuzzBoss

BRAEDEN

The heavy drum of chopper blades overhead matched thundering of my heart inside my chest. The enclosed space of the cabin was barely noticable and neither was the turbulence of a helicopter ride over the state.

I'd never been in a helicopter before, and if you asked me later about it, I'd still respond like a man who hadn't. My focus wasn't on the distance we were in the air, the sounds the pilot made just a few feet away, or even on my best friend who sat squished beside me.

I was sweaty, dirty, and scared as hell.

"Prepare for touchdown," the pilot said, his voice sounding suspiciously like Darth Vader from *Star Wars*.

I braced myself for the second we made contact with the landing pad, a place I knew technincally we weren't supposed to be.

What can I say? Being a star athlete in your home state had some perks.

The second the chopper touched down, Rome and I were on our feet, grabbing up our helmets, and bursting out the door. The whirring blades overhead whipped air around, and I held my breath against it and ducked my head to run toward the nearby door.

The second Rome and I were clear, the chopper lifted up again, but I didn't look back. I barrelled through the wide glass doors and into the sterile-scented floor of the hospital.

"Labor and delivery," I rushed out on my way past a nurse, and she pointed to the stairwell. "Up two flights."

We hauled ass through the door and pounded up the stairwell and burst out onto the floor. Several people nearby jumped at our sudden intrusion and then stared as wel barrelled past. Whispers and excamations filled the hall behind us, and a nurse behind the station desk up ahead smiled and pointed as we approached. "Third door on the right."

Our cleats made loud clomping sounds, and there was a high-pitched squeal when I put on the breaks outside the door and flung the door open to rush inside.

"Am I too late?" I gasped, stumbling farther into the room so Romeo could do the same.

Three sets of eyes snapped to where we stood, and then one last—the most important set—followed suit.

"Just in time," Ivy said from the center of her hospital bed.

I filled my sight with her body, taking in everything from her flushed cheeks, long hair, and very pregnant belly beneath the blanket on the bed.

Monitors were attached around her stomach, and there was an IV in the back of her hand, covered in too much tape.

"Who put that much fucking tape on your hand?" I roared. "That's gonna leave a mark."

"So will the needle it's holding in place," Rimmel remarked dryly.

I glanced at my sister and glowered. "It's a good thing I love you."

"I'm fine," Ivy assured me and held out her hand—the one without the IV. "You got here fast!"

I dropped my helmet on the floor and rushed to her side, taking her hand between both of mine. "Are you in pain?" I worried.

God, I was already feeling queasy, and she didn't even look harried.

"Nothing I can't manage." She smiled.

"Until another contraction comes around," Drew muttered from the other side of the bed.

She gave him a stern look and grimaced.

"We heard the helicopter coming in," Rimmel said.

Romeo stepped up behind her, looking even bigger than her than usual because he was still completely dressed in his football uniform.

We both were. We literally got the call Ivy was in labor and ran off the field to get on Ron Gamble's chopper so we'd make it here in time.

"It's good to know people with connections," Romeo said and kissed her on the head. Then he came over to the side of the bed to stand next to me. "You ready for this, princess?"

A nurse bustled into the room then. She wasn't even through the door and was saying, "Where did all this mud come from!"

She drew up short when she saw me and Rome.

"Sorry about that," Ivy said. "These two can be a little barbaric when they're in a rush."

Rimmel giggled.

"Oh well. Which one of you is the father?"

"Me," I said immediately.

"Come on. I'll get you some scrubs to change into. I don't think you'll be needing all those shoulder pads to meet your child.

Holy shit, I was gonna become a father today.

I tightened my grip on Ivy's hand. "Thank you, but I think I'll stay right here." I wasn't about to walk out of this room and leave Ivy's side for the sake of my own comfort.

"I'll take some scrubs," Romeo said, smiling at the nurse. She blushed.

I rolled my eyes, but then Ivy made a sound and squeezed my hand. Her breathing became more labored and her body stiffened.

"What's happening!" I bellowed.

Drew and Trent laughed. This shit was not funny.

"It's a contraction," Drew said and pointed to a monitor with a bunch of squiggly lines on it. I knew it hurt. I could tell by the set of her jaw, the grip on my hand, and the way she tried to breathe.

"Can't you do something?" I asked the nurse. I did not like this shit. Not one bit.

"Contractions are perfectly normal," she said and wandered over to the monitor.

She wandered.

Like she didn't have anything better to do.

I was gonna blow a gasket. I didn't want to see Ivy in pain.

"Sit down before you fall down," Romeo said, and a chair hit the backs of my legs and he shoved me down.

I hadn't realized until I sat that I'd been swaying on my feet.

Ivy's grip loosened and she looked up at me with tired eyes. "Calm down. Everything's fine."

"Good thing he wasn't home when your water broke," Trent muttered.

I squeezed my eyes shut at the thought. I should have been home for that. I shouldn't have been playing today.

Like she read my thoughts, she said, "You haven't missed anything."

Another contraction seemed to take over, and she made a sound and griped my hand. "Coming faster now," the nurse said. "I'll go get the doctor." Then she glanced around the room. "Maybe we should give them some room."

"With pleasure," Drew said and kissed Ivy on the head. "I love you, sis, but I can't watch this."

She tried to laugh, but it wasn't quite successful.

"We'll be in the waiting room," Trent said, and the two disappeared out into the hallway, the nurse going with them.

I hoped she hurried the hell up with the doctor.

Rimmel rushed to the side of the bed where Drew had just been and leaned toward Ivy. "You got this. We'll be outside."

"Thanks for being here," Ivy said.

The pressure on my hand was gone again, so that must mean the contraction was over.

"You cool?" Romeo asked, his hand falling on my shoulder.

I nodded. "Yeah, I'm cool."

Romeo and Rimmel started for the door, and just as they were about to disappear, I called. "Hey, Rome."

He glanced back.

"Maybe wait outside the door?"

He grinned. "Sure thing."

What? He was the only one big enough to pick me up off the floor if I passed the hell out.

Okay, fine.

I needed my best friend close.

Becoming a father for the first time was the scariest thing I'd ever done.

It hardly seemed like Ivy and I had been married for five months already. It was like I blinked and it was gone. By some sheer luck (or maybe fucking hard work and a really good agent), I was drafted by the Maryland Knights. Another team tried to draft me at the same time, but thankfully, the Knights's offer was higher, so I went to them.

I signed a solid three-year contract, and while I didn't make an excess of forty mil like Rome, I did get well over ten.

It was more than enough to take care of Ivy and the little critter.

I still had no idea if it was a son or a daughter. Ivy was adamant she not find out. For a woman who loved to shop for pink shit, I would have thought she would have been the first to know. But she maintained it didn't matter if it was a girl or a boy because it was mine and that's all she cared about.

Seriously. Who wouldn't marry that?

Romeo continued to declare it was a boy, Ivy insisted it was a girl, and everyone else was just waiting to find out who was going to be right.

Rome and I were back on the same team. We played together better than ever. The Knights were dominating already this season with the lead in just about everything. I even set a new record and so did Rome. Game attendance was up, team morale was up, and Gamble was a happy man.

It was early in the season, but I already knew we were headed for the SuperBowl.

Blanchard asked for a trade, and the powers that be worked it out. I would have played with him and managed to keep my cool. These days, it took more than an ass like him to ruffle my feathers.

I was married with a baby on the way. I had a budding career and an awesome family. I focused on that. Yeah, sometimes I still had dreams about Zach, but they weren't like they used to be. I still worried about Ivy, but I no longer had nightmares she died the night of the crash.

Turns out telling everyone in the family and even sort of admitting to Robert that I did have a choice that night went a long way in helping me put it behind me. No one in this family judged me for the decision I made, and that made it really hard to judge myself.

It was like Ivy said. I was human. I was a real, flesh-and-bone man.

I didn't have to be perfect. Hell, I didn't even have to be free of the darkness I lived with all my life.

All I had to be was genuine. All I had to be was me.

Ivy took summer classes last summer so she could graduate early, so come January, she would be a college graduate. I didn't want her pushing herself like that, but she was insistent she finish as much as she could before the critter came along.

She also started her YouTube channel, and it was already getting hits like crazy. The editor at *People* magazine called her, and they were currently in talks for a new style column called "The Blonde Next Door." Ivy was really popular with the college demographic but also with the elite who followed what celebs were wearing.

I had no doubt when she was ready, she would own a piece of the fashion world. Until then, she was going to build her empire from home with my baby on her lap.

"Braeden?" Ivy said, gripping my hand.

I glanced over at her, noting the worry on her face. "What's the matter, baby?"

"I'm scared."

All the queasiness and fear I'd been feeling left me. I didn't have room to be freaked out right now because I had to be strong for her.

"I know. It's okay, now. In just a few minutes, you're going to have the baby in your arms and fear will be the furthest thing from your mind."

She smiled, a little of the anxiety slipping away. "Having a baby takes a long time. I'll probably be pushing for hours."

What the what?

Why hadn't anyone told me this! On TV, it was a bunch screaming and then a crying baby. All in one scene!

I should have known this shit was suspicious when I walked in and Ivy wasn't screaming.

Thank God she wasn't screaming.

* * *

I shook my head and made a sound. Then I leaned over the bed and spoke directly to my wife's stomach. "Listen up, critter," I said. "Don't you be making your mother suffer for hours before you decide to come out. Football players don't dally at the one yard line."

I nodded and then glanced up. Ivy was watching me with an amused expression.

"What?"

"The one yard line?"

"He knows what I mean." I defended. "Football's in his blood."

Another contraction took over, and her face clouded in a mask of pain. Just as I was about to get the nurse, she came into the room with a doctor wearing a pair of gloves and a cap on his head.

He did a few things down below that I didn't care to watch and then glanced up with some surprise in his eyes. "I think it's time to have a baby."

My stomach flopped.

Another contraction ripped into my wife, and she whimpered.

Everything started happening at once, and people were telling her to push, and she was squeezing my hand until I was sure the bones were shattered.

And then the sound of crying filled the room.

My heart literally stopped.

The doctor scooped up a little baby and placed it immediately on Ivy's chest.

"It's a girl!" he said.

Ivy started crying and pulled the baby close. "Oh my goodness," she crooned. "Look how beautiful you are."

The sound of her mother's voice made the baby stop crying. Her eyes—which were deep blue—focused on Ivy and held on.

"Braeden," Ivy whispered, unable to take her eyes of the baby.

"You did real good, sweetheart," I said, brushing the hair from her face.

The baby knew my voice, too. She turned to me immediately and her lower lip wobbled.

I literally felt like someone ripped my heart right out of my chest.

I had a daughter.

"Let me clean her up a bit and ger her weight." The nurse reached for the baby, and Ivy tugged her closer. I grabbed the nurse's hand and glared.

The nurse didn't seem put off by my animalistic behavior. "I'll just be right there." She pointed across the room. "Then you can have her back for a minute before I take her to the nursery."

"What the hell does she need to go to the nursery for," I demanded. But I did it softly. I didn't want to scare the baby.

"A general checkup. You can come with her." The nurse assured me.

I grunted, and Ivy relented and handed over the baby.

She started crying again, and Ivy started fretting.

I got up and towered over the nurse, watching her with my daughter, making sure she treated her right.

"Well," the nurse said to her as she worked, "you're definitely gonna have a hard time getting away with anything with this one around." She thumbed a finger at me.

"Watch her head," I ordered.

The nurse laughed. "I can assure you I've had lots of experience." When the baby was wrapped up in some generic blanket, she picked her up and held her out toward me. "Want to hold your daughter, Dad?"

I blanched. She wanted me to hold her?

Oh fuck.

I'd never held a baby before.

She started fussing again, and I didn't like it. My instinct was to reach for her, and I went with it. "Watch her head," the nurse said, and I gave her a dry look.

When the nurse stepped back, I stood stiffly, staring down at the tiny little bundle in my arms. I was afraid to move, afraid to breathe. Holy crap, she was smaller than the damn dog.

The baby was still fussing and her lip was wobbling.

"Now don't be doing that," I told her softly. "Just tell me what you want and you'll have it."

The baby stopped fussing and looked at me. I smiled.

The nurse laughed. "Daddy's already wrapped."

"Is she okay?" Ivy worried from the bed as the doctor still worked around her.

"She's perfect," I whispered and walked over to show her.

"You both are," Ivy said, looking at me holding our daughter.

I sat close to the bed, staring down while the doctor and nurse finished with Ivy.

"Is she okay?" I asked, worried when the doctor pulled off his gloves.

He pulled the mask off his face and smiled. "Mother and baby appear to be doing great."

The nurse nodded. "You, my dear, had a quick labor for a first time."

It was because I told the baby. We had an understanding, my daughter and I.

"She's going to be okay, then?" I asked again, wanting to be sure Ivy was all right.

"Yes, just fine."

"Gimme," Ivy said and held her hands out to the baby.

"She likes me," I told her.

She smiled. "I never had any doubt, but I want my daughter before you get to go with her to the nursery."

I sighed. "Fine. I guess since you did all that pushing and shit."

The nurse laughed. "Does she have a name?"

"Critter Walker," I said, gently handing the baby to my wife.

Ivy made a rude sound. "Not."

"I'll give you just a minute with her, but then I really need to take her to the nursery."

"Thanks," I said, watching Ivy with my daughter.

I thought I understood love before, but this was a whole new level. Seeing my wife holding my baby was something so profound I was momentarily struck silent.

"Oh my goodness," Ivy was saying to her. "You are just the most beautiful baby I have ever seen. And look at your hair," she practically sang as she drifted her fingertips over the whispy light-brown downy hair on her head.

She was a beautiful kid. Best-looking one I'd ever seen.

I mean, really, it wasn't a surprise. She did come from my loins.

She was tiny, maybe six pounds. Her skin was all pink, her head was perfectly round, and her cheeks were chubby as hell. Her eyes were so big and so round and so blue that even the whites around them seemed tinted blue.

I watched as she yawned, her tiny mouth opening wide and her hand—which was practically the size of one of my fingers—reached out.

I brushed my finger against it, and her fist closed around it.

There was a light knock on the door, and Romeo stuck his head in the room. "Safe to come in?"

I waved him in. I still didn't trust my voice not to crack when I spoke. Rimmel slipped past him and rushed in first. Her shoulder brushed against my side when she leaned in for the first look.

"Meet your niece, sis," I said.

"It's a girl?" Romeo asked from the foot of the bed.

"She's perfect," Ivy said.

"I thought I was getting a nephew," Romeo said with a hint of jest in his voice. Then he came around the other side of the bed and leaned over to see her. "But she's pretty cute. Guess she'll do."

"You wanna hold her?" Ivy asked him.

Romeo glanced at me, and I smiled. "Better do it now before that nurse comes back. She keeps trying to take my kid."

"You're sure?" he asked.

Ivy laughed. "Here. Watch her head."

Romeo let Ivy put my little girl in his arms and tuck the blanket around her. Romeo was wearing a pair of scrubs already, and he pulled her in against his chest and backed up slowly to sit down in a nearby chair.

Beside me, Rimmel sighed and stared at them both.

I draped an arm across her shoulder. "You're next," I whispered.

She smiled.

Romeo made some sounds I'd never heard him make at the baby, and then he leaned down and kissed her on the forehead.

"Smalls," he whisper-demanded, "I'd like to place an order. I'd like one in blue."

Ivy laughed. "You can't just place an order for a baby."

"Why the hell not?" he demanded.

The baby made a sound, and everyone stopped what they were doing and stared at her.

"What'd you do to her, man?" I rushed around the bed. "What's wrong with her?"

Romeo looked like he was holding a bomb he accidentally detonated. "I don't know."

The two of us stood there and freaked out, trying to figure out what was wrong, and behind us, the girls laughed.

"Babies make sounds, you idiots," Ivy said.

As if to prove the point, she did it again.

Romeo and I both reacted again.

Rimmel laughed and pushed between us. "My turn."

She scooped her up and cuddled her with both arms.

"Now that's a sight I like," Romeo said, gruff.

"I'm your auntie, and I'm going to spoil you rotten," Rimmel whispered. Then she carried her over and handed her to Ivy.

"What's her name?" Rimmel asked.

I started to say it, and Ivy looked at me. "No."

"Aww, baby. Critter is the best I got," I told her.

"It's a solid choice." Romeo agreed. "It would look good on the back of a jersey."

Ivy and Rimmel both looked horrified. I chuckled and went over to sit on the side of the bed and put my arm around Ivy and my daughter.

"I have a name," Ivy said, soft.

"Hit me with it," I said.

"Nova," she answered. "It means *new star*."

"The stars have always been good to us, Blondie," I said. "I think they'll be good to this one, too." I brushed a hand over her downy hair.

"Nova is a beautiful name," Rimmel said and sat down in Romeo's lap. "Fits her perfectly."

Ivy smiled. "I think so. My grandmother's name was Rose. So I was thinking Nova Rose."

"Nova Rose Walker," I said, trying it out. "I guess it is better than Critter."

Ivy rolled her eyes, and Rimmel laughed.

"Do you like it?" Ivy turned her eyes up to me.

My chest constricted with emotion, and I pressed a kiss to the side of her head. "I love it. Nova is perfect."

The nurse came in and busted up our happy time.

She was really getting on my nerves.

But she was learning. Before she reached for the baby, she asked if it was okay. Ivy didn't want to give her up. I could tell by the set of her jaw and the sheen in her eyes.

"Go with her, 'kay?" she asked.

I nodded. "Rome can come, too. Ain't nothing going to bother my little angel with two football players escorting her."

The nurse sighed and accepted her fate without comment.

"Make sure my brother sees her!" Ivy called out as we went from the room, the nurse gently pushing the rolling cart with Nova inside. "And hurry up!"

"Get some rest, princess," Romeo told her. "We got this."

I winked at her as the door closed behind us.

Out in the hallway, Rome clapped me on the back, the sound loud because of all the pads I was still wearing.

"Congratulations, man. She's awesome."

"Thanks," I said and stared down at her where she lay. "We're gonna need to move up the timeline for the family compound," I said, thinking of the place we'd all been planning since we got married.

One big piece of land, several houses, and one stone wall with a gate around the entire thing.

"My thoughts exactly," Rome said, also staring at Nova. Then he put his arm across my shoulders, and we walked down the hallway, our bromance on full display.

"Family just got bigger," I told him.

"There's always room for family," he replied. "Always."

IVY

He stood in the middle of the hospital room, looking like a giant.

All grass stains, sweat, and messy hair.

His purple uniform bulged over the massive pads and protectice gear he wore.

He looked like a warrior who had just stepped off a battlefield.

Except for his face.

It was softened and downturned, his eyes in complete and utter awe.

He didn't hold a sword, or a football… but a tiny baby who stared back at him like he made up her entire universe.

I understood that look.

Because it was one I wore every single day.

The first sight of my tough-looking husband with our daughter in his arms was something I would never forget.

It became a permanent mark—a tattoo on my heart.

And it was only the beginning.

A new star was born today, and despite her small size, to us, she would always be the brightest of all.

ROMEO

I don't know the exact moment we all grew up. When we went from friends to family.

All I know is we chose one another. Love chose us.

Even though we weren't young college students anymore, even though we had jobs, family, and responsibilities, we were still the same. Deep down inside us, we were all the still the same.

We just loved deeper. Bonded tighter. And knew exactly where we belonged.

Our life wasn't over.

It was just beginning.
And it was going to be one fucking beautiful ride.

And they all lived
happily ever after.

#BuzzBoss

Just when you thought this was the end...

**A Hashtag Holiday Short Story
Plus five festive recipes to fill your tummy and
warm your heart.**

Givers Gonna Give...

'Twas the night of game day,
And all through the town,
Lacey glittering snowflakes fluttered around.
They clung to the roads, concealing everything with
white.
It was a beautiful #holiday sight.
The paparazzi were out without any care,
In hopes to catch Romeo and Rimmel, rumored to be
there.
When out on the road there arose such a clatter.
The Hellcat spun out, but it shouldn't matter.
I pulled out my cell to dial in a flash.
But the battery was dead. What useless trash.
The moonlight glistening on the new fallen snow

• • •

Made us forget we needed a tow.
For the season was upon us. Our family was alight.
Our #holiday was destined to be merry and bright.
PRE-ORDER NOW

GEARSHARK *Magazine*

Issue 1

Hits newstands
Winter 2016

AUTHOR'S NOTE

This entire book is a love letter to my readers. A love letter to this series. I don't think I can quite convey how real these characters are to me and how big a part of me they really are. This book was a real labor to complete.

But it was a labor of love.

Even as I just typed the last words on the page and I sit here typing my final author's note of the *Hashtag Series,* I'm not saying good-bye. I can't. Because to me, there isn't a life without a Romeo, a Rimmel, a Braeden & Ivy. Even though their story is finished, they will still live on in the pages of these six books.

I wanted this book to have it all. A little drama, a little plot, and a lot of romance and epic moments. I wanted us all to experience as much as we could with these guys in some of the happiest moments of their lives.

You guys deserve that. You deserve this book to be everything you want it to be, and I sincerely hope this book is the conclusion you were hoping for.

I was scared to write this book because I didn't want to screw it up. I didn't want to let them go. But now that the story is complete, I know there is no other way this could have gone. It's as it should be. The characters made sure of that.

Even though this series is ended, it won't be the last of this family. I'm sure you saw the little teaser image on the previous page for my next book…

GEARSHARK is a spinoff series of the *Hashtag Series.* Maybe you noted in the book that Drew carried around a copy of *GearShark Magazine?*

That's not a coincidence.

Drew and Trent have some stories of their own to tell. I think they need to find their happily ever afters, too. This winter I will be diving into the world of racing (which I know nothing about… ha-ha) and going for a ride with our boys.

I can't tell you yet what is going to happen, but I can promise it's going to be something I've never done before, with some of that hashtag flare we've all come to love so very much.

So even though the ending of the *Hashtag Series* is bittersweet, I hope you will pick up the first issue of *GEARSHARK* when it hits stands and join me in a whole new adventure.

One last thank you to the readers of this series. Words or hashtags cannot express how much I appreciate you. Thank you to the #nerds in my fan club for the neverending support and excitement and for all the pics of hot shirtless men on days when I'm dragging. Shirtless men fix a lot of stuff…

#BetterThanDuctTape

Thank you to Regina Wamba for posting that first still behind-the-scenes picture, which inspired me to create an entire world. Thank you to Cassie McCown for being an amazing editor but an even better friend. Thank you to Melissa Stickney for keeping my fan club an awesome place to be. And of course, thank you to my family who understands that Romeo and the rest of the family are no less real to me than any of them.

So with tears in my eyes and maybe a little heaviness in my chest, I conclude this series.

In the words of Romeo, it's been one *fucking beautiful* ride.

XOXO,

Cambria

Cambria Hebert is an award winning, bestselling novelist of more than twenty books. She went to college for a bachelor's degree, couldn't pick a major, and ended up with a degree in cosmetology. So rest assured her characters will always have good hair.

Besides writing, Cambria loves a caramel latte, staying up late, sleeping in, and watching movies. She considers math human torture and has an irrational fear of chickens (yes, chickens). You can often find her running on the treadmill (she'd rather be eating a donut), painting her toenails (because she bites her fingernails), or walking her chorkie (the real boss of the house).

Cambria has written within the young adult and new adult genres, penning many paranormal and contemporary titles. Her favorite genre to read and write is romantic suspense. A few of her most recognized titles are: *The Hashtag Series, Text, Torch,* and *Tattoo.*

Cambria Hebert owns and operates Cambria Hebert Books, LLC.

You can find out more about Cambria and her titles by visiting her website: http://www.cambriahebert.com.

Lightning Source UK Ltd.
Milton Keynes UK
UKOW02f0617021016